LORD VILE

Beastly Lords Book Three

Sydney Jane Baily

cat whisker press
Massachusetts

ISBN: 978-1-938732-37-9
Published by cat whisker press
Imprint of JAMES-YORK PRESS

Cover: cat whisker studio
In conjunction with Philip Ré
Book Design: cat whisker studio

DEDICATION

To Toni Carol (née Baily) Young

*My loving sister, whom I treasure
and who always has my back.*

OTHER WORKS
by
SYDNEY JANE BAILY

THE RARE CONFECTIONERY
Series

The Duchess of Chocolate
The Toffee Heiress
My Lady Marzipan

THE DEFIANT HEARTS
Series

An Improper Situation
An Irresistible Temptation
An Inescapable Attraction
An Inconceivable Deception
An Intriguing Proposition
An Impassioned Redemption

THE BEASTLY LORDS
Series

Lord Despair
Lord Anguish
Lord Vile
Lord Darkness
Lord Misery
Lord Wrath
Eleanor

PRESENTING LADY GUS

A Georgian-Era Novella

ACKNOWLEDGMENTS

Thanks to my kind and capable editor, Violetta Rand, tidying up after me like the good fairy she is. And a big hug and kiss to my smart and beautiful mother.

PROLOGUE

1849, London

"Why are you 'ere?" Michael Alder, viscount and heir to an earldom he hadn't seen in over a year, raised bleary eyes to the inquisitor seated on a stool beside him in a gin palace in Drury Lane. He felt no compunction to answer. He drank alone.

Turning away, he smacked his hand atop the sticky counter until the barkeeper responded with an enquiring grunt.

Nodding at his empty glass, Michael watched as the man refilled it with gin.

London Dry or Belgian gin? he wondered briefly. Then he downed it. He'd had too many to feel the burning sensation as it hit the back of his throat. No matter. It did the job nonetheless.

"I mean, you're not like the rest of us," continued the voice at his elbow. "You could be drinking brandy at White's or Boodle's." Then the man laughed. "I betcha didn't think I'd even know the names of them fancy clubs, eh, m' lord?"

Couldn't a man get himself positively ran-tan in an obscure and shabby pub without being buttonholed by some nosey bloke?

Feeling a hand stroke his back, Michael turned slowly to see the barmaid with the wide smile and even wider hips tilt her head toward the stairs.

"You won't answer, eh? Too arfarfanarf!" His chatty, unwelcome examiner pointed out the obvious—Michael was well and truly in his cups!

Too many pints of ale followed by too many glasses of gin.

Ignoring the man and nodding at the wench, Michael slid off his stool and followed her upstairs. He wouldn't remember any of this in the morning. All the better.

CHAPTER ONE

Miss Ada Kathryn Ellis, known simply as Ada to her friends, acknowledged a growing sense of deep disappointment. It was the first time she'd allowed herself to do so in months.

Her first Season, which was the previous year, had been all nervousness and learning the correct modes of behavior. This Season, having mastered the art of flirtation and witty conversation, she'd excelled at being in the right place at the right time, and often with a partner whom she didn't entirely dislike, occasionally one whom she even found agreeable.

That wasn't to say she'd found someone to tickle her fancy. Unfortunately, she hadn't, and not for want of trying. *Oh, she had tried!*

To every dinner companion or dance partner, she'd compared one man, a young viscount she'd encountered two years earlier. As she'd not yet been brought out into society, he had been firmly off limits. Thus, at a dinner to which her parents had munificently allowed her access, Ada could only watch Lord Alder from afar.

Fervently hoping he would still be available when she was on the marriage market, alas, she'd seen neither hide nor hair of the viscount this entire Season.

His inexplicable absence hadn't stopped her from participating in all the excitement of London society. However, whenever she thought she might fancy someone, a gentleman with a particularly nice smile or attractive eyes, she weighed his merits against the now nearly mythological memory of Lord Alder.

If only she could see him and maybe even speak with him, then she'd be able to disabuse herself of the ridiculous notion—he was *the one*.

As her friends got engaged, particularly her best friend Maggie Blackwood, who snagged an earl and became the Countess of Cambrey, Ada grew a little less interested in each social event. Perhaps her parents, the Baron and Baroness Ellis, had wasted their money on a daughter who seemed neither a wallflower nor a dazzler. Firmly in the middle of the pack of society misses, Ada was unsure how to proceed as the Season drew to a riotous close.

Should she grab any man who showed an interest in her fair face and large dowry? She could get engaged to a viscount's son, who nearly declared himself before she ran off to the ladies' retiring room in order to avoid the unpleasant task of saying no. There was another, an older bachelor who still had all his hair, a sizable yearly income, and a townhouse on the west side of Arlington Street. She was confident she could be mistress of his house by Christmas, if she so chose. In fact, there were half a dozen others who'd shown an interest.

If only she could decide to settle.

Or should she set her sights on the following year and go home to Juniper Hall in the Surrey countryside? Perhaps cut her hair in the new fashion or take more music lessons? Maybe she should learn to speak French like Maggie or attempt to stop talking so much about her interest in commerce. The latter scandalized her mother, yet Ada found most interesting the rise and fall of commodities on the London Stock Exchange. Fluctuations of price could make or break a man between sunrise and sunset. There was the Spanish panic of 1835. And four years after the 1845 crash, newspapers still wrote about the burst "bubble" from railway speculation. Some very old families, indeed, had been ruined.

Fascinating, Ada thought, whenever she picked up her father's well-read copy of *The Banker's Magazine* or the *Economist,* infinitely more interesting than the silly romantic novels her friends were reading. She could listen for hours to her father espousing about what he encountered on the floor of the exchange, even though he was speaking primarily to her younger brother, Grady.

Gentlemen in search of a wife, however, didn't want a young woman to have an interest in business. It was too manly!

Sighing loudly, Ada let her maid prepare her for yet another end of the Season *soirée.* Yes, the violet silk gown. Yes, hair up in a braided bun with blonde ringlets hanging from her temples past her ears. Yes, the matching lavender silk gloves, because why not? Yes, yes, yes. Except she didn't want to go. Not really.

She looked at her blue eyes in the gilded mirror and hoped they didn't appear as weary as she felt, and then she went to the Fontaine's ball.

With her mother in her usual position seated with the other hopeful mothers nearby, Ada let her card be filled, holding out her wrist dutifully to every young man who asked. *When had this become such a dreary chore?*

The next hour passed in a carousel of dances—the Grand March, then a quadrille, polka, and waltz. When her mother wasn't looking, she had a glass of champagne. Waving to Lady Adelia Smythe, the daughter of an earl but still very friendly and who also hadn't found a match, Ada headed toward her when a man bumped her elbow as he brushed past.

"Well, excuse me," she said loudly enough that he halted and turned.

Intending to take him to task for his rudeness, she pursed her lips and stared up at—

Ada had to stop herself from gasping. *It was he!* At last. *Her* viscount. Lord Michael Alder.

He narrowed his eyes as if studying her, perhaps to see if he knew her. When he didn't, he relaxed and shrugged.

"My apologies."

Good God! He was speaking to her. His voice sounded as she recalled, rich and deep, causing a delightful shiver in her spine.

Say something, she ordered herself, but her tongue was frozen. She could do naught but stare at his handsome face below thick brown hair that curled slightly, giving him a rakish air.

She'd never been close enough before to see how instead of plain brown eyes, his were a striking amber color. Unusual, reminding her of one of her family's cats.

"Are you well?" he asked, undoubtedly thinking her addlepated as she gaped at him.

Nodding, still speechless, she did the only thing she could think of—she held out her wrist with the card dangling from it.

He looked at is as if it were on fire, practically recoiling.

"No," he said, without preamble. "I don't wish to dance."

At her distraught expression, he added, "Not with anyone," as if to soften the blow.

She swallowed. Think of something brilliant, amusing, interesting. *Anything!*

Then he nodded quickly, turned away, and disappeared into the throng.

Blast! She'd lost her one and only chance. Yet it didn't truly matter. Obviously, she held no attraction for him, and whatever words she'd spouted wouldn't have changed that fact. Especially not her personal notion one could become extraordinarily wealthy from investing in the developing technology of undersea cables. The newspapers indicated they would be laid between England and France within two years. She ought to have blandly praised the music, the champagne, or even Lord Alder's ascot, or brought up Dickens' latest.

Expelling an unladylike puff of air, she sent her golden bangs flying high with frustration. Then her next partner found her, perused her card for his name, and hauled her onto the dance floor.

Another eternal hour, during which she tried to spy Lord Alder while she twirled and spun. To no avail. Overheated by the crush of bodies, disappointed in not only this event but the entire Season, and even her future prospects, Ada left the security of the ballroom. In a hasty, ill-conceived moment, she ventured to the other side of the multi-paned glass doors and onto the marble terrace.

Unfortunately, there were couples who must have already publicly professed agreements as to their future associations since they were openly together, alone and unchaperoned. The practice was still frowned upon, but if the couple was engaged, the *ton* deemed it practically acceptable.

One such couple was a mere few yards from Ada and another was at the far end of the terrace. In each instance, the man held the woman close.

Ada rolled her eyes at the sheer awkwardness of being outside in a romantic spot without a suitor of her own. Between the couples were the stone steps leading to the wilds of the topiary and sculpture gardens.

In a flash, she darted down the steps and into the darkness.

MICHAEL STUMBLED OUT ONTO the terrace after one too many dance cards had been dangled before his face, and one too many glasses of champagne had found their way down his throat. In fact, he carried one with him at present.

Downing the bubbly liquid, he set the empty glass on the edge of the terrace's stone railing and made his way down the steps into the silence.

Having stayed away from so-called polite society for many months, he couldn't imagine why he'd talked himself into this particular ball. Actually, yes, he did know. He'd read the guest list in the newspaper, knowing *she* would be there, the woman he'd loved and lost.

Of course, he knew she was married, and happily, too, which he didn't begrudge her one bit. After all, it wasn't her fault his treacherous parents had lied to them both and ended their engagement due to her lack of fortune. Yet, like an animal which can't stop licking a raw wound, he liked to make certain he still fancied her above anyone else.

Seeing her, on the rare occasion he did, confirmed this fact. Seeing Jenny Blackwood, now the Countess of Lindsey, reminded him of what he'd lost and why. It renewed his anger and refreshed his bitterness against those who professed to love him most. His own parents.

Betrayal most foul! Pulling a sterling flask from his pocket, he took a sip of brandy and sauntered onto the brick path leading farther into the garden.

After a minute, he crossed a sickeningly romantic bridge over a tiny fake stream and found himself next to a gazebo, dark except for two torches, lit to show guests they'd reached the end of the garden. Beyond was a brick wall higher than his head.

Taking another sip, he thought he was seeing a vision. Not the first time, either, since his favorite state lately was 'half seas over' if not fully passed out.

Before him came an enchanting creature in such a pale pastel shade, she was practically glowing in the moonlight.

She seemed to float toward him, and as she did, bone deep, he knew he wanted her.

When the torchlight caught her golden crown of hair, he made a sound, alerting the bewitching goddess to his presence. She froze. Yet, instead of fleeing as a sane and reputable maiden should, she took a step closer.

Slipping the flask back into his pocket, he held out his hand. Silently, she took it, letting him draw her close.

"I had no idea when I came out here, I would encounter such a creature as you. You are so lovely."

She trembled.

But was she real? There was more than one way to discover if she were.

Wrapping his arms around her, still feeling her shuddering movements, Michael decided she must be real and quite cold. He would do his best to warm her.

Lowering his head, he brushed his lips against hers. A bouquet of some exotically lush, floral scent tickled his nose, and her soft lips were warm and encouraging.

Mm, she smelled good. No doubt in the cold light of day, she was older than she appeared in the dimly lit garden. Yet for this moment, he would accept she was a sprite, sent for his enjoyment.

He settled his mouth upon hers once again, tasting her sweetness. Tilting his head slightly, he found they fit together perfectly, and when he licked the seam of her lips, she opened them with the smallest gasp. It inflamed him.

Apparently, she was willing.

Glancing around, he took in the glossy white gazebo, also seemingly glowing in the torchlight. Inviting, beckoning, the ideal spot!

With finesse, despite tripping slightly on the threshold, he led her into the secluded place. *How thoughtful of their hosts.*

There was a divan, undoubtedly used for reclining whilst reading a book during the day. What a mundane waste for such a magical place!

It took only a single step and he had the back of her skirts pressed against the settee cushions, and then they were both falling upon it. Too small for stretching out comfortably, yet it offered them a suitable place to engage in a quick sensual dalliance.

His goddess went rigid as soon as she was prone beneath him. He couldn't imagine she didn't want this as much as he did, since he could feel her warm and curvaceous body thrumming under his. She was made for a man to embrace and to enjoy.

"My lord?" Her first words to him were soft and questioning.

Mayhap he was taking too long to please her.

He lowered his mouth to hers again, and as he kissed her thoroughly, she relaxed. What's more, he could feel her heart beating a strong tattoo of desire. His own was doing the same.

Raising himself up and reaching between them, with practiced hands, Michael unfastened the fall of his trousers, letting his manhood spring free.

He watched her eyes in the darkness. Although he couldn't determine their color, he could see them widen with delight. Ever so gently, he lifted the hem of her dress, smoothing his fingers up her stockinged legs until—her fingers suddenly met his, holding her gown in place across her thighs.

Was she truly wanting to stop?

"It's all right," he soothed. "I want you. Beyond anyone else, I want you."

Her voice a whisper, she asked, "Do you know me?"

"Of course," he responded. She was his goddess, a gift to soothe him for all he'd lost. "Do you know me?"

"Lord Alder."

He felt a frisson of surprise. Indeed, she must be a fairy sprite, an otherworldly creature, for how else could she have found him in the darkness?

"Then we are meant for each other," he stated. "Let me love you."

After another moment, her hands fell away, and he pushed her gown and petticoats and cotton shift up to her hips, baring her drawers to him. As expected, she wore two separate legs tied together at the waist, so he needn't even remove them to have access to her coveted core.

Wondering if he could last even for a few moments, he came over her body, fit his stiff member to her warm channel and slid himself inside his magical nymph.

He groaned in delight at the same time as her hands came up to his chest.

Was she pushing him away?

Kissing her, he began to move his hips, and her hands relaxed, while still grasping his jacket. He wished to hear her moan with pleasure, but she was breathing shallowly. He wished he could see and touch her breasts, but he was pressing both hands into the divan for support and couldn't spare one to ease down the neckline of her gown.

"Good?" he asked.

Silence. Looking down at her face, he was unable to see her at all as his shoulders blocked the light of the torches. He thought her head was tilted back in ecstasy and thus continued to pump inside her.

He'd been correct about his own stamina. He lasted barely a minute in the delicious tightness of his goddess. Then with a guttural cry of pleasure, and a whispered name—*Jenny*—he spent inside the mysterious sprite.

Leaving another kiss upon her mouth, he drew back, stood up, and began to fasten his trousers. To his consternation, she lay there, unmoving.

"Are you well?" he asked after a moment, remembering when he'd asked the same to another young miss earlier in the evening, a simpering simpleton who couldn't even speak to him—the opposite to this passionate creature.

His words spurred the lady into movement. Hastily, she lowered her skirts and took his outstretched hand, letting him assist her from the divan.

Then a strange expression crossed her lovely features, visible again in the moonlight now they were standing. She looked down, and he did the same before realizing she was feeling his warm seed as it leaked from her.

"Luckily, you have so many layers, no one shall be the wiser," Michael advised. "You can float back into the ballroom and continue to dance with what I'm confident are your many, many suitors."

"But . . . ," she trailed off.

Was this delightful morsel having a moment of regret? *A bit too late!* He drew out his flask and took a sip. As a gentleman, he offered it to her.

She looked from the silver flagon to his face

For the first time, he felt a twinge of regret. On second glance, she seemed a bit young for this game, but she had to know the rules and the consequences of a tryst in a dark garden. Why else had she let him have his way with her? He certainly wasn't her first.

"I'm sorry if your pleasure was not complete," he said, thinking perhaps his swift climax had robbed her of her own ultimate satisfaction. There was nothing he could do about that now.

Still, she said nothing, and he was growing weary. His sated body yearned for his own bed and a long night's sleep.

"I bid you farewell, dear goddess."

He turned from her, took a few steps, then looked back.

Why was this willing temptress with her plump, kissable lips suddenly looking so damned shocked and teary-eyed?

As he met her gaze, she opened her mouth and found her voice at last.

"Can you possibly mean to simply walk away?"

Ah, he understood. She wanted the promise of something more. She was a society miss, after all, even if one who enjoyed sharing a naughty assignation away from prying eyes.

"I may attend a few more balls this Season. Look for my name on the guest list, and we can enjoy ourselves again. I'll try to last longer next time, my sweet."

Offering her a smile, he winked and took his leave.

CHAPTER TWO

Three years later, 1852
Juniper Hall, Surrey

Ada left her son's room, always thankful how quickly the little boy could fall asleep. *Her dear Harry.* And this was their last night in her parents' country home. Undoubtedly, he would miss his doting grandparents until they met up again in London.

Making her way back to her own bedroom, she glanced over the trunks filled with her clothing and considered whether she'd forgotten anything. With her capable maid, Lucy, having worked diligently, it appeared her chamber was cleared of all her personal effects, except her nightdress and robe laid out for the night.

Ada could finally relax after weeks of preparation. Downstairs, her parents waited in the parlor, so they could spend a last evening before her move to Town. To spare her mother, she and her father would try not to discuss the stock market, their shared passion.

She would greatly miss them, but, as usual, as she thought of her move to London, a thrill of excited anticipation tickled her spine. Her own home, at last.

With her accumulated wealth, she'd purchased a townhouse on Belgrave Square. She might have chosen the locale because of its close proximity to two parks in which she could ride and Harry could play, or because it was not too distant from her parents' townhouse, which they occupied about six months out of the year.

However, there was another more attractive reason for choosing the spacious neo-Classical home. For although *Lord Vile*—as the *ton* had so aptly nicknamed the viscount Michael Alder—didn't live there, he frequented it. Everyone who read the scandal sheets knew he'd had two paramours from among the fifty residences of the square, and was currently keeping company with a widow only two doors down from where Ada would soon reside.

She intended to be the next on his list.

Not only would Ada finally be mistress of her own domain, she intended to become Lord Vile's mistress as well, with the fine distinction of being the woman he kept company with but never bedded. It was the only way she could think to capture his black heart.

How blessed she was her parents had not disowned her after the disastrous breach of sanity three years earlier. Instead, they'd shown incredible generosity. She knew no other parents who would have behaved with such benign kindness.

The alternative, being cast out to fend for herself and her unborn child, would have likely ended in an intentional final swim in the Thames. For Ada had not been prepared to go to a seedy house for unwed mothers, if she could even have found one that wasn't truly a front for a brothel.

The idea of Harry being born as the child of a prostitute could still cause Ada to shudder.

Instead, her mother, Kathryn, had enveloped her in love, and adored her grandson as soon as he made his way into the world. Her father had decided finance and commerce were a "damn sight safer" for his only daughter than so-called *civilized* society. Thus, James Ellis indulged her interest for stocks and trade, teaching her what he knew as a broker in good standing at the London Stock Exchange, having always paid his yearly £5 license fee, on top of his £105 entrance fee, and his £22 subscription. To his credit, he'd never had a default penalty placed against him from all the trading he'd done, and thus, he'd been reelected each year on Lady Day in early April.

When her parents left her alone in Surrey for their London residence, most days, Baron Ellis was on the floor of the exchange at Capel Court. When they were with Ada at Juniper Hall, her father kept up with the markets through the trade reports and the general newspapers.

Not only had he taught her, he'd also listened. As it turned out, Ada had a head for investing. Even better, he had let her invest through him.

In three years, with a singularity of purpose, she'd become a wealthy woman in her own right, while helping her father to grow his own wealth. Eventually, when her brother inherited, he would benefit, too.

Sitting in her father's study together, poring over one of the intriguing reports of the Select Committee on Joint Stock Companies, they shared a like-minded friendship rarely seen between father and daughter. The only time they ever fought was if James yet again asked who his grandson's father was.

"Ada Kate, tell me the scoundrel's name and I'll run him through or shoot him in the heart, or would if he had one," her father promised.

His strong words in no way enticed her to reveal anything about Michael Alder.

She wasn't protecting the rogue. Not at all. Alder could dance with the devil for all she cared. She was protecting her beloved father, who might find himself run through or shot in a duel as easily as being the victor.

And most importantly, she was protecting Harry St. Ange, as she'd named her baby in the church records directly following his birth. He would not grow up a bastard, the result of an unbelievably stupid moment in which his mother mistook his father for a decent human being.

A terrible misjudgment of character.

It took little more than a quiet moment to snatch her thoughts back to that horrid night. Shocked to find *him* at the end of the path, her obsession, Ada had become wool-headed almost instantly. Then his lips had seemed magical as he pressed them to hers. If she were ever to relate the tale, which she would never do to a single soul, she would have said it seemed one minute, Michael Alder's lips were on hers making her feel wondrous new sensations, and the next, he was raising her skirts, and . . . giving her Harry.

She could not regret her boy. Nor the life she'd created since that fateful night. Unable to reenter the ballroom with her hair tangled and her gown in disarray, she'd slipped out through a cast iron gate in the brick wall and found her parents' carriage in the long line. Once inside, she'd begun to shake and hadn't felt warm again until her mother, having eventually been summoned by the footman, took her stunned and sobbing daughter home, got her bathed, and tucked her into bed.

Her disgrace had been obvious, but her parents' love had been stronger.

In the weeks that followed, her folly had become even clearer. Far from being the noble viscount she'd envisioned, Michael Alder had already been given the moniker of Lord Vile by the *ton* for his drinking binges and his treatment of the fairer sex, including preying on debutantes when he wasn't satisfying himself with whores.

Or so the gossips reported in the papers. If only she'd read them prior to that night instead of the stock reports!

She wasn't his first ruined maiden, nor, apparently, would she be his last.

Now, from an elegant home in London, she would live as a mother, a widow as far as anyone knew, and a businesswoman, which no one would ever know. She was simply Mrs. St. Ange, a baron's daughter, no longer grieving a husband lost at sea two years earlier before her baby was even born.

And without anyone's assistance, except perhaps her old and dearest friend, Lady Margaret Cambrey, Ada would exact revenge upon the vilest nobleman in London. If her father had suspected her motive for returning to London, undoubtedly, he would never have let her out of his sight.

"THERE YOU ARE, OLD chap." The voice had Michael coming out of his reverie, thinking of nothing more important than whether to see his paramour that evening. At White's having read the papers and drunk enough tea to float an armada, he was ready for billiards and brandy. Perhaps a hearty meal first.

He smiled at seeing Lord David Hemsby, an old acquaintance from Eton with whom he'd renewed a friendship after he'd stopped slumming in filthy nameless pubs and gin palaces and returned to his rightful place at the gentlemen's club.

Of course, Michael still drank far too much, regardless of switching from low-class gin to the more refined drink of his peers, French brandy. And still, he refused to speak to his parents, who'd sent him into the foul abyss from which he'd barely emerged. And, of course, he avoided any marriage-minded misses who foolishly hadn't yet been scared off by his hard-earned reputation as a reprobate of the first order.

After a certain garden tryst with a woman whose face he couldn't quite recall but whose floral scent haunted his senses, he'd stopped going to the Whitechapel doxies. They never smelled like anything except gin or frying oil. Instead, he kept company with upper-class widows and genuine Cyprians with all their learned charms, and the occasional nobleman's wife, if one happened across his path. The latter was a rare treat, a titillating adventure that had nearly got him killed twice.

His life was playing out as he'd expected it would after the treachery of his broken engagement.

To his dismay, following a dinner with Hemsby, his evening was ruined by the appearance of the Earl of Alder.

Bloody hell! What could his father possibly want after all this time?

David excused himself to find amusement elsewhere. Brandy in hand, Michael stared across the table from the man he hadn't seen in years.

His father's hair was streaked with gray, a few more lines under his eyes, nothing remarkable that would indicate he'd suffered the loss of his son's respect.

"Come now, you've been nursing this grudge long enough. I'm not getting any younger," George Alder said. "You'll be head of the family within a decade if not sooner."

Sooner the better, Michael muttered under his breath. Then he instantly regretted thinking it. He didn't wish his father dead, simply in another city, preferably another continent.

"And your mother wants to see you," his father added, as if they were discussing a weekly visit. "This estrangement hurts her, especially as she knows you've stayed in contact with your siblings."

Rolling his eyes, Michael signaled the waiter for another drink. He didn't care to discuss his missives back and forth with his younger sister and brother. In fact, he didn't care to discuss anything with the earl.

"Is there anything else? Frankly, you're boring me," Michael said, hoping his tone dripped with the professed boredom. "I'm well-aware you're aging. We both are. As for the 'grudge' as you call it, did you ever consider that maybe you ruined my life's happiness, and now I simply don't give a damn what happens to you or the earldom?"

"Balderdash!"

Michael waited. Then he waited some more, staring into his father's golden-brown eyes, the mirror of his own. Nothing more followed.

"That's it?"

The waiter set down another glass of brandy before him and removed his empty one.

His father clucked his tongue. "Don't you think you've had enough?"

Picking it up, Michael shook his head. "No, not nearly." He sipped, then sipped again. "If I understand you correctly, you wish me to return to the bosom of the family? Forgive and forget? Go give Mummy a peck on the cheek?"

"Don't be insolent."

"I'll be any way I like. I'm a grown man."

"Then start acting like one," his father quipped, "instead of a truculent child."

"Nothing you say can bother me." Yet, in truth, he felt like hurling the contents of his glass at his father's face. "You took away the woman with whom I wanted to spend the rest of my life. And you did so in such a cowardly way no one even knew it wasn't *my* doing. Imagine how I felt finding out you broke it off for me after telling me she was the one who ended our arrangement. If I'd known sooner, I would have gone after her and married her."

His father drummed on the highly polished tabletop. Then he signaled for the waiter and ordered his own brandy.

"I will speak plainly. We couldn't afford for you to marry her. It was ridiculous enough for you to consider a baron's daughter. However, your mother and I were willing to consider it when we thought her father had some money. He didn't have a shilling, as it turned out, and that was the end of it."

"That was the end of it," Michael repeated. "For you and Mummy. It wasn't for me. I loved the girl."

His father shrugged.

"I loved her," Michael insisted. "Don't sit there like a cold fish. What if someone had snatched Mummy away from you?"

The earl sipped his brandy, gazed into the tawny liquid, and then back at his son.

"Then I would have done my duty to the house of Alder and married another woman with your mother's charms and an equal dowry. I love your mother, but I would have found someone else to give me an heir, and she would have found another man to wed her. I certainly wouldn't have moped around, fallen headfirst into a bottle, and begun a campaign of carousing that makes your name and the word *libertine* nearly synonymous."

"Shall I tell Mummy you believe her so easily replaced?"

His father's expression tightened.

"*Ah,* I thought not. As pragmatic as you believe her, I don't think she'd enjoy knowing she was merely a fat purse and a breeding cow," Michael concluded.

His father slammed his glass down and stood. "How dare you? You impertinent cullion!"

Michael nearly yawned to complete the farce, but he restrained himself. With other nearby gentlemen's interest perked and watching the scene unfold, his father might jump over the table and try to throttle him. He would fail, but his aging sire could have an apoplectic fit in the process. Not a good thing at White's. It could tarnish his membership after all.

"Very well," Michael said, his gaze locked with his father's. "Why are you here?"

A few long moments went by. Eventually, the earl looked around, stared down anyone still audaciously looking at their table, and then resumed his seat.

"We are going broke."

Taking in his father's words, Michael considered them. He cocked his head, waiting, wanting more information.

The earl sighed. "The family accounts are low and not replenishing with the small holdings we have. We sold the house in France last year and the hunting lodge at Dunk's Green this past winter. Still, I find our situation grows more precarious. As I said, we are going broke."

Michael had rather liked the house in France. Right on the sea. Pity.

"Actually, not to put too fine a point on it, Father, but *you* are going broke. I have money from Grandfather. Plenty of it, in fact."

Did he have plenty? He wasn't truly sure, although it seemed to him he'd lived frugally these past years. He must have saved a lot by not avoiding any events of the past Seasons. Ticket prices for balls and *soirées* weren't cheap. Indeed, if he recalled correctly, the last time he'd attended an event, it had been with the fervent desire of running into his delectable garden goddess again.

When he hadn't found her after two or three attempts, he'd given up. There were too many marriage-minded ladies at those events anyway. It had been much more enjoyable to cozy up to a lonely widow in her luxurious townhouse. They never needed much in the way of expensive things, more desirous of his company than any sparkling bauble.

True, he'd spent some good sterling on the Cyprians, who liked to be kept in an elegant manner and given expensive gifts. And then, there was his penchant for fine brandy.

First thing in the morning, he would head to his bank and see where he stood.

Meanwhile, this tedious *tête-à-tête* with his father needed to end.

"Thank you for telling me your tale of woe. I don't know what you thought I could do for you, but I assure you, I can do nothing. Despite your shabby treatment of me, I hope you fare well." Standing, he picked up his drink and walked away.

Hopefully, David would still be in the billiards room.

"Think of your sister and brother," his father's voice cut across the room.

Michael barely broke his stride as he crossed the carpeted floor.

Yet, when he reached the next room, his father was right behind him. The man was harder to get rid of than the pox. Thankfully, that particular challenge had not been visited upon him.

Whirling to face the earl, Michael kept his tone neutral. "What do you want?"

"You are the heir! Do you wish to deal with this *after* I die? You'll have a grieving widow on your hands, as well as two siblings looking to you for help, one for a dowry and one for an allowance. At that point, we may no longer have our beloved Oxonholt. Thus, your family will leave Kent and come live with you in Town. Won't that be cozy?"

Michael considered all this. "Then don't die anytime soon."

He meant what he said. He wasn't prepared to become the head of the family, nor be responsible for the maintenance of his mother, brother, and sister. He certainly didn't want them in his modest townhouse.

His father's impatience was written upon his countenance.

"It's time for you to start preparing, at the very least," the earl continued. "What do I want from you? I want my eldest son to use his God-given brain for something besides enjoying himself. You used to have a conscience and a purpose. Five years ago, you were talking about railways and mining and even textiles. I think it's past time you started figuring out how to make money the way every man-Jack is doing in this budding nation of ours."

Michael narrowed his eyes. "At the time, as I recall, you turned up your nose at my interest in such middle-class business dealings."

"At the time, I didn't realize servants would demand a raise in their wages or the price of bread would shoot through the roof or the government would start taxing my land right out from under me. I tell you, it's almost not possible to be a landholder if you aren't also a savvy businessman. And that's the truth."

"I am supposed to suddenly figure out the intricate world of business, am I?" Michael desperately wished this entire encounter never had happened and even more desperately wanted another soothing glass of French delight, only to discover he still had one in his hand.

"Somebody has to," his father pointed out, "and I'm too bloody old to start. Come see me in a week and let me know what you've found out."

Michael spluttered his last sip of brandy. "A week?"

"If I give you any longer, then you'll simply dawdle about and put it off. We need action now. I've already waited too long for you to come to your senses."

"Come to my senses? You're not making me want to help you."

"You're not helping *me*," the earl insisted. "You're helping yourself, if you haven't figured that out yet. When your grandfather's money is gone, how long do you think White's will let you stay?" He gestured at the grand establishment around them.

"Maybe more important to you, how will you keep your mistresses? Or have you sunk so low you don't mind them keeping you, like a bloody lap dog?"

"We're finished," Michael told him, turning his back and walking away.

"One week," his father called after him.

ADA WAS IN LOVE! When Maggie came to visit, bringing her little Rosie, Ada simply had to tell her.

"I absolutely love my new home. Look, come see the adorable carving around the drawing room fireplace."

Maggie agreed it was adorable. "And yes, to the pale green draperies," her friend agreed. "They are a far better choice than ivory. Every detail is perfect, and suits you down to the doorknocker. You're creating a wonderful home."

"I thank that clever Mr. Cubitt for developing the square. He's positively ancient, but I wonder if I should visit with him and offer him my honest appreciation."

Ada's friend laughed. "Think of where we were a few years back," Maggie recalled. "Can you believe our lives at present? I was practically penniless in Sheffield, and we were both husband hunting. And now you've bought your own white stucco home in Belgrave Square. Why, there's a duke living two doors down, for goodness sake, and an admiral of the fleet across the way."

Ada laughed. "And you and I both have a child." They beamed at each other.

Maggie and her husband, John Angsley, the Earl of Cambrey, were the only people outside of Ada's own family who knew she'd never been wed and widowed. She'd told Maggie in a long letter from Juniper Hall as soon as she realized she was with child a month after fleeing London.

A month after receiving Alder's terribly cynical wink.

Yet even her friend didn't know who Harry's father was. Ada would take that to her grave.

For one thing, Lord Alder had once been engaged to Maggie's older sister, Jenny, now happily married to Lord Lindsey. Their engagement had not been official, however, since it had never been announced. What's more, Alder had broken the agreement as soon as Jenny and Maggie's father passed away leaving the Blackwood family in debt.

The shallow cad!

Ada hadn't known any of that during the time she'd been smitten with Michael Alder. She'd simply thought him an upstanding viscount with a certain dash-fire that appealed to her tremendously.

Had she known he hadn't kept a verbal promise to wed, she might have looked at him differently. Unfortunately, she learned Jenny's tale far too late to avoid her own ruin.

After finding out from Maggie one day when they were visiting, enjoying their babies, and discussing men in general, how Lord Alder had ill-used Jenny, Ada imagined it would be terribly awkward to disclose who her child's father was. Instead, she let Maggie believe she had loved a man who'd ardently loved her back, and who for private reasons couldn't marry her.

Then she'd created an entirely false and tragic romance to save face and keep Harry's father perceived as a good man. Often, Ada wished she hadn't. It was a burden not to be able to rage against Lord Vile just once to a sympathetic ear.

"How is Jenny?" The question popped out of Ada's mouth unbidden. She still had a fascination for the woman who, unlike her, had moved on from Michael Alder to a full and seemingly happy life.

"Very well. Living in utter bliss with her husband. And like me," Maggie patted her barely blossoming stomach, "expecting again."

Ada nodded, thinking how Harry might wish for a brother or sister who would never come.

"Her third, isn't it?"

"Fourth," Maggie said, then offered a wry grin. "You know Jenny with numbers. She likes to add."

They both laughed. For as Ada had a head for the stock market, Maggie's sister was a skilled accountant.

Inside, though, Ada thought if Michael Alder hadn't broken off with Jenny Blackwood, then those four children would be his, and Harry wouldn't exist at all. Stranger even to think that she and Jenny had kissed the same man.

"Are you all right?" Maggie asked, seeing some change in her expression.

"Yes, thinking how nice it would be for Harry to have a sibling."

Maggie tilted her pretty head. "It could still happen, couldn't it?"

Ada appreciated the softening in her friend's eyes and voice, but she couldn't think of opening her heart to another man, nor ever being used again for a man's pleasure. She was sure *Aristotle's Masterpiece,* the explicit book of relations between a man and a woman, had got it all wrong, for Ada had felt a little pain, certainly fear and excitement, but none of the great pleasure mentioned in the book, which got passed around from sister to sister and from sister to friend in the debutante groups.

Plus, she couldn't recall that night without remembering how her maid and her mother had seen the blood on her undergarments—her utter disgrace had been complete.

No, it had been nothing but shame and humiliation. If Maggie and her sister didn't mind the marital act of procreation in order to have happy husbands and more children, that was their business.

"Next time you see Jenny or write to her, please tell her I wish her well."

"I will," Maggie promised. "Where is your Harry, by the way?"

"We'll go up to the nursery in a minute. I can't wait for you to see the room. It's—"

"Adorable?"

Ada smiled and rang for tea. "Yes, positively. And his nanny is patient and wise. My mother found her for me, and I love her."

Maggie leaned back on the pale, rose-colored sofa. "You seem content. Is there anything amiss?"

"Except for needing to hire more staff, no. Why do you ask?"

"Your missive sounded as though you had something on your mind besides nannies and fireplace carvings."

Ada knew she would need to get to the point, but was having trouble articulating exactly what she wanted from her friend. *What if Maggie said no?*

"Yes, in fact, there is something important I want to speak with you about. However, it's rather . . . how shall I put it? Irregular."

Maggie raised her eyebrows. "Really. How interesting?"

Just then, Rosie, two years old like Harry, got up from where she sat on the soft carpet playing with her two dolls.

"Mama," she said, placing her hands on her mother's lap. "I want a bicky."

"Biscuit, dear. I'm sure Auntie Ada has something for you."

"Oh, I do, and better than a biscuit, too."

Ada opened the top drawer of the lamp table beside her, withdrawing a paper-wrapped chocolate bar. She handed this to the delighted toddler who jumped up and down with glee.

"I hope you don't mind," Ada said to Maggie. "It's from Fry's, and I think they're fabulous."

"It would be a bit late if I did mind."

They both looked at Rosie who'd already proceeded to rip off the wrapping with her chubby fingers and was half-sucking, half-chewing on the sweet confection.

"I don't suppose I'm going to get a bite of that," Maggie said, and Ada reached into the drawer, pulling out another one.

"See what it says? *Chocolate delicieux à manger.* When I saw the French, I thought of you."

"Thank you. Glad to know my fluency is good for something." Maggie took the bar and slipped it into her reticule. "For later. I'll share it with John. My husband has quite the sweet tooth, as well."

Ada tilted her head. "You may be disappointed. It can be a little chalky and even bitter."

They both glanced at Rosie who seemed to have no complaints.

Then Ada had a thought. Perhaps if she helped her friend grow her income, she'd be more willing to aid her in her scheme.

28

"If you're interested in turning that sweet tooth into a little extra income," Ada continued, "I would suggest you approach John Cadbury and see if he wants someone to invest in his business. It's growing, and his workers love him. Also, I have a little inside knowledge Parliament intends to get rid of the high tax on cocoa soon, within a year or so. I think the chocolate industry will blossom."

"Goodness gracious, you are a wonder!"

Ada felt her cheeks warm, and she shrugged.

"You didn't invite me here to give me investment advice," Maggie said shrewdly.

"No, but I also didn't invite you here merely to ask for your help."

"I know, but let's get that out of the way so we can go see the adorable nursery and your lovely boy."

Taking a deep breath, Ada blurted, "I need to figure out how to masquerade as a man."

CHAPTER THREE

Maggie said nothing at first. Ada liked that about her, neither condemning her nor immediately drowning her in a barrage of nosey questions. Instead, she asked a very intelligent one.

"Do you need to *be* the man specifically, or will someone acting on your behalf suffice?"

Ada sighed in relief. "Oh, the latter, as long as I can trust him. And he must seem intelligent and be personable enough that someone else will trust him, too."

"Someone in particular?"

Ada nodded. *Oh, yes!*

"Strangely enough, Jenny was in a similar situation a few years back after my father died," Maggie disclosed. "Remember when we left Town and went back to Sheffield?"

"Yes, of course." Ada had mourned the loss of her friend mid-Season.

"I know you'll keep this in confidence since it doesn't really reflect well on a countess, but Jenny worked as a bookkeeper. She let our manservant, Henry, be the liaison between the outside world of my sister's clients and herself, whom she called 'Mr. Cavendish.' Henry collected people's ledgers and returned them after she was done."

Ada considered. "I don't want anyone to know there is another person involved, namely me, in the background. If I didn't masquerade as a man myself, then I thought to hire an individual who could meet with a specific someone to pass on information as if it were his own."

"Depending on the type of information, that seems so much harder," Maggie mused "What if your 'specific someone' whom you are trying to fool asks a question and your counterfeit man doesn't have the answer?"

Ada could easily see how that might happen. There were so many tricky components to the stock market, which she'd spent years figuring out. On the other hand, she didn't want Alder to suspect there was anyone else he could blame when things went terribly wrong as she intended them to.

"My counterfeit man, as you call him, will know enough to fool anyone. I'll make sure of that. If he doesn't know something, then he'll say, 'That's a trade secret' or something like that."

"I suppose it will work," Maggie agreed. "Before we proceed, I need to know one thing? This is about business, I assume, and your investing skills? It sounds as though you want to impart something you know to someone without them knowing it's you."

"Precisely," Ada agreed.

"No one will get hurt, especially you?"

"Can you be more specific?" Ada asked, prevaricating. "What do you mean by 'getting hurt'?"

"Oh, dear," Maggie muttered. "I suppose I mean no one is going to lose life or limb or go to prison unjustly."

Ada considered. "Then, I can say yes, no one will get hurt, especially me. So how do I find a trustworthy man willing to act a role? Your connections are greater than mine."

"I'll have to ask John."

As Ada's eyes widened in alarm, Maggie calmed her. "Don't worry. He knows everyone, and he won't mind helping as long as no one will get hurt. I believe you intend to help someone who wouldn't otherwise take the help of a woman, am I right?"

"Something like that." *Actually, nothing like that*, Ada thought.

But Maggie was sipping her tea and wearing a dreamy expression.

"Wouldn't it be frightfully romantic if you fall in love with either the counterfeit man, or the other one, the individual he'll meet with?"

Ada recoiled. "No!"

Maggie shrugged. "All right. Don't look so alarmed. I am sensing this isn't about romance."

"No," Ada repeated. "This has nothing to do with an affair of the heart."

In fact, she had to keep her heart utterly detached for the rest of her plan to work.

This was all about cold, hard vengeance.

"AS EASY AS FALLING out of bed," said the man whom Lord Cambrey, Maggie's husband, sent a week later.

Ada was extremely grateful to meet the discreet Mr. Clive Brunnel, an innocuous man of indeterminate age, with an accent marking him as well-educated and an open, trustworthy face. No scars or pox marks visible, either. In a word, perfect for the job.

However, she didn't see her plan as easy. To her, it was complicated and scary. What's more, the time to act was imminent, since she'd found out Lord Alder was asking about potential money-making businesses.

How incredibly fortuitous! She had thought getting the despicable viscount interested in his own financial ruin would be difficult. Then she'd come to London only to find he would make things easy for her, as long as she could steer him away from the Royal Stock Exchange, where she had no connections, and toward the London Stock Exchange, of which her father was a member.

Ideally, her liaison, as Ada now thought of Mr. Brunnel, would himself have been a member of the exchange, either a broker or a jobber. However, none of those men would endanger their good standing, or risk becoming defaulters, by taking purchase requests from a woman. Thus, Mr. Brunnel was a necessary go-between, and she'd told him to deal with an associate of her father, a jobber named Andrew Barnes, who would deal fairly with Clive Brunnel and not charge an exorbitant commission.

"Very well. You mustn't ask me any whys or wherefores. You must simply do as I say."

"Yes, missus. You're paying my fee. As long as there is no bodily injury required, either to myself or anyone else."

"Gracious, no." Ada wondered what he'd been asked to do in the past but didn't really want to know. "You're positive you've never met Lord Alder or his family?"

"No, missus. I'm sure."

"Very good. First, we need to make contact with him. Do you think you could encounter him outside of his club, perhaps seeming to be coming from a meeting? I envision you with papers and a satchel and look very knowledgeable. Perhaps we should get you some glasses."

Clive looked doubtful, but nodded.

"Then you bump into Lord Alder on the doorstep of White's and drop your stock reports and say something like, 'Can't make a fortune for a man if my investments are all on the ground.'"

He frowned.

"I'll let you come up with that part, then. Simply find a way to sound successful in investing, and I'm sure he'll want to speak with you."

"Yes, missus. You leave it to me."

MICHAEL COULDN'T BELIEVE HE'D gone from his carefree existence to worrying about saving the family estate in a week. After a second meeting with his father and the earl's banker, as well as a private meeting with his own banker, Michael was well and truly committed to not ending up as a threadbare, former nobleman, living in a country cottage with a single maid and boiled potatoes for every meal.

Not to mention having his mother and siblings share the same cottage.

He was letting his imagination run wild with how far he could fall, but at least those thoughts inspired him to action. Nevertheless, he had no idea how the hell he was supposed to grow their accounts. He needed help.

Someone at White's would put him on to the right person, perhaps a way to invest in the railways.

As he approached the inconspicuous set of doors, another man was exiting and plowed into him.

In a flurry of apologies, Michael realized what he was helping the individual pick up from the pavement were stock reports.

Fate had stepped in. Hopefully, the man was better with investing than maneuvering the doors and streets of London.

In very short order, he'd turned him around, and they were seated in the room for members' guests.

"Should I be concerned you don't have a membership here?" Michael asked Mr. Brunnel, watching the stranger push his glasses up the bridge of his nose.

The man shrugged, appearing unconcerned. "I know so many here, I come and go as I please without having to pay the yearly dues. Smart of me, don't you think?"

Michael nodded, supposing it was how the rich stayed rich.

"Besides, if I feel like a little social outing, I go to Crocky's. The Shark has enough excitement at his establishment. Better food, too."

Michael couldn't argue with that. Crockford's gaming hall was elegant and served the finest in French cuisine.

"You are not titled, then?"

"No," the man was quick to offer with honesty and a grin. Again, he fiddled with his glasses.

"Nor are you a businessman, Mr. Brunnel?"

"True enough. I have neither shop nor trade. I make my money on the market, the only type of trade I'm interested in. I've already spent years figuring out marketable securities, and it's the quickest way to earn—or lose—a fortune."

"And you can help me?"

Brunnel nodded. "That's what I do."

"Why?"

"Why?" The man pushed his glasses up his nose, then removed them entirely and put them in his pocket.

"Yes," Michael persisted. "If you've made a fortune and can continue to make more, why do you work for others?"

The man hesitated. "You're asking why I do what I do?"

"Precisely." If Brunnel hesitated a moment longer, Michael would show him the door.

"It's entertaining," Brunnel said, offering a large smile.

"Really?" Michael wondered at his answer.

"Yes, rather like some men who spend their time at the races or hunting or at a pugilist club. I'd rather be dealing with stocks, watching them rise and fall. It's exciting to predict and then see your predictions play out. As you surmised, I'm not titled, but I wield a lot of power by handling gentlemen's accounts."

Michael nodded and sipped his drink. "This offers you amusement, then."

"More than that. I've made a lot and intend to make more. If I help you, then I get some of your profit as well."

That made perfect sense. "How do we start?"

Brunnel frowned. "Ask me how I made my money."

"I beg your pardon."

Brunnel cocked his head. "I thought you might want to know."

"All right, seeing as how you want to tell me."

The man grinned again. "I read the newspapers, domestic and foreign. I see trends. I also read the parliamentary notes and upcoming acts and bills. All of this lets me know what's going to be big. When I realized we were going to lay telegraph cables across the channel to the froggies, I invested in the raw materials and the know-how."

Michael was impressed.

"I wouldn't have the head for it," he confessed. "You'll just tell me what to invest in, correct?"

"Exactly so, my lord. In fact, I'll tell you, then you approve, and then I pop over to the exchange and place the order."

"And there are short-term returns? I need to see things happen within months or even less to begin with."

"Certainly. How else could I prove myself?"

"Indeed. And how much will your advice cost me?" Michael braced himself.

"Twenty-five percent."

"Ridiculous! It's my money and my risk. I'll offer you ten percent. Anything else is outrageous usury! Robbery even."

"Hardly that," Brunnel said, looking unruffled. "How about we settle on eighteen?"

"*Hm,* that seems as if it would offer you plenty of the amusement you seek."

"It will suffice," Brunnel agreed. "Remember though, if and when you win, we win together. You lose, you lose alone."

Despite the harsh sound of the man's statement, Michael didn't see how he had any choice. "Then let's start winning, shall we?"

"Exactly so, my lord," the man said again, and they shook on it.

After his new business partner left, Michael considered him. Turning the man's card over in his hands, he wondered if he should investigate Brunnel a little. Yet, he'd all but promised to turn him a profit in a month. If he did, then Michael would trust him with his family's future. If he didn't, he'd beat the tar out of him for good measure and walk away.

It also put him of the mind to go to Crocky's for a little amusement of his own before he visited his latest paramour, a widow residing in Belgrave Square. To that end, a few hours later, after his valet had spruced him up, Michael appeared at the luxurious Crockford's on St. James's Street.

In minutes, he was surrounded by the cream of British aristocracy, young men gambling fortunes in a blink of an eye. Michael swallowed. A few weeks ago, he would have joined them in wagering too much and not giving a fig. Now, he intended to watch more than play, spend his money on a delicious meal and some fine imported brandy. The women here were not for sale but were lovely, nonetheless, so he passed a pleasant few hours until it was time to see his lady friend.

He'd even won a few hands of piquet.

Feeling uplifted by everything he'd accomplished in one day, Michael fairly sprung aboard his carriage for the ten-minute ride around the north side of Green Park, past Buckingham Palace, to the widow's house.

Every home at Belgrave Square was nicer than his own residence, a brick townhouse on Brook Street. This fact didn't bother him a bit. Lady Elizabeth Pepperton was generous with her home, her food, her body, and especially her brandy. Her husband having succumbed two years prior to the fatal disease of old age, this young widow enjoyed the fruits of her short marriage to an aged man.

One evening at a private dinner, Michael had congratulated her on earning such a juicy retirement in the only way open to a woman. They'd gone home together that very night and had spent many enjoyable evenings during the past six months.

They would never marry. His income was insufficient to keep her, and she could never be faithful in any case. She'd admitted as much. With such a solid understanding, he could enjoy her thoroughly for as long as they suited.

Disembarking from his carriage, he was about to scale the three shallow steps to her darkly varnished door and brass knocker when he heard a woman cry out in distress.

Glancing to his right, he saw a vision of golden tresses wearing an elegant purple gown with a matching pelisse, both were the deep, rich color of a woman who'd left her debutante pastel years behind her.

Another woman, clearly a nanny, held a youngster by one hand and a shopping bag in the other. The packages strewn on the pavement were obviously the cause of the lady's distress. Yet her carriage was already pulling away, perhaps heading for the stables in the alley behind.

Trotting the few yards between them, he was bending at the feet of the lady, collecting her packages, even before she could begin to do so.

"Thank you, sir. I'm afraid I had piled them too high, and clearly, I am no architect," she said to his bowed head, her voice having an inviting, lilting quality.

When he had gathered everything in his arms, including a small carpet runner wrapped in brown paper, he looked up.

The expression on her face changed instantly from smiling, warm, and friendly to one of shock. Indeed, shock was the only thing Michael could think of which would cause her smile to falter and disappear and her creamy complexion to become chalk-white.

Perhaps she'd expected someone else, her husband even, and was surprised beyond all reason by a stranger.

"I hope nothing is damaged," he said.

She merely stared at him with clear blue eyes, taking his measure.

He could not in good conscience pile all the parcels back into her slender arms.

"May I carry them into your home for you?" he offered.

"No," she snapped, finally coming out of her daze.

Even her tone had changed remarkably from the softer greeting.

She started to grab them from him, dropping some and becoming more agitated.

"Please, I mean no harm," Michael assured her. "I will simply get them into your front hall. Where is your butler? Why did your footman not stop and help?"

She glared at him, not answering. Walking around him, she reached her front door and thrust it open, tossing the packages she held inside, presumably onto the floor, before returning to retrieve the rest from him.

He bent and picked up another dropped bundle, hoping it was a large bag of tea or a cushion, for anything else would be damaged beyond repair by the rough handling.

Handing it to her, his gloved fingers touched hers. He watched, fascinated, as she froze, staring where they both held the package.

Had she stopped breathing?

"I believe you should have more household help."

Meeting his gaze, her eyes were glittering with . . . anger?

"I believe it is none of your business. Nanny Finn," she said, without looking away, "please take Harry inside."

He glanced past the beauty to watch the other two go up the steps. At the door, the little boy looked back at him with large amber eyes and a curious smile.

Lifting his hand, Michael gave him a wave, which he returned.

The lady gasped again. Snatching the bundle to her chest, she turned and followed them inside.

"You are most welcome," he called after her as the front door closed with a bang.

Hmm, what do you make of that? A hell of a feisty female. He wouldn't want to be her husband. Except she had a delectable figure and pretty, rosy lips.

For all he knew, though, she was dull as mud and a harsh scold. In which case, no luscious curves and pretty blonde tresses would make her desirable.

In a minute, he was in his mistress's parlor seated on her sofa, and her maid was pouring them each a glass of madeira. As soon as the servant left, Elizabeth locked the door and drew the drapes.

Just those two actions stirred his loins, anticipating what would follow. She joined him on the plush velvet seat.

"What do you know of your neighbors?" he asked.

Elizabeth raised her eyebrows questioningly.

"The family at number twenty-seven," he clarified.

"Oh, Mrs. St. Ange. She recently moved here with her boy. I haven't had a chance to meet her yet. How do you know her?"

"I don't. Her packages were all over the sidewalk, and I was kind enough to help her. Odd woman, I thought."

"Really?" She'd started to run her hand along his thigh. "How so?"

"Seemed both furious at me and petrified, too."

Draping his arm around her, he drew her close, not minding at all when her hand brushed the buttons of his pants.

"What of her husband? Is he anybody?"

"No one at all, apparently, for he is dead. She is a widow."

His interest perked, even though he knew himself a scoundrel. Here he was, holding a lush female in his hands, her fingers even then unfastening the fall of his trousers, yet he was fancying his chances with the sharp-tongued golden lady two doors down.

Setting his glass on the table beside him, he turned fully to his fine widow, dragging her gown up her long legs at the same time as he bent low to kiss the soft skin of her neck.

As usual, the only thing missing was the delicious floral scent that had enchanted him three years earlier on the skin of a goddess.

However, as his shaft sprung free and he drew Elizabeth's gown up to her hips to find she had nothing on underneath, Michael had to admit a willing woman with no expectations was a rather fine consolation.

CHAPTER FOUR

*W*hat *cruel coincidence had put Lord Vile literally on her doorstep?*

Ada asked herself this as she turned the page while reading a fairy tale to her darling boy, and she wondered again while eating alone before preparing for bed and a good book of her own.

Alder's townhouse, as Ada had discovered before returning to London, was over a mile away on the east side of Hyde Park so he hadn't simply been happening by. Obviously, he was on the square to pay a visit to his current paramour, who lived a mere two doors down in the same terrace of homes.

Of course, she should have expected to run into him— in fact, that was the point of returning to Town. It was simply the utter surprise Ada found difficult to get over.

To have been caught unawares and off guard—it had been a blow to the calm and tough exterior she'd crafted.

Would it have made a difference had she some warning before seeing him? She wasn't at all sure any prior notice would have helped quell the myriad of emotions which had assaulted her upon seeing his face. She only wished she hadn't let her temper—and the instantaneous flood of rage—get the better of her. He must have thought her either half mad or a shrew, at the very least.

Alder looked the same. Somehow, his unchanged appearance had left her disconcerted since she was certain she no longer looked to be the same wide-eyed innocent who had blundered to her own ruin.

If she'd had any doubt of this, it was put to rest when he obviously hadn't recognized her. Of course, Vile not remembering her was due to a variety of reasons, some unpleasant to consider. The night *it* happened, the garden had been dimly lit, he'd looked at her face for only a short period before he was pushing her onto her back as most of his interest had been beneath her skirts, and he'd walked away so quickly, there hadn't been time for her to make any kind of impression. Besides, he had a flask of alcohol, and was thus bleary-eyed and foggy-brained.

In any case, she was so forgettable, that horrid night, he hadn't recognized her from earlier the same evening, a mere few hours before.

Moreover, from the rumors, Lord Vile had so many women in the interim years even if she'd had three eyes, he was just as likely to have forgotten her.

As she sank into her pillows, book open on her lap, Ada could admit to herself a smidgen of gall. Her pride was well and truly pricked. Yet how disastrous would it have been if he had remembered her! For her plans to work, Lord Vile couldn't think upon the young lady he'd enjoyed and left with no thought to the consequences.

No, she didn't want him to recall anything about the previous Miss Ellis, when as the widow St. Ange, she would make him fall for her and become absolutely devoted, and then she would cut out his black heart.

Still, she wished she hadn't encountered him before she was ready, as it had left her a little uncertain. Never mind. Somehow, she would use it to her advantage.

Opening her copy of Shakespeare's *Othello*, she gazed at the wood-engraved illustrations, considering how one man could be so easily fooled by another into believing something with all his heart.

MICHAEL FOUND HIMSELF THINKING about the fair-haired woman on Belgrave Square. Too much, in fact, particularly when he was supposed to be focusing on the future of the earldom.

Today, he was meeting Mr. Brunnel and finding out precisely what his first investment would be.

"Guano!" the man said with enthusiasm.

"Guano?" Michael repeated. "I'm not sure I understand."

"You don't know what it is? Is that the problem?" Brunnel asked.

"Of course I know what it is. Bat manure," Michael practically growled the words.

This was how he was going to save the Alder name? With the feces from a flying mouse? After a brief pause, he asked, "What are you playing at?"

"Not *bat* guano, my lord. Seabird guano. Peruvian, to be precise. You want a quick return, don't you, to prove I know what I'm doing? This isn't a huge-profit market, like silk, for instance, but it will give you results in weeks."

"Why on earth do we want bird dung from Peru or anywhere else?"

"It's presently the finest fertilizer known to mankind. Rich in nitrate. Hundreds of ships are pulling up to the southern coast of Peru, not just from Britain, but from Germany and America, too."

Michael shook his head.

Clive Brunnel frowned. "You don't want to invest in this?"

"Oh, no, I do. I'm simply surprised. I'm truly starting at the bottom, in the actual dung heap."

They shared a laugh. "Indeed, you are."

In a very short time, Michael had signed a note for the requested amount, and their transaction was complete.

"May I tell anyone else about this?" If the man was fleecing him, he would want it kept quiet.

Brunnel shrugged. "Tell whomever you like. Let your friends in on the stock tip and they'll thank you in a few weeks."

Encouraged by his answer, Michael thought he might tell Hemsby over a glass of brandy and get his opinion, if he had one. On seabird guano!

"YES, MRS. ST. ANGE, just as you said. I told Lord Alder he could tell whomever he wants. And the jobber you recommended was courteous and fair."

"Thank you, Mr. Brunnel. Please come again in three weeks' time? We'll see where his investments are, and then you can set up a meeting with the viscount to impart the good news."

Ada saw him out, as she still hadn't found a suitable butler. Having never set up her own household before, she'd had no idea the difficulty one had in finding staff. She'd interviewed two men who gave her an uneasy feeling, seemingly too interested in her *not* having a Mr. St. Ange, or any man in the house. Moreover, she hadn't found even a footman to augment her carriage driver. And even he was only at her disposal a few days a week.

At least she had Clive Brunnel. The man was perfect for the position as he had a manner that instilled confidence, even if he knew no more about import and export than what she'd told him. He'd helped her begin the ruin of Lord Vile.

Now, it was her turn to take the bull by the horns. To that end, she decided to befriend his current paramour.

This turned out to be easily done. After all, very little investigation beforehand and the good fortune of a home becoming available at Belgrave Square had put the woman within a few doors.

To live so close to where Lord Vile practiced his profligate ways might have seemed a smack in Ada's face if she hadn't intended to use it to insinuate herself into his life.

His mistress could be an easy means of ending up in his company, depending on how openly they flaunted their relationship. For instance, she knew Lady Pepperton liked to host dinner parties, and her escort for the past half-year had nearly always been Lord Vile.

As if out for a stroll, Ada left her calling card with the widow's butler. Observing the sandy-haired fellow, she couldn't help wondering where Lady Pepperton had found him. A good age, neither too young nor too old, the butler didn't feel threatening, plus he undoubtedly could still carry packages and move furniture without groaning about his back.

"Do you wish to wait, madam, while I take your card to her? Her ladyship is at home."

"No, thank you. I would never do so uninvited. I live two doors down. Give her my card, and we shall meet when mutually convenient if she wishes. Please tell her I said precisely that."

Ada wandered home for some soothing milky tea since her heart was beating hard at her boldness. Taking her card over with no expectations was one thing. However, staying for an audience with Lady Pepperton would have marked her as vulgar indeed.

Entering her own gorgeous home, she almost wished she'd feigned a dead aristocratic husband instead of a humble yet wealthy businessman. However, if she'd returned to London as Lady Such-and-Such, eyebrows would have raised and many of the *ton* would have started digging. They didn't like newcomers popping up out of nowhere into their esteemed ranks.

As Mrs. St. Ange, however, she was of no threat and of no particular interest. In other words, invisible. London society would leave her alone except for her own outreaching toward them. Her wealth would help open many doors. To that end, Ada hoped Lady Pepperton would want to meet her at least as a neighbor.

Surprisingly, it happened within hours. A footman walked the two doors down with an invitation to dinner that very evening.

Strange, Ada thought, that the woman had no plans, but then, by inviting her on such short notice, Lady Pepperton must have assumed she had none either.

Since it was dark, Ada had her driver escort her, walking by her side the few steps between her door and the widow's, and then she dismissed him for the night. She would brave the return trip by herself with a quick dash.

She was welcomed inside by the same butler, who also took her cape and showed her into a well-appointed drawing room. Elegant, understated, it looked in many ways similar to Ada's choices in color and style, except there were simply more things. More bric-a-brac and paintings, more rugs and candles.

"My new neighbor," Lady Pepperton exclaimed as she entered, wearing an exquisite buttery yellow brocade gown that hugged her tall and curvaceous figure while the full pleated skirts cinched to an impossibly tiny waist.

Ada felt almost frumpy, inches shorter as she was and wearing a subdued shade of dove gray. However, the lady made her feel like an honored guest, taking both her hands and kissing each of her cheeks.

"Another widow on my block! And not an old stuffy one, either. I'm thrilled."

She sounded as though she meant it.

"Thank you for inviting me to dinner, my lady."

"Oh, you must stop that at once. We are going to be friends, I just know it. Two women of independent means. What matters if I married a lord? You must call me Elizabeth, I insist."

"Very well. And you must call me Ada."

Elizabeth laughed good-naturedly.

"Oh, I'm not laughing at you," she clarified when Ada looked on in confusion. "Your name is simply so short in comparison."

Shrugging slightly, Ada confessed, "I was meant to be Ada Kathryn after my grandmother, but it was such a mouthful, very soon after my birth, my mother shortened it to Ada Kate. My friends shortened it even further to Ada, which suits me fine."

"Perfect!" The widow was a happy person, and everything Ada said or did all evening invoked the same response, starting with her choice of beverage.

"Madeira or sherry?"

"Madeira, if you please," Ada said.

"Perfect!"

And thus it went, throughout a half hour *tête-à-tête* in which they got to know each other, or at least Ada's falsified story of true love and loss. Elizabeth didn't even attempt a pretense of having loved Lord Pepperton.

"He was a necessary means to an end," she admitted, gesturing around herself at the "end" result. "What's more, Lyle didn't mind a bit. He had already married and had no issue. His wife was long dead. I was a decoration and a comfort for his last years, and I never cuckolded him during our two years together."

She said it so matter-of-factly, Ada didn't even take offense at the impropriety of it.

"I knew there'd be plenty of time for amusing myself in that regard *after* he passed."

Oh dear! Ada had never had an acquaintance who spoke so plainly about such a topic before. What's more, Lord Vile was Elizabeth's latest amusement. Later, in private, Ada would consider the emotions brought up by such a strange situation. They had kissed the same man. They'd both done a great deal more than kiss him, too.

For now, she would use it as the perfect opening to bring the conversation around to the lady's paramour. The bullseye for her arrow of retribution.

"Do you intend to marry again?"

Elizabeth immediately shook her head, her dark waves of hair ruffling as she did.

"I have no intent in that regard. Why should I? I have money enough to last, absolute freedom, and my choice of lovers."

Ada felt her cheeks heat up. *Lovers!*

"What about you? You have been a widow you said for two years. Do you want to marry again?" Elizabeth waited expectantly.

"No, I suppose I don't." In fact, Ada couldn't imagine saddling herself with a domineering male. Currently, everything was exactly to her liking, and she answered to no one. Yet, she doubted she would feel the same in Elizabeth's shoes, without a child. Harry had given her purpose, along with her deep-seated desire for revenge.

"You amuse yourself, as you said, with . . . with available gentlemen?" *Good God*, Ada couldn't believe she was asking such a question, but she had to get the conversation to Lord Vile.

Elizabeth nodded. "Exactly so. And since I'm widowed and my paramours are always unmarried, we can go out in polite society and are welcomed practically anywhere."

"Paramour*s*?" Ada emphasized the "s" and then felt like a country bumpkin instead of the sophisticated London woman she'd wanted to project. "Forgive me," she added at once.

Elizabeth only laughed, a lovely sound from a lovely woman, and while Ada admitted she liked this lady, she also felt her self-esteem sinking. How could she ever compete with Lady Pepperton, steal Michael Alder from her, and crush his heart—if he had one—under her satin slipper? Or at least crush his pride?

Moreover, how would she make a move at all if this woman became her friend? She wouldn't want to hurt her in order to hurt Lord Vile. She'd hoped for a hard-hearted, brittle vixen who wouldn't give a fig if Michael Alder left her for another.

Truly, Ada felt her head was becoming muddled.

"Do you know something?" Elizabeth said when they were seated at one end of her glossy, cherry-wood dining table with bowls of light broth before them. "I think finding your own bit of amusement would do you a world of good if you've simply been in mourning and grieving. And how old is your little one?"

"My son is two and a half years old."

"Perfect," Elizabeth said again, with less enthusiasm. "I never wanted children. My mother died from trying to produce another for my father when there were already three of us. Plus, I'm too selfish."

Delicately tipping back her glass of wine, she sipped.

"Shall I help you find someone with whom you may keep company? I have a wonderful companion currently, and he knows many people."

Ada felt a frisson of discomfort.

"Truthfully, I have heard of your association with Lord Alder. I wouldn't want to deceive you. Are you in love with him?"

If her bold question disturbed her ladyship, she showed no sign. Yet she sighed heavily.

"I wish I were. As I said, not in order to marry, which holds no appeal, but I have never been in love. I would very much like to try it, as long as I don't get hurt. And who can guarantee such a thing?"

Lady Pepperton spooned the soup slowly, thinking, while Ada considered her own youthful obsession with Michael Alder. If she hadn't taken an instant liking to him, then she might have been open to one of the other men she'd met during her Seasons.

"I suppose I'm a coward," Elizabeth continued, "but I'm having entirely too much enjoyment to care. Besides, I can't fall in love when I'm thinking of who else is out there. There's always another paramour around the corner."

She laughed heartily at her own words, and Ada couldn't help joining in.

"Not wanting to deceive you either," Elizabeth added, "Lord Alder mentioned running into you outside your door, and I told him your name. I hope you don't mind."

They'd been talking of her already. How odd and also fortunate.

"I don't mind at all." Nevertheless, she mustn't let all this frank and interesting talk dissuade her from moving her plan forward. Especially now she knew Elizabeth's heart was not invested.

"How did you meet?" Ada asked.

"Alder? At a dinner. In fact, I should throw one. I haven't in weeks. I will invite you, of course, and there's another new tenant of the square. He's older than us but not too old. I believe his family is from Cornwall. I'll send my card around there first thing in the morning. Who else? Two other singles and another couple should do the trick. We'll have both a little uncertainty amongst you single eligibles, as well as some safe steadiness with us confirmed couples. And there'll be no one frightening, I promise you, like awful gossipy Lady Turnandy. I tell you, that one is a nightmare."

And Elizabeth launched into a story of how the older woman with the morals of a saint tried to blackball Lady Pepperton from polite society.

"I'm so much more interesting than she is," Elizabeth said without an ounce of hubris, "she found herself thwarted at every turn and facing me at every dinner or ball which I cared to attend. It was perfect! Anyway, we won't have any of her type at our dinner."

Thus, with very little nudging, Elizabeth set about creating exactly the sort of *soirée* Ada had hoped for. Lord Vile would attend. Undoubtedly, he would drink too much and be easily enticed if Ada wore a fashionably low-cut gown. She had two assets she was confident he would admire, if nothing else.

By the time she left after a delightful meal and good company, Ada congratulated herself how things were falling into place. Moving swiftly along the dark sidewalk, she was nearly at her own steps when a voice called out to her.

"You there! Mrs. St. Ange!"

She wouldn't have stopped if the man hadn't known her by name. With the hair on the nape of her neck prickling, Ada turned, already knowing who it was. Obviously, Lord Alder had only just alighted from the carriage that had glided past her. Then, for some reason, he'd come straight after her.

"Our favorite meeting place," he remarked.

Ada tried not to sneer at his supposed wit.

"Do I know you?" she asked blankly.

His friendly expression dimmed. There, that took him down a notch. He seemed to think she should have remembered him. *Ha!* She tilted her chin.

"Well, no, not really," he said. "I helped you with your packages the other day. That was me."

"Indeed," she said, looking him up and down. "Yes, that was you."

If he was waiting for a thank you, he would stand there all night.

"I saw you walking by yourself, and thought I would make sure you reached your home safely."

She made a great show of looking behind her, to her own front door a few yards away.

"I would be inside by now if you hadn't stopped me."

He nodded. "Yes. True. I'm Michael Alder, by the way."

"Yes, I know."

Did he just puff up his chest as if pleased?

"I had dinner with your . . . friend," she clarified. "She mentioned you."

"My friend?" He frowned. "Oh, you mean Lady Pepperton. Yes, my *friend*. She had you over for dinner? I wasn't aware. And why should I be? Good thing I didn't arrive any earlier and interrupt."

"Good thing," Ada agreed.

"On the other hand, I would have been pleased to see you off the street."

"I beg your pardon?"

Lord Vile coughed. "I meant simply I could have seen you properly. More of you, I mean. In better lighting."

She said nothing, as she had nothing to add. He was a buffoon at this point. What had she ever seen in him? How had she thought him remarkable in any way?

"If you'll excuse me." She turned toward her doorway. "We'll meet again."

"Why do you say that?" he called after her. "Are you a soothsayer?"

Again, he was trying to be droll.

"Indeed," she said again, hoping he was half insulted yet intrigued by her disinterest.

"Good night, Lord Alder," she added and slipped inside.

Once safely in the foyer, she leaned against the door and closed her eyes. Her heart was thumping like a captured rabbit, but she couldn't help the smile upon her lips.

In a very few nights, she would be sitting down to a meal with the vile viscount. In front of Elizabeth, she would be cordial, but to him, she would remain cool and, with any luck, alluring.

And if she couldn't tempt him away from his mistress, then there was always the next plan, as soon as she thought of one.

CHAPTER FIVE

Michael was baffled. He'd never had a woman react to him quite so coolly as this one. And he wasn't even trying to woo her into his bed. He was simply being nice to her, picking up her damned packages and making sure she stayed safe on the streets of London.

The diminutive blonde was most probably safe anywhere she went, with her shield of icy indifference. *Who could penetrate that?*

"Indeed!" he mimicked in a singsong voice as he entered Elizabeth's abode, tossing his coat and gloves onto the table in the front hall.

She greeted him with a kiss to both his cheeks and then drew her arm through his as she directed him upstairs. Apparently, tonight, they would be in her bedroom. This meant no leisurely conversation, no meal.

"Is there brandy upstairs?"

"Of course," she said, sounding distracted. "I'm having a dinner party in four, no, in five nights. That will give me time to prepare and to ensure I get the guests I want."

She was speaking to him but looking ahead, lost in her own thoughts.

What if *he* was busy that night? Had she considered that? After all, she hadn't even invited him properly.

"Am I invited?"

Elizabeth stopped in the middle of the staircase. "Don't be absurd. Of course, you're invited. Why, I wouldn't have it without you."

Good, he thought, as they finished the trek to her room. For a minute there, he wondered if she would be equally as happy being a solo hostess for her *soirée*.

"Without your presence," she added, falling back onto the four-poster bed, "I wouldn't shine nearly as brightly. When you show everyone how you adore me, it makes me appear utterly scrumptious."

He was her foil apparently. She didn't want him there for his scintillating dinner conversation, merely to boost her own ego.

"And who would flirt with the female guests during the cocktails and converse after dinner with the men over cigars?" he added, feeling sulky.

Most parties were not for him. Too many of the *ton* looked askance at his years of misbehaving. However, Elizabeth's guests would be tolerant of him, or he knew she wouldn't invite them.

His mistress began to remove her clothing, starting with her slippers.

"Darling, you are essential at one of my *soirées*, like fine wine."

He shrugged, feeling appeased.

"Or like the perfect serving platter or cut of meat. Absolutely essential."

Now, she'd gone too far.

"I say, Elizabeth, you make me sound like an object on your party list, rather than your partner."

"My partner?" She sounded stunned. However, she looked divine. Naked, she lay atop the satin counterpane, clutching her silk shift over her body. Unfortunately, nothing in him stirred.

She frowned. "I had never thought of us as partners."

"No?" he asked.

"No. And you do?" She stared at him, both brows raised.

Admittedly, he didn't. "Not usually, I suppose. Now that you mention it, not at all. Yet for a party, I am your gentleman companion, your cohost, am I not? Others might think of us as partners."

"Everyone knows it's *my* home."

"We could have the party at my townhouse."

She laughed. "Impossible, darling. I want to invite my new friend. Why should Mrs. St. Ange travel across the city to see me at your place?"

"I see." Suddenly, the party was becoming more interesting. Still, Michael didn't want to appear less than a successful viscount in front of Mrs. St. Ange. He didn't even know why. "Because of her attendance, I have to look like a kept man who can't afford to throw a party at my own house?" He knew he sounded childish.

"What on earth are you saying?" Elizabeth cocked her head at him. "Besides, it's not only her. I have another new neighbor I am inviting, and I intend to do a little matchmaking."

That didn't sit well with him either. As if he and Elizabeth were an old married couple, his paramour intended to help other people form love matches.

Maybe six months was too long to be with someone he had no intention of marrying. Perhaps he ought to be considering a little matchmaking for himself.

"You look peevish. Don't say you're not coming to my dinner." Elizabeth stopped hiding her body and set the shift beside her.

He would attend, if only to see how Mrs. St. Ange behaved around other people, for he couldn't believe she could be so abrupt and surly with everyone. More than that, he wanted to see her indoors, without a hat and cape, and in lamplight.

Would she allow Elizabeth to match her with someone? He could hardly give that credence.

"Of course, I'll be there."

Then Michael focused on the irresistible creature before him, except he *could* resist her and without any effort.

"What you mistake for peevishness is actually a headache," he confessed. "I apologize. I shall see myself out. Send word of the date and time, and I'll be there."

With a sense of satisfaction whose origin he couldn't identify, perhaps self-denial, he left.

HOLDING HARRY IN HER arms until her back ached, Ada finally put her boy down. Using him as an excuse not to leave for the widow's dinner could only work for so long. Nanny Finn was waiting for her charge, and Ada's maid, Lucy, was waiting to put the finishing touches on her appearance.

She dropped to her knees in front of the boy, hearing Lucy gasp with dismay. Any creases would have to be removed, maybe the whole gown changed if she ruined it. She didn't care. With Harry's gorgeous eyes, so like his father's, staring at her adoringly, she gazed back at him with equal adoration.

"Mama."

"Harry," she replied. They did this often, stating each other's place in the world and then laughing. She had no idea why it delighted the boy but, as usual, he chuckled.

Kissing his soft cheek, she thanked God for him as she always did.

"I love you, my little man. Will you be good for Nanny?"

He nodded.

Squeezing him tightly against her, not minding when his little fingers got caught up in her lace fichu, which he pulled away from her as she set him free, Ada then stood and let the disapproving maid tidy her up.

"Good night," she called to Harry who waved before taking the nanny's hand and letting her lead him away.

Smart boy, Ada thought. He knew warm milk and chocolate biscuits were in his future. *And what about her?* A nerve-wracking performance at a dinner with strangers.

"The wrinkles aren't so bad," Ada said as Lucy tugged at the hemline to smooth the top skirt.

"Shall I get another fichu for your neckline, ma'am?"

Ada glanced down. The upper curves of her breasts were on display, but no more so than what she'd seen in the fashion magazines and in her brief time in Town.

"I'll go ungirded," she quipped, causing Lucy to frown. "That is, I'm fine as I am."

"Yes, ma'am," the maid agreed. "You're more than fine. You look like a dazzling jewel."

If only she didn't feel like a bowl of undercooked porridge, all mushy with no firmness to hold her up.

"I'm ready," she told her driver, waiting by the front door to escort her the few yards.

In a very few minutes, he was leaving her at Elizabeth Pepperton's doorway, well-lit, and already being opened by the butler.

"What time shall I collect you, ma'am?" her driver asked.

If all went right, she would have an escort.

"You won't be needed later."

In the next instant, she was indoors in the warmth and light, and being led into the drawing room where people were already chatting and drinking. Elizabeth even had a violinist playing softly in one corner.

Ada took in all this in the span of a few pounding heartbeats, and the first person she made eye contact with was Lord Vile, who was standing next to an elegantly dressed couple. Something like the zap of a lightning bolt slammed through her. She didn't even flinch, merely swallowing and letting her gaze roam over the rest of the attendees.

Then Elizabeth was moving toward her, arms outstretched, welcoming her. The conversation had come to a halt upon her entrance, so naturally the hostess took her arm and faced the other guests.

"Let me introduce you all to my delightful new neighbor, Mrs. St. Ange. Alas, she is a widow like myself."

Then with everyone's greeting still echoing in her ears, Ada let Elizabeth take her around the room to meet each guest individually. She knew none of them from her Seasons, and only the bachelor, a Cornish viscount from across the other side of the square, showed a particular interest in her. He was about a decade older than she was but had kind eyes and a surprisingly thick shock of blond hair.

Ada had absolutely no interest in him, unable to concentrate until she reached the other side of the room where her quarry stood. All the while on pins and needles, she was extremely glad of a glass of something red that magically appeared in her hand. She sipped it as she finally reached Lord Vile.

Coughing at the unexpected flavor of berries, she reached her nemesis with tears pricking at the back of her eyes and her cheeks reddened. *Bother!*

"Mrs. St. Ange," Lord Alder intoned, bowing over her free hand. "Are you all right?"

Instead of the cool, sophisticated demeanor she'd hoped to project, she was spluttering.

"Fine."

"Don't you like my festive drink?" Elizabeth asked. "A *cocktail*, I'm calling it, like the Americans say."

"It's delicious," Ada assured her. "For some reason, I assumed it to be wine."

Elizabeth laughed. "Naturally. Where everyone else is serving claret, I chose sloe gin. Speaking of wine, I'll go make sure my selections are already open in the dining room before we go in."

The hostess disappeared from her side, and Ada felt the keen loss of her friendly camaraderie. She would face Lord Vile alone.

"We meet again, and indoors," he said.

For want of answer, she sipped the drink again with better results. It had enough sugar to make it palatable. Two more sips and she was ready to engage in conversation.

"I am often indoors," she offered. "You, however, seem to spend an inordinate amount of time loitering on the square."

He grinned instead of taking offense. She wasn't sure what she'd been aiming for, but his smile tickled her insides, causing an immediate resurgence of anger. She would not be charmed by him, not in the least.

Remember what he did, she reminded herself. *How you had to sneak back to your carriage, a sticky wetness dripping between your legs.*

"I assure you, it was coincidence," he said. "I have other interests besides the sidewalks of Belgravia."

"Truly? How do you occupy yourself?"

His eyes widened.

"A viscount, not yet head of your family," Ada continued, leveling him with her stare. "No apparent responsibilities. Never married, no offspring. Why, it's almost as if you haven't needed to grow up, and thus . . . ," she trailed off.

After a moment of silence—perhaps he was stunned by someone finally telling him what a wastrel he was—Michael snagged a drink off a nearby table. He nearly downed it entirely before he put his unconcerned, affable expression back in place.

"You seem to know a lot about me. Or think you do. Tell me, have you been asking questions?"

Rolling her eyes, making sure he saw her doing so, Ada had her response ready.

"I noticed you answered my question with a question of your own. Thus, your richly full life with all its important interests occupying your time remains a mystery. As for my asking others about you, one needn't do any more than read the dailies. The infamous 'Lord V,' as you're called, is often in the papers."

His smile had decidedly died, and his face was taking on a flushed pallor. No doubt it was her use of the moniker 'Lord V.' She'd heard he absolutely hated it.

"You shouldn't believe all the gossip in the papers, Mrs. St. Ange."

"Indeed, I don't. Or I wouldn't be speaking with you now, Lord Alder." She glanced away from him. "I believe we're being called to dinner. Would you like to take my arm?"

She couldn't believe she was going to let him touch her, but decided it showed him she had no interest and that he didn't affect her one way or the other.

His jaw clenched.

Inside, she felt the smallest of victories. More of a *coup d'état* than a *coup de grâce*, for she was certainly not dealing him a merciful blow with any intent of kindly putting him out of his misery. There was too much more misery she wished to deliver.

Setting her glass upon the sideboard, she waited.

What could he do? He would have to politely take her arm and lead her into the dining room or be viewed an absolute heel.

Still, Ada hadn't expected the strange reaction of her body when he reached for her hand and placed it on his arm.

The scent of him, his warmth, his familiar face, even the width and breadth of his body, all filled her with agitation. In the blink of an eye, she was back in the gazebo, and an irrational part of her brain imagined him drawing her to him and kissing her in front of everyone.

By the time Lord Alder showed her to her seat, pulling out her chair for her, she wanted to gulp for air. Keeping her head down, she sat and didn't even thank him.

Not a very alluring performance, she had to admit. She'd used all the vinegar to put him in his place, but none of the honey she'd intended to keep him off balance and draw her to him.

Sighing, Ada flicked open her white cotton napkin and settled it on her lap. When the ladies were in their places, the men sat. Naturally, the eligible, fair-haired man was seated next to her, as she'd already ascertained he was Elizabeth's choice for her 'match' for the evening.

Be that as it may, when she had collected herself and looked up, Michael Alder at the head of the table to her right was observing her.

Do it, she told herself. *Unsettle the blackguard.*

Gazing directly at him, she lifted her lips ever so slightly in the smallest of discreet smiles, and then she winked.

BLAZES! MICHAEL COULDN'T STOP staring at this beautiful, blue-eyed minx even after she'd turned to her dinner companion, Lord Toddingly, and begun to converse. No one had ever spoken to him thusly, nor ever brought up that horrid nickname to his face. He should be furious. Yet he wasn't.

Her soft little smile and mocking wink carried with them a punch to his gut, as did her lowcut neckline without a hint of a lace fichu. Her bosom was on display, and he, for one, thought it magnificent.

However, Michael didn't know if she hated him or admired him. Maybe she didn't know, herself.

Whatever the case, a lot of sentiment was swirling around from someone who didn't even know him. Someone whom he definitely wished to know better.

The lady on his right, one of Elizabeth's acquaintances, said his name and snagged his attention with talk of cricket, which her husband to her right joined in. Soon, the whole table was debating the merits of George Parr over Fuller Pilch. Except Mrs. St. Ange and her dining companion.

She and the bachelor from across the square, to whom Michael had taken an instant dislike, had their heads close together, discussing something which, evidently, they had no interest in sharing.

This went on through the first two courses, punctuated by her lovely throaty laugh. Each time Michael heard it, he wondered what had inspired it and why it sent a message directly to his groin.

When he could stand it no longer, after the oysters and the mock-turtle soup and just as the fish course was being served, Michael addressed her directly.

"Mrs. St. Ange, how are you liking your new residence on the square?"

She paused a moment, turning slowly to face him, making everyone aware he had disrupted the flow of her conversation with Lord Toddingly.

"I find it very much to my liking. Particularly the helpful people one meets on the street. Of course, one never knows when one might be accosted by a ne'er-do-well right on one's own doorstep."

There, she'd done it again. In the space of two seconds, she seemed to praise him then disparage him.

"All the excitement must be on this side of the square," Lord Toddingly observed. "I've had neither help nor hindrance since I moved in."

And to his dismay, the two started talking amongst themselves again. Michael glanced down the length of the table toward his mistress, only to find her giving him a querying look.

Hm, could she see the storm brewing inside his head? He hoped not.

After the roasted chicken and the salad courses, they had sherbet and strawberries—disappointed, he'd hoped for a sponge cake with thick custard—and then coffee.

At last, he could stand. However, before he could get to Ada's chair, her dining companion pulled it out for her. Michael didn't fail to notice how Lord Toddingly looked down her décolletage. He would have been angry except he couldn't blame the man, and had hoped to do precisely the same thing.

Sighing at the duty coming next, Michael had to play his part and lead the male guests into Elizabeth's library for cigars and brandy. Undoubtedly, they would talk more of cricket. Perhaps one of them was knowledgeable about the stock market and he could learn a little more.

When they returned half an hour later, none of them wishing to linger too long away from the ladies, Elizabeth and her three guests were in the drawing room drinking cognac, which sounded like a fine idea to Michael.

"What has been your topics of conversation?" he asked, sitting next to his mistress for the first time all night.

The women exchanged glances all around and then laughter broke out. Instantly, his gaze was drawn to Mrs. St. Ange, whose cheeks had turned a becoming shade of pink, even while laughing.

"I see," he said. "Gentlemen," he addressed the others, "I believe they've been discussing us."

"Pish," Elizabeth said. "You are not our only source of amusement."

"Then our sometimes-ridiculous behavior wasn't on your tongues?"

"Maybe," she admitted, and the ladies laughed again.

He was pleased to see the violinist had returned. There would be no coercing untalented ladies to play the pianoforte or, worse, sing off-key. He should have known Elizabeth was too kind a hostess to open up her guests to embarrassment.

Still, looking at Mrs. St. Ange, he couldn't help wondering about the dexterity of her fingers or the skill of her lips. *To sing a song, of course!*

"What are you grinning at?" Elizabeth asked him quietly. "Are you glad we threw this party?"

He looked at her, the woman whose bed he'd warmed for half a year and knew it was over. While he admired her, he didn't want to be her partner in any way outside of the bedroom, and now, even that passion was dwindling. This evening, although a success in terms of everyone's enjoyment, felt false. He could be any man she'd placed at one end of her dining table.

"I think you make a divine hostess," he praised.

Her gaze held his for a moment too long.

In another hour, the evening was over, and as he knew would happen, he had to fight Lord Toddingly for the pleasure of walking Mrs. St. Ange home.

After the women had kissed each other's cheeks and thanked Elizabeth profusely, they all stood in a small group in the marble-floored foyer. Maneuvering so he was the one holding Mrs. St. Ange's wrap, Michael draped it around her from behind, feeling her shoulders under his fingers.

Did he feel her tremble at his touch?

Before Toddingly could offer himself as an escort, Michael held out his arm.

She stared at it.

He wanted to close his eyes and say a prayer. She could and probably would humiliate him in front of everyone.

Place your hand on my arm, he urged her silently.

She cocked her head, prolonging his agony. Then she looked at Toddingly, and Michael feared the worst.

"It seems our host is going to do his due diligence and see me safely down the sidewalk. It's all of ten yards."

Michael let out the breath he was holding and felt her delicate, gloved hand rest upon his forearm. He tucked it more securely and they stepped out into the chilly night.

"You needn't have left Lady Pepperton," she said. "Lord Toddingly would have seen me home."

"As you said, due diligence. I don't know him from some lady's pet monkey."

He was rewarded by her burst of laughter at his irreverence, and he glanced behind him to make sure the man in question had gone the other way around the square.

"No more than I truly know anything of you," she pointed out after regaining her composure. "Anything that isn't gossip."

They were already at her steps. *What he wouldn't give to have her alone in a carriage!*

"I protest," he said. "You know I will pick up your packages."

"I'm sure Lord Toddingly would stoop to pick up my packages, too."

"Really, I'm not convinced. His nose is turned so high, he looks like a pug."

Again, she laughed, and he thoroughly enjoyed being the cause of her amusement.

"That's a lovely sound," he blurted, hardly meaning to speak the honest words aloud.

Unfortunately, she stopped, both walking and laughing, and he knew he had to release her at once or appear extremely forward.

And yet, he didn't let her go. Rather, he waited to see what she would do.

"I'm home," she reminded him, staring up into his face and looking far less frosty than she had in the past.

He was beyond tempted.

CHAPTER SIX

At last, Michael let her pull her arm free, but only until he could place his hands on her waist and draw her close.

He heard her small gasp.

What was wrong with him? They were on the street, within feet of a brightly lit lamp cutting through the darkness. Yet, he was fascinated by her, drawn to her.

"Simply take a step back," he advised her. "I will not restrain you. If you don't, I am going to kiss you."

There, he could pat himself on the back for his fair warning and then take the consequences. He hadn't had the reputation of a man who enjoyed women simply dropped upon his head. No, he'd earned it. Woman by woman.

And right that moment, he was desperate to enjoy at least a taste of her.

She didn't move.

Was she frozen with fright or disbelief?

The light was behind him. When he tilted his head slightly, it angled upon her face.

She appeared to be considering, but definitely did not appear frightened.

"I'm not going to move," she said at last.

Triumph rushed through him, and he lowered his head.

His lips brushed hers, softly at first, and then he claimed her mouth more completely. As he always did, he breathed deeply, catching the scent of the lady's skin. As expected, the distinct floral fragrance he remembered from one night in a garden was not evident.

It didn't matter a damn, he reminded himself. That particular female had walked out of his life and never sought his company again. His golden goddess was, in all likelihood, overweight, toothless, and with ten ugly children.

After a few moments, they both pulled back. Before she collected herself, he saw it—an expression of stark surprise. It was quickly replaced by her cool neutrality, and he released her.

She lifted her fingers, and for a moment, he thought she might wipe her mouth. But she dropped her hand to her side.

"Due diligence," she said to him. "Well done. Yet I believe your *friend* is waiting."

With that, Mrs. St. Ange, looking supremely regal, turned to her own front door.

"Good night," he offered, feeling abashed. He ought to have broken it off properly with Elizabeth before kissing this new widow.

When she slipped indoors without responding, he shrugged.

Turning, Michael strolled back along to number twenty-nine, his hands in his pockets.

A BATH! ADA NEEDED a long hot one. Realizing the inconvenience to her small staff especially at this late hour, she couldn't do it. She would wait until morning. Besides, it wasn't as though he'd had his hands all over her body. She would scrub her face with warm water and her favorite Pears soap and brush her teeth with a large dose of paste from her favorite camphor toothpowder.

Once tucked in her bed, she sat staring into the burning coals. She'd expected luring Lord Vile into fancying her, longing for her, maybe even loving her—if that were even possible—was going to be unpleasant at best. Like keeping close company with a snake, she imagined, or a rat.

Instead, his kiss was as she'd remembered. Warm and pleasant, sparking something inside her that felt tingly and exciting. She closed her eyes.

No, no, no! It was all wrong. How could she enjoy the kiss of a man she hated? And that hatred hadn't shifted even a little.

She would focus on her success, causing the horrid man to leave his mistress's side to escort her home. From such a small thing as their brief walk, huge strides could be made.

It was only the beginning, she knew it.

Sure enough, by late morning the following day, a servant had dropped off Lord M. Alder's calling card with a note scrawled on the back.

"May I call upon you at your leisure?"

Oh, you most certainly may, she thought. She was spinning her web like a meticulous spider, and he was flying in unawares.

First thing to remember was not to act in haste or appear eager. She would not even respond for a day.

Secondly, she needed to send a note of thanks to Lady Pepperton for the wonderful evening. If only Ada could dispel the qualms she felt about getting involved with Elizabeth's paramour, but there was nothing she could do about that. Her plan had been in the making long before Lord Vile and Lady Pepperton began an affair.

In the meantime, there was Harry to play with, letters to write, a visit to make to her friend Maggie, and more staff to hire, for those she had were run off their feet.

THE FOLLOWING DAY, AFTER a midday meal at the Cambrey townhouse on Cavendish Square—during which Ada nearly burst with wanting to tell Maggie about her first kiss in years—she was at her writing desk coming up with exactly the right words to disarm Lord Vile.

On her third attempt, she wrote:

> *Lord Alder,*
> *How strange that you should wish to call upon me given your association with Lady Pepperton! What can you possibly mean by such a request? Furthermore, she and I are on a path to becoming friends. Thus, the answer is no.*
> *Mrs. St. Ange*

Let him think on that!

Apparently, he thought quickly, for within an hour of sending over her note to his townhouse, she received in reply:

> *Dear Mrs. St. Ange,*
> *I understand your concern. However, please be assured that my interests at present lie only with you. Lady Pepperton and I have broken off our association on absolutely friendly terms and with no wounded feelings. I await to hear when I may call upon you.*
> *Lord M. Alder*

Hmm. Ada would not respond in a hurry. She wished she and Elizabeth Pepperton were already close enough so she could hear from the widow's own lips whether a break had occurred. Yet, she didn't doubt him. He was vile but, as far as she knew, he was not a liar. Moreover, he knew how easy it would be for her to discover if their association had ended.

The issue, then, was how to proceed and how quickly. Two days later, she finally wrote back:

Lord Alder,
You may call upon me at eleven o'clock in the morning tomorrow.
Mrs. St. Ange

If only she could confide in Maggie what she was doing. Yet, because of her friend's older sister's prior association with Lord Alder, Ada couldn't let her in on the plan. For without a doubt, Maggie would tell her to leave off any entanglement.

Thus, it was without anyone's counsel that Ada waited on the appointed day, seated in her parlor, wearing one of her favorite daytime gowns in a rich coral color. She couldn't concentrate to read despite trying repeatedly, nor focus on anything except watching the clock on her mantle, knowing he would be on time.

Precisely at two minutes to the hour, she heard the clop-clop of horse's hooves out front and knew Lord Vile would be on her doorstep in an instant.

Breathe, she told herself. Shoulders down, face relaxed, and hands purposefully not touching, lest she start fiddling her fingers with nervousness, she waited. There was nothing she could do about the hard and fast beating of her heart, except hope it wasn't as loud as she feared.

Her maid, Lucy, answered the knock, and suddenly, after years of waiting, Lord Michael Alder was calling upon her. As he entered the room, she stood, letting the open book on her lap fall to the floor as if she'd been recently reading and not simply awaiting his arrival with mouth-drying nervousness.

This brought him over to her and to his knees to retrieve it. *Exactly where she wanted him.*

As he rose and handed it to her, he took hold of her other hand and bent over it, brushing his lips across her knuckles, lingering a little too long.

She'd expected this. Still, it sent a frisson of excitement skittering through her. Looking at his brown hair falling attractively over his forehead, she had to remind herself he was skilled and vastly experienced in the ways of seduction. Her defenses were strong, however. Indignation, anger, mortification, even revulsion at the man's decadent way of living—all of these would bolster her.

He would get nothing from her but what she freely gave as bait.

Offering him a cool smile as if unaffected, she withdrew her hand slowly and dropped the book casually onto the couch. If he'd bothered to look at what she was pretending to read, he might have a better notion of her inner thoughts. Alexandre Dumas's *Count of Monte Christo* was the quintessential novel of perfectly executed revenge, and Ada was finding it to be fascinating reading.

She'd been a little shocked to learn the novel's hero, Edmond Dantès, even manipulated the bond market to destroy the fortune of one of his enemies. It was an uncanny coincidence, although her method of passing along advice seemed easier.

Looking past Alder, she spoke to Lucy, "Bring us a pot of tea."

Her maid nodded and hurried from the room. Lucy probably intended to get back quickly to chaperone, but Ada would send her away again. She hadn't crafted this hard-earned persona of an independent widow only to have her maid treat her like a green youth.

"Won't you have a seat, Lord Alder?" Resuming her place, she gestured to a winged chair across from her.

Purposefully ignoring her suggestion, he sat beside her on the couch, with only the leather-bound volume of Dumas between them. Resting one arm along the back of the couch so his fingers touched her shoulder, he turned his body to face her.

"I should have asked if you would prefer coffee," she blurted, then bit her tongue.

Drat it all! She sounded anxious, a little flustered.

"Tea is quite agreeable, until it's time for wine." Glancing around the room, he took it in with a curious, appraising eye. "I wondered what Mrs. St. Ange's private residence looked like."

"I cannot believe you spent a moment wondering about the interior of my home."

He smiled. "I did. A woman's sense of decor usually represents her mind and even her emotions. Don't you think? Particularly her bedroom."

Ignoring the last phrase obviously meant to titillate, she asked, "What does my home tell you about me?" It was the closest she could come to flirtatious talk.

"It is understated, uncluttered, a little stark actually, more so than I expected. Perhaps that is due to your having so recently moved in. Still, I get the sense you are not one to waste space on fiddly jim-jams and useless knick-knacks. You have belongings that matter to you and see no reason for anything else. Do I have that about right?"

She couldn't help but nod. "I believe it is from having a child. After one sees the true importance of another living being, one who is solely dependent on you, then one tends to realize everything else is merely a 'fiddly jim-jam,' as you say."

"I see. So, were I to sire a brat of my own, I might no longer want to keep my Chinese bronzes, and, of course, I'd toss my Ming porcelain into the rubbish bin?"

She smiled, imagining Harry getting his hands upon porcelain antiques. They wouldn't last a minute.

"That's a lovely sight," he commented.

"Excuse me?" *Whatever did he mean?*

"Your smile. Like moonlight coming out from behind a dark cloud."

She was experiencing Lord Vile's flattery. How trite.

"Thus, when I am not smiling, I'm a dark cloud?"

He raised his eyes to her eleven-foot ceiling in mock frustration. Then he looked at her again.

"Let's go back to useless knick-knacks. What do you think of ferns and seaweed? Do you collect them like the rest of the mad Brits?"

"I don't." Although Maggie had said her younger sister, Eleanor, was mad for ferns.

"What about taxidermized cats or squirrels? Any of those stuffed creatures in your curio cabinet?" he asked.

She couldn't help smiling again, but shook her head.

"At least tell me you have a collection of bird's eggs hereabouts." He leaned forward and looked between his own boots to the area under her sofa.

The laugh that escaped her drew his gaze back to her face.

"I must confess, I like it when you laugh. Thus, I will make it my goal."

"Your goal?" she asked as Lucy returned with a tray of tea.

"Yes, to make you happy and, therefore, laughing."

Undoubtedly, he would have been shocked to know his words meant to cajole her caused her stomach to clench. He had brought her such misery, the idea his goal was the opposite nearly had her telling him who she was.

The maid poured them each a cup and stood there, most likely waiting for instructions to take a seat on the other side of the room.

"Thank you, Lucy. That will be all. I'll ring should our guest need anything."

The woman's eyes widened, and Ada feared she would protest. Their relationship had always been informal since she was not nobility and they were close of age.

"Perhaps you can look in on Harry for me," she added.

Lucy pursed her lips. They both knew Nanny Finn wouldn't appreciate Lucy entering her domain or usurping her care of the boy. However, at last, she nodded and left.

"Stubborn for a maid, isn't she?" Lord Alder asked, picking up his teacup and saucer. "Not used to your being alone with a man."

She ignored him and reached for her own saucer. Tea, strong and sweet, was exactly what she needed to get through this first *tête-à-tête* with Lord Vile.

"You asked me what I do with my life," he reminded her. "Let us also talk of yours."

"Are you truly interested?" Ada didn't believe him for a second. Getting under her skirts—or any woman's—was the only thing he cared about.

He nodded. "Yes, why not?"

She could hardly voice her opinion of him, or he would wonder why she'd let him in the door in the first place.

"Why don't you go first," she suggested. "Since I've only recently returned to Town, I haven't done much of anything except settle in here and reconnect with old friends."

Instantly, she wished she hadn't said that. He must never find out her best friend was Jenny Blackwood's sister or he might suspect she knew him previously.

"My own life is not that interesting, actually," he began. "You were right. While you were busy settling in, I was going to my club. I favor White's. I enjoy watching cricket, and I'm not bad with a bat, if I do say so. Of course, horse racing and boating. I like art galleries. Recently, I've taken up an interest in investing."

She clamped her teeth down on the side of the teacup, making a strange clacking sound.

He stared, but she merely smiled.

"What do you mean by 'taken up an interest'?" Inside, she was crowing at her own handiwork.

"I am investing in markets through the London Stock Exchange. It's new to me, I confess."

"And you're doing this for sheer pleasure?"

He laughed a short, brusque sound. "Hardly that."

However, he didn't elaborate on his need for financial success. She couldn't blame him since no member of the aristocracy wanted to admit the need to earn money. In any case, she couldn't push him to say more on the matter without seeming vulgar.

"I'm sure it is fascinating," she told him, wishing with all her heart that she could go into the exchange. As a man, he had the freedom to do so yet didn't bother. The injustice made her want to shake him.

Lord Alder shrugged. "Honestly, I'll learn what I need to know, but I have someone else acting on my behalf. There are a lot of ins and outs, I hear, and a few wrong moves can lose a man his fortune."

Precisely, she thought.

"Really?" Ada batted her eyelashes, which felt ridiculous, but she saw his gaze flicker with interest.

"Do you ride?" he asked. "The weather is fine today."

She couldn't really bear the thought of him poking around her parlor, unsupervised, while she was upstairs with Lucy changing for a ride through the park. Moreover, she'd have to summon her driver to get one of the carriage horses saddled properly. And while she felt comfortable being alone in the safety of her own home, oddly, the idea of their being seen out riding together didn't sit well.

Instantly, she would be considered Lord Vile's latest conquest as soon as people learned of his break with Lady Pepperton.

"I'm not dressed for it," she pointed out. "Does it bother you being here, merely two doors down?"

His blank expression at last registered her meaning.

"No, not at all. Her home is not my home. Besides, Lady Pepperton shall remain a friend, and that is all. Come now, you're not a debutante. You know how these things are done?"

Did she? Actually, she hadn't a clue.

Keeping her face neutral, she offered, "We can plan for horses through the park another day."

"Mrs. St. Ange, I cannot tell you how pleased I am to learn there will be another day for us."

She wished she hadn't said it. Statements like that wouldn't keep him guessing, wouldn't make him doubt his own prowess, and certainly didn't portray her indifference as she hoped. *Drat!*

Then he added, "You *are* dressed for a carriage ride, if I'm not mistaken."

Glancing down at her gown as if she didn't know what she was wearing, she was surprised to hear him laugh again.

"And dressed rather beautifully, I must say. It seems a shame not to show you off."

"From the inside of a carriage?" She might not know much, but she knew what could happen in such close confines. What's more, she had no intention of putting herself in such a position. Not yet.

"We could take my carriage to the Serpentine for a walk," he pointed out.

"It's not that far to walk to the Serpentine and then take a leisurely stroll." She would have to put on her sturdy boots. "There's no need for your carriage at all."

"By the time we have walked to the Serpentine," he pointed out, "we'll be tired of walking, don't you think?"

Ada was confounded. Lord Alder's persistence was beyond reason, but she was simply not getting into his carriage . . . unless . . .

"We could take Harry to the park." She had thought to keep her son far away from his father, but Harry loved Hyde Park and especially the Serpentine. Even Lord Vile wouldn't touch her whilst a two-year-old was in tow. Moreover, Nanny Finn would make an excellent chaperone. Meanwhile, she could continue to try and spark his interest. Keeping him dangling like a fish on the line was of utmost importance.

Lord Alder said only, "Harry?"

"Yes, my son. You saw him the first time you encountered us. When you wouldn't leave my packages alone."

"Is that how you saw it? As if I had a strange fascination with picking up your paper-wrapped bundles?"

He was teasing her. She could tell by the way the skin crinkled at the corners of his tawny eyes.

Then he stood. "All right, Mrs. St. Ange."

Holding out his hand to her, Ada had to take it or seem unacceptably discourteous. He drew her to stand before him.

"I will go on an outing with you and your son, forsaking having you all to myself, but only if you will grant me a boon."

Oh, dear!

"A boon?"

"In the form of another kiss. The first was very sweet, and all I can think about is tasting you again."

If only he'd said such pretty words three years earlier.

"Indeed," she said, somehow summoning the unruffled widow from within the nervous woman who'd only experienced the touch of one man. This one!

"Indeed," he repeated, lowering his mouth to hers without further preamble.

CHAPTER SEVEN

Michael had enjoyed the first kiss, despite its brevity. This time, he intended to make it last. With a hand on her back to anchor her close and his other cupping the base of her head below her jauntily braided bun, he claimed her mouth.

Almost at once, she opened her lips to his tongue. Not in a lascivious way as if she was about to suck him down her throat. Merely in quiet acquiescence to the sensations they were exploring.

He'd kissed many women, oftentimes while in a drunken haze and even more often, not giving a fig for who they were a moment later.

Presently, he was perfectly sober and fully able to experience the thrilling sizzle coursing through him.

Her soft, pliable lips didn't go slack and unmoving. She tilted her head sideways so her mouth fit his perfectly, and then, wonder of wonders, she kissed him back. Her mouth moving ever so slightly, her tongue touching his.

This was not a kiss that led to moaning and tearing off each other's clothing and doing the two-backed beast on her Persian carpet.

No, this kiss was like a conversation, two minds melding as their mouths did the same. A little give, a little take. Awareness of this woman allowing him a taste of intimacy and wanting to offer the same in return.

When the kiss ended, he didn't draw back. No quip or jest came to mind. He simply rested his forehead upon hers, his eyes closed, breathing her in, and feeling extremely grateful she'd entered his life.

"Lord Alder," she said.

Finally, he drew back.

"Yes, Mrs. St. Ange?" He stared down into her blue eyes.

"You are standing on my hem."

Looking down, his boot was upon the bottom of her lovely gown and pulling it taut so she couldn't back away if she wanted to.

He stepped back, wishing she had called him Michael.

"My apologies."

"None necessary but accepted in any case," she told him, looking completely composed as if a profoundly intimate moment had not occurred.

Moving away from him, she crossed the room to the bell pull. Then seeming to change her mind, she went to the door.

"I'll get my son and his nanny." Without looking back, Mrs. St. Ange left him, still standing there, staring after her.

"Due diligence," he muttered the ridiculous term. What had just happened? And why, instead of feeling randy and ready to toss up her skirts, was he looking forward to spending time in her company at the bloody Serpentine? With a child?

In a very few minutes, he found himself in his carriage—luckily, he'd come in his spacious clarence—seated next to a portly woman, introduced as Nanny Finn. Across from him was the intriguing lady and her cute little boy.

"Harry, is it?" Michael said, trying to engage.

The boy grinned, then turned and buried his face against his mother's side.

Mrs. St. Ange merely shrugged. "If he does warm up to you, Lord Alder, you will not enjoy another moment of silence."

Was he supposed to look forward to that?

As soon as his feet touched the ground, Harry was off like a shot, running hither and yon.

"He has a lot of energy, does he not?"

"Yes, rather like a puppy. I believe most children are the same."

"Perhaps most children should have puppies, then, to keep up."

She nodded noncommittally. "I had a dog for companionship when I was a young girl," she said. "An excellent dog he was, too."

Michael imagined her with her hair in pigtails chasing after a furry friend.

"We had two cats," he confessed, "and I don't think they liked me."

This evoked a smile from her, one of so few it spurred him to keep talking.

"Actually, I'm partly jesting. Although my mother did have cats, we also had hunting dogs, as my father used to have a lodge. So, not really pets, I suppose. My brother took to training them nearly as soon as he could walk. I never cared too much for hunting, neither fox nor pheasant, so didn't spend time with dogs. By the time my brother started keeping a few as companions, I was already at Eton."

They were strolling along the footpath toward the northside of the lake, past the Dell and an enormous weeping beech, when it dawned on him the last time he'd been to the Serpentine was also the last time he'd been alone with Jenny Blackwood. Although she was already married, her husband had been across the Channel, or so he'd thought. He'd asked her to meet with him to explain to her how his parents had ended their engagement behind his back.

Some part of him had hoped she would say she favored him over Lord Lindsey and even leave her marriage. Instead, the man had shown up to claim her right on the path near the cafe, and Jenny had never looked back.

He shuddered, recalling the dark days that followed, which became months and then a year of his life. Since then, a couple more had gone by, and suddenly, he found himself glad his father had given him a purpose, albeit one he feared himself unsuited.

"Are you well, Lord Alder? You seem distracted." She didn't look at him when she spoke as she was keeping her motherly eyes firmly on her son, despite the nanny's watchful presence.

"I'm fine," he assured her.

The past was where it should be. Now, he was here at the same place with an entirely new woman, one who stirred something in him for the first time in ages besides base desire.

In fact, he was surprised how enjoyable it was simply to be in the fresh air, walking beside the intriguingly independent Mrs. St. Ange, even while watching her son and nanny gambol ahead. The boy found joy in every flower and bug, and his nanny was young enough to keep up with him.

After Harry had returned to his mother for the umpteenth time to grab her hand in delight only to race away again on his sturdy little legs, Michael wondered if it was at all painful for her to see the spit and image of her husband.

"How did your husband die?"

Mrs. St. Ange hesitated for the briefest of moments, accompanied by a faltering in her step. He hoped he hadn't offended her.

Yet, when she slowly turned her face to him, she looked as serene as usual.

"Lost at sea," she said succinctly.

"Was he on a business trip as a passenger, or was he in the Merchant Navy?"

"Neither," she said. And nothing more.

"The Royal Navy then?" he probed.

"No."

He waited but, as if trying to milk a bull, nothing was forthcoming. Perhaps a different line of inquiry would yield better results.

"Your boy was very young when his father passed on?"

"A baby."

He had never known a woman of such few words. Moreover, he decided he was being an oaf for prying when, clearly, she didn't wish to say more. After all, the unfortunate Mr. St. Ange was dead and gone, and nothing could be done about it.

In fact, although Michael thought it a shame the man would never see his lovely family, for his own part, he was very much alive and happy to be in the widow's company.

Would he be considered a full-fledged cad for benefitting from the other man's tragedy? Inwardly, he shrugged. It certainly wouldn't be the first time.

When the nanny extracted a small wooden boat with a linen sail from a bag she carried, the little boy began to hop up and down with excitement. They all headed toward the water's edge.

Thankfully, it didn't have the strong stench it sometimes did upon the hottest days of summer.

"I keep thinking he should be in leading strings," Michael said.

Nanny Finn shot him a look but said nothing. It was the boy's mother who answered.

She wrinkled up her nose, which he realized was quite beautifully shaped, and said, "Most physicians agree those are not healthy for the child."

"Really?" It was news to him, but what did he know of rearing children? "It seems less healthy for the child to run away from his nanny and get stomped by horse's hooves or run over by a carriage."

He was only thinking out loud, but Mrs. St. Ange's expression of displeasure reminded him once more her husband had perished, and there were doubtless numerous worries in her head over keeping her son safe.

"My apologies. I spoke without thinking."

"Indeed," she said.

With the Serpentine at their toes, Nanny Finn gave Harry his boat, which he promptly tossed upon the waters. Its rough entry caused the sail to get wet, and very quickly, the vessel capsized, lying on its side, just out of the boy's reach. He began to yell excitedly and seemed ready to jump in after it. Fortunately, the nanny had a firm grasp on the back of his blue jacket.

"Drat!" Mrs. St. Ange vowed, surprising him greatly.

When it was clear that Harry understood he mustn't try to reach his toy, Nanny Finn released him. She leaned forward, arms outstretched. However, as her stature was short along with her limbs, she could do nothing.

"Lord Alder," Mrs. St. Ange said, gesturing to the little boat and her now unhappy child, "would you assist?"

"Certainly," he said, without even thinking, although for the life of him, he didn't know what she thought he could do. He wasn't going to wade into the water and ruin his boots.

At this point, the minor current from the gentle spring wind had moved the boat even farther out of reach. Staring at it, he considered his options. If he'd had a brolly, he could use the handle, but he hadn't since there wasn't a cloud in the sky.

Across the lake and past the King's Road—Rotten Road, as they all called it—the Crystal Palace stood as a beacon containing mankind's progress and forward-thinking ideas. Yet here he stood, on the edge of a small, manmade lake wondering how to rescue a child's toy.

Glancing around for inspiration, his gaze fell upon the oak trees nearby. Keeping an eye on the little boat that had settled about two yards off shore, Michael began yanking upon a smaller branch. It was tougher than it seemed and extremely bendy, forcing him to work it back and forth until, at last, it came free, and he ended up nearly toppling over.

Regaining his balance and, he hoped, his dignity, Michael approached the small group of three. The closer he got to them, the more his branch seemed to be a twig.

The Devil! It wasn't nearly long enough.

Another look around yielded no further inspiration. After all, it had taken him a lot of effort to get the spindly stick. He couldn't hope to rip a long enough branch. Probably one of the queen's guards would appear and take him into custody for destruction of Her Majesty's flora if he tried.

"Right," he said out loud, though talking to himself. Sitting down on the grass, he removed his jacket and began to pull off his Hessians.

"What on earth, Lord Alder?" Mrs. St. Ange asked.

Silently, he folded his pants up to his knees before rolling his stockings down and removing them. Rather humiliated by his state of undress, with his calves and toes on display, he continued without speaking. After all, when undressing before a beautiful woman, he was usually alone with her and about to dive into passionate ecstasy, not the bloody Serpentine.

"Are you sure?" she prompted.

"Yes, it'll only take me a moment." Stepping gingerly into the water, he prayed he didn't see the carcass of some unwanted dog or cat float by.

Since it was an artificial lake, the muddy bottom was firm and not unpleasantly squishy pond muck. Yet the water was colder than expected. In three steps, it was up to his knees and his pants were getting wet. *Blast!*

The boat was nearly in reach if he leaned out. Suddenly, he heard horses and a man shouted, "Salutations!"

Turning, Michael recognized Lord Toddingly, Mrs. St. Ange's fair-haired neighbor, upon a gorgeous bay. When he raised a hand in greeting, Michael did the same, feeling a tad foolish from his position.

"May I be of assistance?" Toddingly said.

Without waiting for a response, he urged his horse, scattering both nanny and boy in one direction and Mrs. St. Ange in the other. The horse splashed into the water nervously, as most horses would.

It probably didn't want to be in the stagnant Serpentine, famous for its impurity as a receptacle for God only knew what.

"No, I've got it," Michael protested, knowing nothing good could come of standing at knee level with a large animal in water.

Not heeding him, Toddingly forced his horse to approach Michael, then circle the little boat. At first, its movements sent the boat careening away, but in another moment, Toddingly was on the other side of it and herding it toward the shore.

Meanwhile, all the splashing had soaked Michael up to his waist.

The deuce take the interfering twit!

As he strode from the Serpentine, hoping never to repeat the galling experience, Mrs. St. Ange was able to bend down and pick up the boat that had been forced to shore.

"Thank you," she called out to Toddingly, who tipped his hat.

"My pleasure. A word of advice?"

"Yes, my lord?" she replied.

Michael's annoyance increased at her deferential, grateful tone, one he had never experienced from her.

"They usually work best with a long string attached," Toddingly said, stating the obvious as if he'd discovered how to turn lead into gold.

"Of course," she agreed, gesturing to Nanny Finn who still held the string she'd pulled from her bag but not had a chance to secure.

"*Ah,* I see," Toddingly said as he urged his horse from the water. Dismounting, he ruffled the boy's hair, and Harry was staring up at him like he was a God.

Irrationally, Michael wanted to send the meddlesome lord back into the water with a fist to his smug face.

"So, you were a little hasty, were you?" Toddingly said to Harry, who nodded.

"I threw it," the little boy said in the most words Michael had heard.

"Next time, let your nanny tie it up first, my boy."

Michael sat on the grass again, drawing his stockings up his wet legs, hoping once he had his boots on again, he would regain a measure of his customary poise.

Before he had finished, Toddingly had waved the boat around to dry the sail but declared it useless, exchanged the bit of fabric for one of his monogrammed handkerchiefs firmly tied to the mast, and was attaching the string through a hole in the bow.

By this time, Michael had unrolled his wet pants, donned his jacket, and was standing, arms crossed, watching the proceedings. Glancing up, his gaze caught that of Mrs. St. Ange.

What did she mean by that raised eyebrow? An expression of challenge, perhaps?

"I must be off," Toddingly said.

"Oh, must you?" Michael asked, still looking at *her.*

"Afraid, so, old boy. I've an appointment with my tailor. Henry Poole on Savile Row. But you must know *of* him, of course. Difficult as finding a sinner on Sunday to get a fitting with Poole, so I dare not keep him waiting. I can put in a word for you, if you like."

Michael tried not to bare his teeth. "I have a perfectly adequate tailor, Toddingly."

The man looked him up and down, taking in his sodden pants and crumpled jacket.

"Yes, of course." Tipping his hat to the nanny and Mrs. St. Ange, and with another hair ruffling for Harry, Toddingly mounted his horse.

"Thank you again, my lord," Mrs. St. Ange said.

"I hope you enjoy the rest of your day," he said and rode off.

The man sounded like a bloody shopkeeper, Michael thought. Besides, how was he supposed to enjoy any part of his day in the state he was in? He was most definitely ready to end this adventure.

Yet Harry was already fussing to get his boat in the water. What's more, the nanny complied.

Mrs. St. Ange approached him, and he was positive he detected a hint of amusement.

"I'm so sorry you got wet," she said, not sounding sorry at all. "And what a pity you did so and still failed."

"Failed?" Rather a harsh word he thought for his attempted rescue of the toy boat.

"I mean, if you'd become soaked while retrieving the boat, it wouldn't seem so senseless."

She was right. *Damn it!* And, in truth, his pants were uncomfortable as hell.

"Plus, having Lord Toddingly swoop in," she continued, "like a knight, I imagine he rather emasculated you."

With that statement, she turned to join her son, leaving him with his jaw slack.

Emasculated? Emasculated! Could she be serious? He would like to show her exactly how masculine he was! In private. With her reclining upon a bed, lips pouting from being kissed, eyes begging for him to come to her, her bare skin flushed with desire.

Finally, she'd said more than a few words, and they were insulting!

What's more, she expected him to stand there in wet clothing while her son played.

First things first, he drew his flask out of his pocket, unscrewed the cap, and took a healthy sip. At least he wouldn't catch a chill. He used to keep gin in it but now preferred the smoother pleasure of brandy. He took another drink.

"I believe I will head home to change. I live on the northeast side of the park," he said, gesturing vaguely in the direction with his flask.

Her eyes widened, and if he didn't think it impossible, she seemed delighted.

"I'll send my carriage back to take you home," he assured her.

She shook her head.

"We'll walk from here." Her tone was definite.

What could he say? This was not how he'd hoped their first outing would end.

"As you wish. Goodbye, Harry," he called to the boy, who, to his credit, turned and waved with a cheerful smile. He liked Harry's face and his eyes reminded him of Michael's own younger brother, Gabriel.

She said nothing until he said, "Good day to you, Mrs. St. Ange."

Then she nodded.

He paused. Surely, she could not be so rude. Just as he turned away, however, she added, "Good day."

No "my lord" for him as for Toddingly. This woman was infuriating. Moreover, she plainly had some grudge against him. Even worse, it didn't matter. He still wanted to be with her, no matter how she treated him.

What a half-wit he was!

ADA KNEW SHE SHOULDN'T feel so triumphant, but she did. After all, it wasn't every day one got to see a nobleman in his bare feet or see him set down a peg. Yet that was exactly what had happened to Lord Vile.

Obviously, he had so wanted to be heroic in front of her and her boy. Not because he cared a fig for Harry, of course, but to impress her. Instead, he'd looked foolish.

The outing had worked better than she could have hoped. It had even driven him to drink!

Now, more than ever, because his pride had been wounded, he would attend her and attempt to win her admiration. And she would relish every moment of him doing so.

CHAPTER EIGHT

As expected, within a day, another missive from Lord Vile arrived at her door. This time accompanied by flowers. Spicey carnations and sweet pungent pinks, to be exact.

Having never received flowers from a man before, she admitted to a small sensation of pleasure. Even though she realized he'd done nothing more than send his servant to a flower girl on a street corner to purchase the sweet bunch, tied with a silver ribbon, he'd succeeded in making an impression.

The note was similar to the previous one, except more specific:

Dear Mrs. St. Ange,
Despite failing to retrieve Harry's boat, I hope you will not hold it against me. I would like to call upon you tomorrow at two o'clock in the afternoon for a carriage ride.
Lord M. Alder

Again, he wished to get her alone in a small space. She knew he would kiss her and then attempt to touch more of her. Seduction was his aim, but she intended to hold out for his heart. At some point, she knew she would have to let him take a few small liberties with her person, and she was prepared for that, but not yet.

Tomorrow, he could have another small taste of her, and then she would abruptly be unavailable until after his next appointment with Mr. Brunnel. The good financial news would put Lord Vile in an ebullient mood, and undoubtedly, his black heart would open a little more to her, especially after a few days' absence fueled by anticipation.

Lord Alder,

Given your reputation, a carriage ride seems the height of folly, and I am not foolish. However, I will be ready in my riding habit at two if you wish to bring a gentle gelding for me."

Mrs. St. Ange

She certainly didn't fancy trying to ride her own carriage horse, who was rather round in the withers and swayed in the backbone. If Alder didn't have a horse for her to ride, then they would go for another walk. At least, she was getting exercise.

Before she knew it, it was time for her dinner alone with Lady Pepperton. The widow's invitation had arrived the day before, and Ada saw no reason to avoid her new friend, merely because she was trying to destroy the woman's former paramour.

In fact, their sociable association could only help.

"So good to see you," Elizabeth said. "You look splendid. Come in, come in. Madeira?"

Ada nodded.

"Perfect."

Soon, Ada was ensconced in the widow's drawing room, her feet on a small velvet footstool, sipping red wine, and hearing about the breakup of Lady Pepperton and Lord Vile.

As far as Ada was concerned, Elizabeth had done well to be rid of him.

"What did you get out of your six months?" she couldn't help asking, for it seemed to her this charming woman shouldn't have wasted so much time on such a hedonist of a man.

Elizabeth stared at her as if she were two-headed.

"My dear, it was not about getting anything out of the association. Neither of us needed anything tangible from the other. I didn't expect flowers and chocolates, after all."

Ada felt her cheeks grow warm since she'd already received the former. However, Elizabeth didn't seem to notice.

"The relationship was satisfactory in many ways. I liked having him come to me when I summoned him, I suppose. We didn't talk about much beyond the weather and what we might eat. Nothing of importance because we both knew it was silly to invest too much intimacy in something that was never going to be a sentimental attachment."

Given how Ada's friend Maggie felt about her husband, John, or the deep feeling that bound her parents, Ada couldn't fathom spending six months with someone only skirting the surface and remaining completely unattached.

She was firmly of the belief if she spent time with a man, and exchanged kisses and much more, it would be because she wanted to be with him forever. With the exception, of course, for her enticement of Lord Vile, whom she wanted to punish and then oust from her life as quickly as possible.

"I'm awfully glad your heart was not in it, and that you're not sad."

Elizabeth had a wonderful laugh, which Ada appreciated hearing. "I could never love a man such as Alder. He was too unreliable for my taste. Yet we had a very good time together."

Ada didn't like to think of their *very good time*. She assumed it was something akin to what had occurred between her and him in the gazebo. At least, *he* had seemed to enjoy it. She vaguely recalled the blend of terror and excitement, along with something unfulfilling and disappointing, and then the outright shock of what had occurred. What she had willingly allowed.

Ada definitely wouldn't declare it a *good time* and was still surprised how women sought out the experience.

"So, he is unreliable and shallow, and yet you found him good company?"

"You say that as if it is beyond the pale. I assure you, Alder has some rather good assets. Why all this interest? Are you thinking of taking up with him?" And Elizabeth's lovely laugh broke out again.

When Ada didn't join in and, instead, sat staring straight ahead, the widow said only, "Oh." However, her laughter stopped.

"It's not what you think," Ada began. How could she explain what it was? Simple revenge? Did she even want to? What if Elizabeth felt a sense of loyalty to her former paramour and told him?

Determined to keep her plan to herself and be truthful, Ada said, "I have absolutely no interest in him as a beau, nor would I ever want to have a 'good time' with him."

Elizabeth took her measure, then nodded.

"Either way, I'm not bothered," the widow admitted. "As I said, I could never love him, although I'm convinced I could have made him fall in love with me if I'd wanted to. If he's capable of such."

"He was once engaged to someone I know," Ada blurted.

"Really?" Elizabeth looked intrigued, then she frowned. "He never mentioned it."

Ada shrugged. "Why would he? It meant nothing to him, for he was the one who broke it off. Anyway, it was about four years ago."

"Was it you?" The question came at her quickly.

"No, I swear it." Yet she wouldn't reveal Jenny Blackwood's name either, for it was all water under the bridge.

"Strange," Elizabeth said. "I've never heard a whisper of his close brush with marriage, but then I was abroad for much of the decade before I met my husband, rest his soul. Anyway, Alder's behavior or his *affaires de cœur* wouldn't have stopped me taking up with him."

The widow paused, then raised one saucy eyebrow. "In answer to your earlier question, there was one thing I wanted from him which I hadn't had with my husband, and Alder provided that perfectly."

Ada sighed. They were back to the physical relations between a man and a woman, the mysterious act about which she couldn't fathom what was all the fuss.

"You weren't bothered by his reputation that earned him his nickname? His drinking and whoring?"

Elizabeth cringed at the last word. "I admit he drinks more than some. But I don't think it was gin or enjoying a few harlots alone that earned him his atrocious moniker."

"No?" Ada felt a prickle of discomfort.

The widow shook her head, dark curls swishing about her neck.

"The *bon ton* doesn't care overmuch about a little drinking or whoring, although the places he chose to do both did raise eyebrows, to be sure. No, it was his reputation for preying on gullible young ladies that caught their attention—and even made them fearful. Most of *haut* society still think it vile to seduce an innocent."

"Of course," Ada said, forcing herself not to let her mind wander back to that night, and the terrible shock of it.

"And it's not even for the sake of the young lady," Elizabeth continued. "Basically, everyone's concern is the perceived theft from the future husband of the moment of deflowering. Also, of course, the worry someone's going to end up with someone else's bastard."

Ada swallowed, unable to speak.

Elizabeth shrugged. "As for me, I guessed any man who could seduce a debutante into giving up her most prized possession must be quite skilled at making love."

Ada wouldn't ask if her new friend had guessed correctly as to Lord Vile's skills. She could see the answer on her face. The woman had enjoyed herself. Then Elizabeth sighed.

"The only nuisance in the end of an affair is having to find another man. The tiresome search is on."

Yet her expression, eager and even excited, belied her words. The widow looked all too ready to dive into the hunt.

MICHAEL BROUGHT ADA A gentle gelding as requested. Doing anything else would be ungentlemanly, and he was determined to be a gentleman in her eyes. Except when he was kissing her, as he intended, or bedding her, as he also intended. Not that day, but someday soon.

Obviously, a good rider, she'd effortlessly taken her narrow skirts in her left hand, grabbed the pommel with her right, and placed her left foot in his hand. In the next instant, with his assistance, she'd sprung lightly up and into the ladies' saddle, hooking her right leg over the pommel.

Patient and unmoving, she'd allowed him to secure her booted foot into the stirrup and even arrange the skirts of her riding habit.

When he glanced up at her, she was looking straight ahead while he touched her. Was it because she was moved by his touch or utterly unmoved? He couldn't tell.

"Either north toward Grosvenor Gate or west to Kensington Gardens," he offered as their route, "but I will avoid the Serpentine altogether, madam. On that, I will brook no argument."

"Indeed."

Seemingly, it was her favorite word for irritating him, being noncommittal, and giving him a set-down all at once.

When she said nothing more, he decided they would go west along Rotten Row, skirting the bottom of Hyde Park.

They rode in silence for a few minutes, which suited him fine. He was, as expected, on her right, which gave him a delightful view of her rounded bottom with the habit pulled tightly to her left.

"You cut a fine figure," he said at last, keeping his voice down as they drew alongside the Crystal Palace and the crowds of visitors.

She wore a becoming riding costume of green velvet which he had longed to remove from the moment he'd assisted her into the saddle.

Ignoring his remark, she glanced to her left at the building.

"Incredible," she stated.

"I agree," he said, "but how do you mean?"

She kept her gaze on the structure. "That the builders could design and have it up in nine months. The size of it, the design. Never mind what is inside, although the exhibits are enough to addle the brain, I think the building itself with all that glass and iron is a marvel."

"Again, I agree. How many times have you been inside?"

This brought her gaze around to meet his. "Four times. My father numbers Henry Cole among his acquaintances, so naturally, we were invited to the queen's opening of the exhibition. What about you?"

"I wasn't invited," he said, hoping she realized his sardonic tone was directed at himself. For he'd done nothing in the world of invention to warrant either knowing Cole, who'd practically created the entire exhibition singlehandedly, or being a member of his inner circle.

"I suppose your father is also a member of the Royal Society for the Encouragement of Arts, Manufactures, and Commerce."

"Naturally," she said.

"I have not even sent a Cole's greeting card," he said, "but I have received one," he added, hoping to soften the iciness surrounding her. "For this reason, I am grateful to the man."

"Indeed," she said.

He rolled his eyes. "Pray tell, why are you disgusted with me now?"

"Mr. Cole has done a great deal more than come up with the simple idea of a Christmas card!" she snapped. "Even now, he is developing a Museum of Ornamental Art at Marlborough House. Did you know he invented a marvelous teapot?"

"A teapot?" Michael bit his tongue in order not to mention that one could brew tea in just about anything.

"He's written books, too."

"Truly?" Michael had read a lot of drivel in his day. It seemed to him any Tom, Dick, or, in this case, Henry could write a book.

In any case, he had no doubt Cole was as smart as everyone said. Thus, Michael wasn't about to bring up how much he enjoyed the exhibition's handily placed public toilets. Yet, he had thought they were a treat. A penny well spent, in fact. The seat had been clean, and the attendant had handed him a fresh towel and a comb to tidy himself up while he was in there. He'd drawn the line at the shoe shine, however, as his own valet would have been insulted had a new coat of wax appeared on his Hessians while he was out.

"Shall we go in?" he offered. "I have a few guineas on me."

Mrs. St. Ange raised her chin in the air. "I have a season pass, thank you. And no, I'm not dressed for it."

He never quite understood why ladies in riding habits didn't wish to do anything but ride while wearing them. Perfectly serviceable outfit, as far as he was concerned, but they couldn't stand being without their poufy skirts and their bits of lace, he supposed.

On the other hand, it gave him a reason to ask her to go with him again. And in a carriage.

They rode along, surrounded by other riders, as far as West Carriage Drive, which divided the park from the gardens.

"Shall we keep going?" he asked. "Maybe all the way to the basin?" Where he would keep his boots and stockings on, by God!

Since she nodded amiably, they continued with their horses at an ambling pace. Once in Kensington Gardens, they left some of the other carriages and riders behind, and he started to think he might find a place where he could be alone with her for a moment.

In a small copse of sweet chestnut trees, with the pond just ahead, he suggested they dismount, stretch their legs, and let the horses graze.

She stared hard at him. Finally, she agreed.

"You shall have to assist me," she told him, as if there was any doubt he would.

He got down off his horse in record time, secured its reins to a branch, and then was at her left side, ready to touch her again.

"Leg over the pommel," he instructed, pulling her other booted foot from the stirrup.

"I know that," she snapped, lifting her right leg up and over the high pommel of the sidesaddle. Then, with nothing to keep her up, she slid down the side of the horse into his waiting arms.

"*Hmm*," she said, with her hands resting on his chest, their bodies not merely close but pressed together. She had nowhere to look except at his tidy cravat or up to his face.

With her head tilted up, it was easy. Michael pressed his mouth to hers.

"*Hmm,*" he mimicked against her soft lips.

She didn't seem to mind being kissed, neither stepping back, nor pushing at his chest. He had to admit kissing her was *different*. She made him want to be cautious with her, a little gentle and slow. He'd bedded wenches and he'd bedded aristocratic ladies before, even a duchess! Yet he'd never felt the sense of carefulness he felt with her.

It gnawed at him, telling him she was someone he could—and should—cherish. How strange, considering she was one of the prickliest females he'd ever met.

Giving in to an impulse, he sucked her lower lip, grazing his teeth across it as he released her.

He heard her small gasp. *Was it pleasure? Outrage?*

Belatedly, he realized she couldn't move since the horse was a hairsbreadth behind her. *Bother!* Maybe she hadn't liked it at all but was simply trapped.

Lifting his head, he released her from the imprisonment of being squashed between man and horse by taking a step back. He certainly didn't want to force her. Far from it. He liked his women willing and bursting with desire, and to his recollection, had never had one any other way.

Saying nothing, while her cheeks pinkened prettily, she skirted him, walking away, keeping her back to him.

The Devil! Had he offended her terribly? After tying up her horse, he caught up with her.

"Mrs. St. Ange, shall we walk at least once around the basin and then, if you're ready, we can ride home, perhaps the northern path." He would even deign to go around the blasted Serpentine.

Nodding, looking distracted, she didn't seem to care.

He desperately wanted to do something for her, anything, to get into her good graces.

"I noticed you had no footman or butler to hold the horse's bridle when you mounted. Are you having trouble getting servants?"

"As a matter of fact, I am."

"Where was your driver today?"

"I don't keep him full-time. And I've decided not to bother with a footman. What would he do all day? However, I would like a butler. One who is not *disturbing* in any way."

A disturbing butler? Whatever could she mean?

"No, of course, that wouldn't do."

100

"Exactly. I don't want to feel menaced."

Menaced? What manner of servants had she been interviewing?

"I will make some inquiries. I'm sure I can locate a capable butler."

He felt her hesitate.

"No, don't go to any bother," she said, sounding mulish. "I don't need *your* help."

How quickly her tone and demeanor changed. She needed help but obviously didn't want his.

Very well. He would do it anyway and send some likely candidates to her doorstep. She couldn't stop him from helping. He knew many people and most likely, someone at White's would have a suggestion. Even if he had to poach another man's butler, he would find her a suitable one.

Feeling benevolent, he set about trying to cajole some small measure of warmth from her. And the best way would be to speak of Harry.

"Your boy reminds me of my younger brother."

Again, her steps faltered as if everything he said either surprised or annoyed her.

"How so?" she asked in that manner she had of saying very little.

Never had he wanted a woman to speak more than she already did, until he met Mrs. St. Ange. From her, he would like to hear volumes.

"Peculiarly, Harry looks very like Gabriel, same hair color and eyes. I was six when he was born, so I recall how he was as a toddler, not that I took much interest. As most children, I had my own concerns."

After a pause, she said, "Undoubtedly, there are many little boys who look like Harry."

And nothing more. He would persist.

"I also have a younger sister, Camille. She is five years younger than I am. Now that I think of it, she is most likely about to have her coming out Season."

No wonder his father was starting to worry over money. Tickets, gowns, and all the trappings and amenities could be financially oppressive. Not to mention setting money aside for a hefty dowry. Although with Camille's pretty face, he was confident she would find a match to her liking, even if penniless.

She said nothing, perhaps thinking of her own Seasons.

"Did you have a Season in London? I'm afraid I don't recall meeting you at any social events."

She didn't simply hesitate this time. She turned on her heel, obviously walking back to their horses.

Dammit! She must have had some disastrous occurrence as a debutante. Or perhaps she was shunned by someone at a ball, or maybe her dowry had been a pittance. How was he to know? And how could she still be so affected? After all, she'd ended up marrying the wealthy Mr. St. Ange and landing a large home on Belgrave Square, so why was she practically trotting to get away from him and some long-ago memory?

Catching up with her, he matched his longer stride to her furious marching until they were back at the horses. She untied hers at once.

"Assist me," she demanded.

"Are you unwell? That is, I can see you're physically fine, but—"

Impatiently, she attempted to mount the sidesaddle on her own, getting so far as placing her left foot in the stirrup. However, then she was faced with the task of getting her right leg over the pommel without needing to sweep it over the back of the horse. The apron skirt of her habit made this all but impossible.

Hopping on one foot, her other still in the stirrup, and the horse now getting agitated and moving, she snarled at him, "Are you going to help me or not?"

He'd like to tell her to go to the Devil, seeing as how she'd not said a single kind word to him. However, he stepped up, pulled her foot from the stirrup, and waited with his hands clasped.

She stepped into the cradle of his fingers and let him give an assisting lift. Soon, she was safely in the saddle, and before he could mount his own horse, she was urging hers into a trot.

When they arrived at her home, he hoped he could persuade her to let him know what had bothered her. However, as soon as they got there, she jumped down from the mount by herself and fled.

Astonished by her manners, he watched her open her front door, walk inside without a backward look, and slam it shut.

Indeed!

CHAPTER NINE

It took Ada a day to recover from the callous cad. How dare he ask her if she'd had a Season! She'd simply had to get away from the man to prevent herself from attempting to do him bodily harm.

She'd hoped to have a pleasant outing during which she would leave him wanting more before refusing to see him for a week. Instead, her plan was in ruins. Not only had she run away from him, she'd been irrationally uncivil, as far as he was concerned.

If he didn't ask to keep company with her again, she wouldn't be surprised. But if he didn't, then how could she break his heart?

If he did contact her, instead of not responding for a week, she decided to see him again. *But was it doing any good?*

Each time she was with him, she swore she would be enticing and even lovable, but then, as soon as she saw his handsome face, she would remember the entirety of that awful night. Especially how he'd whispered Jenny's name when he was inside her. And then, the appalling wink, as if they were conspirators in some mischievous endeavor.

She cursed him in the privacy of her room and then wished she didn't curse so much. Always over him, and usually daily.

Vowing to do better, Ada wondered if she should break the pattern of their interactions and be sweet as sugar. *Could she do it?*

When she didn't hear from Alder the next day, she feared she'd ruined everything. And then a surprising thing happened, a man came to her door and said he wanted to apply to be her butler. What's more, she liked him on sight and even more after they spoke. When he said the salary was acceptable and the butler's quarters were more than adequate, she nearly hugged him. He was impeccable, except for one thing.

And it was a rather unusual thing. He was married.

Had she ever heard of a butler who was married?

No, she hadn't. However, at present, he was her best choice, not to mention, her only choice. Moreover, with her servants' quarters barely inhabited, Ada decided to offer an invitation.

"Mr. Randall, if you will take the position, then you may start immediately. I know you said your wife lives in Lambeth, but I see no reason why you should be separated, certainly not with the Thames between you. She may live here, too. If the room I showed you isn't big enough, then you may choose any of the rooms that are empty, although I think that one is the largest."

A man of neutral but friendly expression, for the first time, she saw his eyes crinkle with happiness and the smallest of smiles turn up his lips.

"Thank you, madam. She will be very happy, as am I. However, I believe you are supposed to ask me for my references before hiring me."

Of course, he was correct. Reaching into the pocket of his coat, he pulled out a single sheet of paper, which he handed over.

She recognized the writing at once. Alder!

Barely reading it—*"this man comes highly recommended, yet because of his wedded status, is having a hard time finding placement"*—she knew he wouldn't send someone to her home who wasn't trustworthy, not with Harry there. She just knew it.

How odd! She considered him the vilest of beings when it came to his treatment of her, and maybe all women, yet she trusted his judgment in this.

So be it. She had a butler. When Mr. Randall left to collect his things and his wife, Emily, Ada did a small waltzing dance around her parlor. Maybe she would try to take tea with Maggie and exchange a little gossip.

Then she realized Lord Alder hadn't asked to see her again, and like a deflated hot-air balloon, Ada sank onto her sofa.

Then it hit her like a brick. It was her turn to make an overture. *Of course!* To thank him for finding her that rarest of all creatures, the perfect butler, she would invite him to dinner.

LORD VILE WAS PUNCTUAL to the minute. She wished she could say she liked that about him, but there was nothing she liked about him. Or, at least, nothing she would admit to.

Regardless, she'd dressed to dazzle, as Maggie might say, for her friend was the best at dazzling a man of any woman Ada knew. Thinking of Maggie, she selected the rich blue satin over the more demure rose she'd first chosen, and then she left off the lacey fichu for good measure. Let her décolletage dazzle him, too.

Her new butler announced his arrival and brought him into the drawing room. If she didn't think Alder was already cock-sure of himself, she would think he'd made a particular effort to look more devastatingly attractive than usual. And he'd succeeded.

Standing up to greet him, she allowed him take her hand and kiss it. He had a nice way of doing so, with dry lips and the most enticing soft caress of his mouth across her bare knuckles. Then he released her.

"Thank you for coming," she said, feeling she might choke on the words.

"Thank you for inviting me. I see that Mr. Randall is already in residence."

She could offer a genuine smile over her butler, and did so.

To her dismay, Alder froze and backed up a step.

"Is something wrong?" she asked, putting her hand to her throat. Could there be a small piece of lettuce from her light lunch in her teeth?

"No. It is simply the welcome appearance of your smile. And it's breathtaking."

A small bubble of pleasure floated up inside her at his compliment. She crushed it.

"A drink before dinner?" she offered. "What would you like?"

"I'm drinking you in with my eyes," he said.

His ridiculous statement, so practiced and insincere, brought her entirely back to her senses. *Thank goodness!*

"Nevertheless, is there something you would like to have in your mouth?"

His eyes widened and a wolfish grin appeared.

"Now what?" she asked. "Have I done something else breathtaking?" She hoped her tone was as cutting as she felt.

"There is something I should very much like to have in my mouth, but, undoubtedly, you would find it inappropriate. At least before dinner."

Frowning, she considered her words and realized her *double entendre*, although she still was in the dark as to what part of her he was referring. She almost wanted to ask.

Instead, she spread her hands, helpless.

"Since you made no decision, I shall make it for us both. We shall go in to dinner at once and forego any drink ahead of time. We can as easily speak in the dining room over our meal."

"As you wish," he said, with a polite nod, returning to good manners. Then he offered her his arm.

It seemed beyond strange, letting a man, particularly this one, lead her into her own dining room.

When they were seated, her staff, small as it was, worked like clockwork, serving the courses that her cook, Mary, had prepared. Ada had simplified from the many courses one normally served to a guest. Firstly, she wanted this over sooner than the normal two hours it took to get through appetizers to dessert. Secondly, Mary was less skilled than she'd indicated at her hiring interview. There'd been a few minor disasters, and Alder was the first guest for dinner.

A plate of prawns with a sprig of parsley was set before each of them.

A tad simple, but it looked fine, and Ada ate the first one. She chewed and chewed on the rubbery little morsel, washing it down with a sip of wine. *Drat!*

Peering cautiously at Alder, she saw him working his jaws manfully on the overcooked shellfish.

"So tired of oysters," she commented and popped another shrimp in her mouth as if it were delicious. Then they chewed in silence.

After finishing most of them, Alder sat back.

"I'll leave room for the next course," was all he said.

He was being kind again. She hated that. However, since he had stopped pretending to enjoy the prawns, she could, too.

When the kitchen maid brought out a bread basket *before* the soup, her timing being off, Ada merely shrugged. With tongs, the girl put a crusty roll on Ada's plate. Unfortunately, when she went to do the same for Alder, it slipped, and by the sound it made hitting the porcelain before bouncing onto the floor, Ada surmised they were more like rocks than rolls. Hopefully, a spread of butter would help.

"So sorry, madam," the maid said and bent to pick it up, thought better of it, then used the tongs to retrieve it and slipped it into her pocket.

Ada was only glad the girl hadn't put it back onto Alder's plate. Instead, she carefully gave him another, then set the basket on the sideboard, snatched up their appetizer plates, and hurried back to the kitchen.

"Did I thank you for sending me a butler?" Ada asked.

"You did in your note. I'm glad he worked out. And it's not inconvenient to have his wife here, too?"

"Certainly not. It seems barbaric when married servants are forced to live apart, or worse, forbidden to marry in the first place. Why shouldn't they have a private life separate from their employment?"

He nodded. "Many do not think as you do. Are you a romantic, Mrs. St. Ange?"

She felt her cheeks warm. She could tell him how she used to be a romantic young miss before a so-called gentleman ripped the veil of starry-eyed silliness from her eyes. Romance was the name for a man's false behavior up until he lifted a woman's skirts and got what he wanted.

He was waiting for an answer.

"No." At that moment, the soup was brought in, and she didn't have to say more.

It smelled good. She'd asked Mary to make a basic savory soup of chicken. When Ada looked down, she gasped before she could stop herself, for there were bones, some floating and a few in the bottom of her bowl, visible through the transparent broth.

She wanted to slap a hand to her forehead but feigned absolute calm while surreptitiously looking at her guest to see his reaction.

His gaze darted to hers, and she tried to look nonplussed.

"I've never seen chicken soup served this way," he confessed.

"The bones add to its flavor," she informed him. "Simply leave them in the bottom."

"I assure you, I wasn't going to eat them." However, he did pick up his roll and try to break it open. When he couldn't, he attacked it with his knife, and eventually, it crumbled like toast, with the crumbs flying everywhere across the white tablecloth.

Ada pretended not to notice and took a spoonful of soup. At first taste, it seemed fine, but then the salty flavor hit the back of her tongue and lingered down her throat. It wasn't what one would call pleasant, more like swallowing glass. *The deuce!*

Waiting anxiously for him to dip his spoon into his soup, she wondered if it would be wise to knock the bowl off the table entirely, but she couldn't think how to do it without it ending up on his lap.

As he swallowed, she watched his eyes widen.

A nervous laugh escaped her, which she turned quickly into a cough.

He coughed, too, obviously due to the soup.

They both reached quickly for their wine glasses and gulped it down. Trying to recall the next course, she knew she'd told Mary to skip the fish and could only hope the meat was something even her cook could manage.

Thankfully, when their barely touched soup was taken away, the maid brought in a simple roasted haunch of mutton with creamed potatoes, French beans in butter.

What could possibly go wrong?

Of course, the mutton was overcooked to the consistency of shoe leather. Despite that, hungry by this point, they both consumed what was on their plates. The potatoes were astonishingly perfect. Apparently, overcooking them only made them creamier. Who knew? And the beans?

Ada choked down a mushy and strangely stringy bean.

By this point, there was no use pretending it was good.

Opening her mouth to apologize, she stopped when he held up his hand.

"Don't say it."

"What?" she asked.

"Cooking everything to within an inch of its life somehow adds to the flavor. Is that your contention? Because I can tell you, madam, except for the potatoes, I don't want any greater flavor to come through, not from this meal."

Yet, he ended his complaint with a smile.

What could she do? She offered him a small smile in return.

"Actually, I was going to apologize for this disaster. My cook has made a few missteps, such as hard aspic the other day. I can't for the life of me figure out how she could turn a jellied food quite so solid, but there you are. Anyway, I'm not a fussy eater and hadn't noticed how bad her cooking is."

"I, for one, am thrilled with the meal," he said.

"I beg your pardon?"

He took another sip of wine. "I am grateful to your cook for those are the most words you've said to me at one time."

Ada rolled her eyes. She wished she'd maintained her aloof manner.

"Will you fire her?" he asked.

The notion hadn't occurred to her. Ada wouldn't be able to give Mary good references, and without them, how would she find another job?

"Absolutely not," she declared.

"Then how will you manage? More importantly, how will I be able to accept your next invitation? I could eat first, I suppose, and then come to dinner."

Again, he smiled.

She sighed. "Mary will improve."

"Are there many more courses?" He looked nervous.

"No. Only dessert."

"Thank the good Lord." Then he drained his glass. "By the way, the wine is delightful."

She agreed. They'd had two different types, one with the shrimp and soup and another with the mutton. In each case, the wine was the only thing truly palatable.

The maid entered with dessert.

"What are we having?" Ada asked her.

The girl looked at it and frowned. "Cook said it was raspberry tart, madam. With fresh cream."

She put a plate before each of them, blackish and still smoking, with very thin cream that had run off onto the sides.

"To tell you the truth, madam," the girl added, "I'm not at all sure what it is." With a clucking sound, she left.

Then Ada did something she thought she would never in her life do. She laughed with Lord Vile. She laughed so hard tears came to her eyes as she stared at the mess in front of her.

He slapped the table with mirth. "I'm not eating it, Mrs. St. Ange. I tell you. Not out of politeness. Who knows how I would feel in the morning?"

She couldn't speak as she dabbed at her eyes with her napkin, shaking her head.

Finally, she said, "You don't have to. You've been more than polite during this fiasco of a meal. I don't know what I'll do about her."

He stood and walked around to pull out her chair. When she rose, he took her hand and tucked it under her arm.

"Shall we go back to the drawing room and have a drink?"

Then what? she wondered. Yet, she had to be pleasant.

"I have only port. No brandy."

He grinned. "I shall suffer through it."

She let him pour them both a drink from the sideboard. Then they sat opposite each other, her on the sofa, him in a winged chair, and silence descended like thunderclouds. She recalled what Elizabeth said about discussing merely the weather and what they would eat.

What did she want to talk with him about?

If she were truly interested in him, she would ask about his family, and she supposed she would tell him of hers. They could discuss investing and how the London Stock Exchange came to exist due to a renegade group of traders who either left the Royal Exchange or, more excitedly, were expelled for being rowdy, only to begin trading in the coffee houses of London. They could, if she weren't trying to ruin him financially.

"What do you read?" she asked finally.

He looked surprised. "Read?"

"Yes, you know, like a book."

"Yes, I know what one reads. Frankly, I read the newspapers more than anything else, but I confess to enjoying occasional serial fiction. Why, one can hardly open a magazine without seeing an installment by Mr. Dickens."

"Indeed," she said.

Alder jumped up from his seat and came around to sit beside her, leaning across her startled body to place his glass on the small octagonal table beside her.

"Now don't start that 'indeeding' me again. I thought we were beyond that."

"I have no idea what you mean."

"Why don't you tell me what *you* like to read?"

She stared at him. "Do you really want to know?"

"Yes, definitely," he insisted.

Ada spent a lot of time reading not only the *Economist* and the London Stock Exchange reports but also philosophers, particularly those who discussed economics. She'd read voraciously during her confinement before Harry was born, and she'd read to stave off loneliness afterward, when she refused to see anyone except Maggie and barely left her parents' home in Surrey. It had become such a habit, she read every day. Luckily, it was a luxury she could afford and, therefore, had built up her own library. However, she didn't want to take him into her library. It was too personal.

Thinking to what she'd read recently, she confessed, "I like John Stuart Mill and Karl Marx." As soon as she'd said those names, Ada knew she should toss in something more frivolous and ladylike. "As well as Jane Austen." Although she couldn't think of a single title by that esteemed lady writer.

Alder's eyebrows rose. "They are vastly different texts. I can understand your reading Austen, but I honestly have never met a woman who has read Mill or Marx."

She thought about it. "Except for myself, neither have I."

"I must confess I haven't read any of the three," he said, then shrugged.

As he leaned forward, she gasped softly. He was going to kiss her, and she knew she had to let him if she were to win his affections.

Closing her eyes, she prepared herself.

Nothing happened. When she opened her eyes, he had his drink in hand and was looking at her smugly.

The rat! He knew what she'd assumed and had let her sit there like a ninny. If he hadn't intended to humiliate her, he would have kissed her. He ought to have.

No! That made no sense. How could kissing her be the correct thing to do?

Confused by her own addlepated thoughts, Ada picked up her own drink and sipped, while Lord Vile finished his in two more swallows. Then he rose to pour another one. He held the decanter up in question, but she shook her head.

Was this enough time spent being alluring? Could she end the evening now?

When he sat again, he looked at her profile.

"Why aren't you a romantic, Mrs. St. Ange?"

"I have never experienced romance," she said, then wished she could call back her words. It was the tongue-loosening port after all the wine.

He cocked his head. "Did your husband not woo you properly?"

"I don't wish to speak of him," she said stiffly.

"Fair enough. Let's speak of you. May I call you by your given name?"

"No," she said quickly.

"You may call me Michael."

"I don't wish to."

He sighed. "Why did you leave the country for Town? Were you lonely?"

Was she?

"I suppose I was."

"So, you came to Town to find a new husband?" he asked.

Her laugh sounded like a scornful bark to her ears. "No."

"A paramour, then?"

"No!" She had to get him off this hounding. "I have friends here."

"Anyone I know?"

"No," she muttered. *Drat!* She could not mention Maggie, who, after her flight from London, was the only friend Ada had kept. Bringing up Jenny's sister would be a disaster.

"I'm certain you and I move in different circles." She had to deter him. "Does it seem strange for you to be sitting here in my drawing room of an evening when you could be two doors down?"

"We've discussed this before, I believe."

She shrugged.

"I would have eaten better along there," he pointed out, finishing off his second glass of port. "And by now, we would most assuredly not be discussing books and friends."

Ada's cheeks burned.

"In fact, I would like to demonstrate what I would rather be doing with you than with any other woman."

With that, he leaned toward her and kissed her. She hadn't even time to close her eyes!

MICHAEL BREATHED IN HER scent as he did whenever he kissed a woman, even though he knew she wouldn't smell like his oft-recalled golden goddess. It didn't matter. He very much liked Mrs. St. Ange's fragrance, the popular neroli scent, he guessed. In fact, it was starting to be as dear to him as the lost lady from the garden.

Her soft lips beckoned him each time he was with her, and he exalted in claiming them again, as much as he wished to claim the rest of her.

Did she want him to stake claim to her?

From her behavior and her words, he couldn't tell. However, when her mouth moved against his and her lips opened for his tongue, he felt certain they were moving toward an affair.

Just like his previous one with Elizabeth. Or the one before that with Lilith. The one before that, unfortunately, her name he'd already forgotten.

Even as he explored her mouth and as his hands began to roam, stroking her bare upper arms and then sliding down to rest upon her slender waist, he argued with himself.

An affair with Ada Kathryn St. Ange would not be like the others. He didn't want it to be. With most of his paramours, the relationship never went beyond the confines of the lady's residence. Although he had escorted Elizabeth to events for which a doting male was necessary, those occasions were not initiated by him. He always knew he was providing a service and playing a part.

With Mrs. St. Ange, he truly wished to view the Crystal Palace's exhibition in her company and hear her thoughts on the wonders inside. He imagined seeing an opera with her or something by Dickens at one of the newer playhouses in the West End. He could even imagine going farther afield and taking the waters at Bath or seeing the lochs of Scotland together. With Harry, too, he supposed.

If only she didn't seem to spend so much time disliking him. At least, it seemed she did. On the other hand, she continued to accept his invitations and had invited him here to dine. What's more, she let him take liberties, at least with her mouth. She was a puzzlement.

Feeling her hands at the back of his neck, her cool fingers reaching into his hair, he shuddered and hot desire shot straight to his loins.

How many more times could he kiss her like this and not begin to undress her?

How likely was it she would let him make love to her when she wouldn't even let him use her given name?

Maybe he'd been too tentative in his attentions toward her. Perhaps it was time to push his case, pursue her more firmly, and see if she wanted more.

To that end, he moved his hand from her waist to the underswell of her right breast, cupping it. Despite the layers of fabric, he could feel her heart beating like a war drum. He also felt her freeze like a Michelangelo statue.

Should he continue his ministrations?

When she didn't protest, he brushed his thumb across her nipple, which was easy to feel through the satin of her gown. He could imagine it pebbling under his touch, and he ardently longed to set his lips to the ripe berry.

Breaking their kiss, he nibbled along her chin and down her neck, which she arched, apparently transported by his touch.

Still, she didn't protest. A glance showed her eyes closed, her lips slightly parted, and he knew if his hand ever made it up under her skirts, she'd be damp for him. For his own part, his shaft was pressing painfully against the fall of his trousers.

He slipped his fingers into the neckline of her gown and tried to edge the fabric down so he could place his lips upon her creamy bosom.

Perhaps it was his clumsy attempts to get to her breasts which brought her from her passionate haze, but suddenly, she was struggling against him, trying to sit up with his weight upon her.

The very same hands that had been holding him close were now pressed against his chest and pushing him away.

"Let me up," she demanded.

CHAPTER TEN

Ada couldn't believe she'd given in to the sensual delights of Alder's mouth and his hands. She'd planned to let him kiss her, precisely as he had before. Yet, in a heartbeat, when his tongue had slid into her mouth, she'd gone from being in control to closing her eyes and losing herself to the sensual experience.

Now, with her breasts tingling, still able to feel the path his mouth had taken down her bare neck to her décolletage, and with a distinct dampness between her legs, she was mortified.

This was Lord Vile! Who knew whether in the morning he would remember with whom he'd been the night before? After all, he'd had two glasses of port after an equal amount of wine. As for herself, she was feeling a little tipsy.

She pushed on his chest, and he moved back quickly.

"Did I hurt you?" he asked, his voice thickened.

"No," she said. *Had he really asked her that as if he gave a damn?*

Ada wanted to tell him to go to the devil. Instead, she breathed deeply, arched an eyebrow, and addressed him.

"I'm not prepared to go any further."

That was the truth, so help her.

He nodded. "That's fine. I meant no disrespect."

She stared at him. *Truly!* "That seems hard to believe."

He looked surprised. "Why? Because I am expressing how much I admire you and would like to know you better."

"By tugging at my garments?"

He had the gall to smile. *The rogue!* "Yes, of course. Because I would like to know every part of you better. I am trying to be precisely clear. After all, you are not attached to anyone, nor am I. I imagine you must be lonely at times, having known the companionship of a husband. Surely, you are too young to give up pleasures of the flesh?"

"I . . ." She didn't know what to say. He was obviously far more worldly than she was. He was used to the likes of Lady Pepperton and lived in a world where men and women enjoyed each other without attachment.

In all likelihood, she would fail to work her way into his stone heart before he demanded something she would never give him.

"I think it's time for you to leave."

His expression clouded over. "I am sorry if I've offended you. Frankly, you are a puzzle to me."

She wanted to remain a puzzle, too. Maybe she should let Brunnel exact her revenge on Vile's financial holdings and forego the hope of seeing his heart crushed as hers had been.

He stood. "I had no way of knowing you didn't want, as you say, to 'go any further.' That's no matter. I confess, however, if we meet indoors, alone, I shall want to test your resolve."

He crossed his arms and tapped his chin with one hand. "I've the perfect answer. Let's go out next time. I'll get tickets to a play."

Her head was spinning. She'd expected him to storm from her home when she said she wouldn't let him take any more liberties. Instead, he wanted to see her again, this time out in public.

Spending time together doing ordinary things would certainly demonstrate whether he was capable of forming an attachment of the heart. Yet, if she acquiesced too easily, how would he long for her?

"I will accompany you to a play, but not this week. Not next week either."

"Why?" he asked, looking perplexed.

Why? Was he allowed to ask her why?

"You're being impertinent," she told him, raising her chin.

"I'm not. Why can't you see me this week or next? Do you have another suitor?"

He said it as a jest, which annoyed her.

She remained silent, thinking quick and deceitful thoughts. *Why hadn't she considered this herself?* The surest way to gain his devoted interest was to make him jealous. Even her pause was affecting him, for his easy smile died on his face.

"Well, do you?"

"I refuse to discuss such matters," she said at last. Neither confirming nor denying seemed the best course of action.

"I see. And if I choose to woo another lady, that is fine as long as we do not discuss it."

Drat! It wouldn't do for him to fall for anyone else.

"Absolutely not." She stood and faced him in the center of the room.

He sighed. "You are puzzling me again."

"I am not a puzzle. If you are incapable of self-restraint, if you need to have another paramour immediately, then I suggest you do not contact me again."

He stared into her eyes, until, finally, unable to bear his scrutiny, she looked away first.

"Very well," he said. "It has been a stimulating evening."

Was he leaving for good?

"I look forward to our next one," he added.

She nodded in agreement, inside feeling a wave of relief her plan wasn't ruined, and walked to the drawing room door. She sensed he wished to kiss her again and was fully prepared to endure it.

Instead, he took her hand and bestowed a gentle kiss upon her knuckles, and then, before releasing her, he turned her hand over, and brushed his lips upon the inside of her wrist.

She gasped as a sensation of desire shot straight to her womanly core. *Indeed!*

AT A PRIVATE TABLE at White's, Michael listened to Brunnel explain how much the stock had increased in value and how much he'd made. *From guano!*

Without hesitation, he went along with the man's suggestion of being part of a sugar trading group. Why not? Who didn't love a spoonful in their tea or coffee or a delicious sweet treat anytime? Apparently, all his fellow Brits were enjoying it by the sackful.

Brunnel accepted both a glass of brandy and Michael's signature, and then went on his way. Efficient and capable. The absolute opposite of Mrs. St. Ange's cook.

Each time he ate, Michael recalled the meal of four nights' earlier, and he was determined to do something about it. Not only for Mrs. St. Ange's sake but for his own, too. He intended to dine with her again as he worked his way from the ground floor to the upper chambers. Eating her cook's fare would do more to spur on indigestion than ardor.

Mrs. St. Ange would not accept another cook. She'd made it clear she had no intention of firing the incompetent woman in the kitchen. There was only one answer, short of murdering the cook whilst she shopped for perfectly good food to ruin. He would send his own wonderful cook knocking on the backdoor with an offer of assistance. Maybe Mrs. St. Ange didn't need to know.

He thought better of his last idea. If she found out he'd gone behind her back and interfered with her staff, she'd undoubtedly have a fit of pride. Moreover, he rather hoped to get credit for having done a good thing, just as he had by sending over the well-trained Mr. Randall.

Thus, feeling beneficent, he sent his skilled cook, Mrs. Beechum, letter in hand. She was at Mary's disposal and would teach her whatever she could, daily, as necessary.

After all, he nearly always ate at his club, and he was paying his cook anyway. He wouldn't have to pay her any extra for cooking at someone else's home. Moreover, she'd been pleased to do it, to get out of his kitchen and have a bit of company and help out a fellow cook.

He waited for a grateful missive from Mrs. St. Ange in return.

Nothing for three days, and then, when he started to think he might drive to her home and see if her lights were on at night, or even send another message, perhaps with a few suggestions for plays, finally, he received a brief note:

Mary is pleased to meet Mrs. Beechum, and she sends her gratitude.

Mary sent him her gratitude! But not a word of thanks from the mistress of the house. *Naturally!*

He would wait before tendering her another invitation, as she suggested, although he couldn't help but wonder what the infernal woman was playing at. Didn't she find both his company and his kisses agreeable? Didn't she want more of both?

It had been over a week, and he longed to see her face, pretty even when she was scowling at him.

After a meeting with his father, during which, he found himself promising to visit with his mother within a fortnight, Michael felt he'd waited long enough. Tomorrow, he would purchase two tickets and then let his mysterious lady friend know when.

"Father, do you know anything of the family of Mrs. Ada Kathryn St. Ange?"

The earl steepled his fingers, looked toward the ceiling, wrinkled his forehead, and then said, "No. Never heard of this person."

"What about any St. Ange's?"

His father shook his head. "I don't believe so. What's the husband's given name?"

"He's dead, and I don't know."

Michael only knew Ada's given name because he'd asked Elizabeth.

"Another widow?" His father's tone was disparaging.

"She doesn't need my money, if that's what you're worrying about."

"Of course not," the Earl of Alder said. "With the way you've taken to this moneymaking endeavor, I'm not going to spend a moment worrying about financial matters. Proud of you at last," he added, causing Michael a moment of rancor.

Oblivious, his father lit a cigar and puffed thoughtfully.

"I'm only thinking of the future. My legacy, and yours. To that end, it's about time you considered courting a woman whom you wish to marry. Not playing around with any more of these widows simply because you like what's under their skirts."

Michael gripped the polished handrails of his chair. True, Elizabeth and the others had been for physical sport alone. Yet, he hadn't even experienced what was under Ada Kathryn's skirts and he liked her anyway.

His father blew a perfect O of smoke, then added, "After all, any wife will have the same attraction in that particular regard. At least enough for you to beget an heir, and then you can go back to enjoying widows, for all I care."

How warm-hearted of him.

Picking up his glass of brandy, Michael downed it. Their latest frank discussion was over. *Thank God.* He left determined to discover more about Mrs. St. Ange. In any case, who cared about her husband? The man was in Davy Jones's locker, after all.

If Michael wanted to figure out where she had come from, whether she'd had a Season, and if she had a past before Mr. St. Ange, then he needed to learn her maiden name.

How on earth would he do that?

A WEEK LATER, HE was no closer to solving that puzzle. No one had heard of Mr. or Mrs. St. Ange. However, she was finally ending his misery. And strangely, not seeing her had turned into precisely that—misery. Each day, he awakened thinking how nice it would be to spend time with her. Each evening, he sat at Whites with Hemsby or at home alone, wishing she was beside him. Or better yet, under him. Or on top of him.

He'd never experienced anything like it.

Finally, they were going out together. She was amenable to opera, and thus he had purchased tickets to the Royal Italian Opera at Covent Garden for a performance of Rossini's *Semiramide.*

When he went to collect her, Mr. Randall showed him into the front hall, where she was ready to leave, her cloak already draped about her shoulders.

Clearly, he was not to be invited into the drawing room for a drink, which pained him slightly. However, he would get one at the theatre before the curtain rose, which cheered him. Plus, patting his pocket, he felt his customary flask.

In any case, they would, for a short while, be alone inside his two-seater carriage. The brougham was certainly cozier than a drawing room, and still very private with his discreet driver perched on top.

He held her hand as she set her foot on the step and climbed in, then he entered and sat beside her. If he'd brought his larger clarence, she would have had the opportunity to sit opposite him, and he knew she would have done so.

Instead, he had the extreme pleasure of feeling her arm and thigh pressed against his. He was being a rogue for taking advantage, but he'd waited over two weeks to be close to her again. He was going to enjoy every moment.

"How are Mary's skills coming along?" he asked, remembering her cook's name and giving Ada the opportunity to thank him.

She pointedly stared out the window, her head turned from him.

"Improving," she murmured.

"Mrs. Beechum said she is a willing pupil who only needs some training."

Slowly, Mrs. St. Ange faced him.

"Is Mrs. Beechum in the habit of discussing what occurs in my household?"

He opened his mouth, then closed it. Finally, he shook his head.

"No, I assure you. That's all she has said."

"Indeed." She straightened her shoulders, and he expected her to turn away again. Instead, she took a deep breath as if steeling herself against an unpleasant task.

"I-I . . ."

What was she trying to tell him?

"Yes?" he prompted.

She looked as if a foul odor were under her delicate nose.

"I thank you for sending her."

Another sigh from her as if that had been a monumental task, and then she did turn away from him.

Blast! This wasn't going at all as he'd hoped. How could he get her to relax and be friendly with him when she couldn't stand to offer even a simple thank you?

The only time she'd seemed at least willing and not hostile was when he kissed her.

Tapping her shoulder, as she turned to him, he gently took her face in his hands, leaned forward, and kissed her.

She froze at his touch, but she didn't pull away, so he persisted.

The usual delight at kissing her rushed through him, despite there being nothing *usual* about it. This cool, composed woman lit a unique passion in him each time he touched her.

Slanting his mouth against hers, he felt the heat of desire shoot through him, flooding his groin as she parted her lips, soft and yielding. He wanted to sink his fingers into her shiny blonde locks, but he never knew a woman who would appreciate getting her hair mussed on the way to the theatre.

Instead, he wrapped his arms around the back of her and drew her against him. Still, she didn't protest. In fact, she gave the smallest of moans.

He wanted to give her pleasure, to delight her so much he cracked her icy shell. To that end, he reached for her skirts, still stroking her back with his other hand.

However, the moment he began to raise her gown, she protested.

"No," she murmured against his mouth, despite seeming content to remain in his arms.

"Let me touch you," he whispered.

"No."

He could tell she wasn't unaffected by his ministrations, for she was breathing heavily and leaning into him.

"You will enjoy it," he promised.

"No."

Drawing back slightly, he looked down at her.

"But you like my kisses?" he asked, even though he was positive she did.

If she said no, he would know her for a liar.

After a brief hesitation, during which her cheeks grew slightly pink, she agreed. "Yes."

"I will never force you to do anything you don't want to do. I simply hoped we could pleasure one another."

"No." Her entire body stiffened, and the cool Mrs. St. Ange was back beside him.

"May I kiss you again?"

For an answer, she turned away.

The devil! Next time he kissed her, he would do naught else. No matter how much he wanted to do more, he would restrain himself. His instincts told him she was worth the wait.

Pulling his flask from his pocket, more than ever, he needed a drink.

CHAPTER ELEVEN

A da hated the truth, but she enjoyed Lord Vile's kisses. His were the only lips she'd ever known, and she couldn't imagine anyone's kiss being better.

However, she hoped a kiss given with love, not simply desire, would be superior.

Had Lord Vile ever kissed a woman with love in his heart?

She doubted it. Except maybe for Jenny Blackwood, and Ada didn't know if they'd ever done so.

When Alder put his hand on her skirts, however, he went too far, doing the very thing she'd dreaded he would if she was alone in a carriage with him. Oddly, though, she'd felt no fear. She knew he wouldn't assault her or do more than she allowed.

How or why she knew this, she hadn't a clue.

He had done vile things, but from what she could tell, he had some moral guide. Besides, a man as attractive as Michael Alder had no need to force a woman. She was certain every debutante he'd debauched had allowed him without protest, exactly as she had done.

What was one's virtue when faced with his gorgeous eyes, sensual mouth, and wicked hands? Luckily, she was now immune to his charms.

Going to the opera, however, was an utter delight. She'd never been to a theatre while not in the company of her parents. She liked stepping out of the carriage holding his proffered hand, then walking into the lobby on his arm. Alder attended to her every need, handing her coat to the clerk and procuring their drinks. She had a glass of champagne, he had two.

With all her senses on high alert, she didn't miss the fact hardly anyone spoke to them. In fact, it was clear when women saw him, they began speaking about him behind their fans or gloved hands. And the gentlemen scowled. His behavior had well and truly alienated him from his peers. Most of the *ton* probably feared for their wives, sisters, or even daughters. It was a wonder he hadn't been killed in a duel.

As to her, she was merely a baron's daughter who'd had a couple Seasons three years ago, the second one ending in her flight from London. There was little reason anyone should notice her, except she was obviously Lord Vile's companion. At least for the evening.

They climbed the stairs to the next level and he led her to the Alder family box. After they entered, he drew the curtain closed behind them, and she went directly to the railing. All around the theatre were boxes of earls and dukes and marquesses. The royal box was empty, although all the regular seats, including where she would have sat with her parents, were filled.

The noise from the audience was an excited rumble, perfectly mimicking how she felt—dressed in one of her best gowns and seated in a private box. It was, she realized, one of the most thrilling nights of her life.

And it was with Lord Vile!

She watched him remove his opera hat, put his thumbs to the top and his fingers to the brim and press it flat before sliding it under his seat. Then they sat in silence as the lights were dimmed and the curtains drew back.

The opera made her exclaim in wonder at the music and song and nearly cry, and all the while, she and Alder sat close together, unspeaking, their shoulders occasionally brushing.

Ada fanned herself against the warmth of the building, especially up where they were seated. Thank goodness she'd worn a gown with short bell sleeves and her silk gloves rather than satin, which could become so hot as to make one's palms moist.

As they clapped at the end of the first act, she wondered what Alder had planned for intermission. Would they stay sequestered in his box or would they return to the lobby and mingle?

"You look lovely," he murmured close to her ear, sending a shiver down her spine. "I want to show you off."

Retrieving his top hat and giving it a sharp snap against his leg, returning it to its tall form, he stood and offered her his hand. Soon, they were descending to the lobby, where they parted with the promise to meet near the bar. In the lady's retiring room, Ada heard "Pepperton" whispered close by and knew the theatre goers were wondering what happened between Lord V. and Lady P. to end their affair. Smugly, she also knew she would never hear her own name on anyone's lips. *Who knew of Mrs. St. Ange?*

When she turned too quickly, she caught two ladies staring at her. Letting them wonder who she was, with a polite nod, Ada left the room.

Finding him standing at a high table near the bar where a glass of wine awaited her, she also noted an empty one, which must have been his. Presently, he held a glass of brandy, swirling its pale amber liquid. His smile appeared when he saw her.

Ada wrinkled her nose in displeasure, realizing he had wanted a drink as much as he'd wanted to display her, for he'd certainly downed the wine quickly.

"Something not to your liking, Mrs. St. Ange?"

About to ask him how he could drink strong liquor at all hours, suddenly, she heard her name called from a few feet away.

"Ada!"

Her heart started thumping. *Good God!* It was Maggie, Countess of Cambrey, but more importantly, formerly Miss *Blackwood*, one of Jenny's sisters.

Stupidly, she hadn't thought to ask her friend, but of all the venues, what terrible fortune that Maggie and her earl were at this one!

What could she do? It was too late to hide.

With a drink in one hand, she couldn't hug her best friend, but leaned forward to kiss her on both cheeks. Maggie's husband, John Angsley, the Earl of Cambrey, took her free hand and bowed over it.

And then they realized whom she was with.

"Oh!" Maggie said and nothing more, her sparkling eyes wide with surprise.

John was less subtle. "What the devil?"

Moreover, he didn't bow to her companion, nor even offer a nod of acknowledgement. Instead, his expression was livid.

"Ada, what on earth are you doing with this scoundrel?"

She glanced nervously at Alder, but he took no offense. He simply raised an eyebrow and looked to Ada for her response.

How could she answer while telling them nothing? "Lord Alder has brought me to the opera."

That was the simple truth and gave none of her plan away.

Clearly, John wasn't satisfied. "You know this man's reputation, do you not? You know how he treated Jenny."

She noticed Alder flinch out of the corner of her eye. Apparently, he was not utterly unaffected by his own poor standing among his peers.

"And his treatment of other women after her." John was bristling now.

At this rate of escalation, Ada knew she must diffuse the situation or risk fisticuffs.

"Be that as it may," she said to the earl, "we are simply enjoying an opera."

John scowled, but Maggie looked thoughtful. Her friend was quick-witted, and Ada had no doubt she would know there was more to this than met the eye.

Vowing to tell her some part of her plan, but in private, Ada considered how to separate them all before anything too telling was said. What if John or Maggie brought up Clive Brunnel?

However, the Earl of Cambrey wasn't done being protective.

"I think you are making an error in judgment. Do your parents know with whom you keep company?"

Any moment, John would say her family's surname, and she didn't want Alder to know anything about her real life or her past.

At last, Alder set down his empty glass as he spoke.

"Since Mrs. St. Ange is a widow, I doubt she has to answer to her parents regarding her companion, either for this evening or for anything else."

Oh dear, that sounded intimate, almost as if they were paramours.

"And she certainly doesn't have to answer to you," he finished.

John's jaw clenched. He was forbidden from saying anything about the pretense of her marital state to protect Harry being labeled a bastard. Nevertheless, he was clearly bursting to give Alder a dressing down.

Maggie rested a hand on her husband's arm, and glances went between the two of them and then back to Ada.

Meanwhile, Alder took her free hand and placed it on his arm. "Intermission is over. Are you finished with your wine?"

"Yes," she said, and set her glass upon the table.

Looking at the Cambreys, he nodded to Maggie. "Countess, I hope your sister is well."

John made an exasperated sound, but Alder ignored him and led Ada away, even as she offered a reassuring smile to her friends.

"That was interesting," Alder said when they were far enough not to be overheard. "They are special friends of yours, I take it."

There was no use denying it.

"Lady Cambrey is."

"Which means you are well aware of a history between her older sister and myself, whom the earl so indiscreetly mentioned."

"Yes," she admitted.

"Does that have anything to do with your predisposition against me?"

They'd reached their seats.

"What do you mean?" she asked, arranging her skirts and not looking at him.

"You often seem annoyed with me, or an even stronger emotion. Does that have to do with your friend's sister?"

Looking directly into his eyes, she replied, "No." Ada could be absolutely truthful. His breaking off his engagement with Jenny had nothing to do with how she felt about him. She had plenty of fuel for her own angry fire.

After a moment of silence, he asked, "Will you tell me about your parents?"

"I have two," she muttered.

The lights went down, and the opera's second act began.

BACK IN LORD VILE'S carriage, Ada wondered if the journey home would be more of the same, with him attempting to seduce her while she tried to maintain the illusion of being a possible conquest in his eyes while fending him off.

Instead, he left a little space between them and began to speak nearly as soon as the brougham began to move.

"Normally, I wouldn't bother defending myself because there are too many offenses of which I have been accused. However, in this case, I want to tell you what happened with Lady Lindsey, seeing as you are a friend of her sister."

"That's unnecessary," Ada told him. She really didn't wish to hear his excuses.

"Be that as it may, I like you. I never thought to speak of what happened again since it ought to have no bearing upon anyone except the lady in question and myself. However, if you count her sister among your good friends, then I suppose it does have some import."

Distractedly, he pulled off his hat and ran a hand thorough his already unruly hair, causing it to stand on end in places.

"It is a short tale. I liked Lady Lindsey, at the time Miss Blackwood, and offered for her hand. We never got as far as a formal arrangement or a public declaration. My father sent me to Kent, where we have our family home as well as other holdings. By the time I returned, she and her family had gone back to Sheffield. What's more, she was under the impression due to her family's financial ruin, that I had callously broken off our engagement, as was every person with a wagging tongue."

"None of this is news to me," Ada said.

"Yes, but you see, *I* did not break off our engagement at all. It was done in a letter forged by my father in my name. At the same time, he told me *she* had broken it off. By the time I found out otherwise, she was married to Simon Devere, Lord Lindsey."

His words certainly put the event in a different light. Ada didn't know what to say. It was a strange feeling when a long-held belief turned out not to be the case.

"Why don't you tell everyone the truth?"

Leaning back, he crossed his arms. "Unnecessary. Lady Lindsey knows, and that's enough. I don't give a fig what the *ton* thinks. Besides, as I said, I've committed plenty of other offenses."

He certainly had, including the one perpetrated upon her person, who stupidly, naively, went willingly along with him.

"Even her sister doesn't know," Ada pointed out. "Nor, obviously, Lady Cambrey's husband."

"I suppose not, but Cambrey would have other reasons to dislike me, as does Lady Lindsey's own husband."

"Really?" She wanted to hear all of it.

"Unfortunately, I couldn't rest with Lady Lindsey believing me such a cad after I'd truly cared for her, so I contacted her when she was in London. We went walking. Alone. Her husband caught us. I think if she hadn't been so calm and so clearly uninterested in me, Lord Lindsey and I might have decided upon a duel right then."

Ada processed this new information. Alder had wanted Jenny to know the truth. How strange he had cared whether she thought him a cad or not.

"You loved her?" she asked.

"Yes," he said simply.

Oh dear!

"When next I meet up with Lady Cambrey, may I tell her the truth," Ada asked, "about you and her sister and your father's perfidy?"

He shrugged. "It doesn't matter to me in the least what anyone else thinks. I'm telling you because," he turned to her, yet she couldn't see his eyes in the darkness, "because I like you. Moreover, I suppose I want you to like me, too."

She almost felt sorry for him, but that could never happen.

MICHAEL THOUGHT BETTER OF inviting himself in for a drink. If she said no, then it would push them further apart. Deciding to wait for the next opportunity, he walked her to her door, lightly brushed his lips upon hers because, truly, he couldn't help himself, and bid her good night.

He would begin his wooing of the inscrutable Mrs. St. Ange the next day, starting fresh. He hoped his suit would go better now she knew the truth. For if she'd been influenced by her friendship with the Blackwood sisters, then this could only benefit him.

Moreover, he could make more inquiries with the small piece of information. Ada Kathryn was a contemporary of Lady Margaret Cambrey. Those who knew the latter and came out the same Season might know of the former, too.

The next day, he went to Almack's. While no longer the pinnacle of a debutante's Season, and certainly having lost its sheen of exclusiveness, still a few years back, it would have been a must for young girls coming out. What's more, the Lady Patronesses, now mostly retired from their duties, would have records of everyone who had come through its doors. Whether they would share that knowledge remained to be seen, but he would try his damnedest to get it.

To that end, Michael directed his brougham to King Street and the unpretentious Palladian building standing sentry to the hopes and dreams of many a young lady.

Personally, he'd never cared for the plain brick structure, thinking something which decided the social fate of debutantes and bachelors—including the ruin of so many who couldn't gain admittance—ought to be grander on the outside.

Inside, he could see it was due some redecorating, although it retained the shabby gentility of a grand dame of the aristocrats. In fairness, it was midafternoon, and thus, perhaps not looking as good as it did when made up for the evening, like most women he knew. He hoped he would find someone there who could assist him.

As it turned out, there was an office on the ground floor. Whereas the former patronesses met and made their decisions elsewhere than the actual structure, Almack's had a secretary of business, and he was diligently at his desk.

Getting directly to his business, Michael requested whether there were any written lists of attendees, particularly to the Wednesday evening balls during the Season.

The balding man looked down his nose, passed his pince-nez, and shook his head.

"I couldn't say, my lord."

Michael rolled his eyes. "That tells me nothing. Are there records you cannot share with me, or are there no records at all?"

"I couldn't say that either, my lord. Here is a list of our former Lady Patronesses. You may call on any of them at your leisure, and theirs, of course. I would suggest Lady Cowper has a good memory."

"I'm not trying to go back to the time of our Regent, good man, only about three, maybe four years."

"Then one of the Willis cousins who now own this establishment may be able to help you."

He handed him two business cards, one with Charles Willis printed on it and one with Frederick Willis."

Michael was beginning to feel like one of London's constabulary, a veritable detective in the making. He also felt a little underhanded. After all, if Mrs. St. Ange wanted him to know about her past, she would tell him. If only he could have a friendly chat with the Countess of Cambrey.

Obviously not! Jenny's sister was as likely to flay him alive as speak civilly to him.

In short order, he turned up at the home of Frederick Willis, and with good fortune, the man was home and agreed to see him.

"Good day, Lord Alder. To what do I owe this visit?"

He ought to make chit-chat about the important position of Almack's in the social fabric of London's society, but he hadn't earned the moniker of *Vile* for nothing. Besides, he'd never once attended a ball in the expansive ballroom stretching a good one hundred feet, if he'd heard correctly. He'd also heard the refreshments were dreadful and not worth the price of admittance. Moreover, there was no alcohol on the premises.

Facing three or four hours without a glass of brandy or gin, pretending to be interested in debutantes any further than idly imagining what each might look like bare, Michael had positively no interest in Almack's.

Except as how one lady might have enjoyed herself there.

To that end, he got to the point.

"Do you have records of the Almack's attendees from, perhaps, four years ago?"

"I believe we do, but those records are private, my lord."

"How private?" Did Willis want money for the information?

"I'm not sure I understand the question. Are there degrees of privacy, my lord?"

Michael sighed. Wasn't the man going to invite him to have a drink? After all, this sussing out information was thirsty work.

"I will have a glass of brandy if you will have one, too," Michael said evenly, as if he'd been asked. It seemed a good a way as any to receive a drink.

Frederick Willis looked utterly nonplussed.

"I won't actually, my lord, but I'll be happy if you'll accept my hospitality." The man didn't bother calling a servant. He opened his sideboard and drew out a glass and a decanter.

In a moment, Michael was seated with brandy in hand and a delightful warm trickle going down the back of his throat. Was there anything better than that feeling?

It was usually followed by strong desire for a woman, which brought his attention back to Mrs. St. Ange.

"There is absolute privacy," he said, returning to Willis's point. "Then there is discretion. I would think this information belongs to the latter category. I am not asking you to print the names in the *Times*, merely to tell me the last name of a debutante. Since people's last names are public and since many people would have been in attendance on any given Wednesday at Almack's—around six hundred, yes?—then I can't imagine this one young woman's attendance or name could even be categorized as confidential, let alone private."

He relaxed, crossed his legs to rest one booted foot upon his other knee, and sipped his brandy.

Mr. Willis hesitated, pondering Michael's words. "I suppose you are correct. However, I can't start poring over records right now. We have the Lady Patronesses' subscription books, with names of those who were issued vouchers, and, of course, the list of the far fewer people who had strangers' tickets."

"If I give you the given name, can you find me a surname?"

Willis frowned. "There are many ladies with the same given name, I assure you. You might as well walk along Knightsbridge Street calling it out."

"This one is unusual, I believe, and I only need you to look through three years of balls, I would guess."

The man sighed. "I will need a few days and—"

Michael waited for him to name a price. With his stock earnings, he would be able to pay.

"And naturally, your sincere promise you won't tell anyone where you got the information, particularly if it leads to trouble."

Relieved Willis wasn't going to fleece him, Michael drained his glass, stood up, and stuck out his hand to shake on it. "I give you my word."

Frankly, he was surprised the man would accept the vow of Lord Vile. Perhaps his reputation was wearing off. After all, it had been over a year since he'd been accused, falsely, of corrupting a debutante and even longer since he'd last been found in a drunken heap on the steps of White's.

"And the given name of the young lady you seek?"

"Ada Kathryn."

CHAPTER TWELVE

Ada entered the Cambrey townhouse on Cavendish Square, hoping she was not about to be hauled over hot coals by her best friend.

Without preamble, except for hugging and settling into the parlor with a cup of tea, Maggie was ready with her questions and her suppositions.

"I think you are up to something big, and Mr. Brunnel has something to do with it. Are you going to spill the pail of milk, or do I have to pry it out of you?"

"That makes no sense," Ada said, stalling. "How could you pry milk from a pail?"

"Never mind that! Tell me. Why were you with Lord Vile?"

An easy question. "He asked me to the opera, and I wanted to go."

Maggie narrowed her lovely eyes. "How did you meet? Where? Why didn't you tell me? You know how he behaved with Jenny."

Should she take each in order?

"We met because I dropped some packages in front of my home. There is nothing to tell. And, yes, I know what you *thought* happened with Jenny."

"If he has said otherwise, then he's lying!" Maggie insisted. "Everyone who knew Jenny also knew Vile had verbally asked for her hand."

Ada sipped her tea. "I know. He doesn't gainsay it, either. However, he said *he* didn't break it off with her. His father did while he was away."

Maggie frowned. "Why wouldn't he have told everyone if such were the case?"

"He said he told Jenny. She was already married to Simon at the time."

"*Hmm*, I will ask my sister. Be that as it may, he hasn't been shunned merely because he broke off with Jenny."

"I know," Ada muttered. *Only too well.*

"Then why would you let yourself be associated with him? In public?" Maggie persisted. "He is infamous!"

Shrugging, Ada leaned her head back on the sofa.

"No one knows me," she said. "I was barely out in society. I don't have friends among the *ton*. You weren't an aristocrat when we were trying to find eligible men, if you recall. Yes, people saw me at the theatre, but who am I to them? A nobody. They know only him."

"They will try to discover who has replaced Lady Pepperton."

Ada lifted her head. "I haven't replaced her." She felt her cheeks growing warm. "I certainly do not have the same relationship with Lord Vile that she did."

"No one will believe such is the case, and rumors will spread like wildfire across London Bridge, as will the curious questions. People will want to discover who you are. What's more, there are certainly enough of us around from our coming out Season who do know you. Someone is sure to say, 'Oh, yes, the beautiful blonde woman is Ada Kathryn Ellis, Baron Ellis's daughter.' All the inquiries about the deceased Mr. St. Ange will begin. And then there's Harry."

Ada's stomach flipped uncomfortably. Could Maggie be right? Would people care who Lord Vile's latest companion was?

"What should I do?"

Maggie shook her head. "John was most displeased the other night. He doesn't want to see you hurt any more than I do. I suggest you don't see Vile again. You haven't told me why you did, or why you needed Mr. Brunnel."

Ada sighed. "I have my reasons for spending time with Vi . . . with Alder, but I am not in any danger of being hurt by him. I promise you that. In fact, nearly impossible as it is to believe, he has been nice."

"Nice?" Maggie's tone was incredulous.

"Yes. He found me an excellent butler, for one. And he is letting his cook teach mine, who I admit is quite abominable in the kitchen."

Maggie's expression clouded over. "How long have you been keeping company with him? It sounds as if you've known him a lot longer than simply one evening attending the theatre."

Ada nodded. "A few weeks."

"What!" Maggie guzzled her tea as if it were a fortifying liqueur, then set the cup down on its saucer with a clank. "And during all that time, he has been simply *nice*? Do you expect me to believe he hasn't tried to have his way with you? The man has a reputation for an insatiable appetite. Not for food, either!"

"I know!" Ada was becoming a little irritated. Maggie might be married, and a mother, and a countess, but she was not Ada's keeper.

She, too, was a mother with a good head on her shoulders, from what her dear father said. And although she was not experienced where men were concerned, she was not a ninny either.

"Do you intend to let him court you?" Maggie persisted.

That was precisely what Ada intended, but she didn't have to tell Maggie, who would disapprove strongly unless she also knew the plan for revenge. And even then, Ada suspected her friend would think it too risky.

"Not really courting," she muttered quickly, trying to put an end to her friend's questions. Better to divert her.

"As for Brunnel, he is simply passing on some trading information in my stead. You know I could never do it myself. Who would take a woman seriously talking about the stock exchange?"

Somewhat mollified, and then instantly distracted by the feel of her baby moving inside her, Maggie agreed to let the topic of Lord Vile go with one last warning.

"You said you will not get hurt, but you are a sweet person, Ada, and he is definitely not. Moreover, he is—how shall I say it?—worldly. And that's the nicest word I can think of for such a jaded, decadent rapscallion! I know you've had a child, but you still seem as innocent as when we were debutantes."

They smiled at each other, recalling their carefree days, and then they began to consider baby names in earnest.

WHEN MICHAEL RECEIVED THE news of an increase to his account value due to sugar trading, he wanted to celebrate. Moreover, he wanted to do it with Mrs. St. Ange. Knowing he should send a message first, after a few drinks at White's, he ignored propriety and drove to Belgrave Square.

Alighting from his carriage, Michael hastened to the door, all his thoughts firmly focused upon seeing her.

"Randall," he greeted the butler, trying to push past, at least into the large foyer.

However, the man was formidable, managing to fill the front door frame and not allowing Michael to bluster his way inside.

"Madam isn't expecting visitors this evening, my lord."

He appreciated learning she wasn't waiting for some other man either, but he didn't want to simply be *another* visitor.

"Randall, I promise I won't step a foot past the hall if you let me in and tell Mrs. St. Ange I'm here."

Still, the man hesitated. He knew his job well, but did he have to do it so superbly when it involved Michael, who'd found him the damnable job?

"Look here, old boy, I am confident she'll be happy to see me if you let her know I'm here." Michael wasn't confident at all, and this could be an occasion of great humiliation.

The butler sighed, then stepped aside.

Immediately, unthinkingly, Michael started for the parlor.

"My lord," Mr. Randall intoned, "you promised. I must insist you wait here while I let her know."

Chastised by the butler!

The problem was the port decanter was in the parlor or in the drawing room. He didn't remember which.

"I'm very thirsty, Randall. Would you be so good as to bring me a glass of port, unless you have any French pleasure?" Maybe, knowing he liked brandy, Mrs. St. Ange had bought some. "If you do, I'll wait right here."

"That's highly irregular, my lord."

At that moment, one of her maids appeared, a duster in one hand. Stopping short at seeing him when she was supposed to be invisible to guests, especially while holding an instrument of cleaning in her hand, she tucked the feathered wand behind her back and looked to Mr. Randall.

"Rachel," he hissed, "you should use the back stairs." The unfortunate girl turned to flee. "Wait," the butler halted her. "Since you're here, fetch Lord Alder a glass of port while I speak with our mistress."

Expecting all to be done as he'd commanded, Mr. Randall went steadily up the main stairs, neither hurrying nor dallying.

Michael admired his aplomb. Undoubtedly, it had bothered the man to no end even to permit anyone entrance after his mistress had retired upstairs.

In very short order, the maid returned with a generous pour of port. He hoped no one taught her in the near future how to dispense for a guest because this was precisely the plentiful amount he enjoyed.

Feeling a little strange loitering in the foyer drinking alone, nevertheless, he would stand by his word and remain where he was. Glancing up the main staircase of the home that was extremely similar in layout to Elizabeth's a mere two doors down, he could well imagine Ada Kathryn's bedroom. At least, he could guess its location above. However, he didn't yet know her tastes enough to imagine her bed. Wood or iron? Lacey hangings or a damask pattern?

In a few minutes, with his drink nearly gone, Michael was now leaning against the front door and had practically designed her bedroom in his mind. What's more, he could easily picture her stretched out upon a counterpane of ruby satin. He was wondering whether it would be worth the wrath of Mr. Randall to breach the sanctity of the upper floor and see for himself what her room looked like when he heard footsteps.

Looking up the staircase, Michael saw her. Despite the ten minutes she'd had to prepare for him, she looked a far cry from her theatre-going attire. Her hair was up, but in a haphazard manner. She wore a plain gown of midnight blue cotton, probably soft and comfortable, and for some reason, her basquine, her skirts, and even her sleeves appeared wet. Despite it all, she looked beautiful.

Taking the stairs at a quick pace rather than an elegant descent, in a moment, Mrs. St. Ange was before him, her eyes flashing.

"Lord Alder. How positively surprising!"

Her tone left no doubt as to her displeasure. Luckily, the port had warmed him against her frosty reception.

"I half expected you to send your butler back downstairs to turn me away, especially after such a delay."

"How canny of you, for I nearly did. However, your appearance here, uninvited as it is, made me think there was some matter of importance you wished to tell me. Why else would you break the rules of a civil society? I came down as soon as I could."

She flapped her arms around, and he assumed she was attempting to dry her sleeves. Yet, her movements also brought attention to the dampness of the front of her gown.

"What on earth were you doing up there?"

She glared at him as if he were a half-wit. "Bathing Harry, of course."

"Bathing Harry," he repeated. He pondered a moment. "But you have a nanny. I've met her. Quite stout and capable-looking. Is she ill? Has she gone on holiday?"

"Nanny Finn is putting my son to bed presently. I bathe Harry because I enjoy it. He is a little mischievous, of course, as all boys are."

She let her gaze linger on his empty glass. "And thus, I am slightly wet from his splashes. I don't mind. We have a jolly time of it."

He shook his head. "Amazing."

Without being asked, she was leading the way into her drawing room. Over her shoulder, she said, "How so? A mother bathing her child. What of it?"

"Oh, I'm certain you're correct. All across England, indeed, let's add Scotland, Wales, and Ireland to the mix. Throughout the British Isles, dear mamas are bathing their sons and daughters. I would wager, however, you are the only one in London with servants at your beck and call, particularly a nanny, who is yet doing the bathing herself."

She stared at him, frowning, perhaps considering if he were correct.

Then she shrugged. "Would you pour me a drink?" And she gestured to the sideboard before plopping herself onto one of the sofas.

"Of course. If you can turn your hands to wrinkly prunes for your boy's amusement, I can stretch my elbows to pour you a drink. Port or port?"

"Port, if you please," she said, going along with his joke. Then she examined her hands, and he laughed.

"I was only teasing." He poured her half what the maid had given him and then he poured himself another of equal measure. "Not a wrinkle in sight."

Sighing, she then stifled a yawn, apparently tired, her defenses down, or he doubted he'd be in her parlor.

"Well, I don't care what you say," she stated. "I love Harry more than anyone on earth, and I take pleasure in watching him play. Why should Nanny Finn have all the enjoyment?"

"I suppose it is not so different from when I used to groom my horse as a youth. We had stable hands, naturally, but I took pleasure in brushing my favorite mount."

Her mouth had fallen open slightly, but as she took her drink from him, she started to smile. He loved seeing her normally serious face looking relaxed and amused.

"No, Lord Alder, my son and your horse are not in quite the same category, but I do believe you understand my meaning. I would have changed out of these damp clothes except you were uninvited, and, frankly, yet another change today before my nightclothes was unwelcome."

He grinned at her, trying to picture what she wore to bed.

As if reading his mind, she blushed, dipping her head to hide her face. In the next instant, having collected herself, she raised her gaze to his, sipped her drink, and straightened her shoulders.

"Why did you come?"

The cool lady of the house had returned.

"It seems a tad impetuous now, but I am growing my family's fortune by way of the stock exchange. I have met with some success, and I wanted to share the news with someone."

Seeing her nod, without any great interest, he decided to speak more frankly.

"No, not with merely anyone. That would be a lie. With you. My first thought was to tell you."

Her eyebrows rose. "I see. And what about your family? Wouldn't they like to know?"

Feeling deflated by her lack of enthusiasm, he shrugged and tossed back his drink.

"I'll tell them soon enough, and yes, my father especially will be pleased."

After a moment's pause, she raised her glass to him. "In that case, let us toast to your success. I am . . . happy for you."

Except she'd had trouble with the word *happy*. *What a strange woman!*

"I suppose while we are telling each other our news," she began, "I should confess I had tea with Lady Cambrey the other day, and the topic of you arose."

"Really?" He would like to have been a fly upon the wall.

"Naturally, she was surprised to see us together at the opera, given your . . . ," she trailed off. "Anyway, I did tell her you hadn't treated her sister badly the way she believed."

Thinking of Jenny, he looked to the decanter a few feet away. How differently he would have led the past few years of his life if they'd married and begun a family. Imagining what might have been used to sting, rather like splitting open an old wound. What's more, that path of thought usually led to a strong drink. And another.

Strange to find, tonight, the missed opportunity of Jenny Blackwood didn't torture him as it used to. Moreover, a third drink so quickly, especially in this lady's presence, might be ill-advised.

"And what did the countess say?" he asked.

"Not much," Mrs. St. Ange said. "She will ask Lady Lindsey to confirm your tale for she couldn't give it credence out of hand, even coming from me."

Michael shrugged. "Not when you received the information from me."

She didn't even look abashed when she said, "Precisely."

After all, he knew his own reputation as a rogue. Why would any of the fairer sex take him at his word?

"Did she say anything else about me? Perhaps give you some advice?"

Mrs. St. Ange glanced away from him. Now, she did look disconcerted. Clearly, their discussion about him had included the usual warning one lady gave to the other over his wicked ways.

And yet, Ada Kathryn had come downstairs in her damp gown to see him and was presently looking at him with her big blue eyes.

Impulsively, he crossed to where she sat and joined her. Without even thinking about it, he took her hand in his, simply wanting to touch her.

"After the earful of poison she must have given you, I'm shocked you didn't send Randall back downstairs to heave me to the pavement."

"Poison, you say, but *not* lies?" Her gaze was fixed on his.

"Most likely the awful truth," he admitted. "I haven't hidden who I am or what I've done. So probably Lady Cambrey knows as well as anyone."

She nodded, looking neither impressed by his wickedness nor fearful. Instead, she simply looked enticing, with her disheveled tendrils falling all about her face and with her water-stained gown.

Michael bent closer. He hadn't planned on kissing her again so soon, but now it seemed inevitable. As soon as he'd directed his carriage toward her door, he'd intended for them to end up closeted together and kissing. He simply hadn't known it until that moment.

Breathing in her scent, he enjoyed her fragrance of fresh soap, no doubt from Harry's bath. Her hair was already unkempt, so he didn't have to worry about messing it up further. Rather, he could give in to his desire to slide his fingers into it and cradle her head while pulling her close.

To his delight, she relaxed against him as soon as his lips touched hers.

WHEN ADA HAD HEARD Lord Alder was in her foyer, she'd known they would end up kissing. It seemed unavoidable whenever they were alone. She'd not only come to expect it but to anticipate it with pleasure.

She would be lying to herself if she said she didn't enjoy kissing him tremendously, even though she knew she was doing it only to ensnare him.

When his hands sunk into her hastily styled hair, shaking out pins and letting loose tendrils, she felt a quiver of excitement. As his tongue swept familiarly between her lips to taste her, she slipped her hands behind his neck, interlacing her fingers and holding on tightly.

Every nerve in her body became alert. She could feel her stockings snug against her toes, and her basquine felt too small across her breasts. Where her thighs pressed together, she trembled against the urge to open them. Already feeling the heat at her apex, she closed her eyes and imagined Michael Alder touching her there, precisely in the spot where she was on fire.

She moaned, and taking it as an invitation, he pressed her down the length of her sofa. Hovering over her, boldly, he palmed both her breasts, his thumb swiping across her nipples, before he continued his exploration. Resting on one arm, he reached down between them to her skirts, beginning to pull them up.

Feeling the cooler air on her ankles and calves, her body clamored for him to continue. So strange, this treacherous longing that gripped her, considering how disagreeable the actual act was.

Why was her body overheating, practically melting beneath his touch?

She felt his hand under her gown, brushing her left knee and then tracing a path up her thigh.

"Yes," she hissed against his mouth.

In another instant, his fingers would touch her womanly mound, thread through her curls, reach her core. She had vowed it would never happen again.

Inside, her rational brain was trying to be heard. Remember, this is Lord Vile. He takes what he wants, without thought for the woman beneath him.

"Ada," he murmured against her neck, and she rejoiced in her given name upon his lips.

She nearly whispered his name back to him, but then his fingers touched her most intimate place, silencing her.

Clenching her fingers into the cloth of his jacket, she sucked gently on his probing tongue. And then, deftly, softly, he stroked her. She bucked under him.

Her body was throbbing with need. Of course, she'd touched herself there before, but lying prone, having a man's strong fingers playing over her as if she were a stringed instrument was entirely different.

Ada couldn't move, couldn't stop him because the sensations were so overwhelmingly delicious. Pure pleasure. Wavering between holding her breath and breathing deeply, she didn't even mind when he tugged at her bodice, exposing her breasts. His mouth left hers to kiss a path down to her décolletage.

Eyes shut tight, head arched back, and with something deep inside her coiled and ready to spring, when Michael latched his lips upon one of her nipples, she cried out again, "Yes!"

To the ministrations of his lips upon her flesh, he added his clever tongue. All the while, his fingers at her core moved rhythmically, a little faster, a little more intensely.

She wriggled against him, not to stop him, only to help herself to a culmination that was just out of reach.

And then as he fastened his teeth gently onto one of her nipples, he slipped a finger inside her slick channel, even as his thumb continued its sweet stroking of the bud between her legs.

"*Oohh,*" she moaned as she felt the tension inside her reach its peak and then, wonder of wonders, release like a fast unraveling spiral.

It was glorious!

It was exhausting!

As if she'd been on a journey far away, she felt herself return to her own drawing room, her own sofa. Opening her eyes, she looked down the length of her body at the same time as Lord Alder lifted his head from her breast to meet her gaze.

Thankfully, he didn't add to her immediate mortification with a smug expression. Perhaps he seemed a little pleased with himself, yet he had the good grace to quickly remove his hand from her private area and begin to sit up. At the same time, he drew her skirts down.

Scrambling out from under him, breathing hard, she sat up. What in blue blazes had happened to her control? And, sweet mother of God, how had she gone so many years without such an exquisite sensation! The explicit book, *Aristotle's Masterpiece*, had been right all along.

Lord Alder remained silent, staring at her as if she were a specimen under a microscope. *What was he thinking?* She couldn't ask him.

She'd known she was in danger of going further than a kiss, but she'd never intended to be transported to such giddy heights. Gracious! She'd let him touch her. He'd even bitten her.

Glancing down, she realized the bodice of her basquine still rode low, exposing one of her breasts and half the other. With a fierce yank, she pulled it up, at the same time, standing and facing away from him.

Her hands were shaking.

What should she say?

Why didn't he speak?

"That was . . ." *Dammit!* She couldn't say it was unwanted or even unpleasant. Undoubtedly, he could tell by her body's reactions how very pleasant and wanted it was.

Yet it had been inappropriate. Entirely so.

"You shouldn't have," she said finally, a lame half-hearted protest.

He chuckled softly, and she whirled to face him.

"Are you laughing at me?" She didn't think she could bear to be the object of his humor. If it was the case, she would banish him forever from her life.

"No," he insisted, standing up and swiftly moving to take her in his arms.

"I was thinking how you may be right. I should not have done that, for now my discomfort nearly matches your pleasure."

Frowning, she felt wooly headed. *What was he saying?*

He took her hand and placed it on the fall of his pants, so she could feel . . . *Oh dear!* His manhood bulged against the fine wool fabric, hard as a stick.

With her fingers against him, he groaned, and her gaze flew to his.

"You must know what it does to a man, to see the woman he desires reach her fulfillment under his touch. And then not to have any release himself."

She should know. That is, if she'd truly been a wife.

It seemed painful. *Would he explode?*

"Will you be all right?" she asked.

This brought another slight laugh from him. "Eventually, yes. Everything will, uh, calm down. Perhaps another drink," he suggested.

She supposed if they were true paramours, after she'd found her release, as he called it, then they would have done what they'd done in the gazebo and—

Yes, she remembered his extreme pleasure that night. He'd groaned and shot his seed inside her. Glancing again at his pants, she realized another Harry was just on the other side of Lord Alder's trousers, waiting to reach her womb.

She could use a drink, too, something to dull the many conflicting thoughts and feelings.

Silently, she poured them both a generous amount, but she couldn't sit. At least not there, on the sofa where he'd only just . . .

"Drink up," Ada told him handing him his glass, before she took a generous swallow, letting the tawny-colored liquid glide down the back of her throat. "Then you must go."

CHAPTER THIRTEEN

M ichael had never been dismissed so quickly. True, he'd jumped up from any number of females' beds as soon as he'd spent inside them, and he'd left while they were still basking in the aftermath. This was different.

How he longed to embed himself deep inside her and finish off the yearning built up over the past weeks. He had a feeling he might have been able to do it, too, right when she was quivering with pleasure at his touch.

Except he knew if he had, he would never be allowed to see her again. She was a skittish wild creature, as it turned out, and he must continue to take it slowly if he ever hoped to have her spread naked beneath him, her soft thighs wrapped around his waist while he pumped into her.

She would enjoy it. He would make certain. For his part, he would be ecstatic.

But, alas, not yet.

Finishing his third glass of port, knowing it was his pent-up, unfulfilled desire keeping him stone sober, he took his leave.

When at home, retired to his own bed, he had to stroke himself to climax, all the while thinking of Ada Kathryn. Her own release had come so quickly and intensely, no doubt due to the length of time since her husband's death. It was obvious she hadn't been with a man in a long time.

All he could think of as he finished himself off was how her skin had tasted and how beautiful she looked, particularly at the moment of her fulfillment.

He hoped to see it happen again. Soon.

The next morning, he received a letter from Frederick Willis.

The list of *Ada Kathryns* who had attended a ball at Almack's was short indeed, namely one, Ada Kathryn Ellis, daughter of Baron and Lady Ellis.

Staring at the paper, he felt a twinge of unease. Why was he searching out her past? What could he hope to accomplish?

Yet, now he held a nugget more of information he hadn't had before. *Ellis*. Nice enough name. It didn't smack of anything unacceptable. Perhaps an old Welsh family.

In any case, he could either surprise her by letting on he knew her name, which he already guessed she wouldn't like as she seemed an extraordinarily private person, or he could dig deeper. *To what end?*

Because she'd come to mean something to him, and the idea she would never let him be her paramour didn't sit well with him. He wanted to dispense with the awkwardness, wrap his arms around her, and make passionate love to her.

He had a suspicion she didn't like him for some reason other than his exceedingly debauched past. Could her life prior to marrying Mr. St. Ange hold the key?

First, unfortunately, he had to go to his family's seat in Kent. His mother was clamoring for a visit, ever since he'd accepted the task of growing the family's coffers. Moreover, he wanted to see his siblings.

Thus, the very next day, he strode into the front hall of Oxonholt, their West Kent house, which he hadn't set foot in for four years. Formerly a royal deer park, now simply a royal pain in the ass. Already too large for their modest family and dwindling accounts, nevertheless about seven years earlier, his father had commissioned the renowned French gothic revivalist architect, Anthony Salvin, to build the mansard dome and the chateau tower.

What on God's green earth did they need a tower for? Weren't they a modern family for pity's sake? Michael still rolled his eyes at the foolishness of it.

In any case, the house looked the same as when he'd last seen it. Exactly the same. Outdated, rather ugly wallpaper, landscape paintings by some unknown artist, scuffed floor in need of a good polish, but with the hundreds of feet of wood in the home all in need of beeswax, that was understandable.

His father had run out of money after the renovations, no doubt, and this was how it would remain until Michael infused the estate with new income.

Even the butler, Mr. Tulsey, was the same. He welcomed the prodigal son home without even raising an eyebrow or creating the slightest crease of interest in his unflappable face.

"Is Lady Alder somewhere about?" Michael asked him.

"Yes, sir. In the parterre gardens. Amongst her roses, my lord. Shall I announce you?"

"No, I can find my own way. But I would like a brandy when you get a minute. No, make it madeira. Don't want to upset Mummy at this hour. A good-sized glass, mind you, Tulsey. I'm very thirsty."

"Very good, my lord."

And Tulsey disappeared with the perfect speed ensuring he didn't look hurried yet imparting confidence in Michael he would have his drink shortly.

Precisely as the butler had said, his mother was in her rose garden, pruning the bushes.

"Mummy," he called out to her.

She shrieked unnecessarily, dropped the snips she held in one hand and the basket from the other. Instead of running toward him, she covered her face with her hands and began to sob.

Michael couldn't help rolling his eyes at her histrionics. True, it had been a number of years, but he hadn't come back from the dead. It was, in truth, merely a quick jaunt from London.

Making his way toward her, he wasn't sure what to do once he was standing before her. In the end, he patted her shoulder, and she lowered her hands. In the next instant, she gave him a smack across the cheek.

Good God! Where was Tulsey with that drink?

She looked aghast, perhaps due to her own erratic actions, then she reached out and hugged him, pressing her face against his chest.

"My son! My son!"

Again, he patted her back, somewhat gingerly. This was the woman who had ruined his happiness, after all. But now he knew the reason—fear of financial ruin—Michael supposed he almost understood his parents duplicitous and underhanded scheming.

Hearing footfalls behind him, he stopped patting, hoping she would take her cue and release him. She didn't, not until he tried to turn, and then she looked past him.

"What is that, Tulsey?"

"His lordship's madeira, my lady."

At last, she took a step back, and Michael could breathe again. He could also turn and take the glass from the tray.

"Do you want anything, Mummy?" he asked, taking a sip. *Ah, refreshing!*

Frowning at him, she shook her head. "That will be all," she told the butler, who disappeared at once.

"Don't you think tea or coffee is more appropriate at this hour?"

He stared down at her. "Don't you think not stealing a man's fiancée out from under him is most appropriate at any hour?"

She sighed and tossed her hands up. "Really! It's been nearly four years, hasn't it?"

Stooping, he picked up her snips, tossed them in the basket, and then handed it to her, all the while careful not to spill his wine.

"I hear you wanted to see me. Was it simply to smack my cheek with motherly affection?"

She paled slightly. "I cannot believe you stayed away so long. Do you know how much I missed you?"

"You had Gabriel and Camille." And he'd had his gin and his wenches. It seemed like a fair trade.

His mother pursed her lips. "One child doesn't replace another one. That's nonsense."

"I see." He supposed she was correct. "Where are they anyway?"

She tilted her head, staring at him. "Did you truly come here simply to see us?"

He stopped scanning the property for signs of his siblings and looked at her.

"Why yes, of course. Why else?"

She pursed her lips for a second, then blurted, "Not to ask for money."

He barked out a laugh.

"No, indeed not. Apparently, in this family, I'm the only one who not only has some but can make more."

"Your father mentioned something about your going to the market. Is that paying off, then?"

"Mummy, I am not 'going *to* the market.' I'm investing *in* it. But never mind. Explaining trading and stocks and the exchange is not my strong suit, either. All you need to know is it's going well. I hope we shall continue to have an earldom for many years to come."

"That's good, dear." She appeared entirely unconcerned. Perhaps his father hadn't explained the dire circumstances in which they were in danger of falling.

"Michael," came a soft voice.

Whirling, he caught sight of Camille hurrying toward him.

"There's my girl," he said, feeling utterly fond of his sister, who looked, at that moment, rather wild. So much so, he handed his mother the wine glass, knowing what was coming.

Brown hair flying loose and her hands fisted in her skirts to hold them up, Camille was tearing across the back terrace toward them. Down the stone steps in a flash, and she was in his arms.

"You're here" she said, at last. "Mummy, Michael is here. In Kent!"

"Yes, dear. He was born and raised here and was bound to return at some point."

Their mother, over the shock of seeing him, went back to cutting her roses.

"Let me look at you." He held Camille away from him. "Are you excited for the upcoming Season? Father told me you are coming out."

"I am!" She jumped up and down, more like a child than a young lady hoping to marry. "I cannot wait for my first London ball."

"*Ah,* yes." He thought of the many he had attended and of what often happened in the larger homes with many dark rooms and in the gardens. "Hopefully, I can be your chaperone, along with Mummy, of course."

Camille merely shrugged. "I cannot wait to start ordering gowns and move into a townhouse. Will we stay with you?"

He flinched. The large Alder townhouse had been sold years ago. Michael had been a small boy at the time. Probably the family had needed money then, too. His father stayed at his club when he went to London, and his mother never went.

Luckily, Michael had been deeded his own small place from his grandfather, who'd kept it for his mistress! He could not imagine his mother and sister living there with him, but it might be the only option.

Unless he continued to make money at the exchange.

"Where's Gabriel?" he asked.

"Where he always is," their mother piped up.

Camille offered a fond smile. "Let's go find him." She grabbed his arm.

"You'll stay for dinner," his mother called after them.

And it was as if he'd never left the bosom of the family.

When alone with his sister, her sweet face resting against his shoulder, Michael relaxed. The first meeting with his mother hadn't been terrible at all, apart from her sobbing and smacking his cheek. He'd seen Camille and Gabriel at least once every six months, since their home was under two hours from London, making sure they understood two things: one, he loved being their brother and would always look out for them, and two, they shouldn't trust their parents.

They had to learn it sometime, and better from him than being blindsided by parental craftiness.

"When you are displayed upon the marriage mart," he told his sister, "you must take precautions."

Camille giggled. "Oh, I know. Never be alone with a man. Never let him kiss me. Never dance more than twice with the same one unless I want us to be linked."

Michael laughed. How many times had he caused a young lady to break all those rules, and then some?

"Yes, that's all good advice," he admitted, hoping his sister had better luck than the ladies he'd compromised, "but I meant precautions against our parents. I now know exactly what they are like, and they will try to pawn you off, even sell you, to the wealthiest eligible man. Whether you like the fellow or not."

Camille's footsteps faltered, and her expression went from delighted to devastated in a heartbeat.

Dammit! He'd spoken too plainly.

"Don't worry, dear sis, I won't let you be married off to someone you don't like."

"Promise?"

"As long as you don't put yourself in a situation where marriage is the only alternative."

She laughed. "You never let that stop you!"

He halted in his tracks, right as they reached the stables courtyard. *What had she heard?*

"What do you mean?" he asked.

Offering him a knowing grin, Camille said, "I'm sorry to be the one to tell you this, dear brother, but the doings of Lord Vile have even reached us here in the country."

He shook his head. "How did you know it was I with that godawful moniker the *ton* slapped upon me?"

"Easy. Every time Mummy came across anything in the papers about you, she circled it for Father to see. It was always about 'Lord A, also known as Lord Vile, until it simply became Lord V.' It doesn't take an Oxford intellectual to know who's who."

They entered the stables, which to Michael, had always been a place of refuge. He'd told Ada about grooming a horse. He hadn't told her how he'd broken a series of them in his youth, creating damn fine riding mounts from practically wild beasts.

Following him around when he was old enough was always his younger brother, Gabriel. Whereas Gabe also had an excellent hand with equines, canines were his passion. Thus, it was no surprise when they entered the ancient building, nodding to the first stable hand they saw, to find Gabe surrounded by a pack of hounds. Not merely surrounded, either. He was seated on the floor, legs crossed, and a quick headcount told Michael there were eight dogs in continuous movement around him.

"You're like their sun," Michael called out over the din of the barking animals.

Gabriel caught sight of him and shot him a smile that looked so like Camille's. Strangely, also reminding him of little Harry's.

"Hark," he called out, and there was blissful silence except for the whinnying of a horse in one of the stalls.

"That's a good bit of magic," Michael said now that he could be heard.

Getting to his feet, his brother with the darkest brown hair in the family said, "Here's another bit. Sit."

Every last canine bottom hit the cobbled floor.

"What do you think?" Gabe asked, stepping through the devoted dogs to reach his brother.

"I think that's bloody amazing," Michael admitted.

Gabe grinned. "I may make my living train hunting dogs since I don't have the burden of lounging around as the heir apparent."

"Why you!" Then, as always happened, they had to scuffle around and mess up each other's hair before he let his brother declare it a mutual victory, even though Michael could wipe the floor with him. What's more, Gabriel knew it.

"Anyway, I think it's a fine idea," Michael said. "People will always need well-trained dogs." Then he thought of Ada and Harry.

"What about a family pet? Any of these mutts good for that purpose? Sitting by the fire, letting a lady rest her feet upon him, or playing tug-of-war with a young boy and going for a stroll on a leash through the park?"

As he stopped talking, he realized his brother and sister were staring at him.

"Now what have I said?"

Camille spoke first. "You sound as if you're a married man with a family. That's all."

Michael felt his face get hot. *He had, hadn't he?*

"Are you?" she pressed. "Are you marrying that woman?"

"Which woman?" *Did his entire family already know he was trying to woo and bed Mrs. St. Ange?*

"'Lady P' is how she's referred to in the papers. Mummy says it's Lady Pepperton."

He pressed his lips together. He wouldn't discuss his personal life with his siblings and especially not his parents.

"Well?" Camille prompted, all the while with Gabriel looking on interestedly.

"No. And that's all I will say."

His siblings glanced at one another.

"Anyway," Gabe said, "they're not mutts. They're foxhounds, every one. They'd be fine as pets, very sociable, too, except they can be loud. Listen to this." He turned to the pack. "Sing!"

They began to bay. The hair on the back of Michael's neck stood up.

"If it's a town pet," Gabe continued as if he wasn't being accompanied by the loud canine sounds directly behind him, "you might not want him singing next door to your neighbor."

"Make them stop," Camille protested.

"Hark," he said just as before, and they fell silent, all of them with their eyes fixed on the youngest Alder, awaiting his next command.

"Also," Gabe continued, "if they lose their training, they may start following a scent and wander for miles."

"The baying alone is enough to put me off," Michael said. Maybe Ada and her son simply needed a rabbit or a parrot.

"I trained a pack of spaniels a couple months back." Gabe was clearly warming to the topic. "For flushing out pheasants, you know. If you confess this dog is really for a nice lady and her son, I'll show you something you'll like."

"Very well," Michael agreed, enjoying the light in his brother's eyes. "Yes, I have a lady friend, and she has a two-year-old boy. Now, show me what you've got."

"Come on." Gabe turned and led them out the other side of the stables into the paddock. "Where are they?"

With his two siblings, Michael stood and surveyed the grassy field. In the far corner, three dogs were running around.

"They probably have a rabbit at their mercy," Gabe muttered. "Come," he called out and, instantly, the three dogs came at a run.

"Why do they stay in the paddock?" Michael asked his brother, since the fencing was meant to contain the horses only.

"Because I tell them to," Gabe said, pride in his voice. The three newcomers jumping excitedly around them.

"The red setter there is Rufus, the retriever is Myrtle, and this fellow," he bent to pick up the smallest of the three, a black and white spaniel, "is Dash."

"Dash?" Michael repeated.

"He's lovely," Camille said, leaning toward her brother to pet its head. "Mummy's cats probably wouldn't like him in the house, though."

"Sold all the rest of the litter. He was the runt, but he's grown up fine," Gabe said. "He'd make a great city pet. Happy simply to be with people or even sit on your lady friend's lap like a cat."

"Really?" Michael couldn't imagine the handsome animal settling onto a lap. He seemed so full of vim and vigor. But he could well imagine him on the floor playing with Harry. "You'd part with Dash?"

"For a small sum," Gabe shot back.

Michael threw back his head and laughed. His brother was going to make a fine businessman.

"Also, I'd like to meet your lady and her son someday."

"Oh, yes," Camille agreed. "I would, too."

Thinking how unlikely that was, with Ada being so prickly, he readily agreed.

"Deal," he said.

After an excruciating meal with his parents, questioning him on what he was doing with his life, made bearable only because of his siblings' presence, Michael decided to spend the night in his old room. Gabe could tell him all he needed to know about caring for Dash. After, Michael could share a bottle of brandy with his father while filling him in on the good news from the stock exchange, a topic too vulgar for the dinner table with females present.

After dinner, Dash was brought into the house to get acclimated to the civilized world, although Michael thought the spaniel was already better behaved than many people he knew.

"He must stay in your room," Lady Alder said. "I don't want my pussycats frightened."

By the time he went to bed, with Dash on the rug by the fireplace, Michael was exhausted but excited. He felt like old Father Christmas, bringing a present. Moreover, he couldn't wait to see the look on Ada's face

TO THAT END, MICHAEL went straight from Oxonholt to Belgrave Square, arriving by late afternoon.

Mr. Randall opened the door and immediately dropped his gaze to the dog sitting at Michael's feet.

"Good day, Randall," Michael intoned, excited by seeing Ada again. "Is she home?"

"If you're referring to her ladyship, my lord, yes. However, once again, she isn't seeing visitors, not uninvited ones."

"Bathing the boy?" Michael asked.

Randall frowned. "No, my lord. I believe she is reading in the library."

"Please tell her I'm here, and I come bearing gifts." After all, she was probably engaged in one of those silly romance novels with which all the ladies were obsessed. Even more so if it were gothic *and* romantic. Nothing like a dark and freezing castle, a lady in distress acting ridiculously, and a couple of ghosts clanking around to evoke notions of romantic love. At least, that's what he heard.

"Yes, my lord," and Randall closed the door before Michael could bargain with him to let him wait in the foyer.

"Well, Dash, we wait. I don't suppose we'll see a glass of brandy or port out here, will we?"

No matter. Retrieving his flask from his pocket, he had a few sips, and was just putting it away when the door flew open.

It was Mrs. St. Ange, herself.

"Are you insane?" were her first words, as she stared down at the dog. "Mr. Randall told me what you'd brought, but I couldn't credit it until I'd seen it with my own eyes."

"Yes, a dog for you and Harry." He thought Dash was making a good first impression.

Her mouth formed an "O" and then tears sprang to her eyes.

Michael hoped those were tears of happiness, but he started to feel doubtful as she put a hand to her mouth and shook her head.

"No, no, no."

"I'm sorry, Ada. I didn't mean to upset you." Yet for the life of him, he couldn't imagine how he had.

Her eyes locked with his, and then she collected herself, narrowing her gaze.

"I never gave you leave to call me by my given name. Nor could I imagine you'd show up without warning and bring us a dog. A sweet-looking, soft dog! How dare you!"

The next thing Michael knew, he was staring at the firmly slammed, darkly painted front door. If he'd been a step closer, his nose would have paid the price. Little Dash even jumped back in alarm.

Exchanging a glance with the spaniel, Michael shrugged.

"I'm afraid, dear chap, I have no idea what that was about. I guess, for the time being, you're coming home with me."

CHAPTER FOURTEEN

Ada ran back to the security of her library, trying not to think of the adorable dog on the other end of Lord Vile's leash.

""*He* should be the one collared and restrained," she muttered, thinking of the arrogant man.

What an oaf! How dare he assume she'd want a dog? Moreover, how dare he do something so thoughtful for her and Harry. She could not possibly have any idea how to handle it.

He was Lord Vile, practically a drunkard and definitely a despoiler of women, including herself. After his last visit, she'd half expected him to send a note apologizing for being so forward. Instead, he brought her a dog.

She'd told Maggie he was being nice, but this! This was beyond the pale.

Her fingers had itched to reach down and touch the dog's soft-looking fur. Now she wanted to tear her own hair out. Or Michael Alder's.

What's more, he'd had his charming smile upon his face, hiding the villain behind.

With a vicious oath, she cleared the table of all the business newspapers, sending them swirling to the floor with a single incensed sweep of her hand.

Each encounter with him made it harder to hold onto the darkest part of her anger, the simmering rage that gave her strength. Without it, she would find everything she was doing to ruin the man's life a difficult burden.

Bending down, she began to pick up the papers. It wasn't like her to have a fit of temper. She and Lord Alder had had a brief conversation about dogs, hadn't they? Was that why he'd brought her one? Harry would adore it. Moreover, so would she? If only she could tolerate the gift bearer.

Accepting the dog would make her beholden to him, or at least, it would soften her hatred.

Blast the man!

"Mama!" It was Harry. He came bounding into the room ahead of Nanny Finn. "Doggy!" he yelled in delight before crashing into her skirts.

Crouching down, she hugged him while sending a searching look to the nanny.

Nanny Finn shrugged. "We were upstairs, and he saw his lordship approach with the dog. I'm sorry."

"It's not your fault," Ada assured her, but Harry was looking at her with his big amber eyes, the same way his father had just looked at her before she'd slammed the door on him. No doubt Michael Alder was perplexed by her seemingly irrational and inexplicable actions.

"Mama! Where is doggy?"

Oh dear!

The boy had no siblings, no father, and now she'd deprived him of a cuddly spaniel. Of course, they could go buy a dog if she had any idea where one procured a trained one. It wasn't as if there was a corner shop filled with pets.

Smiling at the odd notion, she straightened. Given a few minutes to think about it, she was beginning to believe she would accept the gift. Maybe it would even help with her plan to make Lord Vile fall hopelessly in love with her. Although how, she had no idea.

"Nanny Finn, I believe our household needs a dog. Shall we go to Lord Alder's and claim that one?"

The nanny looked at her strangely. "I'm sure Harry will enjoy growing up with a dog, madam, but I must tell you, I'm not picking up after it. My responsibilities stop with the child."

"Yes, Nanny Finn, I understand." If need be, Ada could make Rachel or even Mr. Randall clean up after the dog until Harry became old enough in a few years. Most likely, her butler wouldn't mind.

"All right, we'll do it. Let's all get changed for an outing."

Ushering them before her from the room, she rang for Mr. Randall.

"My driver isn't coming today, is he?"

"No, madam."

"Can you hail us a Hansom cab? We're off to Brook Street."

Then she considered the tight fit of her, Nanny Finn, Harry, and then a dog.

"On second thought, see if you can get us a hackney."

"Yes, madam."

By the time Harry was made presentable and she'd changed into a suitable day dress, the hired carriage was waiting. She'd also had the unpleasant task of sending Lucy two doors down to ask Lady Pepperton for the exact number of Lord Alder's residence.

Showing up uninvited was bad enough. Feeling queasy at the vulgarity of her task, Ada would have to apologize for her rash behavior—apologizing to *him!*—which was even worse. And what if he'd already given the dog to someone else?

It was the worry the spaniel would no longer be available that spurred her on to complete this distasteful mission. Harry was bouncing excitedly at her side. If Alder hesitated due to her slamming the door in his face, she was confident he could not disappoint Harry.

In fifteen minutes, the driver, with instructions to wait, let them off at Alder's townhouse in the heart of Mayfair.

Ada stood on the step, stomach churning with apprehension, holding Harry's hand like a talisman, and Nanny Finn firmly at her back. She pressed the bell, then used the knocker for good measure.

In a minute, the door swung open and a tall, thin man looked down at her.

"Yes, madam?"

"We are here to see Lord V—," she caught herself just in time, "Lord Alder. He is not expecting us exactly, but he has our dog."

That sounded a good a reason as any to give the servant so she didn't seem like an ill-mannered intruder.

"I see, madam. Won't you come in. I'll tell his lordship you're here. For your dog," he added, opening the door wide.

Stepping into his home, she wondered how many women had crossed the same polished wooden front hall. Doubtfully any of them had a son and his nanny in tow. Ada couldn't help noticing the stairs to the upper floor. To Vile's bedroom, which, if even a few of the paper's accounts were true, saw a lot of comings and goings.

After what had occurred in her parlor, however, she realized a bed was incidental.

The butler showed them into the front room, a parlor that was not lavish yet neither sporting shabby furnishings that might make one cringe. All three of them remained standing in the center on the rug, although Harry was tugging on her hand.

One of the double doors reopened, and the first thing they saw was a streak of black and white fur rushing in, followed by Lord Alder. Harry broke free of her grasp and was on the floor with the spaniel before Alder even had a chance to greet them.

After glancing at the boy and dog already becoming playmates, he took Ada's hand and bowed over it, just as if she hadn't behaved abominably a short while earlier. Just as if he hadn't had his hand up her skirts before that. Then he nodded to Nanny Finn.

"May I get you ladies anything?"

She wanted to scream. He was not only being a gracious host, he was including her nanny.

Finally, Ada found her voice. "I . . . I . . ."

Unfortunately, she couldn't find her words. Flustered and loath to give him any satisfaction or gratitude, she snapped her mouth closed.

"Tea?" he offered, and by the slanted smile, he knew she was discomfited.

"Yes," she ground out. "That would be lovely."

Then she recalled the nature of their visit and her desire to keep it short. *Don't be intimidated by him,* she schooled herself. *Ignore appearances.* He has behaved terribly in the past. Standing a little straighter, she stopped being a mincing coward.

"Actually, we came only for the spaniel. Harry saw it out of the window and assumed it was for him."

"It is," Lord Alder confirmed.

"We cannot stay for tea. We came in a hackney. It's waiting, so we must go at once."

Ada felt better already. They could attach the same leash she'd seen Alder holding and be gone in under five minutes.

"Nonsense, I'll have Lawrence send it away," he said smoothly. "We're civilized people, aren't we, Nanny Finn? We must have tea."

Then nanny, bemused at being addressed, merely nodded.

Ada clenched her hands at the implied notion she wasn't being civil.

"That won't be necessary," she said.

"I insist." With that, Alder stuck his head out the door of the parlor and had words with his butler. When he returned, Ada was seething.

"I must protest, for we shall now have to go to the trouble of procuring another carriage."

"Nonsense," he said again, making her want to bop him on the head with her reticule. "Tea along with biscuits, of course, are in order while I tell you about Dash."

"Dash?" Ada had lost control of the situation, and it galled her.

"The dog." Lord Alder turned to Harry whose cheeks were now being washed by the spaniel's tongue. "Your dog's name is Dash, unless you wish it to be otherwise."

"Dash!" Harry repeated, proving he was listening.

An easily spoken name, Ada thought, even for a boy not yet three.

"Very well, my lord. We shall stay for tea."

Without being invited, she chose a seat on the dark blue sofa and nodded to Nanny Finn to join her. As soon as her bottom touched the damask fabric, however, she recollected what had happened on her own sofa, and nearly jumped up. She could only imagine the many scenes of sensual relations that had been played out right where she sat. *Vile!*

Shooting a glance at their host, she found him staring at her and wondered if his thoughts had gone where hers had. Next thing she knew, her cheeks were heating up.

Drat the man!

Taking a quick look around the room, she deemed it unlikely a woman had ever lived there. The merely functional furnishings included two wingback chairs, various tables dotted about, a mirror, a landscape painting, and a sideboard nearly groaning with the weight of bottles and decanters. *Good God!*

She stared at it, not having ever seen so much alcohol displayed.

When she looked back at Alder, she realized he had followed her gaze and a slight red flush appeared on his cheeks. *Was he blushing now?*

Clearing his throat, he sat in one of the chairs.

"I'm glad you came. I was about to write a note expressing my hope you would see fit to accept Dash and, naturally, I was also going to apologize for being too forward."

Ada's breath caught and her gaze darted to the nanny then back to him, her cheeks now scalding hot as she pressed her lips together. *Was he mad bringing up what had occurred in her drawing room?*

His eyebrows drew together in puzzlement at her reaction, and then, as if realizing what she might think, he added, "For bringing the dog to your home, I mean."

Of course! She was being too sensitive. He'd probably already forgotten the incident, which, to her, loomed huge in the experiences of her life. For him, it was undoubtedly a minor trifle.

Precisely that, in fact! He had trifled with her!

"Mama," Harry shrieked with delight, snatching her attention. He was on his back with the dog half-planted on his stomach. "Doggy!" he squealed.

Her heart melted. Truly, what a wonderful gift! Deciding to put aside her rancor for the moment, she began her questions as the tea tray was brought in.

"Where did you procure him?"

Alder picked up a biscuit and crossed his legs before answering. "My brother has a way with dogs. He trains them."

"Yes, I believe you mentioned him before."

"I visited my family, and Gabriel had recently trained a pack of spaniels, for flushing the birds from the bushes. He'd kept this one and said he would make a good pet. I thought of Harry."

That made her flinch, and her heart started beating faster. She didn't want Lord Vile thinking of Harry.

"And your brother had already named him Dash?"

"Yes, I believe the queen has a similar dog with the same name, and my brother has an odd sense of humor."

"It's a fine name," she murmured. "Did he recommend anything in particular for feeding him?"

"Meat and vegetables," he said, "at least twice a day, and not too much bread or biscuits."

She tried to remember what the cook fed her dog as a child, but she couldn't recall ever noticing.

"Until Mary gets better at cooking, I suppose Dash will have plenty of scrapings off our plates." She hadn't meant to make a joke, but Lord Alder laughed.

"I hope Mary is improving or the dog will grow fat."

She wanted to laugh, too, but tamped it down.

"Luckily, you've got the green on your square and Hyde Park close by," he pointed out.

"When I take Harry out to the park for a breath of air, I don't mind if we take the dog," said Nanny Finn, who even then had stretched out her hand to let the dog sniff it.

"Thank you," Ada told her, sipping the tea, which was perfectly brewed. It tasted delicious except she didn't want to enjoy his hospitality, not even his wretched tea.

"He's got a rather plain collar," Lord Alder pointed out. "Not like the jewel-encrusted ones I've seen fashionable ladies with in the park."

Nanny Finn chuckled.

"I meant their dogs, of course, not the ladies. He's also got a leash, a plain but sturdy one. And he is to have water available at all times, according to my brother."

The brothers had discussed the dog and what Alder must impart to her on its care. The brothers might have even spoke about her and Harry!

Ada set her cup and saucer down and stood up. She knew she was abrupt, but she couldn't take another moment of this domesticity in his presence. He was even charming her nanny.

Of course, Lord Alder jumped up, too. When he stood, the room seemed to shrink, and she was glad of a small table between them.

"Perhaps you could give us the dog's trappings," she suggested, "and we'll leave you in peace." Then she remembered the hackney. "Also, if you could have your butler hail us another carriage."

He shook his head. "My driver will return you to your home. I'll get Dash's things. First, shall I tell you what commands he knows?"

Without awaiting her answer, he went to the boy and dog.

"Come," he said, and Dash jumped off of Harry and rushed over to Alder.

"Sit." And the spaniel sat.

Harry clapped. "Come," he yelled, and the dog returned to him.

"I'm impressed with your brother," Ada admitted.

"If he starts to bark loudly, then I suggest you try, 'hark.' At least, that worked on the foxhounds. It made them stop and listen."

"If he barks too loudly," said Nanny Finn, "he'll feel the end of my foot."

Ada hid her smile at her no-nonsense nanny.

"We shall try 'hark' first, of course," Ada said. "About his leash?"

To her relief, they were soon at the front door, Dash in collar and leash, which Ada held the end of, while Harry held his nanny's hand.

"Your carriage awaits, Mrs. St. Ange. Incidentally, my siblings would like to meet you."

She felt as if the floor tilted under her, and she nearly dropped the dog's leash.

"Whyever for?" came out of her mouth before she could think. Her next thought was even less kind. *Not in a hundred years!*

Alder smiled, and it looked so genuine, if she didn't know him for a cad and a libertine, rather than a kind, dog-gifting man, she might have fallen for him.

"Gabriel wants to meet the person who has his dog, of course, and Camille, she's simply curious about my . . . friends."

"I see," Ada said. She didn't want to tell him then how unlikely it was such a meeting would ever occur. After all, they were supposed to be forming an attachment. "Please do give your brother my thanks for parting with Dash. Good day."

With that, she turned from his handsome face, his attractive smile, and his knowing eyes.

"Come along, let's go home."

WATCHING THEM LEAVE, MICHAEL felt a prick of something—perhaps envy—at her word, *home*. Tonight, he pictured her tucking Harry into bed before sitting in her library or drawing room, maybe a glass of port in her hand. She would pick up a book or her needlepoint, if that was her fancy. The fire would be crackling beside her, and Dash would sit on her glorious lap, where he, too, would like to lay his head.

He intended to go to White's and play cards with strangers, some who barely tolerated him, and drink. The brandy made it bearable. In fact, enjoyable. It was always a satisfactory evening, particularly if he ran into Hemsby. Usually, in months past, he would then head over to Elizabeth's afterward, or previously to Lilith's.

Yet the notion of *home* intrigued him. He had one, he reminded himself, as he took the stairs two at a time to change for the evening ahead.

Had Mr. St. Ange appreciated what he had? Had he sat with Ada Kathryn of an evening and then taken her upstairs to the bedroom to make passionate love? Did she even now spend her evenings thinking of her dead husband, perhaps desperately missing him, still loving him?

It all seemed so grown up, compared to his existence. When he believed he might have to keep Dash, he'd been a tad nervous. Of course, he would have made his butler care for the dog, but knowing there was a creature whose responsibility ultimately fell upon his shoulders had given him pause. *Imagine having a child!*

Recalling Ada's words at Elizabeth's party. "You haven't needed to grow up," she'd said, and she might have been correct. When his father had admonished him as a 'truculent child,' he'd dismissed him, too. However, Michael did do as he pleased, rather like a willful child.

Thus, why did he keep finding himself wanting to assist her in any way he could? Maybe he *was* maturing.

"Fenley," he called to his valet. "Bring me some brandy. I'm becoming far too introspective."

Soon, he would begin to reap the rewards of his generosity. After all, how could she turn him away after he'd made her son so happy? When he next kissed her and reminded her of the bliss she'd found at his touch, certainly she'd be willing to reciprocate.

Tonight, though, he would ask at the club if anyone knew of the Ellis family.

CHAPTER FIFTEEN

How had they ever lived without Dash? He kept Harry constantly amused and laughing. In fact, he kept them both happy with his dark, button eyes glistening at them, his playful nature, and his lovely tail, thankfully not docked, swishing back and forth displaying his own joy. Moreover, she loved the white streak between the black markings on his head, making it look as if Dash sported a very neat parting of his fur.

Every time she encountered this new furry member of their family, her heart warmed. Even Nanny Finn had obviously taken to the dog, never once complaining about him being under foot.

To think Lord Vile had accomplished this. *The devil take him.*

It had been difficult, indeed, to respond to his next missive inviting her to a concert. A little distance was needed after what had happened on her sofa.

He was too skilled at the art of seduction, and she was too inexperienced to resist. Perhaps if she'd had a few years of such sensual encounters, she would be able to easily rebuff him. Instead, her body melted under his touch and clamored for more.

Even while writing back to him from the safety of her own library, she imagined a repeat performance. Lord Alder could press her down upon her writing desk, lift her skirts, and—

A knock at the door interrupted her erotic reverie.

"Come in."

Mr. Randall entered with a letter on a silver tray. Another unwanted letter, she was certain of it.

"How does Mrs. Randall like your quarters?" she asked, hoping it wasn't too personal a question.

He appeared momentarily nonplussed. Then he bowed slightly. "Very well, madam. Thank you."

"She's working at a shop, isn't she?"

"Yes, madam. At the Burlington Arcade at a milliner's shop."

What more could she say to stall receiving the letter she knew was from Lord Vile? Nothing. Holding out her hand, she accepted the missive from his gloved hand.

"Thank you."

He left her alone to open it.

Dear Mrs. St. Ange,
I hope you are well and Dash is behaving himself.

Ha! She knew he would mention the dog at once. He thought her beholden to him and wanted the debt repaid.

It seems a long while since you came to my house. I hope soon we can meet again. I take it you are not interested in ballet at the Royal Lyceum. Perhaps your heart has a secret wish to go someplace to which I may escort you. You need only let me know.

Ever your servant,
M. Alder

Ever her servant! What rubbish. He was the most self-serving man she'd ever met. Except for finding Mr. Randall, giving Mary cooking lessons from his own cook, and, of course, Dash.

Lord Michael Alder was certainly an enigma.

Sighing, she picked up her pen. At least she didn't have to respond to his previous invitation to a concert. She could combine her dismissals of both his invitations in one fell swoop.

Then she hesitated. Her plan had to move forward, and most advantageously *before* her parents came to town in a month or so.

She and Alder would have to get together again, for she wanted a declaration of love. Nothing else would do. Nothing else would allow her to toss his heart onto the ground and stomp it beneath her slipper, or rather, beneath her favorite sturdy walking boots.

Where could they go? Some very public place which allowed for little physical contact. Perhaps the upcoming Derby, heralding the true beginning of the social Season, or the Ascot. But what could they do in the next week? Perhaps a lecture at the Royal Society of which her father was a member. She could easily get tickets, and Lord Vile wouldn't dare act up surrounded by the intellectuals of London, would he?

On the other hand, better they do something which Harry and Nanny Finn could also attend. Their presence insured Lord Vile's good behavior.

Smiling to herself, she wrote him a brief note inviting him to the zoo. After all, he was a beast and ought to fit right in with the lions and the lone hippopotamus on display.

Thus, two days later, he picked them up in his carriage.

His first words were, "How is Dash?" as if to remind her of his thoughtfulness. Again.

Ada let Harry answer him and continue to chatter on, barely making either sense or sentences, all the way to the zoo, which as it was in Regent's Park, took nearly three-quarters-of-an-hour through traffic.

Since it was not a Monday, entrance cost a shilling each for the three adults and six-pence for Harry. Naturally, she let Lord Alder pay. Also, naturally, she walked beside him while Nanny Finn walked with Harry. Congratulating herself for coming up with such a benign outing, suddenly, she felt Alder take her arm and tuck it under his.

"This was a grand idea," he told her. "Also, very wise of you not to bring the dog. I'd hate to see him slip his leash and end up being eaten by a bear."

"Indeed," she muttered, wondering if she could wrench her hand free while still appearing friendly. She guessed not. Thus, she settled into the disconcerting situation of his closeness, his warmth, his easy chatter, his pleasant scent of sandalwood, and his undaunted effort to amuse her.

While unnecessarily keeping an eye on Harry, who was under the watchful gaze of Nanny Finn, Ada found herself enjoying the day, particularly the hummingbird exhibition. Of all the large animals on display, it was this tiny, gorgeous, jewel-toned creature which caught her admiration. What a pity they were all stuffed and mounted. And why weren't there any in England?

"Why do you suppose we don't have these wonderful creatures in all of Britain?"

Alder appeared to really consider her question. Finally, he shrugged.

"I suppose the beauty of an English lady is so exquisite, they cannot compete and thus do not try."

She gaped. "That is the most ridiculous statement I've ever heard."

"Really? Why, I'm positive I can come up with something far worse. Let me think a minute. Elephants were clearly put on earth to give us something to ride in India, and every British home should have a well-behaved monkey."

"No, stop. I'm sure you can be far more ridiculous, but why don't we have hummingbirds?"

He looked back at the exhibit, focusing on a spectacular blue and green specimen.

"I would wager the answer has to do with their wings, Mrs. St. Ange, and the size of their bodies. We are an island surrounded by water. They aren't natives to our land and cannot get here since they can't store up enough food in their small bodies for the journey. Moreover, they can't have bigger bodies because their wings are so small."

Staring at him, she felt like a child whose parent had just pointed out the obvious. In that instant, she saw him in a new light, as a contemplative man. She swallowed an unexpected lump in her throat, thinking how nice it would have been for Harry to have a father who brought him a dog and could explain bird populations.

Harry did have such a father.

She shook her head to clear that unwelcome notion.

"Are you all right?"

"Yes, fine." She licked her suddenly dry lips. "I don't know why I didn't think of that myself. Obviously, they're not like geese."

"No," he agreed, staring at her mouth. "Not like geese."

His gaze remained trained on her lips until it flickered up to her eyes.

In that instant, she knew if they'd been alone, he would have kissed her. Luckily, there were hundreds of people at the zoo, as well as Nanny Finn and Harry a mere few feet away.

"Shall we?" he said, making her startle.

"Shall we what?" Ada couldn't look away from his fine eyes.

"Move along to the next exhibit."

What an addlepated ninny! "Yes, of course."

Alder took her arm again, which she minded less and less.

"Let's look at something more interesting to Harry, shall we? Perhaps the rhinoceros. I bet he'll enjoy that."

WHAT WAS WRONG WITH him? When Ada had first sent him a message about the zoo and taking Harry, Michael had been disappointed. His goal was always to get her alone. Smelly animals and hordes of families would hardly spark desire.

And yet, he found himself thoroughly enjoying the experience. Harry was a whirlwind of excitement. Every animal sparked his *oohs* and *aahs*, even a pigeon crossing his path. That gave Michael a good laugh.

Moreover, spending time with Ada Kathryn in a relaxed way only made him like her more. Of course, he still sought the ultimate prize of an invitation to her bed. As it turned out, though, he'd been wrong about the zoo. Desire could certainly be sparked in the ordinary moments.

He could see in her eyes only a moment ago, if they'd been alone, she would have welcomed a kiss. *How wonderful!* What's more, even in a perfectly ordinary day dress, without a hint of décolletage, she was positively the most desirable woman he could imagine. The bonnet perched on her head at a jaunty angle might look silly or frumpy on anyone else. On her, it was endearing.

What was happening to his practiced rakish ways?

With that, he realized a sip of brandy was in order, and he used his free hand to slip his flask from his pocket. His choice was to use his teeth to open it or break free of Mrs. St. Ange's lovely arm. In the end, he did neither, managing to hold the silver flagon and unscrew the cap with the same hand. Luckily, he'd had the forethought to purchase one with a secure chain, so the cap didn't go flying off into some animal compound.

Had that been the case, he would have been forced to drink the entire contents at once.

Tilting it back, he let the liquid hit his tongue and then trickle down the back of his throat. There was hardly any more delightful flavor than good French brandy. Next time he saw Brunnel, he would ask about investing in its import.

Feeling her stiffen at his side, he realized she was watching him.

As they had clearly shared a moment with the dead hummingbirds, he felt it appropriate to offer her his flask.

He certainly didn't expect her to blanche as if he'd held out a bucket of flaming dung.

"It's brandy," he explained, as she pulled free of him. "Not gin."

The way her gaze went from the flagon to his face seemed oddly familiar, as if he'd seen her eyes do the very same before. A shiver of apprehension coursed through him.

How strange. For he was certain he hadn't offered her a sip during any of their other meetings.

Without saying anything, she turned away, taking the necessary steps to catch up with her son.

"Are you happy, darling?" he heard her ask Harry.

The boy nodded enthusiastically and reached for her hand. They spent another hour roaming the zoo, most of it with him trailing along behind the happy threesome. *What had he done wrong?*

Surely the woman wasn't a member of the temperance society. He'd seen her drink wine and champagne, and even Elizabeth's sloe gin. Perhaps it was drinking in a public place which had put her off.

Shrugging, he decided to set his concerns aside. What he'd found with this mercurial creature was, at any moment, she might pull away from him, even seem angry or as if she couldn't possibly stand to be near him. Then, in the next, she would let him kiss her soundly.

And since kissing her was about the finest thing he'd ever experienced, he would settle for this uneasy relationship, which kept him on edge. At least until he could slake his hunger for her.

Her shriek brought him out of his fantasy. Since she was standing next to Nanny Finn, he assumed it was to do with Harry, and his heart began to pound. Nanny Finn was bent over double. Had she been injured? Then he realized she was tying her bootlace. *Where was Harry?*

Ada was looking around wildly, but as Michael hurried to her side, Nanny Finn straightened up. Lo and behold, there was the boy, safe and sound, hidden by her round body and the shape of her skirts.

"He's fine," he told Ada because she still seemed distraught. "Harry is safe."

"My reticule!" she exclaimed. "A man just snatched it and ran off." She held up the strings on her wrist. "A cut-purse at the zoo. I should have been more careful."

How had he missed such an occurrence?

"What did he look like?"

"Why?" she asked.

"I'll go after him."

She rolled her eyes. "He could be miles by now."

"He will be if you don't hurry and tell me what he looked like."

She crossed her arms. "He's the one running for the zoo's exit with a lady's purse in his hands."

Michael gave her a wry smile. "How about the color of his clothing? I'll take a quick look near the ticket booth."

Seeing he was serious, she lowered her arms. "He had on a brown cap and wore . . . oh, I think a dark blue coat. It happened so fast. It's really not necessary."

"Stay here so I can find you."

With that, Michael took off toward the entrance to the zoo through which they'd come. No harm in trying. Theft was rampant in London, and he understood the desperate poverty causing it. Why, he would bet pickpockets had fleeced a third of the people at the theatre the night he'd attended the opera with Ada, but that didn't make it right.

Especially when it happened to the woman whom he considered in his care for the day.

Reaching the gate in record time, he went a few yards outside the park and looked around. No one was running away. No one looked the least bit suspicious.

After another moment, he showed the ticket-taker his ticket and re-entered, standing by a tree to observe the crowd.

And then he spotted the thief. Michael was certain of it. Brown hat, navy coat, strolling determinedly toward the exit. The man was clever, walking slowly, whistling to himself as if he hadn't a care in the world. In the interim minutes, he might have even had time to steal another purse.

Intercepting the man at the last moment, Michael pushed him against the back of the ticket booth. Laying his forearm across the thief's chest, he pressed it up against the man's neck.

"'Ere now, what you up to?" the man asked, sneering up at Michael.

He was a rather rough-looking individual close up, and Michael was all too close, smelling the gin coming off his skin. He was also younger than he seemed at first, as well as rather thin.

Michael felt a little sorry for him. Even his malnourished stature spoke of his poverty.

"You've taken my lady's purse, and I want it back."

"You're bleedin' mad, you are." The thief started to struggle, but Michael had him firmly pinned.

"I saw you," Michael lied. "Just give me her reticule and there'll be no trouble."

The young man sighed, as if giving in, and then when Michael barely relaxed his hold, the thief tried again to break free.

He nearly succeeded, but Michael hadn't been in pub fights in the alleys of the east end, filled to his own brim with gin, without learning something—even when he'd lost a fight or two.

188

As the thief took a step away, Michael grabbed his arm, twisted it behind his back and once again, pushed him up against the ticket booth, this time face-first.

"You've got five seconds to tell me which pocket, and after that I decide whether to call a constable or bash your head against this hut until you crumple to the ground. Then I take the purse anyway."

"All right. Left pocket, inside."

Distasteful as it was, Michael fumbled around inside the man's jacket until he located the interior pocket and the reticule. Drawing it out, he made sure it still had items inside. No doubt the man hadn't wanted to stop and sift through it for coins until he was safely away from the zoo.

"You might try the stock exchange," Michael said as he released the thief and backed out of hitting range. "Far better return than being a cutpurse."

The man swore loudly before spitting at Michael's feet. Then he ran away.

There but for the grace of God go I. Truthfully, not that much separated him from the thief except a better class of drink and the good fortune of birth. That, and Mr. Brunnel's sound investment advice.

In a very few minutes, he was returning the reticule to a wide-eyed Ada Kathryn St. Ange.

"I'm stunned," she admitted.

He gave a chivalric bow.

"Truly, is there no end to your heroic deeds?"

He began to smile, feeling satisfied, when he realized her tone held mockery.

"Aren't you pleased to have it back?" He knew his tone held a note of irritation, but for God's sake, the woman hardly seemed grateful.

"I am fond of this reticule, but only because it matches this gown."

"But . . . but." He stopped and took a breath. He refused to splutter indignantly while the nanny and little Harry looked on.

"What of its contents? It feels as if you've got a goodly amount of coin in there."

She laughed. "Oh, no. I keep no coins in there. I have a pocket sewn into my skirt. Those are just a few things of Harry's, a couple marbles, maybe a toy soldier or two, already sadly armless." She started to tip the contents into her palm. "Oh, and a few of his favorite rocks."

"His rocks!" He nearly smacked his own forehead. He could have been injured or beaten a man. Over a reticule of marbles and rocks.

Ada beamed down at her boy as if had been the one to rescue the reticule.

"Harry, tell Lord Alder thank you for saving your toys."

The little boy turned his lovely eyes up to him and grinned. "Tank-oo."

Michael knew he'd been made a fool of and she was laughing at him behind her placid expression. Nevertheless, to see Harry's sweet expression, he would do it again.

"You're welcome, Master St. Ange." He saluted the boy.

His lovely mother cocked her head at him. Maybe he'd softened her heart a little after all.

ADA SUPPOSED SHE SHOULD be glad Vile wasn't injured. It would be hard to exact revenge if he'd been pummeled by a pickpocket and left too hurt to woo her properly.

Moreover, he had behaved chivalrously, even if he'd only saved Harry's toys. He hadn't known it to be so.

What would he do next? Adopt a few of the city's many orphans? Help those still suffering in Ireland? Thankfully the famine was nearly, miraculously, at an end, and Vile needn't go down on his knees planting potatoes.

She strolled beside him toward the gate, silently admonishing herself for making light of any of the troubles of their modern world. Best to count her blessings and pray for the rest.

She stumbled upon a loose paving stone, and Michael grabbed her elbow.

Her heart squeezed tightly, and her own thoughts echoed in her head: *Count her blessings and pray for the rest.*

She glanced at Lord Michael Alder, who, realizing she was staring at him, regarded her in turn. When she said nothing, merely offering him a nod, he smiled and tucked her hand under his arm until they reached his carriage.

She had plenty to be thankful for. Suddenly, her vengeful plan seemed petty, and she was of half a mind to forego it entirely. Alder could drop them home, and she need never see him again, nor offer him any explanation.

"I have an invitation to proffer," he said, startling her.

"Do you?" Another frivolous excuse to get her alone, no doubt.

"I think you will like it. My parents and my siblings live out of town but not too far. In West Kent. It's a lovely ride there, and Gabriel has those dogs we discussed. I'm sure Harry would love to see a whole pack. We can take Nanny Finn, of course, and even Dash—"

He broke off when she stopped walking.

"Is this one of those times when I've thoroughly annoyed you beyond reason? Are you going to lock me out of my own carriage?"

Blast the man! She couldn't help the smile that appeared on her face at his teasing words.

"You are asking all of us?" *Like a family outing!* If Alder only knew Harry would be meeting his paternal grandparents, and an aunt and uncle.

Was it possible any of them would see the resemblance? She doubted it. After all, they didn't know Alder had a son, so their eyes wouldn't see Harry as such.

She was ever so tempted. *What manner of family had created this puzzling man beside her?* And his controlling parents, who'd ruined his chance of happiness with Jenny

Blackwood, what of them? Someday, she might want to tell her son more about that side of his family.

For Harry's sake, if only so she could say she let him meet his father's family, she would do it.

"Yes," he said. "All of you."

"I think it's a grand idea." She began to walk again.

What's more, Lord Vile wasn't even trying to get her alone to make love to her again. She was almost disappointed at his lack of effort to seduce her.

However, after Nanny Finn and Harry got into the carriage, she let Lord Alder help her in and distinctly felt his hands upon her rear, an unnecessary touch considering she didn't need to be shoved in like an ornery pig into its sty.

By the time he sat opposite her, a smirk upon his too-handsome face, she wondered if she'd agreed too quickly. Lord Vile had to have more in mind than visiting a pack of hounds.

CHAPTER SIXTEEN

T The next meeting with Brunnel was as exciting as the last. Michael's accounts were up, thanks to guano and sugar. He now understood his country had an insatiable hunger for both, as well as for tea, silk, and cotton. It was simply a matter of knowing how to buy into the market.

It was too bloody easy!

"Why isn't everyone doing this?" Michael asked at the conclusion of their business.

Brunnel offered a knowing smile. "I have spoiled you, my lord. Because *I* know how to invest and with whom, you think it's a certain gain. Many are trying what you're trying but losing money, even going bankrupt."

Michael felt a twist in his gut at the idea of such a disaster. Not only what terrible straits it would put him in, but for the first time, he considered Gabriel and Camille. No doubt it was because he'd seen them so recently. If Gabriel didn't have a place to train dogs, what would he do? If Camille couldn't come to London for her first Season, she would be crushed.

"Can you assure me I won't become bankrupt?"

Brunnel's face grew serious. "Of course not, my lord. That would be foolish of me. If anyone were to make such a claim, you should run in the other direction. I can only tell you to look at my results so far."

Michael nodded. The man hadn't steered him wrong. Why would he? If Michael lost, Brunnel lost.

"Very well. You seem to have things well in hand with silk and all that," he trailed off a moment, thinking of presenting Ada with a bolt of shimmering silk to drape across her body. "Shall we meet again in, say, three weeks?"

In three weeks, Michael hoped to have accomplished more than simply adding to his fortune. He fervently hoped to introduce Ada to his siblings and, because he had to, his parents, as well. It was the respectable thing to do to gain a lady's affections, even if he had no interest in marriage.

Their outing to Oxonholt, the Alder home, was arranged for the following week, giving him time to write to his family and set the date. He had a feeling Harry would adore Gabriel.

When Mrs. St. Ange agreed so readily, he hadn't been required to use any persuasion. He'd been prepared to mention Camille and her need for advice on how to comport herself during the Season. Usually, women enjoyed gossiping and giving advice. He held back on mentioning his sister, however, for he knew the Season was a touchy subject with the prickly Mrs. St. Ange. Something had occurred leaving a bad taste in her mouth regarding the *ton*, he was sure.

Something which he would like to know. *Had she behaved inappropriately?* It was hard to give credence given her composed demeanor, but it was a possibility the fledgling Ada Kathryn Ellis had committed a faux pas. She'd only attended Almack's once, and none of his friends knew her. One chum at White's remembered the name, and believed he'd even danced with her. *No help at all.*

When he dug deeper, asking if anyone's sisters or mothers recalled Miss Ellis, one fellow came back with the nugget that his sister recalled Ada had nearly completed a second season when, abruptly, she left London with her family, never to be heard of again. Whether that was due to her parents or to her, the lady didn't know.

The only thing Michael knew for certain was Ada was firmly linked with Jenny Blackwood's middle sister, Margaret, whom everyone seemed to know. Now the Countess of Cambrey, she had not only been a sparkling debutante, she'd been proposed to in front of Queen Victoria at the Duchess of Sutherland's ball.

Given that momentous occasion, how could anyone be expected to recall other less fortunate young ladies?

On the day of the outing, he picked up the St. Ange party in his spacious clarence. Dash jumped in without assistance, although Michael enjoyed helping Ada. Her trim waist or soft bottom seemed always to be under his hands when he did.

To his delight, she seemed relaxed and enthusiastic. A couple hours later, when they passed the open gates, with half a mile more before his house came into view, Dash gave a few barks, perhaps remembering his former home. They all laughed.

A streak of pride ran through him as his family estate, encompassing over seventy acres, appeared through the oaks at the end of the lane. The expensive dome and tower of Oxonholt actually looked rather impressive after all.

"We'll go inside first," he said as he offered everyone a hand down and lifted Harry to the ground, making sure to hold onto Dash's leash so the dog didn't run off to find his old pack. "Then we'll go to the stables where Gabriel is probably training."

As soon as they entered the front hall, his mother appeared from the parlor, followed by his sister. Introductions were made all around.

"What a dear little lad," Lady Alder said. "He looks so like my own boys. Perhaps all little boys do," she added.

Addressing him, she said to Harry, "I heard you like your doggy, yes?"

Harry nodded, eyes wide, then hid behind Ada's skirts.

"Yes," Lady Alder confirmed. "Very like all little boys. Now my Camille here, she was a chatterbox at every age."

Camille blushed. "Better a chatterbox than a saucebox, mother."

"I would say you have that covered as well, my dear. But neither will suit you well when you get to London."

Camille blushed more profusely.

To Ada, Lady Alder said, "We are preparing for our daughter's first Season."

Ada nodded and, in a serious tone, said, "These days, a young lady must speak her mind and hold her own against a world in which we have so little control over our lives."

Surprised silence ensued from both his female family members.

"It's almost heartbreaking how the social Season is built up as the highlight of a girl's life, as well as the critical moment to catch a husband." Ada was speaking directly to Camille now. "You will be expected to be perfect at all times, even to the point of hiding your true nature, no matter how wonderfully unique, in the guise of being potentially the ideal wife. At the same time, you must stave off the advances of the bachelors who prey upon innocence and would no more take a wife than fly."

Michael realized his mouth had fallen open. Apparently, he'd been right. She'd had a rather trying Season.

"Luckily, as in your case," he pointed out, "ladies do find husbands outside of the London Season."

For a moment, Ada's pursed lips and pale face warned him she might be about to unleash another tirade. Then, she visibly relaxed, glanced around her as if realizing she might not be in the appropriate venue for discussing her opinion, no matter how valid, upon the *ton* and the Season.

"I apologize if I spoke out of turn," she said, glancing from his mother to his sister, who looked more impressed than daunted. "I hope Miss Alder has a wonderful time in London."

Lady Alder cleared her throat. "I appreciate your warnings, and we shall endeavor to guide our Camille through a successful coming out, even if that doesn't mean an engagement."

Ada nodded, and Michael decided they'd better at least get out of the foyer.

"I'd like to show Mrs. St. Ange and her son around the property, and of course, go see the other dogs."

"Of course," Lady Alder agreed. "Perhaps a tour of the house first. We have some lovely paintings in the upstairs gallery. After you've been to see Gabriel, we'll sit down to a meal. Camille, will you go with them?"

"Yes," his sister said, still gazing at Mrs. St. Ange as if she were otherworldly. "I believe I will."

Michael knew Harry wouldn't care to see the paintings, so as soon as his mother left them, he began by dividing the party.

"Camille, why don't you take Harry, Dash, and Nanny Finn to our nursery and let the boy see our old toys and then to the kitchen for some of Cook's sugar biscuits. I'll show Mrs. St. Ange the upstairs gallery and the conservatory and any other highlights and meet you at the paddock."

Camille returned a grin so like his own, he thought she must know exactly what he was up to—getting Ada alone.

"Yes, dear brother. We'll see you in about twenty minutes at the paddock."

"No hurry," he murmured, taking Ada's arm. "I think the old hobbyhorse is still upstairs, and Harry is the perfect size for it."

With that, he steered her to the main staircase.

"Paintings first," he offered.

ADA FOUND HERSELF ALONE with Lord Vile not ten minutes after entering his family home. *How conniving of him.* On the other hand, she deemed his sister and mother to be quite pleasant, considering she'd nearly ventured into an all-out lecture.

At lunch, she would rein in her tendency toward giving her opinion on the terrible pitfalls of a girl's first Season, keep her mouth closed, ears open, and find out more about the Alders.

"I have nothing but fond memories of growing up here," he said as they climbed to the first landing.

"I can see why. Your home is lovely."

"Thank you. I stayed away for a while and only saw it myself recently for the first time in years."

"When you picked up Dash?" she surmised.

"Yes."

She wanted to ask him why the estrangement occurred, although she guessed it was due to his father being conniving in his own way. Lord Vile had paid the price by losing Jenny Blackwood. And over what? Why had his father ended his engagement?

They had reached the start of the long gallery.

She recognized a Constable painting, confident it was a Dedham Vale scene, and a Turner painting, which looked a bit blurry in comparison. Then there were the mandatory ancestral portraits.

To her horror, there was a man and a woman in eighteenth-century garb with a boy who looked the spit and image of Harry. No doubt Michael Alder had seen it a hundred times, but things oft seen became nearly invisible. Moreover, that was before he met her son.

If he glanced at it now, he might see the incredible resemblance and would know Harry was of the same kidney, as it was said.

Spying a painting on the opposite wall, a castle on a craggy hill, she exclaimed over it as if it were a masterpiece.

He told her about it, something an uncle had painted from his travels to Scotland, and then she dragged him farther along, not letting him go back to the family paintings opposite.

Unfortunately, the far end of the gallery was dimly lit. Almost as if either she or he had intended to be alone in a dark corner, that is precisely where they'd ended up.

"You were quite assertive in your advice to Camille," he said, resting one hand upon the wall at her head level.

"As I said, I spoke out of turn. I'm used to living independently, I suppose, and not holding my tongue."

When she said the last word, his glance darted to her mouth. Unthinkingly, she licked her lips.

He groaned. "If you do that, I am bound to want to kiss you."

"Oh." She sucked her lower lip into her mouth and sunk her teeth into it to keep from saying anything more.

"And if you play with your lip like that, I'm going to want to do the same."

Sighing, she asked, "What can I do that doesn't inflame your passions?"

"Nothing," he said, then lowered his head until his mouth hovered close to hers. "I am constantly inflamed when near you."

Then he kissed her.

She didn't protest, far too used to his kisses by now to be affronted and too fond of them to want to stop him. It occurred to her this was precisely the type of situation a debutante would find herself in at a London ball. If only they'd had such an innocent breach of decorum instead of what actually had occurred in the infernal gazebo.

She let him slip his tongue between her lips because she liked it. As much as she hated him for what he'd done in the past, he didn't repulse her. The man she was coming to know, with all his flaws, also seemed to be kind and thoughtful. Moreover, her body craved his touch.

As his hands slipped to her waist and drew her close, trapping her between his body and the wall, she felt the familiar sizzle of desire streak through her. At the same time, she reminded herself his acts of kindness were all calculated to gain access to her person.

With her head pressed against the wall, held there by his firm lips, she couldn't pull away, couldn't do more than enjoy the kiss. And then he moaned into her mouth, and she felt a twinge of excitement, low in her stomach between her hips.

At last, he drew back.

"Kissing you is like finding a ray of sunshine on a particularly cloudy day."

She laughed, and then put her hand to her mouth at his chagrinned expression.

"I'm sorry, Lord Alder. You don't seem like the type of man to express yourself in poetic reverie. Not unless it is a practiced line and designed to gain you some advantage."

"You've wounded me," he said. "You are correct in the former. I am not given to flights of poetry. But I didn't practice it, nor do I see any advantage to having you crush my attempt at paying you a sincere compliment."

"Crushed, are you?" She considered. "Your kiss was pleasant and your compliment, if sincere, was very kind. I have never been called a ray of sunshine before."

He smiled. "With your crowning fair-haired glory, I find that hard to believe. Since you called my kiss pleasant, and I was aiming for earthshaking, I shall have to kiss you again. I believe we have at least seven more minutes."

Before she could think of a rebuttal, he lowered his mouth to hers again. This kiss was designed to impress and overwhelm her. After he ravaged her mouth and stole her breath, leaving her sucking in air, he kissed his way along the line of her chin and down her neck.

She loved the feel of his mouth on the skin at her throat. To her amazement, he nipped at it, then immediately licked the same spot, causing a shiver to race down her spine.

Pushing aside her lacey fichu with nimble fingers, he rained kisses across the top of her breasts until she would have gladly pulled her satin bodice down to give him better access if she didn't have to appear in perfect order for lunch. His hands roamed over her body, settling on the curve of her bottom through her skirts, pulling her against him so she could feel his arousal.

It matched her own!

If they weren't in his parents' upper hallway, if her son weren't somewhere nearby, she would give in to his seduction and look for the nearest bedroom.

"I wish to God we had planned to spend the night," he said, practically reading her mind.

"Frankly, I'm shocked you didn't plan it that way."

Breaking the moment of intense passion, he blinked at her, then started to laugh, leaning against the wall beside her.

"I nearly did," he admitted, his hands on his knees as he chuckled. "A tired horse, a cracked carriage wheel, easily arranged."

"Why didn't you?"

"Honestly?" He stopped laughing and looked at her. "Because I like you too much."

Her heart skipped a beat. A step closer to a declaration of love.

"And I figured you wouldn't be happy being away from home without your toiletries and Harry's things."

"My toiletries?" she repeated.

He straightened and took her hand. "All those mysterious things ladies need at night and in the mornings. Plus, your maid to do your hair."

"My hair?" She reached up to make sure it was still in good order.

"Yes, so if I stranded you here in the country, with an angry nanny, an irritable little boy, and without your toiletries and maid, I don't believe it would have done me any good."

While she felt a little insulted at his idea she couldn't survive without a few luxuries, she was also pleased.

"You are surprisingly astute for a man and a bachelor."

"Thank you. Do you want to see the conservatory or would you like to get outside and see Gabriel and the dogs?"

"Your brother and the dogs, please."

She was relieved when they went down a different staircase, and not past the likeness of Harry. Descending into a carpeted hallway, just before they turned a corner, Alder grabbed her to him and kissed her again, causing her to melt instantly and grasp his jacket with her trembling fingers.

As he broke it off, she felt off-kilter, her lips seemed to be buzzing, and she nearly grabbed ahold of him again to steady herself.

"Why did you do that?" Her voice sounded strangely light and breathy.

"Because I may not get another chance all day, and certainly not in the crowded carriage on the way back to London. Thus, unless you invite me into your home tonight, I don't know when I'll have the opportunity to touch you again."

He made perfect sense, but she wasn't sure how much of this pendulum of desire she could take, swinging from passionately kissing to speaking as friends.

Taking them past the foyer, he led her downstairs to the kitchens. Harry was seated at a table, Dash at his feet, and they both seemed to be munching on something. Camille was speaking to Nanny Finn, but they all looked up as Michael and she entered.

Ada felt as if their dalliance upstairs was written all over her face, for Camille narrowed her eyes and Nanny Finn looked away.

Michael Alder seemed utterly unperturbed. Addressing Harry while petting Dash's head, he asked, "Are you ready to go see some more dogs, young man?"

"Yes!" Harry cried out, causing Dash to start barking.

"Come along, everyone, let's go find Gabriel."

As they moved toward the kitchen door, Ada felt a hand on her backside, giving her a gentle squeeze, and she nearly exclaimed aloud.

Shooting her elbow out behind her, she made contact with Lord Vile's midriff as hard as she could.

"Oof," came the satisfying sound in her ear.

Ignoring him, she rushed ahead to walk with Harry.

"Isn't this merry?" she asked him.

"Yes," he said again.

In another moment, her son saw the foxhounds and took off running. Then Camille dropped back and took her arm.

"I'm very glad Michael brought you to visit with us. He's never brought a lady friend here before," she added significantly.

Ada wondered how much Camille knew about her brother's broken engagement.

"We came so Harry could see where Dash was bred and trained," Ada explained, hoping to downplay any expectations this young woman might have for a romantic ending to Michael and Ada's relationship.

"Be that as it may," Camille said, "Michael has also never shown much of an interest in Gabriel's dogs before, not enough to choose one to gift to someone in Town. He must like you and your son very much."

What could she say? She simply smiled.

"I understand what you were saying earlier in the foyer," Camille added, "and I am positively not pinning all my hopes on the Season. I want to dance and meet new people. I am not ready for a husband, and I refuse to be forced into accepting one, either by my parents or by putting myself in an untenable situation."

"Good for you," Ada said. "You sound as if you have a good head on your shoulders, which is what it takes to maneuver in society."

"You did well, it seems."

Ada nearly choked. "Alas, I did not." She almost bit her tongue for having blurted that truth.

"How can you say that?" Camille wondered. "You married and have a sweet son. And don't you own your townhouse in London?"

"Yes, you're absolutely right. I did well. However, I didn't find my husband in a London ballroom." She'd better stop talking before she said too much or had to lie too deeply. Glancing behind her, she saw Michael closing the stopper on his ever-present flask. He must have just had a drink.

She added, "You will enjoy some lovely dances and make new friends as long as you don't spend your time looking for a man."

"Thank you for the advice," Camille sounded genuine. "There's Gabriel now."

Harry had already rushed forward to meet the young man surrounded by foxhounds. Dash had also run into the middle of the dogs, apparently recognizing his old pack. Her little boy was laughing in delight as the hounds pranced around him.

"Hello, everyone," Gabriel greeted them, reaching a hand out to his brother and then nodding to Ada.

The exact same beautiful golden eyes as Michael and Harry! It was truly a wonder no one had noticed.

After a few moments, Gabriel pointed out the other dogs running in the field behind him. "These hounds aren't really Dash's pack. Those two are."

"Rufus! Myrtle!" he called, and a red setter and a retriever bounded toward the group. Dash took off at a run toward them and soon was rolled on his back by the bigger dogs, his legs kicking happily in the air.

Ada smiled at how different Dash's pack looked from him. *Weren't dogs wonderful?* They didn't have to be born into a family, they simply accepted the one they were given. And now Dash had accepted them as his family in London. Another blessing in her life.

Then an older man stepped out from inside the barn, and Ada felt her world spin. She knew him. She'd sat next to him at a function at the Royal Society for the Encouragement of Arts, Manufactures, and Commerce, squeezed between him and her father. They'd talked over her all night, before a lecture and after. He'd remarked on her interest in commerce and trading.

Walking toward them, the Earl of Alder greeted his sons and his daughter. Then he turned to her and the light of recognition lit in his eyes.

"Why, I know you, don't I? You're Baron Ellis's daughter."

CHAPTER SEVENTEEN

Regaining her composure, Ada smiled at him. He was an older version of Michael in every physical regard with a sprinkling of gray about his temples.

"Yes, I am."

Quickly, she considered any possible ramifications to this unexpected disclosure. Michael never knew her surname when they met during the Season. What did it matter if he knew who her father was? Or that she liked lectures? Neither of these facts could endanger her plans.

"How are your parents?" the earl asked.

"They are both well, my lord. I expect them in London within a month."

"Your father wouldn't miss the new lectures at the RSA, would he?"

"No, my lord."

"And what about you?" the earl asked. "Will you be there?"

All the while, she could see Michael regarding her with intense curiosity. *Drat!*

"I'm not sure."

"It's been a few years, hasn't it? But here you are. What a coincidence? So, you're my son's lady friend?"

She felt her cheeks warm. It was a nice way her family had of addressing her. How much better than if they said what they were thinking: *Michael's lover.*

"Yes. He's been extremely kind to me and my son."

"Oh, right. You're widowed, I heard. My condolences. And here's the little chap."

Harry was currently rolling on the grass with the dogs as if he were one of them.

"Ha!" the earl said, with a laugh. "Just as Gabriel used to do. Looks like him, too."

Her heart skipped a beat. Luckily, Harry's eyes were closed as he belly-laughed with Dash and the others scurrying around and over him. Moreover, she was certain he would eat either in the nursery or in the kitchen, and not under the scrutiny of his grandparents.

"Are you keeping up with your interest in the stock exchange?"

The earl's words came like lightning from the sky, unexpected and dangerous.

There was only one thing she could do. Lie.

"I'm not sure I know what you mean, my lord. How could I understand anything so . . . complicated and forbidden?"

He nodded. "True, true," he said jovially. "We must make allowances for the weaker sex. Yet I believed you followed the market."

Shrugging noncommittally, she observed, "Seeing how women cannot go on the floor of the exchange, my lord, I am restrained from following the market."

That sounded plausible, she thought, offering him a tight smile. If he mentioned her reading the financial papers, though, she might give up the ruse.

"True enough," he said amiably. "Still, I know you have a good head on your shoulders. Maybe my eldest son can tell you what he's learned about buying and selling stocks lately. Quite a crack capitalist so far. He's growing the fortune for the entire Alder estate. Isn't that right, Michael?"

She turned her gaze to the stock market "crack capitalist," and he smiled blandly.

"I know very little," Michael admitted, "but I am happy to share my knowledge with Mrs. St. Ange should she be interested."

Having settled that matter, the earl went on about his business, polishing his hunting rifle or some such manly thing. *The weaker sex, indeed!* It was as if she were also the dumber sex, the more foolish sex, the incapable sex.

What a load of gibberish! Why, she had managed to mother a child, make a fortune, buy her own home, and was now helping the ailing Alder family not to lose theirs. Until she took it all away from them.

Oh! Standing in their midst, her plan to build up Michael's fortune, which turned out to be bound up with his entire family's, only to then destroy it, didn't seem so justified. Not at that particular moment anyway.

Camille took her arm again as they walked back to the house for lunch.

Blast it! Ada admonished herself for ever having come to Oxonholt. She should certainly never have agreed to get to know these people.

How could she take sweet Camille's gown and ticket money?

What if they lost their home and Gabriel had nowhere for his dogs?

The lunch was tasteless, yet not in the way Mary's cooking was unpalatable, but because each bite was spiced with guilt. This family had made her feel welcome, and while she kept in mind how his own father had forged a letter breaking Jenny's engagement if not her heart, still, Ada's grudge was not with them.

If there was a way to exact her revenge on Michael without hurting his family, she would.

"Why don't you all spend the night?" his mother asked, as the last course was served. "Otherwise, you will have to get on the road before dark, or I will worry myself to death about highwaymen and such. If you stay, we'll have some gay amusements tonight and, in the morning, we can walk down to the Saturday marketplace. It's very jolly."

Camille clapped her hands, reminding her of Harry in her enthusiasm.

"Oh, do say you will. I have many more questions about the Season. Mother can't recall hers, and everything has changed since the Dark Ages anyway."

"Camille!"

Ada hid her smile as Lady Alder muttered, "Dark Ages, indeed!"

Before she could speak, however, it was Michael who came to the rescue. "There are no highwaymen between here and London, for God's sake. No one's heard of such a thing in decades. Besides, Mrs. St. Ange and her family are not prepared for an overnight stay."

"Nonsense," the older woman rebuffed him. "We are civilized people. We have whatever anyone could need for spending a single night, including for the boy. And only think how he will enjoy the jugglers tomorrow."

"Jugglers, Mummy?" Michael raised an eyebrow.

"Yes, at the market. Very amusing as if they have five arms. Moreover, we can all get to know your lady friend better."

Ada looked at Michael again.

He seemed to be asking her whether to continue fighting or to give in.

"After all," Lady Alder added, addressing Ada directly, "your son is here and even your dog, everyone you care about really, so what matters if you wear the same gown tomorrow?"

She gave an endearing smile, behind which was the determination and fortitude of a Roman gladiator.

At this point, to turn her down would be terribly rude. Ada could only imagine since she was the first woman Michael had brought home, his mother wanted to study her, get to know her, probably ask about her finances, too, for that matter.

So be it. She knew Harry would enjoy himself, but Nanny Finn might be another matter. Hopefully the woman had all she needed in the bag she always carried.

Glancing at Michael, Ada gave him a subtle nod.

"Very well," Michael told his mother. "You may have your way."

"Really!" Lady Alder admonished before smiling satisfactorily and sipping her wine. "Nothing to do with having *my* way. We shall all enjoy it, shan't we?"

Lord Alder seemed unperturbed in either case, but took his two sons off for a chat in his study after the meal.

Ada let Camille and Lady Alder pepper her with questions about life in London, although she constantly reminded them she'd only been living there a few months and her last season had been three years prior. Even so, she had some knowledge of Almack's having attended once, and Lady Grishom's famed *soirée*, as well as the safest boating area on the Thames.

Luckily, the ladies were too well-bred to pry about her late husband, or she would have had to invent an entire courtship and marriage, which so far, she'd managed to avoid with vague statements. They passed the rest of the afternoon before dinner with a more thorough tour of the estate, including the fastidious parterre gardens and the orchards.

After Ada saw Harry settled in with Nanny Finn, she found herself again seated in the dining room for the evening meal. It certainly felt strange to be wearing the same clothing, as the other two ladies had changed, but she'd at least washed her face and hands and combed her hair in the bedroom they'd given her.

Dinner was delicious, and the talk was all of national matters, such as their new conservative prime minister, the Earl of Derby, the terrible Holmfirth Flood causing the fatal collapse of the Bilberry reservoir, and the rather late opening of Parliament.

When they reconvened in the drawing room, Ada was amazed to discover the Earl of Alder was a natural entertainer. To everyone's delight, he recited from a Shakespearean comedy doing all the parts, and then gave a rousing rendition of one of the chorus sections of Aristophanes, *The Wasps*.

Ada sat transfixed, determined to lay her hands upon some old Greek comedies to read at home.

"Bravo," she said, clapping when he was finished.

Camille played the pianoforte with above average skill. No doubt, she'd been instructed since birth how, in order to catch a husband, a lady must be able to play a parlor tune to amuse him and his guests.

Ada was glad she could play the stock market instead.

Then it was time for cards.

At that point, she began counting the minutes until bedtime, until Lord Vile showed up at her door, inflamed for her, as he'd said. It was inevitable.

MICHAEL WAS OF TWO minds, be a saint or a sinner. Pretend to be someone he was not and perhaps disappoint the lady, or be himself, knock upon her door, and enjoy each other immensely. After all, they were protected from repercussions by being ensconced in the bosom of his family.

He tapped on her door on the stroke of midnight when the house was otherwise silent.

There was no answer.

Hmm. Had she fallen asleep waiting for him? Earlier, she'd seemed almost disappointed he hadn't arranged for this precise situation of being forced to spend the night, which had then been gifted them by his mother.

Maybe he'd read Ada incorrectly? Her lips, her eyes, her body, each time he touched her, told him she was ready for more.

He knocked again a little more loudly, his bare feet growing cold in the drafty hallway. He cinched the belt of the robe he'd found in his old room.

Another excruciatingly long moment and then the door opened a crack. In the dim light, all he could see was one eye looking out at him.

"Yes?" she inquired, as if there was any doubt why he was there.

He nearly chortled at the absurdity. He could ask her for a pound of bacon, he supposed, or tell her he was there to muck out the stables.

"May I come in?"

She hesitated. Not a good sign. He'd been right. Her mind, perhaps even her morals, warred with her body. In his experience, it was an unnecessary battle. Pleasures of the flesh didn't hurt anyone and certainly lifted the spirits.

Trying to be patient, he said nothing more. He didn't even put his hand to the doorframe. He had never forced a woman to endure his company, never needed to, and couldn't imagine one would gain any pleasure from an unwilling bed partner. He wanted her panting and open to him.

Another long moment passed, then she stepped back, pulling the door open until there was room for him to slip inside.

Surely, that was acquiescence enough. In a heartbeat, he swept her into his arms, closed the door with the sole of his foot, and moved with her toward the bed.

"I cannot wait a second longer," he whispered against the skin of her collarbone.

In answer, he felt her hands creep up his chest to rest behind his neck, her fingers entwining in his hair.

Yes!

He let his hands roam over her body, which was finally unencumbered by the fashionable layers of the day, clad in only her shift. Skimming up her sides, roaming over her round bottom, the first thing he noticed was her glorious hair hanging in a braid down her back. He made quick work of removing the ribbon from the end and loosening the skeins so he could run his hands through the long silken gold waves.

He could feel her pulse where his mouth touched her neck. It was beating an erratic tempo. Normally, the woman he was with would either have begun to remove her garments, or his, or given him leave to do the same.

She merely remained silent, except for her quickening breath in the darkness.

Dammit all, he wanted to see her properly. Striding to the window, kicking his toe upon a chair leg, he started to swear violently.

While hopping in pain, he started to yank at the heavy drapery to let in the moonlight, when incredibly, she began to laugh.

"I imagined the infamous Lord Vile would be more practiced at seduction," she intoned, her voice throaty, making his groin tighten, even as her use of the despised nickname annoyed him.

With a final tug, he had one of the panels pulled back and the light shone in, striking her. He put his foot down onto the thick carpet and simply stared at the vision before him. She was a goddess.

He sucked in a breath. Something in his memory stirred, but before he could grasp it, she moved toward him. As the moonlight gave him an enchanting peek at her dusty nipples through the fine lawn of her shift, all his thoughts were overtaken by her beauty.

Her blue eyes, lit by the moon, sparkled at him, her hair appeared burnished, and her skin seemed to glow.

"You are so lovely," he murmured, thinking even too loud a voice could destroy the moment.

"I've heard that before," she said.

A strange answer, as if taunting him with her past—no doubt her devoted husband had worshiped at the same alter Michael was about to show utmost reverence.

"I'm confident you will hear it again." Ignoring his throbbing toe, he concentrated instead on his aching staff, approaching her.

"I've longed to see your bare flesh," he told her.

She didn't respond, but she didn't stop him either, as he pushed her shift off one shoulder, then the other, until it dropped to the floor.

He groaned, and her nipples puckered. Instantly, he bent low to take one in his mouth while cupping the sweet weight of her breast with one hand and grasping her bottom with the other.

Feeling her fingers fist in his hair, he didn't mind the twinge of pain as he sucked and licked, then transferred his attentions to her other nipple. She writhed against him and pressed her lower body against his as if seeking relief.

His loins were on fire. Sweeping her into his arms, he laid her on the bed and got beside her, resting on his elbow so he could look at her. She stared up at him, and if he didn't know she was a widow and a mother, he'd say she was the picture of innocence.

Perhaps it was her clear blue eyes and her pale hair fanned out around him. She looked positively angelic, which only fired his lust further.

Skimming his hand across her breasts again, marveling at her satiny skin, he was rewarded with her soft moan.

When he stroked down her gently curved stomach to the treasure between her legs, she raised her hips.

He simply couldn't resist the offering. In a quick movement, he situated himself between her legs, gently

214

opened her petals, and blew a breath upon her succulent nubbin.

"Oh." It was an entirely sensual sound.

Dipping lower, he touched her with his tongue, rewarded as she bucked under him and, once more, sunk her fingers into his hair. As he tasted her, she pulled and tugged. He might be bald before the night was over, but it would be worth it. She was so accepting of his ministrations, seemingly so ready and sensitive to each touch.

When he pulled the hard bud between his lips, he felt her desire moistening her. In the next instant, she let her hands fall to the sheets as she quivered, ground herself against his mouth, and experienced her release.

Good God! Had a woman ever spent so quickly in his arms?

Yes, she had, on her own sofa a few weeks earlier.

How could the cool, unflappable Mrs. St. Ange hide such a passionate nature?

For his part, the throbbing between his legs had become nearly unbearable. Shrugging out of his robe, he rose up on his knees between her legs, looking down at her.

Her eyes were still closed, her lips parted, her body flushed, exactly like a woman ready and willing to be plundered.

Yet, as he fit the head of his yard to her core, she stiffened, eyes snapping open, boring into his. Twin blue flames, entirely alert, her entire being no longer languid and relaxed.

"No," she said, one of her hands laying across her naked breasts, the other going to the curls between her legs to shield herself.

"No?" *What could she mean?*

Then she started to struggle, pressing her thighs against his as she tried to close her legs.

"No," she repeated, and he moved to the side, while she sat up and grabbed for the counterpane to cover herself.

Was she a tease? Had she planned all along to enjoy herself and then leave him with the bluest of balls, aching for release within her?

Despite knowing her to have a spine of ice when she wanted, he had never guessed her to be so cruel.

What could he say?

"You want me to stop, correct?" For he had to be sure this nightmare of frustration was truly happening.

"Yes. Only think of the consequences."

He could hardly form a rational thought.

"Consequences?" he asked, then had to adjust how he was sitting, so his shaft wasn't bent painfully against his leg.

"I already have Harry," she said after a pause.

"Oh." It all came clear. She was concerned she'd have a child out of wedlock.

He relaxed, confident he could ease her mind, and then finally ease his aching groin.

"I will not spend inside you. There will be no child."

She cocked her head as if she'd never heard of the method.

"Before I climax, I'll withdraw entirely," he clarified in case she truly didn't know a man could do that.

Her doubtful expression changed to one of bemusement.

"Are you saying a man doesn't have to leave a woman with his seed to grow inside her unless he wants to? Or is utterly careless?"

Was that a bitter note upon her tongue? Hadn't she wanted her son? Had her husband forced her to become pregnant?

Michael reached out to stroke her face, and she flinched, then stilled when he made contact. Touching her skin lightly, he traced the contours of her cheekbones and then her chin. So exquisitely lovely. So young to have already known such sorrow as a dead husband.

"I want only to please you," he told her, "and to make you happy."

She shrugged. "You often amuse me."

Not exactly what he was hoping for. She was resentful, he could tell that much. Would she confide in him, especially after he'd so intimately pleasured her?

"Will you tell me more of your life?"

Instantly, he saw he'd erred. Her expression cooled, and with it went his ardor. It wouldn't take much to bring it back. If he kissed her again and stroked the skin of her bare shoulder—

"I think you had best be leaving now. I don't intend to risk all on your *withdrawing*, as you say. I have no reason to trust you will do so or, even if you do, that it will work."

"That's absurd, I—

With the sheet still clasped over her breasts, she managed to cross her slender arms, looking formidable despite being bare and sporting tousled hair.

He sighed. "Let me only kiss you again, my sweet."

At his words, she pursed her lips.

Reaching into his robe, he pulled out his flask and took a sip before offering it to her.

Another wrong move.

Holding the sheet with one hand, she pointed her other toward the door. In a tone more ice queen than warm goddess, she uttered simply, "Get out."

CHAPTER EIGHTEEN

As if Ada had been mesmerized by one of the lauded hypnotists or mystics she'd read about in the London papers, she suddenly snapped out of her trance.

She wanted to slap his face as soon as she heard him call her "my sweet," the very same thing he'd said the terrible night he'd ruined her.

And now, as then, he'd offered her his flagon. She cared not a fig if it were gin or brandy. He drank too much in any case and would end up in a ditch.

As Alder shrugged into his robe and got off her bed, she thought better of his offer since she was starting to shake.

Holding out her hand, which he didn't immediately understand, she pointed at his flask, then crooked a finger.

He gave it to her. With a quick tip of her head, she took a healthy swallow, letting the warmth of the brandy soothe her. She took another sip before handing it back to him and wiping her lips with the back of her hand.

He started to speak, and she shook her head. Staring at him, she willed him to leave without another word. Whatever he said could only hurt her more, already terribly disappointed in herself for caving in to her yearnings and to his practiced touch.

He padded to the door.

Hurry, she urged, for she wanted to bury her head under her pillow and have a good cry.

But he turned. "I care very much for you, Ada Kathryn." With that shocking admission, he left.

"HARRY," ADA SNAPPED AT her son for the umpteenth time. "Don't yank on the leash."

Marching up to him, she untied it from her son's hand and slipped Dash's leash over her own wrist. The poor dog didn't need to end up with a broken neck!

Harry began to cry, but Ada moved away, leaving Nanny Finn to deal with her devastated son. A second later, feeling as if she were wicked Napoleon himself, she returned to his side, dropped to her knees on the grass, and embraced her little boy.

"I love you so much, dear one."

His arms went around her, and she squeezed him tightly.

"May I please have Dash for a little while?" she asked, looking into his tearful eyes. "That way, you can more easily eat . . . ," she paused and glanced around the stalls, "a juicy apple?"

Harry scrunched up his face, his nose flattening slightly in a way she loved.

"No?" she asked "How about a sultana bun?"

He beamed his artless smile at her, and she kissed his cheek, straightened up, and took hold of his hand.

"We're going to the baker's stall," she announced to Lady Alder who was admiring the floral arrangements at another stall. The woman had either not noticed her guest's agitation all morning or had chosen to ignore it.

Ada didn't bother looking for Michael, who had given her a wide berth for which she was exceedingly grateful. After a restless night considering her life, her faults, and her weakness for this one man, she'd awakened feeling testy and uncertain and desperately wishing she were at home.

When she'd heard his knock the night before, which she'd been dreading and expecting in equal measures, at first, she'd considered not even answering. Let him stand in the hall and wonder if she wanted him.

Yet to move her plan forward, she'd had to engage with him. Truly, she'd meant only to let him kiss her, to tease him a little, to make him want her even more. Instead, she'd behaved like a wanton woman from the moment he'd touched her. Her cheeks heated every time she recalled letting him remove her shift and then lying naked before him. And what he'd done to her.

Making her way across the small marketplace of the Alder's closest village of Hadlow, Ada knew Nanny Finn trailed behind. No doubt the woman believed her mistress had quite lost her marbles for her erratic behavior. Cross and crotchety one minute, sweet as syrup the next. And giving her son a tongue lashing and then a treat.

Inside her own head, it was equally hurly-burly. She'd barely slept for thinking of Alder's parting words and of how close she was to his ruin.

And yet, she'd given in to his touch.

Pulling out six-pence from her purse, she handed it to the baker in exchange for the bun. Harry was thrilled and tucked into it with gusto.

At least she'd made things right with her son.

Glancing around, she spied the Alder men and Camille watching the cricket match on the village green. Lady Alder joined them.

Sighing, Ada supposed she ought to do the same out of respect to her hosts. Yet it would put her in close quarters with Michael.

Michael, whose lips and hands had made her . . .

She turned away and walked in the other direction. How would she manage in the close confines of the carriage back to London? What if Lord Vile smirked?

"Mrs. St. Ange."

And what would happen when they were back home? Would he expect to enter her bedroom there, as well, as if she were his paramour? How long could she put him off and still keep him coming back to her?

"Mrs. St. Ange!"

A few more steps and they were at the other end of the stalls.

Ada looked to Nanny Finn, struggling on her shorter legs to keep up with her, and next to her was Harry, still eating while having to run.

"Yes," she said at last, halting at the relative safety of the table where the butcher and his wife were selling sausages and meat pies, a fair distance from the Alders.

"Madam, the dog!"

At the same moment, Harry yelled out, "Dash!"

Ada looked down at the empty end of the leash. *Drats!*

"He went that way," Nanny Finn said, pointing past the stalls to the cricket field.

Sure enough, the spaniel was running toward the ball.

She could only hope the dog didn't get hit with a bat or trod on by one of the fast-running players. Unfortunately, Gabriel Alder hadn't gone with them. She was certain with a single word from him, the dog would be back where he belonged.

"Dash!" Harry cried out again and took off.

"No," Ada yelled, colliding with Nanny Finn as they both dove for the boy, who darted nimbly under the table of meat pies and toward the edge of the marketplace.

"Harry," Ada cried out to him. But he continued to run.

"Naughty boy," Nanny Finn said, but Ada could hear the panic in her voice as they both tried to see the quickest way through the maze of stalls.

They needed access to the field, which apparently, only a two-year-old and a dog could get to under the tables and through a hedge.

Beginning to run, Ada judged it quicker to continue on rather than to go back the way she'd come. Soon, she'd cleared the market stalls and rounded the hedge and was at the far end of the field. There was Dash running in happy circles, barking madly, interrupting the game.

One of the players, however, threw a spare ball to the far side of the field to get rid of the nuisance, and the dog took off away from her.

"For pity's sake!" Ada exclaimed as the game resumed.

Suddenly, heart-stoppingly, there was Harry, about to come up behind the wicket and the batter, whom she feared hadn't seen her little boy.

She kept running straight toward the game, all the while screaming his name.

And then, out of nowhere, tall, solid Michael Alder had taken to the field, yelling "Halt!" just as the pitcher wound up to throw.

To her relief, everyone did exactly as ordered. The batsman lowered his bat, the pitcher lowered the ball, even the dog seemed to stop barking. And Harry suddenly looked around him, realizing he was in the middle of trouble.

She was still yards away as her son put the tips of his fingers into his mouth in a familiar gesture when frightened. In the next instant, Michael scooped him up with a "Sorry, lads, carry on," and headed toward her.

Their eyes locked, and he offered her a comforting smile.

Seeing Harry carried on Michael's hip, her son's arms around his father's neck, her stomach did a strange flip and tears filled her eyes.

As soon as he was close enough, Michael put the boy down so she could scoop him up, although he was nearly too big for her to carry.

After a moment's hug, she set Harry on his feet and stayed beside him, her second time on her knees on the grass that day.

Looking up at Michael, she said, "Thank you."

He nodded, then with a light tone added, "I would fire your nanny, if I were you."

"I suppose you have a spare one of those to send my way, as well," she joked back until her heartbeat slowed. Harry was safe. That was all that mattered.

Nanny Finn arrived, breathing hard at the unaccustomed run.

"So sorry, madam," she began.

"It's not your fault," Ada said. "Who could imagine he would go under the table?"

"Dash," Harry said, reminding them of the little troublemaker who'd started it all.

Michael glanced around. "If my brother did his job, I'm sure we can get him back."

He peered toward the distant edge of the field where the dog seemed to be playing by itself with no recollection of its owners.

"Dash," he yelled as loudly as possible over the sound of the cricketeers and the few noisy spectators. The dog lifted its head at hearing its name. "Come!"

Instantly, and to Ada it looked like pure magic, the spaniel began running toward them at full speed.

"Thank goodness," she said.

"Yes," Michael quipped. "I'd hate to have to tell my brother we'd lost him in such a short time. I'm certain it would reflect poorly on us and not the dog."

Ada stayed on her knees as Dash arrived, nearly knocking her and Harry over.

"He acts as if *we* left *him*," she said, slipping the collar over his head and tightening it. "No more disappearing acts, thank you."

Standing, her gaze met Michael's and, to her relief, some, if not all, the awkwardness had vanished, along with her exasperation.

"Shall we join the others for the rest of the match?" he asked, taking hold of Harry's hand as if it were the most natural thing in the world.

She exchanged a glance with Nanny Finn, who shrugged.

"Let's get some lemonade along the way," Ada suggested, since her nanny still looked a little out of sorts.

Thus, as they sipped lemonade and strolled to meet up with the rest of the Alder family, Ada felt a sense of peacefulness overtake her. She needn't make any decisions regarding her plans at that moment. The future was uncertain, true, but Harry had been welcomed by his father and his father's family, even if none of them were the wiser—an unexpected outcome of insinuating herself into Lord Vile's life.

BEING WITH MRS. ST. ANGE was rather like being on a small boat in a rough sea, going up and down, and wavering between frustration, gladness, fear, and astonishment. In a word, exhausting!

Also, utterly refreshing. And who would have thought he would be the hero of the day, rescuing both boy and dog? Their ride home was uneventful and quiet, as Harry fell asleep leaning against him, with Dash draped across them both.

If he wasn't careful, he would turn into an entirely domesticated male. He ought to go out carousing that very night to shake it off. First to White's and then to one of the private Cyprian clubs where a luscious willing woman would be only too happy to share a few hours of pleasure.

Except as he rode along with the St. Anges, sharing an occasional word with Ada Kathryn when she wasn't reading from the newspapers his father had given her, he realized he didn't want to carouse. This woman seated across from him, next to a snoozing Nanny Finn, had so taken hold of his senses and captured his interest, he couldn't imagine being with any other.

Even after the previous night's debacle, which had begun divinely only to end with him in absolute confounded desolation.

Pulling his flask out, he had a sip of brandy from his father's well-stocked sideboard, a gift which he considered far better than newspapers. This small taste of delight engendered one of Ada's sharp, disapproving glances.

After another draught, he put it away, sighing to himself.

He would like to stay in her good graces long enough to win her—

Stop! Michael told himself, staring at her bowed head as she read an article. He'd nearly contemplated winning the lady's heart, as in having her *fall in love* with him. *What a piss-poor idea!*

Shaking his head, he rested it on the leather headrest and closed his eyes. If he didn't look at her, he needn't think about her.

He didn't know how long he'd slept when he heard her voice and opened his eyes. She was in a discussion with Nanny Finn. When she saw he had awakened, she tilted her head, considering him.

"Would you care to have dinner with us, Lord Alder? Since it will be nearly that time when we arrive home."

Her question filled him with warmth. And hope. How different an invitation than one he would receive from Elizabeth. She'd never invited him without needing his presence either for escorting her or for her bed. They never dined together merely for the pleasure of each other's company as he and Ada already had.

At least the food would be better this time, if Mrs. Beechum had done her job training Mary.

"I would like that very much." After all, "us" meant only the two of them.

Thus, instead of being given a quick dismissal, Michael found himself seated in Ada's dining room, discussing what she thought of his family and their estate, the events of the week she'd read in the paper, and how they hoped the food would taste as good as it smelled.

With a glass of wine in hand and a perfectly creamy potato soup in front of him, Michael was relieved Ada no longer seemed upset the way she had at breakfast, when she wouldn't even look at him. *Thank God for the naughty dog.*

"Does Harry ever eat with you in here?"

She shook her perfectly lovely head. "Not because I wouldn't like it. But he gets fidgety, and it seems more torture for him than a privilege. In a few years maybe."

She had a wistful look on her face.

"What are you thinking?" he asked her, hoping she would tell him without hesitating and arranging her answer.

To his surprise she did. "That it would be lovely for him to have a brother or sister in the nursery."

As soon as the words were out of her mouth, however, her blue eyes widened, and she gasped softly. To cover her embarrassment, she took a sip of wine and looked down at her soup bowl as if it was the most captivating sight in the world.

Obviously, with her husband dead, she wasn't going to give Harry a sibling anytime soon. She must have been thinking of it after seeing him with his own family. He could ease her mind.

"I was so much older than my siblings, who are quite close in age, it was almost as if I was an only child. Look how I turned out." He smiled.

To his chagrin, she raised to him what could only be described as a horrified expression, staring with even wider eyes than before.

"What?" he asked.

She shook her head, shoveling in some soup and clamping her lips around the spoon, as if to keep from speaking.

"Come now," he urged her. "You've always spoken plainly to me. Brutally so, in fact. What have you to say?"

"Only that you've turned out incredibly selfish, self-centered, self-serving, and even self-destructive." She paused, then added, "Only from how little I know you, of course."

Good lord! She certainly didn't mince her words. Taking a breath, he picked his serviette off his lap and dabbed at his mouth before placing it back. He had nearly picked it up and tossed it on the table.

Part of him wanted to stand, give her a dressing down, and walk out. Yet he feared if he did, she would never contact him to apologize, and he might never see her again.

How could he respond to a hostess who had so insulted her guest?

"I see."

She chuckled. It sounded cynical to his ears.

"And now you're laughing at me?" He reached for his wine and drained the glass.

"Well, you seem offended, which *is* laughable. As if your own behavior were a mystery to you, and as if you weren't aware of what people call you."

He considered this. She was right in some respects, although she probably imagined he'd lived his life even worse than he had. Perhaps far worse. Moreover, he had let people call him Lord Vile and not gainsaid them because he simply didn't give a damn.

Except he did when it came to her. He didn't care what other people called him, but Ada . . .

"What do *you* call me?"

She sobered and tilted her head, taking his measure with those intelligent eyes of hers.

"I call you Lord Alder, of course."

He waited while her maid filled his glass and left the room.

227

"In your head, I mean. What do you call me when you're alone?"

She paled slightly, which he found interesting. To his way of thinking, it was an admission she did, indeed, think of him.

However, all she did was shrug. "Don't you think my cook has improved tremendously?"

He kept her gaze captive a moment longer, then he nodded and looked at his soup. He ate a few more spoonfuls.

"I do. Thanks to me, a selfish, self-centered oaf, we aren't dining on gruel and pig slop."

With a rich, full sound, Ada laughed. He enjoyed it this time, far more than her mocking laughter.

"It wasn't that bad," she protested.

"Yes, it was. Truly, it was." He nearly warned how she might start eating more and putting on a few pounds now that Mary could scrape a decent meal together. Yet—despite being considered vile—even he knew discussing her physical appearance, particularly her weight, would cause her to summon Mr. Randall and toss him out.

Besides, he could easily recall her perfect shape, how much he enjoyed looking at her, touching the fullness of her breasts and the curve of her waist and her smooth, slender thighs.

If she only knew what he was thinking, she certainly would have her butler throw him to the pavement.

He wanted, instead, to be invited to her bedroom, and on a regular basis, too. *How could he accomplish such a feat?*

"You've met my family," he began. "May I meet yours?" He actually surprised himself, but found he very much wanted to meet them. At the moment, she was still a singular mystery. Perhaps if he met her parents or saw where she was raised, he could understand her better.

A long silence followed his request.

"They are not in London at present," she finally responded.

"Nor was my family."

She visibly sighed. "My parents' home is farther away than yours."

"Surely you take Harry to see his grandparents periodically."

She sipped her wine. "I have only recently moved here. I have no plans to visit them anytime soon."

"And if you did, I take it, I would not be welcome." He was starting to think he should have fought the *ton* at the outset of their nasty name calling.

She hesitated again. He couldn't imagine what she was pondering.

"Perhaps when they next come to London."

He waited for her to finish the sentence, but she didn't.

That was it, the vaguest of suggestions. At some point in the future, her parents might come to London, but she would give him absolutely no assurance he would get to meet them.

Perhaps, as an independent woman, she preferred a more direct approach.

"I would like your leave to call you Ada without the uncomfortable feeling I am overstepping. Given all we have already experienced together, I believe that's a reasonable request."

She stared at him, blinking her lovely blue eyes.

Eventually, after a visible swallow, she nodded slowly.

Good God! One would think he'd asked her some extraordinary favor.

"Of course, I insist you begin calling me Michael."

Her eyes widened, and he thought she was going to refuse as she had done before. *What would he do if she did?* Nothing. She could call him whatever she liked, and he knew he would still be happy just to be in her presence. *How odd!*

"Very well."

He was surprised by the tone of her voice, neutral not forced, and how she'd managed the words without choking.

They were making progress. Yet if she'd always been so difficult and skittish, he had to wonder at the power of her former husband to breach her walls and become close enough to ask her for her hand.

What had she seen in Mr. St. Ange which had caused her to marry him? He longed to ask. If he ever did get to meet her parents, he might become as nosey as a maiden aunt.

In any case, they were on a first-name basis at last. As the next course came in, smelling delectable, he decided to try it out.

"Ada," he began, watching her purse her lips, "how can I further my suit of you so we can reach an understanding?"

"An understanding?" she repeated.

"Yes, that we are a couple, linked in our own minds and in society's. I want to make no more missteps, but I fear I don't even know when I am making one."

"You assume I wish to become a *couple*, and to do so with you. What if I don't want to with anyone? Perhaps I don't wish to have an understanding."

It was his turn to sigh.

"We are having dinner together. Moreover, in the privacy of your home and my parents', we have—"

He broke off as she paled. He'd better not speak words of intimacy or she might toss her plate at him.

"We have been alone," he finished lamely, leaving out all reminder of what they'd done when alone.

"Yes," she agreed, hissing slightly.

"You seem to want my company." Actually, it was more that she seemed to tolerate him, but he had too much pride to say that.

"Yes," she said more softly, as if loath to admit anything.

He wanted to tear his hair out. She would give him absolutely no encouragement and no direction, not even the smallest hint she wished to become his exclusive paramour.

"Is there something you wish me to do in order for us to become a couple?"

What a convoluted, needlessly difficult situation!

"Michael," she said, trying out his name.

He liked the sound of it on her tongue. Of course, it made him think of making love to her. Everything about her made him think the same as if he were a randy schoolboy.

"If I were a debutante or even on my second Season, meaning if I were simply any innocent woman, not a widow and a mother—"

"Yes," he interrupted, "I understand the concept of a virginal lady. Please go on."

Her cheeks pinkened, as if she were indeed the very embodiment of a virgin.

"Well, if I were such, then how would you go about forming an understanding with me? Certainly not in any of the ways you have so far," she added. "They would all be considered too forward, including this meal tonight."

He considered her point. How did a normal man and woman form an association? They didn't, he supposed, unless it were leading to an engagement, as he'd tried with Jenny, and then a marriage.

Marriage with Mrs. St. Ange? Is that what she was meant? Every day and night together, living in the same house? Even raising Harry as if he were his natural father.

He grabbed his wine and took a large sip. Yet, the dread of such a permanent and encompassing relationship did not materialize. He'd felt it before. Not with Elizabeth, for she never wanted any such thing. But with a few women before her who'd grown too fond of him and hinted at a permanent arrangement. Then, instantly, terror had gripped him, and he'd seen the woman's many flaws, the things about her that annoyed him to the point of distraction. He'd always broken it off within hours.

Another sip of wine, still, he felt none of the heart-pounding trepidation, only the desire to know Ada better.

"I suppose if you were, as you say, an innocent, and if I wanted to form a lasting attachment, then I would properly woo you with flowers and poetry, sweet treats and outings, always with a companion so as not to sully your reputation.

He paused. "In fact, I have done many of those things, have I not?"

"You've done some of those," she granted, "as well as other things you definitely wouldn't do, or shouldn't, when properly wooing."

She was right about that. And without any regrets, either. However, he wanted to move on. He wasn't content to hope for an occasional crumb of intimacy. He wanted to drop a kiss on her delectable lips whenever it suited him without fear of recrimination. He wanted to make love to her and know in the morning, she wouldn't be so distraught she'd plunge a knife into his chest.

"Are you saying I am going about this all wrong?" he asked. "Are you asking me to become a formal suitor, to woo you *properly,* with the intent of getting engaged? Is your objective to be married again?"

As he said the words, he realized with stark clarity he would find that particular outcome perfectly acceptable. *Yes,* he could see himself spending his life with her. He'd never met a woman he enjoyed more, and he hadn't even bedded her yet.

What's more, the fondness he'd developed for her, which seemed to grow with each meeting, might even be . . . love.

CHAPTER NINETEEN

At first, Ada thought she would have to curtail the discussion. She didn't wish to speak of a future with Lord Vile, certainly not an understanding they would become paramours. However, the more she let him think and question, the closer he got to understanding what she wanted was his heart.

He simply didn't realize what she wanted to do with it.

Thus, when he asked her about marriage, instead of calling him impertinent, she hesitated, hoping she appeared to be pondering what she wanted. Eagerness at this stage might still ruin the game.

At last, she answered his questions.

"I'm saying I wish to be treated as any respectable woman, not as if, because of my previous marital status, I'm ripe only for a tryst or for being your paramour. If you think that means an intent to marry, that is entirely your conclusion."

She watched him drink his wine, at least his second glass if not his third, as he kept his gaze locked on her.

What was he thinking behind those tiger-colored eyes?

"I believe I see the difference at last," he said. "One engages only the body and the mind, of course, and the other engages the heart."

She nearly fell off her chair. He had come to it at last. Nodding her approval, she said nothing. He was doing so well on his own, she didn't want to interrupt.

"It's not a foreign notion to me. As you know, I *was* very briefly engaged. Like you with your Mr. St. Ange, I, too, had my heart involved in the process. I found the experience unsatisfactory at best."

Unsatisfactory. A strange word for having one's parents ruin one's intended marriage. In any case, even if his heart had been bruised, it was nothing compared to how he'd devastated her.

Her good humor died, as it always did when she recalled that night. She'd practically worshiped Michael Alder, only to have him use her like a handkerchief, easily tossed aside.

Moreover, he was still treating women the same, even now. How easily he'd left Elizabeth Pepperton to begin something with her.

"Your heart," she mused, trying to picture the tiny, black, hardened organ in his chest. "You spent six months with Lady Pepperton only to walk away as if she were less than nothing to you. That type of arrangement doesn't interest me either."

He frowned.

"You are correct in one regard. My heart was never involved when it came to Lady Pepperton. Nor hers with me, to be fair. However, you are entirely incorrect regarding what she means to me. We were friends and still are. She knows she can call on me if I can be of service."

She coughed, letting her imagination run wild.

"Not *that* type of service," he added, reading her thoughts correctly.

They were going in circles. Ada had always been of the mind Lord Vile didn't have a heart. That was until he'd told her he hadn't ended his engagement with Jenny over her change in fortune. On the other hand, she needed him to have enough of one so she could break it. A truly heartless rogue would never feel the pangs of unrequited love she hoped to inflict.

To that end, she would follow Alder's logic.

"You are correct in thinking I don't wish for an arrangement involving only the body and mind. However, I have no inclination toward marriage, either."

"Getting the heart involved without the goal of marriage? How forward-thinking of you," he declared.

Vengeance was as old as time, she mused. Not forward-thinking at all.

It was also far trickier than she'd imagined. For there were so many redeeming qualities about this man, as long as her heart was positively not engaged. As long as she saw him for what he was.

Tonight, as with each time they were together, she would have to bend and give a little, usually more than she intended, and then send him on his way. It had become easier and easier to give a little more because it seemed she was the one receiving pleasure each time.

However, giving him pleasure in return was beyond her. It would mark her as low and common, and it would almost seem as if she forgave his earlier indiscretions.

Which she could not.

After their dessert, a perfectly edible strawberry mouse, Ada rose from the table wondering how long she would have to entertain him in the drawing room before he started to kiss her. For when he did, she could send him home.

To her amazement, as soon as they left the dining room, he went toward the front door.

Mr. Randall appeared out of nowhere as he always did when people were coming and going.

"Randall," Michael said, "My coat and hat, if you will."

"Are you leaving?" she asked him, feeling quite astonished at his abrupt departure.

"Why, yes. It's been a long day, starting in Hadlow this morning. I assume you are ready to settle into your own bed."

The word conjured up the scene from the night before and what he had done to her on the bed, as she was certain he knew it would.

Feeling her cheeks grow warm, she glanced away when Randall returned.

Quickly, Michael shrugged into his overcoat and donned his hat.

"May I call on you again soon?"

How strange, but she felt a sense of disappointment he wasn't trying to make love to her, not even a chaste kiss on the cheek. What was he playing at?

Remember you don't really want him, she reminded herself. *This is only a ruse.*

"You may," she told him. "Perhaps next week."

"Perhaps tomorrow," he corrected. Tipping his hat, he departed.

Tomorrow? As quickly as the disappointment arrived, it dissipated. She was actually looking forward to seeing Lord Vile. That could not be good.

Heading upstairs, she ordered Lucy to draw a bath and, as soon as possible, sunk into the hot water, feeling exhaustion close over her. Michael was right. It had been a long day, and she was starting to let the charms of the man muddle her thinking, and her feeling.

Including, she realized, starting to think of him as *Michael*.

After a good night's sleep, she would be herself again.

WHEN HE SENT A message in the morning he would be stopping by after lunch, Ada nearly went out for a stroll simply to spite him. However, she reminded herself of her aim. The sooner she achieved it, the sooner she could end this charade and never see him again.

That was what she wanted, after all.

Thus, when he arrived at the door midafternoon predictably holding flowers, she had already steeled herself against his charm while, at the same time, plastering a pleasant smile upon her face.

Taking the flowers, she sniffed them once, and then handed them to Mr. Randall.

"You're welcome," Michael quipped.

"Oh, I see. You want me to gush over them despite how you practically spelled out your plan as a suitor last night. Why, I wouldn't be surprised if you had a Cadbury's chocolate bar in your pocket wrapped in a poem of your own creation."

The sheepish look upon his handsome face was positively precious to behold. She had guessed correctly. A sweet treat was nestled in his pocket next to his ever-present flagon of brandy.

All he said was, "Of course, there's not a poem in my pocket."

Then he treated her to his broad grin, which annoyingly made her insides flutter.

"I'm still working on it and left it on my writing desk. And I have Fry's chocolate in my pocket, which I shall now give to Harry and not to you."

She liked how he included Harry so naturally.

"You didn't tell me what you wished to do today. I had no idea how to dress."

"You are dressed beautifully as always," he said, his gaze traveling over her violet day dress, from neckline to hem with approving eyes.

She felt warm all over. In that instant, she decided as soon as she'd finished with Lord Vile, she might ask Maggie to begin the hunt for a suitable husband for her. She had never noticed a sense of loneliness before she'd taken up with Michael Alder, but she knew she would miss having a man pay attention to her and keep her company. And kiss and touch her.

At present, though, she couldn't imagine any other man doing those things except the one who currently stood before her.

Obviously, she had grown attached to the only man she'd spent time with in the past three years, and he was most certainly the wrong man.

"There is so much to do in London, but I admit to a weariness with always having to *do* something. Would you be amenable to simply walking along Bond Street and looking at the shops?"

She stared at him. *Had a man ever asked a woman such a question?*

Then she remembered Mr. Randall's wife.

"That does sound agreeable," she said. "I would like to go to the Burlington Arcade."

"Really?" he asked. "It can be a bit rough around the edges."

Shrugging, she insisted, "Nevertheless, Mr. Randall's wife works in a shop there, and I would very much like to go. They have a café there, too."

"Then it's settled," he agreed. "Are you ready, or do you need to bathe Harry?"

She laughed. "No, I don't. And yes, I'm ready."

"So only the two of us? What about your reputation? Last night, we discussed the necessity of a chaperone."

She took her cloak from Mr. Randall and let Michael drape it around her shoulders.

"If I were an innocent young lady, as we discussed last night, then yes, I would take Lucy, my maid. But I'm not. Shall we go?"

Mr. Randall held the door, and Ada was never more glad of her invented dead husband than when he gave her the freedom to go out without being watched over like a child.

New Bond Street was lively as usual with members of the *ton* parading up and down its length, and Ada was distracted by every shop window, many full of luxury items one could never truly need.

She stopped to exclaim before a colorful display of leather bags and silk reticules, silver saltshakers and candlesticks, everything so artfully arranged, she thought it looked like a painting.

"Aspreys," he said, glancing at the sign overhead.

"Oh, yes." She knew this store. "They won a medal at the Crystal Palace!"

"Did they?" Michael mused.

"Yes, I remember the name on a ladies dressing case."

"Well, if you need a case or a bag, this is the place to get one."

They wandered on with her stopping every few feet until she realized she must be quite a tiresome companion. In her own defense, the last time she'd gone to a shopping district, it had been for necessities for her new home, and she'd gone mainly to Market Hall in Covent Garden. All practical purchases. This was far more pleasurable.

Moreover, she'd never in her life strolled along looking through shop windows with a gentleman. There was something comfortable in how the other couples looked at them, smiled or nodded, and moved on. True, she may have detected a scowl or two, and she believed two ladies crossed to the other side of the road after studying Michael's face. It might have been her imagination.

Nonetheless, she felt more a part of the greater fabric of London society right then than she had in previous weeks, and she didn't want to return to a life of seclusion and isolation. He was correct—her life had been lonely.

Once again, she considered asking Maggie to be a matchmaker.

Every once in a while, if she lingered, Michael offered to buy her something.

"No, thank you," she said each time. She didn't need any of the baubles and curios that caught her eye. Moreover, she couldn't possibly let him spend the money she'd helped him earn, not when she planned to take it all from him.

It was the latter fact which put a slight damper on her enthusiasm. Here they were, having a particularly enjoyable outing, and it was all pretend. The next time she walked along this street, she would most probably be alone again.

"Why the sigh, Ada?"

She jumped at his use of her given name, but let him thread her arm under his.

"I didn't realize I had." She certainly couldn't tell him why. "We are nearly at Old Bond Street, and the arcade is just around the corner."

He steered her to the left, and they entered the Burlington Arcade of indoor shops from its north entrance, nodding to a Beadle—one of the arcades private police force—as they entered.

"Mr. Randall's wife told me this building is one-hundred-and-ninety-six yards long."

"Fascinating," he quipped.

"It's modeled after the covered shops in Paris."

"Truly?" He didn't sound impressed.

She nodded to another Beadle whom they passed as they began the long parade past the many storefronts.

"I suppose with the jewelry stores, they are a necessity," she mused.

He chuckled.

"What is amusing?"

Gesturing to the second story, he said, "They deter thieves, no doubt, but they also keep the business on the upper floors from getting out of hand, or from spilling down here to the reputable areas."

Glancing up, she frowned. "Don't the shop owners live up there?

"Some, but many rooms are for harlots and their customers."

"Oh!" she exclaimed, staring curiously at the second level with windows overhanging the arcade. At that moment, above her head, perhaps men and women were engaging in the act!

"Just promise you won't ever come here in the evening."

She nodded unthinkingly, only afterward considering it was none of his business where she went, or when.

"Let's find Mrs. Randall, shall we?" he asked, and they continued along the promenade, past sellers of shoes and shawls, flowers and books. Next door to a fine men's haberdashery, Ada stopped to peer into a shop that dressed women's hair.

"I suppose if you don't have help at home," Ada said, a little disturbed at the notion of a stranger doing her hair and practically in a public place, too.

Another few doors down, they spotted the milliner's shop at which Emily Randall worked, with a sign out front that looked like a bonnet with ribbons.

"I'll wait here, shall I?" Michael asked.

"If you like," she agreed. "I'll only be a minute. I suppose I should purchase some ribbons or a hatpin at least while I'm in there."

"Take your time. I'll stroll a little farther and return in a few minutes."

They made their plans like a couple, she thought, entering the shop. How nice it would be to think of him coming back to collect her and then going home together to dinner.

"Good day, Mrs. St. Ange," Mrs. Randall greeted her. "How nice of you to come."

It turned out to be a lovely shop overflowing with merchandise and at good prices. Ada tried on a few hats, and although not intending to buy one, she did, along with a new pin to hold it on as she was forever losing them.

Even so, she was back outside in short time and wandering along, looking for Michael.

He emerged from a print seller a few yards ahead, bowing slightly as two women passed him. They averted their eyes and walked more quickly. As they approached her, Ada distinctly heard, "Lord Vile."

Halting, she cocked her head to catch the discussion as they walked by.

". . . Shouldn't be out in public," said the first lady.

"What a reprobate! Why, I believe I felt his eyes upon my person."

"Truly, he shouldn't loiter here with moral folk. The East End is where he belongs."

Goodness! To think people recognized him, the way they did Queen Victoria or Prince Albert. Maggie had been right. He was infamous!

She turned away from them and went to Michael, awaiting her with a package tucked under his arm.

He greeted her with a smile, something she now looked forward to.

Drat!

"We both found something to buy," he said, taking her hatbox with his free hand before she could stop him. Just like a gentleman.

"Yes, there was a perfectly lovely hat. What did you get?" she asked as they began walking toward the southern doorway of the arcade.

"I won't show you until we get home."

Home! He said it as if it belonged to them both. How unsettling.

But all she said was, "A surprise?"

"Indeed."

She laughed at his use of the word she'd used so often to dismiss him.

"Very well."

He looked confounded. "Aren't you going to pester me with questions and beg to know the contents?"

"No."

"You are an unusual woman to be sure."

She wondered briefly how many women he'd presented with a gift, only to have them shred the brown paper immediately. In her life, Ada had found surprises often turned out to be unpleasant, and thus, she had no desire to hurry toward its discovery.

They stepped out of the covered mall and turned right toward Old Bond Street again.

"Now comes the hard part," Michael intoned, looking at the mass of carriages, some trying to move through the traffic, some parked at the curb awaiting their owners. "But my driver has a knack for finding a place to wait and, even better, for finding me when I need him."

They stood together, looking up and down the crowded thoroughfare. He even handed her the hatbox and package so he could wave his arms over his head, not minding how he looked half a fool, causing Ada to giggle.

Then he took to saying, "there he is!" as a carriage approached, and then "evidently not" when it passed them by.

He did this three times until, smiling at his teasing, she whacked his shoulder with her reticule, and he dissolved into laughter.

"What a display!" said a woman's voice nearby. "Lord Vile, himself, laughing like a lunatic!"

CHAPTER TWENTY

Ada whipped her head around to see a well-dressed woman with a man wearing a top hat at her side, both with matching disapproving faces. They had stopped on the sidewalk to gawk.

Making sharp eye contact with the woman, Ada expected them to move along.

Instead, the lady took a step closer. "I don't know whether to feel sorry for you, young lady, or scorn you."

Feeling Michael stiffen at her side, Ada said, "I beg your pardon?"

At the same time, Michael added, "Madam, whoever you are, it isn't your place to pass judgment of any kind, neither pity nor scorn."

The man in the top hat tapped his cane upon the pavement to get Ada's attention.

"Are you ignorant of this man's reputation?" he asked. "Do you, perchance, need our help?"

"Or are you one of Lord Vile's doxies?" asked the woman loudly. "In which case, you should take a step backward and get into the gutter where you belong."

"Here, now," Michael said, stepping between her and the odious woman. "I suggest you hold your tongue and move along."

"Oh, really?" The woman glanced at the man, most probably her husband, then back at Michael. "*You* are telling *me* to move along?"

"Actually, no." Michael's tone had gone quietly menacing. "Not until after you apologize to this lady."

"A *lady*, is she?" the woman sniffed.

"I warn you, madam," Michael said, then to the man, he added, "Is this your wife?"

"She is," he said, puffing up his chest. Ada wasn't sure if he was doing so out of pride or in anticipation of an insult.

"My sympathies to you, then," Michael said.

Ada nearly smiled as the woman stamped her foot in outrage while her husband's face reddened.

"May I suggest you rein her in," Michael added, "as she is making a spectacle of herself? Not only that, with her girth, as you can plainly see, she is blocking our fellow citizens."

"Oh!" the woman exclaimed.

"How dare you!" said the man.

"I do dare, sir! What's more, I am demanding an apology, or you and I shall settle this like gentlemen."

Ada watched the stranger's face pale at the implication of a duel. However, his wife only smirked.

"Lord Vile thinks he's a gentleman," she said. "How absurd!"

"He has better manners than you," Ada said, stepping around Michael's protective arm to face the harpy. "You don't know me, yet have insulted me here in public. You have shown plainly who is the guttersnipe!"

"Are you defending Lord Vile?" the woman asked.

Ada put her face close to the woman's. "Simply because Lord Alder allows the gossips to demonstrate poor manners with name calling, it does not give you leave to do the same. In my company, I will not tolerate such discourtesy. If you wish to see vileness, madam, I suggest you go home and peer into your looking glass."

Then Ada looked at the husband. "What's more, Lord Alder is an excellent shot, almost as good as he is with a sword."

After a long moment in which the man considered Ada's words while his wife raised her chin ever higher, he muttered, "My wife meant no disrespect to you, madam."

His wife nodded, then realized what he'd said. "What are you saying, Horace?"

"He is trying to save himself from being slain," Ada told her pointedly, at which the woman blanched.

"My companion is correct," Michael added. "Also, you are still blocking the passers-by."

Michael's driver pulled up and jumped from the dickey to the street, opening the door. "Ready, my lord?"

Ada let Michael help her into the carriage, while she could feel waves of rage emanating from him.

Before he climbed in behind her, he paused and addressed the husband.

"My condolences to you for having such a shrew of a wife. At least you may rest assured, she will never fall prey to the likes of me. I only ever pursue attractive ladies, either in face or in manner."

He entered the carriage, and the driver swiftly closed the door on the distasteful scene, including the couple's outraged faces.

They stared at each other for a long moment, and Ada shook her head.

Michael reached over and took her hand.

"I'm truly sorry."

"Don't be silly," she said. "You can't help the rudeness of other people."

She was still trying to get her thoughts straightened out and come to terms with having defended Lord Vile. *What had happened to her desire to bring him to his knees?*

"You stood up for me as any proper second would at a duel, and I thank you for that. Obviously, I wish it hadn't been necessary." He shook his head. "My previous bad behavior has touched you, which I never would wish in a month of Sundays. For that, I am truly sorry."

"Pish," she said. *Yes, she certainly had stood up for him. Why?*

"Pish," he echoed, offering her a sheepish grin.

Staring at the handsome man before her, holding her hand, apologizing, smiling, she found her head was spinning.

"So how would you have fared? In a duel, I mean?"

He offered her a wry grin. "You may have exaggerated my abilities a little. I am more than a fair shot, but I haven't picked up even a fencing sword in years. Perhaps I should get back into practice."

Then he withdrew his hand from hers, leaned back, and pulled out his flask. After taking a sip, he offered it to her as he always did.

Shaking her head, she stared out the window, perfectly aware he continued to drink until they reached her home.

Maybe if he cleaned up his reputation and stopped seeing other men's wives, as she'd heard from Maggie, then he wouldn't need to worry about his abilities with a sword. But that was not her problem.

When they stopped, he jumped out first and helped her down before reaching back into the vehicle for their belongings.

It was obvious he intended to come inside, and she didn't mind. He followed her into the parlor, and Harry and his nanny entered a moment later, along with Dash.

"There he is," Michael said in a booming voice. "The little man."

To her amazement, Michael bent low, and father and son greeted one another with a hug. Then Harry hugged her tightly and held on.

"Sorry, for intruding, missus. He was ever so excited to hear you return."

Ada stood straight, keeping her hand on Harry's head.

"Nonsense, Nanny Finn, it's fine. My son can always come and see me."

In another minute, though, Harry was pushing away from her and shouting about a biscuit, running from the room and taking his entourage, both woman and dog, with him.

"He has a lot of spirit," Michael said.

"Indeed," she agreed, then realized what she'd said, and they both started to laugh.

"Shall we have a drink?" Michael asked.

"Tea?" she offered, knowing it wasn't his intention.

Sure enough, he wrinkled his nose. "I was thinking more a glass of madeira. It is nearly the hour."

Whatever hour he had in mind, it was always near it. She hesitated a moment, and then rang for wine. However, after it was brought to them and she watched him relish his first taste of it, she said, "You drink too much."

He froze, glass in hand, staring over the rim at her.

Then he cocked his head. "Do you think so?"

"I do, in fact."

"Do you care?" he shot back so quickly she nearly answered without thinking.

Yes, she thought. *Of course, I care. You are my son's father. You have become my friend.*

Yet all she did was shrug and sip from her own glass for her answers were too disturbing to contemplate.

She *cared* about Michael Alder, quite apart from him being Lord Vile, the object of her vengeance. If she examined her feelings thoroughly, there was now a soft spot in her heart. Sighing, she stood up and went to the bell pull.

"Will you stay for dinner?" she asked.

"That is the most apathetic dinner invitation I've ever had. Complete with a long-suffering sigh."

Ada couldn't help but laugh.

"Will you anyway?"

"Yes," he agreed.

She told Mr. Randall there would be a guest for dinner.

"Shall we look at our purchases?" Michael asked. "Since we had to endure that odious couple to get them, I hope they are worth it."

He handed her the hatbox from Mrs. Randall's millinery.

"You first. Let me see what you consider to be a lovely hat."

Feeling a little embarrassed, Ada pulled off the lid and drew out a pale violet silk structured bonnet dressed with rich purple ribbons with small yellow silk flowers adorning the brim.

He seemed to be considering it. At last, he said, "I believe that does qualify as a lovely hat. Do you want to put it on and show me how it looks?"

"No, thank you." She didn't think it would be appropriate to mess up her hair by showing off her new hat. But for a long moment, she held it above her head so he could see it properly, then she put it back in the box.

"What's in your package?"

"Actually, it's yours," he confessed. "Or rather, I bought it for you. Open it, please."

He'd bought her a present?

Peeling back the brown paper, it revealed felt stuffing to protect the contents and under it was more brown paper. She tossed the stuffing aside and worked on the next layer.

"Oh!" she exclaimed with delight at seeing a framed print of the Crystal Palace.

"I hope you like it."

"I do," she said, staring at the intricate pencil drawing, which had been colored in. "It looks so true to life. Such a beautiful structure."

He fairly beamed at her.

"Your happiness makes me happy," he said.

He was gushing. What's more, he sounded as if he was quite sincere.

Tears pricked her eyes. This man had now given her two of her favorite things, Harry and this print. And Dash, for that matter.

She didn't even mind when he refilled both their glasses, even though she'd taken only a few sips of her wine whereas he had drained his.

"Where will you hang it?" he asked, sitting closer beside her so their thighs touched.

As he took it from her hands and placed it on the table in front of them, she considered for a second about whether to hang it in the library. Then, without warning, he took her face in his hands and kissed her.

Surprised at this sudden turn of events, Ada stiffened until he hummed against her lips.

Relaxing at once due to the pleasant sensation and opening her mouth to his tongue, she let him kiss her and continue to kiss her until there was a tap at the door.

"Dinner, madam," said Mr. Randall, not even raising an eyebrow at the close proximity of his mistress to her guest.

It was futile to try to scoot away or pretend they were having a game of charades.

"What was that?" she asked as they rose to their feet.

"What?" He blinked innocently at her.

"That humming you did at the beginning."

The right side of his mouth turned up in a charmingly crooked smile.

"Did you like it?" he asked.

"I'm not sure."

After picking up both their glasses, he nodded for her to proceed him.

"Then I will continue to do it until you are sure," he said to the back of her.

She smiled, rolling her eyes while he couldn't see her doing so.

MICHAEL BYPASSED WHITE'S AND went straight home from Belgrave Square. After a glass of brandy, he went to bed, realizing he actually felt as comfortable in Ada's house as he did in his own. In fact, more so because she was there, with her glow of warmth, so different from the cool person he'd first imagined her to be.

She had a beautiful laugh.

She had a beautiful everything, for that matter. Even that hat, which had puzzled him since it seemed like every other hat in a milliner's window. When she held it over her shining golden hair, however, it transformed into a glorious creation.

"You are besotted," he told himself.

He hadn't felt this way since Jenny Blackwood. No, that was a lie. He'd never felt this way before or since. He'd admired Jenny more than any other woman he knew at the time. Moreover, he was certain he would have loved her, positive he could have been a good husband.

With Mrs. Ada Kathryn St. Ange, though, he was already half in love if the fast beating of his heart whenever he was about to see her was any indication. Moreover, he desired her with a bone-deep yearning he'd never experienced. He'd fully intended to treat her as an innocent, to court her properly, but once they were alone again in her parlor, he'd simply had to kiss her.

He wanted to do so much more, of course, but there was a scintillating thrill in simply holding her sweet face and pressing his lips to hers. He could have done it for hours if Randall hadn't interrupted.

After dinner and after Harry had come running in for his own hug and kiss wearing his pajamas, with an exhausted-looking nanny waiting in the doorway, they'd played cards. Ada had taken delight in beating him at Écarté, and he'd equally enjoyed watching her play her trump card and win.

Each time she laid down a winning hand, she gave a little victorious wiggle of her body, which led his brain to think of other enjoyable pursuits.

Still, he was content. He, who for a very long time never went more than a night or two without enjoying a woman's touch, almost as an exercise in pride to prove he could. Truly, bedding women had become routine, another thing to do in the evening after drinks and cards, and billiards and more drinks. Not as routine and mundane as bathing or combing his hair, but not the exciting act it used to be.

And now, he was content to play cards with the most desirable woman he knew and, of course, to kiss her.

Groaning, he realized *content* was not exactly the right word. He was fairly bursting to get her into bed again, having enjoyed a sampling of her at his parents' home. In the back of his mind, however, he had an inkling he might like a far more permanent arrangement than he'd at first dreamed of.

Tupping her, even once, had seemed like an admirable goal. Now, offering for her hand seemed like a better aim. The notion of joining their lives so they could enjoy each other daily brought him nothing but happiness.

Except what had happened that day might happen again. In fact, he was confident it would. They would be out in public and some dunce would decide to hurl insults. Ada would be tarred with the same brush, simply for being near him.

Strangely, she hadn't seemed to mind. But would she ever consent to be the wife of Lord Vile?

If any woman would, it seemed it would be her. So strong and calm when faced with adversity.

He drifted off to sleep imagining Ada as Lady Michael Alder, and little Harry also taking his name.

"YOU SEEM QUITE DISTRACTED, Mrs. St. Ange."

Ada looked up from her notes, nodded at Clive Brunnel, and considered her situation. This was the time when she had intended to give him the bad stock tip to pass along. Michael so trusted Mr. Brunnel, if he told him to put everything into one commodity, he would. She could ruin him on a whim.

She'd dreamt of it for years. Even in the throes of painful and terrifying childbirth, she'd imagined Lord Vile's destruction.

"What shall I tell him to buy?" Mr. Brunnel asked.

Hesitating, she looked at her list. It was so easy, but at that precise moment, she hadn't the stomach for it. Maybe if he wasn't the heir to the Alder earldom, maybe if his family weren't counting on him for their future happiness. If only she hadn't met Camille from whom only yesterday, she'd received a letter asking if she could visit Belgrave Square when she came to London.

They ended their meeting with her advice to purchase stocks in the wool market, which Mr. Brunnel would pass on to Lord Alder immediately. Safe, solid, with no danger of loss.

If she must delay his financial ruin with her sudden trepidation, perhaps she could, at least, bring to a close their romantic association. He definitely seemed smitten with her. Without doubt, very soon, Michael would declare his feelings, and then . . . then she could break his heart and thrust him from her life forever.

So why, when he invited her to go riding on Rotten Row the next day, did she acquiesce with pleasure instead of stoic resignation?

When they set out, the day was fine, and Hyde Park was crowded with nobility on horseback.

Ignoring anyone who looked at her sideways, perhaps recognizing her companion as the dastardly Lord Vile, she wondered at the difference between his former actions and the way he'd behaved since he'd first stooped to pick up her packages

"You have done nothing recently to warrant the nickname with which you've been saddled."

"Truly, I have not," Michael agreed with a careless shrug.

She shook her head at his complaisance. "Is there nothing you can do to restore your good name?"

He laughed. "I suppose if it bothered me enough, or the lady I am with," he added, "then I would consider what I could do, if anything. Does it bother you?"

"Actually, no. It was more for your sake that I wondered."

"You really don't mind that a woman just turned her head away from us with her nose so far in the air I thought she might tumble backward off her horse's rear end?"

Ada chuckled. "I am secure in my reputation," she assured him.

"Besides, what could I do to make amends in the eyes of London's stylish and snooty? I can't undrink the many drinks I had in the gin palaces, any more than I can un-bed any of the . . . ," he broke off and coughed, looking discomfited.

She assumed he was going to say whores, or maybe a more polite term. However, that wasn't the worst of it. Ada recalled what Lady Pepperton had said. *Did he really not know why he was considered so vile by civilized society?*

"Nor can you restore to any innocent ladies their virtue."

She was surprised she'd been able to say those words without an angry tone. However, she realized the truth was the truth, and it was pointless to spend her life thinking reparation could be made where, plainly, it could not.

Abruptly, Michael leaned over to grab her horse's bridal, while at the same time, pulling back on his own reins so they stopped together in the middle of the path.

"What are you doing?" Ada exclaimed.

Looking at his face, she snapped her mouth closed, having never seen him with such an expression before— outraged and defensive.

"I don't wish to argue with you, but the *ton* has given me a name which can be taken in many ways. While I will freely admit to enjoying more than my share of gin and, if you'll excuse my saying so, women as well. If they think me vile for my behavior, so be it. However, my reputation for preying on innocents was unfounded entirely. I have *never* robbed a lady of her virtue, nor taken anything from anyone that was not freely given."

Ada felt a familiar trembling start. The disagreeable sensation had happened directly after their tryst in the gazebo, persisting that entire terrible night while she sat in the carriage with the stickiness drying between her legs, waiting for her mother. The trembling had returned every sleepless night for months while she lay in her bed, berating herself for her stupidity.

How many times had she recalled how she'd allowed him to maneuver her into the compromising position? She'd been entirely passive as he'd enjoyed himself.

Why? Because she'd been obsessed with him, admired him, practically worshipped him. And because she'd been too naive about what would happen when she acquiesced.

After Harry was born, with her son to think about, as well as building a fortune, and then planning the move back to London, Ada hadn't felt the quivering helplessness in a long time. She didn't like it one bit!

In a swift move, she unhooked her left leg from the stirrup, lifted her right leg up and over the high pommel of her sidesaddle and dismounted, leaving him with two horses and riders passing him on both sides.

"Ada," he called after her as she took a few unsteady steps away, nearly getting run over by other riders until she began to pay attention to where she was going. When she was off the path and next to a tall silver maple, she stopped, gasping for breath.

In a few minutes, he was beside her, leading both horses. Dropping their reins, he grabbed her hands.

"Are you all right? You're shaking. I snapped at you, and I apologize. I didn't mean to upset you. I don't give a damn what anyone else thinks, or even what they call me, but I don't like knowing you think badly of me. Especially when it is for something I didn't do."

Staring down at their entwined hands, she nodded, unable to look at him. She feared if she stared into his luminous amber eyes, he would see the truth—that she had been one of those innocents.

It was true he hadn't attacked her or stolen her virtue, and maybe he hadn't forced himself on any of the young ladies whose furious parents had made mention of Lord Vile in the papers. It didn't excuse him, though. For he had a way about him, almost a hypnotic power when he started kissing. At least, she felt that way about him.

How could he *not* know how mesmerizing he was when he was dealing with a virginal miss? What defense did an innocent have against his skillful lovemaking?

"I swear to you, Ada, I've never coerced an unwilling female, and certainly not an innocent. I had no need, there were plenty of young ladies willing to—"

"Stop," she said loudly, wrenching her hands from his, then childishly putting her palms over her ears. "I don't wish to hear anymore."

He fell silent, looking utterly miserable.

"I've made a mess of things." Stepping back, he yanked his flask out of his pocket, thumbed it open, and took a long drink.

Her old companion, *fury at Lord Vile*, returned when seeing him drink from his blasted flask. At least, she'd stopped trembling, which gave her strength again. Stepping forward, she poked her finger on his chest, right below his cravat, emphasizing her next words.

"How would you know?" Her words were like blasts from a gun.

Closing the flagon, he looked at her in confusion. "How would I know what?"

"How would you know if the young woman under you was a virgin or not, whether she was willing, confused, or simply scared?"

"How would I—?" he began, but this time, she slapped her entire hand against the lapel of his coat.

With each word, she smacked his chest with her palm. "Drinking. As. Much. As. You. Do. How. Would. You. Know?"

He stared at her, and she stared back, until his eyes widened.

Finally, he shook his head. "I am never so foxed I don't know what I'm doing or with whom."

"Maybe," she said, recalling that night in the Fontaine's garden, how he'd spoken so fancifully about her as a sprite, a fairy, or even a goddess. He had certainly been tipsy. "And maybe not."

Turning away from him, swallowing the remains of her anger so it wouldn't choke her, Ada snatched up the reins of her horse, put her foot to the stirrup, and awaited his assistance in helping her into the sidesaddle.

Wordlessly, he did so, then he regained his own saddle, and they set off back the way they'd come toward Belgrave Square.

What more was there to say? He spoke with utter conviction. However, she was proof he was wrong—she was a virgin he'd deflowered without even realizing.

Struggling in her thoughts with how to return to the even keel they'd been on before this painful ride, how to tamp down the rage and the sadness, she didn't notice the carriage drawn up outside her home until she was nearly upon it.

And then, very clearly, she saw the monogram upon the vehicle's door, JRE.

Her parents had arrived.

CHAPTER TWENTY-ONE

In case any of her neighbors were watching, Ada didn't slide down the side of her horse as she had at Rotten Row in the park. Instead, in ladylike fashion but with great impatience, she waited for Michael to dismount and help her down.

They shared a glance, and she realized she needed to smooth things over now before they greeted her parents. Or, on second thought, she could send him on his way with all due haste, which would be prudent.

Since she had no footman, it was Michael's man who was waiting to take charge of their horses. Appearing from the shadowy area by her steps, his footman swiftly took hold of the reins and started to walk them away and around the back, where there were small stables for the entire terrace of houses.

"Hold," Michael said to him. Then he looked at her. "Am I coming in? It appears you have visitors. I can leave at once."

She hesitated. "My parents have returned to London. I knew it was imminent."

At his expression, she added, "They don't live with me. They have a townhouse on Hanover Square."

It was why Ada and Maggie were the oldest and dearest of friends, having grown up as neighbors. Did he recall that was where Jenny and her family had lived before her father's death? He'd probably visited the eldest Blackwood sister there.

He simply nodded, looking, she judged, rather lost. Maybe he was still wondering what terrible deeds he'd done while inebriated.

Her front door opened, but instead of Randall standing in the doorway, it was her mother.

"Come in, come in. Hurry! I've been waiting to see you. How Harry has grown! I've missed you so much, my girl."

Drawn by her sweet mother's words, Ada rushed into her embrace. They entered the foyer, arms still around each other, and she could hear her father's booming voice laughing with Harry.

Crossing to the parlor, she heard footsteps behind her and knew Michael had followed. In the next instant, she saw her father seated on the sofa but bending low to pet Dash while Harry ran in circles holding a new toy.

"Papa," she greeted. But it was her son who ran to her.

"Look, Mama, look," and he thrust a carved wooden horse, realistically painted, toward her.

When she reached out to admire it, he snatched it back, cradling it to his chest.

"*My* horse," he said.

"Did you thank Nana and Grandpapa?"

Her father stood up by this time. "He did, Ada. He's a good boy."

Giving her a brief hug, he looked her up and down. "You look well, daughter. London suits you so far."

She felt her cheeks grow warm, only thinking of what she'd been up to in the past weeks.

"It does, Papa."

His eyes narrowed curiously as he looked past her.

"Whom have we here?"

"My apologies," she muttered. "Mummy, Papa, this is Lord Alder." Her mother wasn't much for the gossip rags and her father never read that section of any newspaper, so she felt fairly safe in giving them his name. There would be no thunderstruck expressions or insults hurled.

Michael stepped forward to offer a sincere bow of his head to her parents, who now stood side-by-side, clearly curious and inspecting the man with whom their daughter had been out riding.

"A pleasure to meet you," Michael intoned, easily slipping into his charming self. "Did you only just arrive from the country?"

"Yes," James Ellis answered. "We didn't even go to our own home yet, so eager was Ada's mother to see her."

Kathryn Ellis smiled. "You were just as eager, dear."

"Would you care for tea or coffee?" Ada asked before her parents began to argue over who was more keen to see her.

"Oh, I did ask Lucy," her mother said. "It should be ready shortly. I hope you don't mind."

"Of course not."

"Your own home and so many changes," Kathryn continued, lifting a delicate brow and glancing between Ada and Michael.

Ada most certainly didn't want her parents coming to the wrong conclusion, not when it was so temporary.

Just then, Harry let out a loud shriek of pure joy simply playing on the rug with Dash and his new toy. Nanny Finn, who had been seated unobtrusively in the corner, stepped forward.

"Shall I take the young master upstairs, madam?"

"Yes, thank you," Ada agreed, ruffling her son's hair as he went past making neighing sounds.

She rather hoped Dash would follow so she didn't have to explain why a stranger had given her a dog, but the animal was too interested in sniffing her parents' shoes, undoubtedly enjoying many scents they'd carried with them from Surrey.

Silence descended, and Ada realized Michael was hovering at her elbow. *What could she say without being rude?*

"Will you join us for a refreshment, or do you have to *leave*?"

If he heard her emphasize the last word, he didn't let on. His face lit up, and she knew he was going to accept the invitation, when all of a sudden, her brother entered.

"Grady!" she exclaimed. "I was wondering where you were," she lied. With Michael meeting her parents, she'd forgotten entirely her younger brother would be there as well.

They hugged, and she introduced him to Michael.

"Where were you?" she asked her brother as the tea was brought in.

"I hope you don't mind, sis. I had to stretch my legs, and with the size of this place, I could take a walk without going outside. You've done really well!"

She shrugged slightly, feeling absurdly pleased by her younger brother's praise.

"There's also a lovely grassy patch in the center of the square. Perfect for Harry to play in."

"And for your dog," Grady surmised, eyeing Dash curiously.

She knew he was about to ask where the dog came from.

"Why don't we all sit?" she blurted, and before she knew it, her family was seated with Lord Vile, of all people, who looked as pleased as Punch, from the puppet show she'd recently seen in the park with Harry.

At that moment, she did feel rather like Punch's long-suffering wife, Judy.

How was she to get out of this farce before someone said something she would need to explain?

Almost at once, it got worse.

"You are here too early for Parliament, Lord Ellis," Michael pointed out. "Do you have other dealings in London, or did you come expressly to see your daughter?"

Her father smiled, and she knew he was about to launch into his favorite topic. Sure enough, he responded, "My primary interest in London is the stock exchange. Always has been. Miss it like the devil when I'm in Surrey."

Ada's teacup rattled in her hand. She couldn't stop the course of the conversation.

"Really? How fortuitous!" Michael exclaimed. "I have recently begun to invest, and it's working out quite well."

"Fabulous," her father said with his usual enthusiasm for the topic, giving a little clap of his hands.

Her mother sighed, and her brother, whose interest lay in becoming a barrister, leaned back against the sofa cushions, firmly settling in for the long discourse. Even Dash lay across Ada's slippers as if knowing it were time to nap.

"What markets have you got into so far?" the baron asked.

Michael listed off three or four, all with her father nodding his approval.

"With your interest in stocks, you are keeping the right company, then," her father said, with a knowing tilt of his head.

Michael fell silent, his expression blank.

"I'm sorry, sir? I don't understand."

"Not to imply you *are* keeping company," Baron Ellis added as his wife poked him in the ribs with her elbow. "I merely thought . . ." He nodded toward Ada, who sat in an otherwise comfortable wing chair, but feeling as if she were resting on hatpins.

How she wished she could somehow transport herself across town or perhaps to the bottom of the Thames.

Michael looked at her inquiringly. She shrugged and offered the vacant stare of a female who didn't know a stock from a stork.

"Has anyone tried Mary's raspberry jam biscuits? They are quite delicious," she asked.

Grady leaned forward and snatched one up, taking a bite. "They are!" he exclaimed.

Michael still stared at her. If recalling what his father said when she'd met him, he might suddenly wonder what she did, indeed, know about investing.

Time for an entirely new topic.

"Have you found a place for Grady to apprentice, or is he going to study common law at a university?"

Her mother narrowed her eyes, obviously reading her daughter like a penny paper, recognizing her diversionary tactics, but her father merely shrugged.

"We will spend some time making the rounds," he promised, winking at Grady. "We'll find him a place."

"Solicitor or barrister?" Michael asked her brother, who responded as to the latter for he quite liked the idea of arguing before a judge.

Crisis averted, Ada thought.

"My brother is frightfully good at arguing," she said with a gentle smile, for she loved Grady wholeheartedly, despite how they fought during childhood. "And I'm positive the wig and gown will suit him."

Grady made a face, and everyone laughed.

"If only both of my children could do what they were born to do," James Ellis lamented, and Ada froze. *Crisis returned!* "As much as Grady will make a fine barrister, Ada should be allowed to—"

"No," she yelped, interrupting her father.

In the shocked silence that followed, she felt her heart beating nearly out of her chest. She was certain he would have revealed her fervent wish to go on the floor of the exchange and be a broker.

"Dash," she said weakly, pointing at the dog, who'd jumped up at her tone. "I'm afraid one of his toenails went through my slipper."

Reaching down, she patted his silky head. "Not your fault, pup," she murmured.

It's my fault. This letting-things-happen attitude, *laissez-faire* as the French economists termed it, was what got her into trouble in the first place in that cursed gazebo. This was *her* home, and it was up to her to take control.

Abruptly standing, Ada sent her parents a warm smile. "You must wish to settle in at home. I shall come visit and bring Harry in the morning."

Grady jumped up, obviously relieved.

"Wonderful. Let's go," he said to their parents. "I've some chums I wish to visit tonight."

"Tonight?" Kathryn repeated, sounding scandalized.

"Mother, I'm eighteen." Grady kissed Ada's cheek and left the room.

"He'll be halfway to Hanover Square before he realizes you're not in the carriage," Ada said, trying to hurry her parents along.

In a flurry of kisses and hugs, Baron and Baroness Ellis were in the foyer.

However, at the door, they hesitated, her father looking pointedly at Michael. In all good conscience, her parents couldn't leave their daughter alone with a strange man.

Luckily, even the jaded Lord Vile understood.

"I, too, must take my leave," he said, and she breathed a sigh of relief.

After a bow to each of her parents, Michael turned to her.

Was he going to take her hand and kiss it? Clenching her hands at her sides, she nodded awkwardly at him.

"I'll walk you all out," she offered, stepping in front of him, feeling eyes upon her as she linked arms with her mother.

Randall opened the front door, and they all stepped outside. Her parent's carriage was already at the curb, door open, and her brother hopped about impatiently.

"Come along," he urged them.

"Bring Lord Alder's horses," she said quietly to Randall.

"I've sent for them already, madam," he told her. "His footman is coming at once."

Her parents couldn't linger without appearing rude, so with another farewell and more nodding and waving, the Ellis family drove out of sight.

Hearing the clip-clop of the horses, Ada and Michael both looked to the corner as his footman came back from the stable riding one and leading the other.

Taking her hand in his, Michael brushed his mouth against her knuckles. Then he lifted his head and looked her in the eyes.

"Today was a strange outing. It didn't go as planned at all."

She couldn't help but wonder what he'd hoped would happen.

"I was uncertain of the day my family would return to London," she admitted.

He shook his head. "I meant *before* that."

Ada stayed silent. She'd known what he meant. It had certainly become strained when they'd begun discussing the extent of his vileness and his drinking. Frankly, she didn't want to think about it again.

"Your family," he said, "they seemed pleasant people."

"Even my brother?"

"Even him. Not so different from Gabriel." He tilted his head. "I would like to speak with your father about my investments some time."

Ada gave what she hoped was a placid smile. Placid and utterly ambiguous.

"I should go look in on Harry now," she said.

"I am dismissed," he surmised.

"Indeed."

ADA WAS HIDING SOMETHING, wasn't she? Michael had experienced the same feeling when she'd exhibited such a strong reaction during their discussion of the Season. It had driven him to Almack's and the discovery of her maiden name.

But all inquiries regarding Ada Kathryn Ellis had come to naught. No one had any knowledge of a scandal linked to her name. No trysts had been discovered and reported by gossips. Nor even a disastrous blunder on her part, such as misspeaking a nobleman's title or wearing the same gown to two similar events or dancing twice in a row with the same man. Nothing!

So why did mention of the Season make her prickly?

Moreover, she had behaved strangely in the company of her parents.

Michael supposed the best thing to do was to ask her. If he intended to make her his wife—which had somehow become his unstated, barely believed goal—he ought to be able to ask her anything and receive an honest answer.

After all, his own foibles were not only on display and generally discussed, but even printed in every blasted gossip rag.

And still, she'd befriended him, if that was the correct term for their strange relationship.

Hemsby was a friend in the normal sense. Even Elizabeth Pepperton was a friend in the sense of him wishing her well. Yet Ada was a puzzle. She seemed to like him and despise him in equal measures, to want to spend time with him as well as to push him away.

Yes, a forthright talk was in order, and there was no better place than Dolly's Chop House, in his opinion, over steaks and wine. For if they had a talk in the intimate surroundings of her home or his, he would probably start kissing her before their conversation had begun.

Quickly, he sat down and penned an invitation to her. No play, opera, or ballet, simply dinner if she was amenable. He found out by return missive she was.

As with every time he anticipated seeing her, he felt joyful. And his anticipation was never disappointed. When he showed up on her doorstep, Ada appeared in a deep blue dress, showing off her small waist, with a sculpted à la mode neckline, low enough to give him more than a hint of her full breasts. Staring into her intelligent eyes—always with something slightly mysterious sparkling within them—Michael felt grateful she deigned to keep company with him at all.

Moreover, she got into his cozy brougham without protest.

Progress, he thought, as they set out through Westminster, past the abbey on the left and the palace on the right, which was ten years into its rebuilding after the last fire.

"We are dining at your home?" she asked.

To keep her from thinking where they were going, he kissed her, then he kissed her again, humming against her lips because now it was their special way.

When he drew back, the first thing she did was look out the window to see they'd proceeded along the Thames as far as St. Paul's.

Exclaiming aloud, obviously bursting with curiosity, she asked him outright, "Where are we going?"

He merely smiled, causing her to ask him half a dozen more times, sounding like Harry when curious about something.

"You'll see," he responded to each question.

"I thought we'd be eating at your home," she said again when they'd entered the Blackfriars district, and her excitement was visible. "I'm not sure I would have worn this gown when meeting new people at a dinner party."

"Then I'm glad we're *not* doing that because I love your gown." And he wasn't about to share her with others at a boring dinner party.

Alighting from his carriage onto Paternoster Row, they slipped under an arch to the nearly deserted Queens' Court Passage, which a little later would be busy with men going out to dine. There, under a large lamp, was the entrance to Dolly's Chop House, which for all his life, he merely thought of as Dolly's.

As he tried to usher her inside, she gasped and planted her kidskin boots on the cobbled lane.

"What are you doing? I cannot go in there."

"Normally, no, but tonight is special. The owner, Thomas Howell, is an old friend of my father's. Trust me," he added, holding out his hand to her.

After the briefest of hesitations, she took it. Michael kept talking as he drew her inside the old establishment, watching as she whipped her head this way and that, taking in the main dining room, currently deserted.

"In an hour, maybe a little less, this place will be stuffed to the gills with men of commerce, as well as barristers and noblemen. It's very popular and the steak is absolutely outstanding."

"Less than an hour?" Her voice rose to a nervous squeak, glancing again at the heavily-paneled room, rather dark, even a little dingy.

"Not to worry. Mr. Howell agreed to close his coffee room for a couple hours tonight, so we could dine privately."

"Why on earth would he do that?" she asked, snatching a menu off a table as she passed, examining it like a child with a new toy.

"Because I said his steak was no better than what my cook could make, and I knew my lady would say the same."

Michael led her past leather chairs and heavy oak tables to a smaller room on the left, in which he could smell the coffee from earlier in the day.

"Mr. Howell told me to bring in my lady at once to sample his fare. He'll visit us later, and you must tell him if it's the finest steak or not."

Her amused smile told him she found the entire situation agreeable. Many women would not. They would have refused to set foot in there on pain of loss of reputation.

"He also has a popular cigar room. He calls it his 'City House of Commons' for all the members who come in to hash out the same things they're debating in Parliament. I wish I could take you in there to listen for an evening. Quite remarkable."

He pulled out a chair for her and then sat opposite, watching as she removed her gloves and placed them in her lap.

"Probably as exciting as I imagine the stock exchange to be," she said.

As soon as she spoke, her cheeks blushed a pretty pink.

"Your father must have told you many interesting tales," he guessed.

Before she could answer, their waitress came in. He'd seen her before but not enough to know her name.

"Good evening, my lord," she began, "and my lady," she added, nodding to Ada. "Mr. Howell said you'll be wanting our finest cuts."

"The fish soup first," Michael said. "And a baked potato each with our beef," he added, while Ada looked on, eyes wide, lips pressed together but smiling, clearly not daring to speak.

"It's all right, luv," the waitress said to her. "Sometimes we get an actress in here, or an opera singer."

If possible, Ada's beautiful blue eyes opened even wider.

He was thrilled to see her appear so amused.

Then the waitress asked about what they wished to drink. He cocked his head at Ada.

"Spanish red?"

ADA NODDED AND FINALLY found her voice. "Yes, please."

She was unable to keep the large smile off her face. Tonight, she was "his lady," and they were dining out!

It was silly really. It wasn't as if she'd never been out of her own home to eat before, but, truthfully, it was usually at a private residence or at a confectioner's shop or, in the summertime, now she was back in London, she would go to a tea garden along the Thames.

"I've eaten in a tavern in the country," she told Michael, recalling when she'd been traveling with her parents and brother before her first Season, and they'd stopped for meat pies.

He nodded seriously as if that were an accomplishment.

"Once my mother went to a ladies dining room in Bath, but I've been out of Town for practically all my adulthood, so have never . . .," she trailed off and stopped her prattling. "Thank you. This is a very special treat."

"I've never considered it before, but it shouldn't be, should it?" Michael said, leaning back as the waitress returned with a basket of bread. "I hear they have more family dining in France. I don't know about America. But with all those people touring the Crystal Palace, someone wrote an article in the *Times* the other day about the lack of places for couples to dine. If they're looking for better than pub food, that is."

"It must happen sometime," Ada agreed. She was simply thrilled for the novel experience. "Maybe by the time Harry is grown, he'll be able to take his wife out to dine wherever they wish."

They laughed at the notion of things changing so quickly. Then the food arrived, and Ada didn't speak again for many minutes. The soup was good, but the steak was divine, and somehow tasted better for being eaten somewhere other than her own dining room.

Although full, she let Michael order a heavy pudding for them to share for dessert because, clearly, he was enjoying the experience of dining out together, and they might as well make it last.

Then he ordered brandy for them both, and she had to quell the prick of displeasure it gave her. Unfortunately, brandy now seemed a reminder of his darker side, of the reprobate lurking within the thoughtful man she had come to know.

"The painting in the main room, is that Dolly?" Ada asked, taking a forkful of the sticky, sweet cake with sultanas soaked in . . . brandy!

"So I've been told." Michael grinned. "Not the most attractive woman, to be sure, but she had an idea how to cook up good food and the even better idea of hiring only lovely waitresses and bar maids to keep her male patrons happy."

"Is that why you come here?" Ada asked.

"That was over a hundred years ago, silly woman." He sipped his drink. "Howell told me Dolly was actually Queen Anne's favorite cook, and the queen gave her the place to open and run as she saw fit."

"A true business woman, and so long ago." Ada shook her head in wonder. "And there are still waitresses."

"And waiters, too, I assure you. They probably sent us a woman so as not to alarm you."

Rolling her eyes, Ada was about to point out the ridiculousness of what society imagined might alarm her female sensibilities when a man ducked his head into their private room.

"Alder!" the stranger greeted, and Michael stood up at once, sticking his hand out to shake that of the newcomer. "Good to see you here. Glad you could come to my humble chop house."

She reasoned at his words he was Mr. Thomas Howell.

Then the man with his slightly graying hair and lively eyes turned all his attention to her.

"And whom have we here?" He reached down, clearly wanting to take her hand, which she lifted to him. "This beautiful creature can only be Lady Alder."

She froze, Michael sat back down heavily, and then silence descended on their private room.

CHAPTER TWENTY-TWO

After a second, this experienced man of hospitality realized he'd blundered.

"Forgive me. She is not your wife," Thomas Howell surmised, speaking to Michael but still looking at her.

Ada felt her cheeks heat up, with the owner still half way to taking her hand.

"I have no wife," Michael said at last, and the man's head swiveled between them.

"You mentioned *your lady* to me, and then I discovered this lovely one seated with you, looking as delicious as a fine beef steak. Of course, I assumed you had an ounce of sense. But if you had, why wouldn't you have married her already?"

Michael coughed, and Ada knew he was covering a laugh.

"Thomas Howell, this is my *friend*, Mrs. St. Ange."

"Oh, a missus? She is your paramour, then?"

Ada's cheeks veritably flamed, and Michael coughed again.

"A widow," he told Mr. Howell, and, having explained their relationship, he picked up his glass of brandy again.

Ada began to feel this was becoming too personal. No wonder women didn't go out to public places for dinner, if their entire social and marital status had to be declared and dissected.

"A widow," Mr. Howell repeated, taking her measure.

At last, she found her hand engulfed by the owner's larger one before he kissed it, right on the back of her knuckles.

"Good evening to you," he intoned, finally addressing her directly. "And my condolences."

"Good evening," she returned, "and thank you for your sympathy, but I am out of mourning."

It was actually a little alarming after all to be in an unfamiliar setting with a strange man.

"Your lady has a lovely voice," Mr. Howell said, still holding her hand but addressing Michael again. Then his face grew serious as he gazed at her.

"I must ask you, did you find the food to your liking? Was every last morsel satisfactory? Moreover, was it better than any steak you've ever had before?"

As she opened her mouth, he added, "Don't rush into speech, dear woman. Think on it a moment. Let me look at you while you consider."

Michael was chortling now, and Ada realized Mr. Howell was teasing a little, but she sensed he truly wanted an honest answer.

"I am not rushing to judgment, sir, when I tell you everything was to my liking. Beyond satisfactory, in fact. As to your final question, the one I believe evoked my being brought here, I can honestly say, yes, it was the best piece of beef I've ever tasted. Cooked perfectly."

He closed his eyes as if in ecstasy. When he opened them, he gave her a small nod and released her hand at last.

"And *his* cook," he gestured to Michael, "cannot do better?"

Oh dear! Ada hated to lie, but she'd never had a meal from Michael's cook. Still, the woman had taught Mary, and

Ada knew Mary couldn't have seasoned and cooked a better steak.

Glancing at Michael, who had an eyebrow raised, clearly wondering how she would respond, she said, "To the best of my knowledge, sir, no, his cook could not."

"Ha!" the man exclaimed, then clapped his hands. "In that case, your meal shall be on the house, by which I mean free to you, dear lady. Only hers, mind you," he said to Michael.

With a wry smile, Michael nodded. "I understand. And we thank you for letting us dine here."

"Oh, yes," Ada said, "I've had a wonderful evening."

"Come back again. This coffee room is hardly used as most of my customers go straight from dining to the smoking room, as you'll notice on the way out."

At the doorway, Mr. Howell hesitated and looked back at them.

To Ada, he said, "I don't know what you're doing with this rogue. If I wasn't already chained, and happily so, I would sweep you away, dear lady."

Considering he was old enough to be her father, she merely smiled politely at his flirtatious charm.

To Michael, he added, "You would do well to marry this one. Snatch her up and chain her while you can."

With a final bow, he exited, leaving them staring at each other.

"Mr. Howell has quite the personality," Ada said. And what vivid imagery of snatching and chaining. Not at all what she thought about marriage.

"He does." Tilting his head, Michael was obviously considering something. But all he said was, "Are you ready to go?"

"Yes." Pulling on her gloves, she waited while he rose and came around to pull out her chair.

Once back in his carriage, she relaxed and let him pull her against his side, his arm draped around her. When he rested his chin against her temple, she felt . . . cherished.

Realizing that detail flustered her. Lord Vile was not supposed to be kind and warm and caring. He was supposed to be manipulative and selfish, wanting only to get her out of her clothing.

"Since it is early still," he said, his tone soft, "will you come back to my home? It would be a change from my always haunting your parlor."

Ah ha! There was the man she expected, hoping to get her into his bedroom.

Instead of being immediately defensive, however, she decided to acquiesce. She could sense his heart was engaged. Perhaps more time alone would be the impetus for him to have deep affection for her—or what passed for affection in his world.

As the driver directed the horses onto Newgate Street, turning left, Ada couldn't help looking to the right, toward Cheapside and just beyond that, after the Bank of England, the London Stock Exchange.

Soon, they had traversed London, along Holborn to Oxford Street, and then onto Brook Street where Michael's townhouse awaited, lamps already lit. He continued to hold her close, but strangely, he didn't try to kiss her.

Was she really going to do this? Going into his home without a companion certainly marked her as something less than respectable. Even a widow was not supposed to go into a gentleman's residence unless she didn't mind being considered his mistress.

Everything was the same inside as the previous time she'd entered, except without her son and nanny. Without their presence or even Dash's, the place seemed like a lifeless tomb.

Once seated in the drawing room, Ada couldn't help making an observation.

"You don't spend much time here, do you?"

He brought her over a glass of brandy without asking, and she took it from him.

As he sat beside her, he answered, "You're correct. I don't. How did you guess?"

"Meaning no offense, it simply has that air about it, as if it's been closed up for a month and no one remembered to air it out."

"Stuffy and dusty, then?" he asked.

"No, not that. There's a smell a place gets when no one lives in it."

"Musty, like a tomb?" he offered helpfully.

She laughed. "Whichever way I say it, I sound insulting, so I'll stop. You spend more time at your club, obviously, and perhaps in other rooms than this one."

"I would like to show you another room," he confessed.

"Indeed." If she went to his bedroom, she had no doubt they would make love. A crackle of desire was always merely a touch away.

"I believe I could entice you tonight," he said, "yet I find I don't want to."

She stayed silent at his strange words, both self-assured and dismissive. He would explain himself in due time, so she sipped the brandy and waited.

To her surprise, he laughed. "I like that about you. Your cool head. Some women would have found what I said insulting."

Ada shrugged and took another sip.

He set his own glass down. "Let's address the first part."

With no more warning than that, he leaned close and kissed her.

As soon as their lips touched, yearning flared within her—stark and strong. She nearly dropped the glass, but he took it from her, setting it aside before beginning a slow and thorough pillaging of her mouth.

With her eyes closed and her senses heightened, Ada relished the familiar roaming of his deft hands, and almost involuntarily, she laced her fingers behind his neck, holding him to her.

When at last he pulled back, he rested his forehead upon hers.

"You make my entire body hum."

Her eyes still closed, she smiled at his unexpected statement. Then she told him the truth.

"Mine as well."

"We *could* go to my bedroom," he offered, and she drew away, opening her eyes to his.

"You think you can entice me to your bed with a single kiss? Maybe you can," she conceded. "What about the second part? *You don't want to.* Is that true?"

He groaned and reached for his drink, finishing it in one go.

"I want to have you in every way possible," he confessed, making her insides flutter. Reaching up, he stroked the side of her face.

"But you wouldn't be happy afterward. I've learned that about you. Thus, I wouldn't be happy with myself."

He sounded awfully insightful and selfless, which only made her want him more.

Michael sighed. "You want a respectful, proper courting, not a quick roll, no matter how delightful it would be. And you deserve such. Howell could see your worth in one glance. I feel the same."

She expelled a breath she hadn't realized she was holding. Lord Vile was showing a tender, considerate side, making it extremely difficult to hold onto her vengeance.

Her head spinning with confusion and her body sizzling with desire, she reached her hands out to him. "Kiss me again."

Ada didn't have to wait long. In the next moment, he gathered her in his arms and claimed her mouth again. His tongue slipped inside to dance with hers, causing a pool of heat to gather low between her hips.

Arching against him, crushing her sensitive breasts to his chest, all the while, she felt his hands stroking her back through the thin satin fabric of her gown.

She wanted his hands upon her skin. Moreover, she wanted to touch his bare flesh, feel his heat and his strength.

About to demand he show her his bedroom, she nearly cried out when he broke away and stood up.

His breath was coming harshly, and her own lungs felt too small.

"Bringing you here without intending to ravish you was a tactical error," Michael confessed, snatching up his empty glass and returning to the sideboard.

Glancing at her own half-filled glass, she frowned. The feelings coursing through her were unsettling and, yes, frustrating as anything she'd ever experienced, but she had no desire to dampen them with liquor.

Why did he turn to the soothing substance every time something seemed tense or pleasurable? Apparently, it was his answer to every emotion.

She watched him pour a large draught into his glass, emptying the decanter. When he upended the cut crystal carafe, so every last drop fell into his glass, Ada couldn't hold her tongue.

"I've said it before, and I'll say it again. You drink too much. You will undoubtedly end up with a distended liver, or some such malady. And you'll become puffy and have a red nose."

"Like Mr. Moore's jolly old elf," Michael quipped. "That's not so bad. Children love Father Christmas."

"It's not funny," she insisted, standing and crossing to him. "After a few glasses, you are *too* jolly."

"I didn't realize one could be too happy." He took a sip of brandy and smiled.

"You'll get gout and have trouble walking."

His smile faltered. "Will I?" He took another sip.

Sighing, Ada paced the room. Many people drank brandy, even more drank gin. And at every party or dinner she'd ever been to, there was always wine and champagne. Be that as it may, she'd simply never been around someone who seemed to always want his next potation.

Michael narrowed his eyes at her. "Last time you said I drank too much, I asked you a question to which I received no answer. I shall ask again, do you care?"

The devil take him! Why did it matter to the man if she cared?

Clearly, since he'd asked her twice, it did matter. Even more apparent to her was how much she, in fact, cared for him. All at once, she thought what an unpleasant void there would be in her life if Michael Alder were not in it.

"I do," she muttered, stopping her pacing and crossing her arms in front of her chest. She cared, but she didn't have to like it.

He blinked and said nothing. Then he looked at the glass in his hand. Quick as a whip, he hurled it into the fireplace where it shattered, spraying the bricks and the coal with brandy, causing the flames to flare and jump.

Startled, she jumped, too.

"A bit drastic!" she admonished him, although inside, a sense of relief washed over her. "If you intend to destroy every glass you have, may I suggest instead you simply don't refill the brandy decanter."

"I really wanted that drink," he said at last, his tone a little exasperated, perhaps with regret over his impulsive action.

"There's always your flask," she pointed out, feeling as if she were challenging him.

He tilted his head. "There is, isn't there?"

Then he sighed, a heavy-hearted sound, and reached into his coat pocket. Withdrawing the silver flagon, he stared at it.

She found herself holding her breath until he lifted his head, looked into her eyes, and then handed his flask to her.

"Why don't you keep this for me? You can put lemonade in it if you like, to refresh yourself when you're out walking or riding."

She smiled at the notion of taking a beverage with her, but studied the silver object in her hand. It was about half full by its weight and engraved with the initials *MGA*.

"*G?*" she asked.

"George, after my father."

She nodded and tried to tuck the flask into her own hidden pocket in the side seam of her skirt. It was heavier than the handkerchief or coins she usually kept there, and too wide. Feeling a little awkward under his watchful gaze, she went to her reticule and tucked the flask inside. As soon as she was home, she would put it away in a drawer.

Glancing at his sideboard, knowing what was inside, she said, "I'm not sure this really solves anything."

"Were we looking for a solution to something?" he asked, taking a seat on the sofa.

It seemed very familiar of him to do so while she was still standing, even a little discourteous, but she took a seat beside him.

"What I mean to say is, I'm certain you have more brandy in your home. As well as wine and maybe other spirits. How will you manage to abstain, or *cagg* as they say, even for a short while?"

He merely shrugged, perhaps hating the idea of going without liquor.

"When I leave, will you ask your butler for another bottle to refill your decanter?"

Michael looked thoughtful. "It had occurred to me, of course. Are you asking me to stop drinking completely, or simply the brandy?"

"I didn't ask you to do anything."

He pursed his lips at her sidestepping.

Relenting, Ada added, "But if I were to want anything, it would be for you simply not to reach for your flask a dozen times when we are out, and not to have a glass of brandy as soon as you step indoors. Or, more precisely, a few glasses of brandy."

"I see. I didn't realize I was doing both of those things."

All the more reason to stop, she thought.

"I don't see any reason, however, why we can't have a glass of wine with dinner," she conceded. "Or champagne at a party."

He nodded. "That sounds reasonable."

She glanced at the fireplace again. "I suppose your butler won't be pleased with the shattered glass."

"It is a bit out of character for me, but Lawrence won't mind."

His face looked boyish, tugging at her heart.

No, she caught herself. It was enough she cared for him, like a friend. She would not let her heart get further entangled.

"I should go home now." Although at home, Harry had Nanny Finn, who was probably readying him for bed, and Dash, whom everyone adored, was most likely in the kitchen with Mary. *Was there really anyone at home who needed her at that moment?*

"I don't think you should," Michael said, and she stilled at his soft tone. "You've taken my brandy from me, and now you intend to deprive me of your company, too. That will make the evening intolerable. Besides, it's still abysmally early. If we were going to a ball, we'd still be getting ready and have the whole night ahead of us."

She crossed to the fire, seeing shards of glass, now blackened amongst the flames.

"Yet we are not going to a ball. So, what shall we do with ourselves?"

He shook his head. "I know you well enough by now to know you are not being coy. That is not a masked invitation for me to take you upstairs."

True, but she could admit to herself she might accept if he did.

"What would we do," he pondered, leaning back, crossing his arms, "if we were to simply stay indoors of an evening? Besides the obvious."

Ada considered the options, finding it to be a pleasant exercise, thinking about companionship, specifically with

Michael. Her parents kept company together nearly every night. Her mother loved knitting and needlepoint, as well as puzzles from the newspaper. Her father was often writing letters or reading. Sometimes, he even drew small ink drawings. They talked about whatever caught their fancy.

"My parents play cards," she offered. "Écarté, such as you and I already played, as well as double dummy. Of course, there are so many amusements when there are more than only two."

He looked curious. "I suppose if we invited over your best friend and her husband, we would all play cards and charades, and maybe a few forfeits."

Ada considered a small dinner party with the Earl and Countess of Cambrey. If her beau were anyone other than Lord Vile.

"Do *you* have some friends?" she asked.

His laughter came out like a short bark. "Meaning you don't think the Cambreys would want to spend an evening with me?" He shrugged. "I have a few friends, but I don't know their wives at all. I suppose we would get to know them together. That is, if anyone deigned to enter the home of Lord Vile, even if I had a civilized, reputable wife such as you."

How on earth had they got to talking about her as his wife?

"I like chess," she said, firmly bringing their discussion back to games, "and if I'm too tired to think properly, then checkers."

"And backgammon?"

"Yes, of course." She'd played many hours with Grady.

"I have a set here somewhere. Shall we play?"

Nodding enthusiastically, she watched him get up and yank the bell pull before going to the cupboards at the other end of the room. He began to rummage through them.

When a maid came in, he asked her if she'd seen his backgammon set.

"No, my lord, but I'll ask the others."

In a few minutes, the board had been retrieved, and they sat in front of the fire with it open before them.

"I don't suppose a glass of madeira is in order," Michael remarked as Ada shook the dice in a little leather cup.

She shook her head. "You don't want fuzzy thoughts when you're playing against me. How about a good strong cup of milky tea?"

Feeling quite at home, she rang for tea and biscuits, and they proceeded to play well into the evening.

CHAPTER TWENTY-THREE

Michael got up the next morning feeling one all-encompassing emotion, guilt! He'd insisted on escorting Ada home rather than sending her on her way with his driver. That was easy—it was the correct, upstanding, and gentlemanly thing to do. Moreover, he'd garnered another kiss or three in the carriage.

However, as soon as he'd walked through his own front door, tossing his hat to the side, he'd asked his butler for a glass of brandy. Taking it upstairs with him, he'd sipped it slowly while his valet helped him undress, and he'd enjoyed the remainder while sitting in front of his own fire, contemplating the success of the evening.

From Dolly's Chop House to laughing hard as they both tried to solve the *Weekly Dispatch*'s puzzle to being equally matched at backgammon—there was nothing about the evening he would change. Nothing he wouldn't want to repeat over and over.

Except the absence of his brandy.

At least, he hadn't ordered the decanter to be refilled. Truthfully, he wouldn't do that in case Ada saw it again.

Nevertheless, he was a grown man who liked brandy. *Was there anything wrong with that?* He wasn't rolling on the cobbled streets like an admiral of the red with no sense of propriety. He wasn't befuddled or listing sideways when he walked. It was only a glass or two of brandy. Or occasionally gin.

So why had he awakened with the overarching feeling of guilt as soon as his eyes lit upon the glass he'd left on the mantle in his room?

Dammit! He had let her down. She hadn't specifically said not to drink, but she'd seemed so impressed when he'd said he wouldn't. *Wait, had he said he wouldn't?*

No, he was fairly certain he hadn't. Problem solved, then.

Today, he would take a break from brandy since she had his flask. Hopefully, they would dine together again for he felt no lessening of desire to spend time with her, even without the pleasures of the flesh. Or the French liquor.

And when they did have dinner, they would have a glass of wine. He remembered her promising they could.

He might ask what she thought of him having a glass of brandy at his bedtime.

Upon second consideration, he decided he wouldn't ask. He didn't need to. That would be emasculating and, frankly, ridiculous. If he wanted brandy at bedtime, it was up to no one but himself. Even if they married—the idea came so easily and often to him now, always making him smile—she would either accept it or not. Or he could drink it in private if it caused her distress.

Satisfied he'd solved the issue, and tamping down his unnecessary guilt, he decided to go directly to Hatton Garden, the area of London with the best jewelers. Practically retracing their ride home of the prior evening, he wandered the shops in the shadow of St. Paul's until he entered Mayer and Sons.

"I'm out of my element," he said to the clerk, a middle-aged man with a looking glass contraption strapped to his head. "My lady is fair-haired and seems to favor pale purple frocks. Does that help one to choose a ring?"

The clerk's nimble fingers bypassed the tray of emeralds and rubies, past the sapphires and pearls, until he reached a small selection of rings with rich purple stones.

"Perhaps something here, my lord."

"I haven't seen many women wearing these," Michael pointed out.

"Correct, my lord. The amethyst is not as popular as a traditional emerald or sapphire but beginning to find favor."

He liked that at once. For his Ada was unique, and any old stone wouldn't do. Then Michael saw it, a gold setting with a large amethyst encircled by diamonds.

If he spent his entire newly built fortune on it, so be it. He could always earn more in the robust market of the day.

Slipping the black velvet box into his pocket, he signed the credit slip with a feeling of glee. To celebrate, he went to his club at noon and had brandy with Hemsby.

WHEN MR. RANDALL ANNOUNCED Lord Alder's arrival at seven o'clock, she realized she'd been waiting for him, trying and failing to read the evening newspaper as the appointed time for his arrival got closer. Moreover, her heart sped up at the sound of Michael's footsteps in the foyer.

Glancing at Dash who seemed to give her a knowing look in return, she stood up, just as his familiar face came around the door, followed by the rest of him. Ada couldn't deny a flood of gladness and had to restrain herself from rushing over to him.

"Mary has outdone herself," she declared without preamble. "Just wait until you—she broke off as he drew something out of his pocket. It was a small parcel, wrapped in paper.

"What have you there?"

"Remember, I am courting you properly and respectably as if you were an innocent. I've brought a sweet treat, of course."

He handed her the package, and she tore it open.

"Both Fry's *and* Cadbury's!" she exclaimed.

"Their chocolate is equally popular, it seems."

"Are you trying to fatten me up, like a Christmas goose, or are these for Harry?"

Michael laughed, a familiar sound to her now, and she recalled the night before when she'd laughed so hard with him, she'd nearly cried.

"Your shape is already quite pleasing but were you to grow fatter, there would simply be more of you to love."

They both stared at each other in silence as the word seemed to echo in the high-ceilinged room. The skin on the back of her neck prickled, but she took a deep breath. It was only an expression, after all.

"I'll share with Harry in any case," she said, setting them down on the side table. "He'll suck on a bar from end to end without stopping. Sometimes Mary shaves one into warm milk for us both. Sometimes, she melts it with butter and cream, too. Come, sit down. Would you like anything?"

As soon as she asked, she wondered if he would request brandy. By the slight cock of his head and the questioning raise of an eyebrow, he was obviously thinking about her offer.

"I'll have whatever you're having," he said at last, bending down to stroke Dash.

Well done, she thought.

"I was considering a glass of wine before dinner," she confessed.

No harm in that, she hoped. Not unless he wanted two glasses before, two during, and two after dinner, in which case, it would be the last time she suggested wine.

At that moment, her little boy appeared for a goodnight kiss and hug. Nanny Finn hovered in the doorway, as Harry climbed upon Ada's lap.

With her arms wrapped around her son, she said, "Lord Alder has brought you another treat."

"Chocolate?" asked the little boy, looking toward Michael.

"I'm afraid he's going to be spoiled," Ada pointed out, "expecting a sweet every time you visit."

To her surprise, Michael crouched down and opened his arms. To her even bigger surprise, Harry kissed her cheek before pushing off her lap to go to him.

Scooping him up, Michael held him high overhead, with the boy laughing hard. Swinging him down and then up once more, Michael whistled a happy tune, causing Dash to bark excitedly. Then he swung Harry down again, before sitting next to Ada and letting the boy stretch across his lap.

"You are a big boy, aren't you, Harry?" Michael asked.

"Yes," her son declared, still grasping his jacket.

"Then I think you can handle my bringing you a sweet treat sometimes but not *every* time? Yes?"

"Yes," her son said again.

Ada felt her laughter bubble up. "I think he would say anything to be agreeable at this point."

"Maybe," Michael agreed, snatching up the two bars from the side table, he asked Harry, "Which one?"

"Both!" he said with enthusiasm, and they all laughed again.

"One is for your beautiful mother," Michael told him. "The other is for you."

Tentatively, Harry reached out and took the Cadbury chocolate, then he kissed Michael's cheek, scooted off his lap, and ran out of the room.

"Oh, dear," Ada said. Then to Nanny Finn, she added, "Hopefully, you can get it away from him after only a bite or two."

"We'll see," the woman said and hurried after her young charge.

Ada and Michael stayed seated closely, side by side, even when the maid came in with their wine.

"Oddly, I was just reading how well Fry's did at a trade fair this year at Bingley Hall." She gestured to the newspaper she'd discarded. "Have you heard of it?"

"No," he said. "Tell me."

"Built specially for exhibits, it's up in Birmingham. Like our own Crystal Palace, only far less ornate and intended to be permanent. Apparently, chocolate bars and sweets in general were great crowd pleasers. Fry's business is run by the founder's sons now. Can you imagine they went all the way from Bristol to Birmingham for this trade fair, and they've pledged over two hundred new types of sweets in the next decade?" She shook her head in wonder.

"I can't imagine what they shall come up with," she added, "but it will be fun to find out."

He nodded thoughtfully. "So, they will take control of the sweets market, do you think?"

She leaned toward him, enjoying finally discussing something of substance with him.

"Not necessarily. The Cadbury brothers also had a display and their factory is actually in Birmingham, thus they were the local favorite. Moreover, they're opening either an office or a warehouse here in London, perhaps with a plan to gain a majority of the market."

He blinked at her and sipped his wine.

"Why aren't you saying anything?" she asked.

"Because I am too impressed for words."

Michael's praise caused her to feel warm from her head to her toes.

"How could a regular man," he wondered, "make a profit on England's love of chocolate?"

"Oh, that's easy," she retorted. "Buy shares in cocoa beans. You can find the name of a reputable importer by . . ."

Ada had started speaking before she'd even considered her words. And then she trailed off and fell silent as Michael's eyes widened.

"I mean, you might want to ask a broker of stocks," she finished, then leaned back, leveled him a cheerful, hopefully somewhat vapid smile, and went back to sipping her wine.

"I'm starting to get the idea you have learned a little something from your father," he suggested.

She shrugged, hoping it was entirely dismissive.

Now, how to change the topic without being too obvious?

"Speaking of my father, he took Grady to the Old Bailey to see if it sparks him. A friend of my father's, one of the older judge's clerks, gave my brother a complete tour, from the courtroom to the barrister's changing room."

"What did your brother think?" Michael asked, draping an arm along the back of the sofa, and playing with the tendrils of her hair.

She shivered. "Grady declared he wished to skip being a barrister and go straight to being a judge or even the Sheriff or Lord Mayor, because their accommodations were so nice. He especially liked the Lord Mayor's dining room."

Michael nodded. "Perchance he'll be the Lord Mayor one day. And why not?"

"Why not, indeed," she agreed.

At that moment, Mr. Randall came in to announce dinner, and Ada felt assured Michael had forgotten her sudden interest in stocks.

Two hours later, and another glass of wine each, not that she was counting, they were in the drawing room, considering cards or chess.

"Either one is fine," Ada told him, "I always enjoy myself when I'm with you."

The statement reverberated in her head, as she realized its truthfulness.

How could she have let the impossible happen? She had developed a *tendre* for Lord Vile.

ADA'S WORDS MIRRORED HIS own feelings.

"I feel the same way," Michael admitted. "What's more, I look forward to each time I get to see you and regret every moment I'm not in your company."

He might as well get to the crux of the matter that had been on his mind all day.

While she went to the sideboard to retrieve a chessboard, he took a deep breath and dropped to one knee in the middle of her soft Persian rug. Then he waited for her to turn around.

She didn't. She seemed to be arranging the pieces on the board before lifting it up.

Finally, when he was beginning to feel ridiculous, he cleared his throat.

Turning, she had the chessboard balanced between her hands, saw him in what he hoped was a gallant position, gasped, and promptly dropped it.

The crashing sound startled him into nearly standing, but he held his ground even as two pawns and a bishop skittered over toward him.

Speechless, she stood before him, little wooden chessmen all around her and the oak board cracked but not broken at her feet. He hoped it hadn't been important to her.

"I apologize for startling you," he began. "I should have begun with a pretty speech and then dropped down here *after* I had your full attention."

He took her mild expression as encouraging. At least, she hadn't fled the room.

"I suppose I have never done things quite conventionally, but now that I think of it, the first time we met, I was at your feet. Thus, here I am again."

Her smile faltered and she frowned.

"When I picked up your packages," he reminded her.

"Yes," she nodded. "I remember."

Her tone was too serious, too much like the Mrs. St. Ange of weeks past.

"In any case, I'm down here on this rug, which I can see is clumpy with dog fur, by the way. You might want to have a word with your maid."

All at once, she giggled despite the seriousness of the situation, and he felt his heart lighten.

"Go on," she urged, clenching the skirt of her gown with fisted hands.

"Yes, of course." He realized his heart was beating at a fast pace. Moreover, he hadn't prepared what he wanted to say at all. After he'd purchased the ring, he had believed himself ready.

"To put it plainly, I am on bended knee, amongst the tufts of Dash's discarded fur, to ask you for your hand and to find out if you'll take my name."

He paused, experiencing a measure of shame. "True, it is not the upstanding name it was when first bestowed upon me, but with your guidance, I shall endeavor to improve its reputation. Already, since being seen with you, less and less do I hear whisperings of Lord Vile when I walk into a room."

She said nothing, but he could see she was thinking. Undoubtedly, she had many opposing thoughts going through her head at once. He hoped the favorable ones overcame the others.

Michael had envisioned touching her as he made his proposal. To do so now, he would either have to stand and then kneel again when he reached her, or work his way over to her on his knees across the chess pieces. Both options seemed ridiculous. Instead, he held out his hand.

If she came to him, perhaps that would be a good sign.

After a brief hesitation, which felt like eons while he waited, she crossed the vast distance of four feet and laid her hand in his. He covered it with his other one for a moment, closing his eyes.

Damn if he didn't feel lucky and grateful already.

Then, when he looked at her again, he brought her hand to his lips.

Kissing first her knuckles, he then couldn't help turning her soft, unblemished hand over and kissing her palm, seeing goosebumps erupt across her forearms.

That was a good sign, he thought.

She shivered, which made him look up at her again.

"If you become Lady Alder, you may still be given the cut direct, the cut indirect, and, I daresay, the cut infernal and the cut sublime, as well. I hope all that nonsense stops eventually, but I cannot promise you some won't always enjoy a cup of scandal-water and whisper about *Lady Vile.*"

"Indeed," she muttered, and he couldn't help grinning.

In the next instant, though, he had to tell her the words that had been running through his heart and head for days.

With a voice thick with emotion, he told her, "I love you."

CHAPTER TWENTY-FOUR

Those were the very words Ada had been waiting to hear for a long time. However, they didn't evoke the response she'd planned and rehearsed. This was the moment when she was supposed to laugh at him, ask precisely how much he loved her, and then tell him she despised him in equal measure.

Instead, she tugged on his arm until he stood in front of her.

"Michael Alder, it's true you've made a bit of a mess of your life for a few years, but you seem *mostly* respectable at present."

She was truly surprised at the answer she wanted to give, but she gave it anyway. "Yes, I agree to an engagement."

He looked surprised, too. "I honestly wasn't sure you would." Then he rubbed his hand around the back of his neck as if stretching it.

"I noticed you didn't say you will become my wife, but you are an honorable person. I assume if you agree to an engagement, you'll follow through to the wedding."

That was a valid assumption, and one anyone might make. Nevertheless, she simply couldn't promise. Ada found she couldn't speak the words agreeing to become his wife. Some part of her still held onto the tattered remnants of her vengeful plot. She'd lived with it for too long to release it immediately.

Yet, over the course of their engagement, she hoped to let go of the last of her anger. Moreover, if they were to marry, she supposed she would have to tell him everything. For, at that moment, he assumed they'd met for the first time here on Belgrave Square.

She thought about how to respond to the words of love he'd given her. She knew what she felt in her heart—believed it to be love—but it was not pure and full. It was imperfect and dulled by years of resentment.

What could she say?

"I feel very strongly for you, too. I believe it is love."

His expression, a little tense with apparent apprehension, softened. He raised his hands to hold her face still, and then he kissed her, ending by nibbling on her lower lip.

"Oh, I really like that," she confessed.

He laughed softly, then he stiffened.

"What an imbecile! A dunce! A dullard!"

"Whatever is the matter?" Ada asked, as he released her and dug in his pocket. "More chocolate?"

"Hardly," he exclaimed. "I was going to present this to you while I was down on my knees, but I got all muddled. I guess I'm a little nervous."

Michael started to sink down again to his knees, but she stopped him.

"I think we can stay standing. We can even sit on the sofa, if you like."

He waited while she sat and then he took a seat beside her. Grabbing her hand, he placed a black velvet box upon her palm.

"Open it," he urged

This was not anything she'd imagined happening to her when she planned her move back to London. Not after only a few months of being here, and absolutely not with Lord Vile. The entire situation was dreamlike.

Still, she opened the lid and gasped at the beautiful ring nestled there.

"Do you like it?" he asked eagerly. "I have never chosen jewelry for anyone before. It was rather enjoyable."

She thought it prettier than any ring she'd ever seen. It seemed he knew her tastes as well as she did.

"Beyond liking it," she told him. "It suits me perfectly. I wouldn't have chosen anything else. Thank you."

"The jeweler may have to adjust the fit. Shall we try it?"

Nodding, Ada let him slip it onto her left hand. It was a little large.

"Why don't you wear it on another finger, if it fits. At least for now. And then we'll go together tomorrow. I believe they have a way to determine your size."

"Yes," she said, still looking at the rich purple depths of the largest stone. "Maybe they use a tape measure, like a tailor would, except tinier."

She let him slide the ring on and off each of her fingers until it rested snugly on her pointer finger. When she looked up, their gazes locked.

"You seem rather shocked," he said, "as if you had no idea I would ask."

She couldn't tell him her astonishment was entirely directed at herself. She had actually agreed to become Lord Vile's fiancée. *Had she lost her reason entirely?*

"Should I speak with your father?" he asked. "The only reason I didn't go to him first was your prior marriage. I believe at this stage of your life, you are permitted to decide for yourself whom you shall marry."

"True." And thank God he hadn't gone to her father. Baron Ellis would have investigated all he could about Viscount Alder and discovered him to be Lord Vile. Even if her parents didn't connect Michael's despicable reputation to what had happened to their daughter in the garden, still,

296

they would have warned her off of him. Two rogues in her life would have been two too many.

"We'll talk to my parents together sometime soon," she said.

"As you wish," he agreed. "I will wait to tell mine until then, although if I encounter Camille in the meantime, she will suss it out of me."

Ada smiled. She might gain a sister. As well as a brother and new parents and become a viscountess.

Gracious! Why couldn't she catch her breath? Suddenly, this notion of marriage seemed overwhelmingly real. Reminding herself she had agreed only to an engagement, she calmed.

From then on, Michael came over to dine nearly every day. Moreover, ignoring any disapproving glances, they went everywhere together, often with Harry and Nanny Finn.

Over the next few weeks, they went to the Adelaide Gallery and had their likenesses taken as photographic portraits for a guinea each. They went to the British Institution at Pall Mall to see artists, both dead and living. They went to the Coliseum, or the Cyclorama, as Ada had always called it, to see the plants and flowers, as well as Hornor's sketches of the panorama of London displayed under the domed rotunda.

Michael was easygoing and a delightful companion. He carried Harry upon his shoulders when the boy got tired. He insisted Ada write a list of places she wanted to go for there were so many, they might forget. Through it all, they ignored when anyone looked askance at them, usually exchanging a mutual glance.

What could he do, after all, except continue to be a normal man?

If people expected he would suddenly lunge at a woman or pull out a gin bottle in the middle of the Museum of Practical Geology, what could either of them do to alter such expectations?

While he professed to not being much of a dancer, when she bought tickets to a ball at the Lowther Rooms, Michael agreed with a half-hearted shrug. Finally, on King William Street, Ada got to dance in the arms of her viscount. She felt as if she were back at her first Season.

Closing her eyes, she let him lead her, trusting entirely he wouldn't allow her to crash into another pair of dancers. The experience almost erased that terrible night. *Almost.*

"I don't know why you don't like to dance. You are a fine partner," she told him.

Shrugging, he said, "Truthfully, I never saw the point in it. Even before I earned a reputation which made me an object of derision, I didn't like people looking at me, waiting for me to make a misstep. Worse, during a Season, I had to hold women in whom I had positively no interest. Insipid girls, giggling ones, clutching and grasping ones, ones who stood on my feet. All hoping to dance their way into a marriage proposal, I suppose."

He put his mouth close to her ear. "Tonight, dancing only with you, wanting you desperately to be naked in my arms, it is a heady experience. Dancing has become an exciting prelude to what we can do with each other. Either tonight," he paused to gauge her reaction, "or after the wedding vows."

Ada knew her cheeks were scarlet. Each dance after that seemed more like lovemaking, especially with his glittering gaze firmly upon her and his wicked smile sending shivers down her spine.

Unfortunately, by the time they left, she'd realized a ball with many of the *ton* present was where Michael received the most rebuking looks, as well as insults either muttered under someone's breath or hurled aloud.

Compared to how happy she was with him, however, it was a minor irritation, and she did her best to send a quelling glare to whomever was speaking ill of her fiancé.

Moreover, to her delight, Michael seemed to have stopped drinking. She realized some of the times when he'd been silly or giddy, he had been a little soused. Now, without the constant access to a flask in his pocket, he had a smarter humor, and they maintained the restraint of merely a glass of wine with dinner. He didn't seem to mind, either.

A WEEK LATER, INSTEAD of an obscure dance on the outskirts, they had tickets to a ball at Stafford House next to St. James Palace, hosted by Queen Victoria's special friend, the Duchess of Sutherland. Sometimes there was only one or two balls a year at Stafford House, and they were always spectacular in every respect.

Ada was thrilled to go without the worry of a dance card or unwanted partners. And Michael, who had never been there before, was actually looking forward to it. Three years earlier, Maggie and John had become engaged in the grand ballroom in front of the duchess, most of the upper echelons of English nobility, and the queen herself.

Ada had been in attendance the night of Maggie's triumph, watching along with everyone else as the Earl of Cambrey publicly declared his love. She could not have imagined then how her own romantic illusions would be destroyed a mere month later.

Passing through the entrance of the buttery-colored stone building, they turned in their cloaks, and Ada changed into her dancing slippers. Then they ascended the magnificent, bifurcated staircase. Some of the attendees chose the left stairs, but she and Michael, who looked so handsome she knew he could have no equal there that night, took the right.

The Earl and Countess of Cambrey would be there tonight, as they had returned to the venue each year since their engagement, and Ada hoped to run into them. It wasn't as crowded as the last time Ada had attended, when she and Maggie hadn't been able to find each other for hours.

Upstairs in the massive chamber housing the ball, the excitement was practically palpable. Music already floated through the room, as did a veritable army of servants. And instead of only the usual champagne and lemonade, some waiters carried trays of liquor. Ada learned this when an excited older lady, called out to one, "Come back with that Dutch Courage," as some called the aromatic gin.

Very unusual, Ada thought, not only because of the cost, but also the unspoken agreement that these large gatherings were made for dancing and socializing and most definitely not for becoming rowdy and drunk. If this many people started to become unruly, it could be a disaster. Moreover, they would spill out into the streets of London, causing mayhem in their carriages.

Ada took the glass of champagne Michael handed her.

"They're serving Plymouth gin with lime juice in honor of the Royal Navy," he informed her. "I just learned that from Lord Dunford. Maybe one of the duchess's sons has joined up."

A slight apprehension skittered along Ada's spine, but Michael was holding merely champagne in his hand.

In a few minutes, they were enjoying their first dance, and then another. After a third, she excused herself to the ladies' retiring room, only to finally encounter Maggie.

Squealing their excitement, they ran into each other's arms, drawing attention, although no one would scold the Countess of Cambrey for unseemly behavior.

The other ladies might very well reprimand the fiancée of Lord Vile, Ada thought, if her friend weren't beside her and if anyone knew of her engaged state.

"I can't believe I've found you," Maggie declared. Despite starting to show her state of pregnancy, her gown was the height of fashion, and she was beaming with happiness.

"I love this place," she confessed. "Well, I don't mean in here, exactly," Maggie added, gesturing around her where women were smoothing their hair or adjusting their gowns.

"I mean Stafford House, of course. It's so busy, I wonder if I shall ever find John again tonight."

Ada felt equally joyful. "I hope you've designated a place to meet."

"Yes, and you?" Maggie looked questioning. "You are here with your fiancé?"

"Of course." Ada said. She'd told her best friend, and no one else. After all, they'd shared everything over the years.

She only wished her friend's countenance didn't dim at the mere mention of Michael, or her tone sometimes become disapproving.

"Be happy for me," Ada exclaimed all at once.

Maggie lowered herself onto one of the tufted seats before a looking glass, careful not to wrinkle her dress.

"I am happy for you. In fact, it's time we got the men together. John will come around when he sees Lord Vi—I mean Lord Alder behaving like a gentleman toward you."

Occupying the empty divan beside her, Ada spoke to her friend's reflection.

"He does behave very well. What's more, he's suits me in all manner and aspects. You know that feeling, don't you?" she asked Maggie, who was patting her hair as she gazed at herself.

Her friend nodded. "I know it well."

"And you can't imagine any other man knowing you so well or being quite so funny or charming or so dash-fire handsome?" Ada continued.

Their eyes met in the mirror.

"You really love him, I take it."

Ada nodded. "Yes."

"Then let's go find John and we'll go together to where you are to meet up with Lord Alder. By the end of tonight, perhaps they will be if not fast and firm friends, then at least amiable acquaintants."

Linking arms, they left the room and strolled the perimeter of the throng until they came upon Lord Angsley, Earl of Cambrey at the designated spot.

"I feared I might never see my beautiful wife again," John quipped. "But now I know what took her so long. And she's doubled the beauty by bringing you." He bowed to Ada. "How are you? Would you like some champagne?"

"I'm well," she said, "and no to more champagne. Thank you."

"Maybe gin, then?" John asked, holding up his own glass.

She laughed. "Have you ever heard of such a thing before?"

"No," he agreed, "at least not at a party of this scale. Must be costing the duke and duchess a pretty penny."

Taking her husband's glass from him and setting it down, Maggie offered him a dazzling smile. "We were thinking of going to find Ada's *fiancé.*"

Ada was certain her friend's voice thickened on the last word, as if it might stick in her throat. *Would anyone ever accept Michael as a reformed rake?*

John grimaced. "If he is lost, may I suggest we leave him that way?"

Ada rolled her eyes. "Obviously, you admire your own sense of humor. However, I ask only that you give him a chance. You know me. I wouldn't have become engaged to the man if I didn't think he had a core of decency."

"And then there's her gorgeous ring," Maggie chimed in, snatching up Ada's hand and holding it in front of her husband's nose. Plainly visible through the pastel-colored, silk net glove was Ada's engagement ring, now perfectly sized to her finger.

He peered at it. "There's no question Alder has taste. I mean, he chose to set his sights on Ada Kate, didn't he? Very well. Let's go find him. I assume you have some idea where he will be."

"We thought it would be far easier to find one another downstairs, near the back terrace."

The three of them traversed the picture gallery, went down the stairs, crossed the inner courtyard to reach the back of Stafford House.

"I've seen so much parquet, marble, and gilt, my head is spinning," Maggie said.

"Truly, those arched windows in the ceiling of the picture gallery are brilliant," Ada added. "It must be full of light all day."

"Personally, I'm particularly partial to the dark cozy alcoves along the second-floor gallery," John said, and Ada noticed he shared a private look with Maggie. Apparently, more had gone on at Stafford House than the exciting proposal in the great hall.

"Why don't you two stay here, and I'll bring him over."

She felt as if she would be taming a wild tiger and luring him into the civilized world of the Cambreys. Michael would be hesitant at best. Moreover, he wouldn't want to be surprised by all three of them seeking him out.

Of that, she was certain.

Ada would warn him first, and then they would all go back upstairs and enjoy the dancing.

Leaving Maggie and John in each other's arms, swaying to music only they could hear, Ada searched the back entrance and then pushed open one of the many doors leading to the back of the house.

Stepping onto the veranda, scanning the length of it, she gasped. There was Michael, *her* Michael, wrapped around a woman whose back was toward her. As Ada watched, he leaned in closer—*was he nuzzling her neck?*—and then he gestured out into the garden.

The floor beneath Ada seemed to shift, and she found it difficult to take a deep breath. Immediately taking a step backward to remain hidden in the shadows of the portico, she could only imagine how awful it would be if he were to glance up, see her, and stutter out a ridiculous explanation.

Who was this woman in her fiancé's arms?

Her brain tried to make sense of it, first thinking this was simply his sister. But she was definitely not Camille. Then she decided it was not Michael but a doppelganger. However, watching for a moment and hearing him laugh at something the woman said, she knew without a doubt it was him.

A sharp pang of jealousy lanced her. It was an extremely unpleasant, painful sensation. Moreover, it made her angry as a wet cat. She was Ada Kathryn Ellis, who'd made her way in the world quite well, better even than most men of her class. If Michael Alder wanted to hang upon some young miss at a ball or kiss her on the veranda, she wasn't going to let it affect her.

The woman was nothing to her, nor was he, for that matter. He didn't mean a damn thing!

How had she forgotten how vile he was?

Even then, he was probably scheming to get the girl alone in the garden.

She was done with this charade of an engagement. It was time to end it.

Turning, she headed back inside. Head down, thoughts whirling, she momentarily forgot about her friends until Maggie called out to her as she nearly passed them by.

"Did you find him?"

Hesitating only an instant, unable to look at them, Ada shook her head.

"No," she replied because it was the easiest thing to say. "I have to leave. I'll talk to you anon."

Hurrying now, she heard Maggie call out to her and then John did the same, but she had started to run. She needed to be alone.

In a short time, Ada was in a hired Hansom cab and nearly home. A bowl of Mary's excellent rice pudding with sultanas and nutmeg as well as a cuddle with Dash would put her to rights.

She was correct on both counts. Sitting in her library, an empty pudding dish beside her and Dash lying across her feet, Ada contemplated the last few months of her life. She'd lost nothing by her association with Lord Vile. Thankfully, with the little wisdom she hadn't forsaken while foolishly growing fond of him, she had at least not let him bed her. At least not entirely.

No! She needn't feel humiliated. Moreover, she would never tell him she was the girl from the gazebo. How smug he would be if he learned she'd let herself get caught up by his charm again after how he'd treated her. But she would never tell.

As Ada turned up the lamp and opened the newspaper, Lucy knocked on the door and entered with unwelcome news.

"Lord Alder is in the foyer, missus."

"Tell him I have retired."

"Yes, missus."

Lucy went away, leaving Ada curious as to his purpose. He'd been ready to pounce upon the woman he was with, already at the stage of nuzzling her neck. Unless he'd acted very quickly indeed, he should still be with her with his hands under her skirts.

How she wished she hadn't given Mr. Randall the night off when she assumed she'd be out until all hours.

Biting her bottom lip, knowing he was yards away on her doorstep, she tried to think of something else. Like the stock exchange. Or cutting Dash's toenails.

Loud footfalls in the hallway, stopping outside the library door, caused her to stand, while Dash jumped to his furry feet. Unless Lucy was now wearing Hessians, it could only be—

The sharp rap on the door made her startle. Before she could respond, Ada heard him.

"I wish to speak with you. I will not be turned away."

Impossible! How could he breach the sanctity of her home uninvited? Beyond discourteous, it was nearly criminal!

Even worse, before she had time to reply, he opened the door.

"How dare you!" she exclaimed, and her tone caused Dash to begin to bark.

Michael's eyes narrowed, taking in her appearance.

"How dare I? Are you ill? Do you have a headache?"

"No," she bit out, and to Dash, she said softly, "hush."

"Then I am utterly perplexed," Michael continued. "Why did you leave the ball and without a word to me? I was worried out of my mind."

Michael bent down to pat Dash on the head. To her, he seemed amazingly nonchalant, as if less than an hour earlier, he hadn't had those same hands on an unwitting female.

Ada raised her chin. "I don't have to explain myself to you, Lord Vile."

He jerked his head back as if struck and rose to his feet. "What has gotten into you?"

"Some common sense," she all but hissed. "We are finished."

Again, he looked stricken and confused.

"Ada, what are you saying? I love you, and you love me."

In her mind, she saw him once more with his arms around the stranger. Had they taken the few steps into the garden? Had he kissed that woman the same way he kissed her?

"*Ha!* Don't be ridiculous," she spat. "Who could love you? Your parents did Jenny a favor."

She was gratified to see his stunned expression. At last, he was paying the price for what he'd done to her.

"Love you?" she repeated. "I *tolerated* you and let myself be seen with you, despite the awful stain to my reputation, only to determine if you had a heart worth shattering. Tonight, I have my answer."

He said nothing, standing stark still in the middle of her library rug, jaw clenched, staring at her.

She considered how swiftly he'd changed while she had been away, talking with Maggie, merely half an hour at most. What had spurred Michael to become Lord Vile again, going after whatever skirt came too close?

Approaching him, she leaned her face close to his and sniffed.

"Gin!" she proclaimed, easily able to detect the nearly perfume-like scent of the juniper liquor, plus she could smell the fresh aroma of lime.

He blanched. "Yes, I had a glass of blasted gin. And what of it? I am entirely sober, I assure you. I had no idea a drink of liquor would unleash this tirade against me, or cause the loss of your affections. I don't believe you could have loved me if such is the case. I promise you my love for you is stronger than a single mistake."

If only it were as simple as a single drink of gin. In fact, if Michael were inebriated, at least he could use it as an excuse, but he was right. He seemed quite sober.

"As for your loving me," Ada said, looking him right in his glorious amber-flecked eyes, "I don't think you know how to love. But I'm certainly glad to know you feel *something* for me. If breaking our engagement hurts you even a little, that only makes it all the sweeter."

Saying such hateful words made her own heart ache, and she desperately wanted to be alone.

Watching his now beloved face was painful to her, especially when his countenance went from one of confusion to hurt. If she didn't know what a beastly cad he was, she would be in tears.

"I want you to leave now and never come back. My door will not be opened to you again." She pulled the ring off her hand and held it out to him.

His gaze went from her to the ring, which he didn't take. Instead, he looked away, at the bookcase, at Dash, at the rug, as if it were too difficult to look directly at her.

Turning away, he started to leave without another word, and a flash of fury ignited in her chest. If he had loved her at all, he would have fought to save what they had.

In two steps, she went to her writing desk, snatching his flask out of the top drawer.

Following him out of the room, Dash circling her feet, she called to him when he reached the front door, "Michael."

He turned back. "Yes?" His voice was barely above a whisper.

"I think you'll be wanting this." And she hurled the flask at him, feeling a small measure of satisfaction when it thumped against his chest. He caught it before it fell.

"In fact, make sure you have a large glass of brandy wherever you're going. Or better yet, an entire bottle."

With that, she went back into the library and slammed the door.

Unfortunately, she'd spent all her anger, and the next emotion flooding her senses was even less pleasant.

Placing the ring on the round oak table in the midst of her papers, she felt the heavy mantle of sorrow descend upon her. When her tears began, she feared they would never stop.

CHAPTER TWENTY-FIVE

Everything seemed topsy-turvy. What had happened to his rational, sensible fiancée? Tonight, they were supposed to show London's highest echelon they were a couple. In some ways, he had hoped—with Ada Kathryn at his side—their appearance at the premiere event in London would redeem him in the eyes of the *ton*, and finally, they would cease with the nasty moniker.

Instead, Ada had been spiteful and shrewish. What's more, she'd said she had never loved him.

She had even seemed to believe him roaring ran-tan—on a single glass of lime juice-polluted gin! *Absurd!* On second thought, perhaps he'd had two glasses at Stafford House, but she had disappeared at the ball and never come back. While he'd waited, he'd accepted what the servants had offered.

Hunching over the bar, he took another sip from the glass in front of him. More gin, and it was positively delicious. Definitely better for not having tart citrus in it.

Why had she pretended to like him? Even to love him? What nonsense had she spouted about shattering his heart if he had one?

He was rather unhappy to learn he had rather a large heart, and at that moment, it hurt like hell. Or it had until the gin eased his pain.

How could a woman who in the beginning had been so cool and calm, who'd then warmed up to being his ideal wife, now become a raging scold?

He couldn't imagine what had caused her to be in such high dander.

And would he truly never see Harry again? He'd come to enjoy his time with the boy. Yes, *dammit*, to love him even as he did the boy's mother.

"Well, this is a nasty turn of events!" he muttered aloud.

Then he felt a hand on his shoulder and turned.

Ah, one of the establishment's jaded whores whom he'd tupped in the past after a long night of drinking. Or, at least, it might have been her. It had been a couple years since he'd been to this Drury Lane tavern.

Then she smiled, displaying the familiar hole where her tooth was missing, and cocked her head toward the stairs.

After Jenny, he used to think all women were the same, especially when on their backs, so what did it matter? He'd spent too many nights in this pub and others like it.

Then one evening, he'd met a goddess in a gazebo, a lady scented with the most beautiful fragrance, with a golden halo of hair and translucent pale skin. After her, he'd left the bawds behind for the well-bathed Cyprians and the aristocratic widows. Until Ada Kathryn.

"Come on, luv," the saucy strumpet beckoned. "I 'aven't got all night."

She probably did, in fact, have all night if he had enough coins on him. But he couldn't summon an ounce of desire for her.

"Not tonight," he said, reaching into his pocket and drawing out a shilling.

With a shrug, she took the money and disappeared without a thank you.

What was he doing there anyway?

Moreover, what was he going to do next?

First, he was going to get out of this hell hole that smelled like piss and looked worse than it smelled. He was going home, glad his driver was somewhere close, for he wasn't sure he could quite remember where home was.

In the morning, he would try to recall what Ada had said and think if there was a way to win her back. For the life of him, he couldn't imagine a tomorrow without her.

IT HAD BEEN TWO days since the Sutherland's ball. London was still abuzz with the success of it, and the papers were filled with gossip.

Lord V had been seen, purportedly with a respectable widow, who the writer was sure wouldn't be respectable for long if Lord V had his way. Witnesses had declared she'd left alone, as had he. No doubt they'd met up afterward, surmised Lady D and Lady M.

Rolling her eyes at the ridiculous statements, Ada could not ignore the irony of being part of the rumors surrounding Lord Vile only after she'd broken free of him.

And apparently no one had noticed him on the terrace with another unfortunate female, or it would surely have been mentioned.

At least, she needn't worry about being the widow linked to him ever again.

And then Mr. Brunnel was shown into her parlor. She didn't have the heart to meet him in the library, where she hadn't done more than put the ring in a drawer of her desk before vacating the room. She could still feel her anger and sadness well up when she passed the door. Moreover, all too easily she could recall the look of bewilderment on Michael's treacherous face.

The devil take him! If he hadn't already.

"Tallow," she told Brunnel, barely seeing him, her voice sounding as hollow as she felt.

"Yes, missus. I'll tell Lord Alder we're selling all the other stocks and buying tallow."

She nodded and excused herself from the room.

Her next visitor, for tea the following afternoon, was Maggie, with whom Ada didn't wish to discuss her strange behavior at Stafford House, but had it dragged out of her nonetheless.

"I *knew* it," Maggie said predictably upon hearing her tale.

And then Ada firmly and quickly changed the subject, unable to bear either her friend's censure or her sympathy.

Each day for the following week, she expected Michael to return and beg forgiveness, and also each day, she dreaded he might. Missing everything about him—his smile, his laugh, his thoughts, and especially his kiss—she could imagine forgiving him if he asked.

Was love a terrible weakness then? It seemed so.

"From Lady Cambrey," Mr. Randall said, bringing her a note.

Dearest Ada,
Dinner at our home tomorrow at six o'clock. Please don't say no and do bring Harry.
Love, Maggie

Ada sighed. Maggie was not going to let her waste away on Belgrave Square. Straightening her spine, she realized she didn't intend to, either. The next night, in a suitably reserved dark blue gown matching her mood, with Harry and Nanny Finn in tow, Ada alighted from her carriage at the Cambreys' townhouse. Unfortunately, to get to Cavendish Square, they'd had to cross Brook Street, not far from Michael's home. It had stung enough to make her annoyed at Maggie for summoning her to dinner.

Ignoring the bounds of propriety, Harry ran on ahead into the open door of the parlor whilst Ada and Nanny Finn gave up their coats to the Cambreys' butler.

"Chocolate," Harry cried out excitedly, then there was a familiar laugh. Ada's heart seemed to skip a beat.

The thread of utter disbelief quickly wove through her mind. It simply couldn't be.

Feeling light-headed with trepidation, knowing she must be imagining things—after all, this was Maggie and John, who disliked Lord Vile intensely—Ada approached the doorway.

Then she heard his warm voice as he spoke to Harry.

"Not until after your meal, yes?"

"Yes!" Harry was agreeing, as she entered the room. She saw two things at once—her son was in his father's arms, and Harry was already tearing open the chocolate bar.

Then her gaze took in Maggie, seated, her fingers entwined, her hands in her lap. When their glances met, her best friend's cheeks pinkened, obviously with guilt. John, looking more than a little discomfited, stood by the fireplace. Their own little Rosie was not in evidence.

Finally, after she'd looked everywhere except directly at *him*, when Harry called out to her, she had to look in Michael's direction again.

"Mama, mama. See the chocolate!" Harry's voice was full of sheer delight.

Her eyes met Michael's, which were soft and beseeching.

However, it was to Harry she spoke. "I see, dear one, but you heard Lord Alder. You can't have any chocolate until after your supper." Reaching out, wishing she didn't have to get so close to Michael, she held her hand out to Harry.

Reluctantly, he turned over the bar to her, which she gave to Nanny Finn, who stood behind her.

"See, Nanny will keep it for you while you eat with Rosie."

To Michael, she said, "Set him down, please."

When he did, she reached for Harry's hand and gave it a little squeeze before bending low to kiss his cheek.

"Go with Nanny now and see your friend."

Nanny Finn nodded to her and took Harry away to find Maggie's daughter in the nursery.

Waiting until the door had shut behind them, Ada took a deep breath and turned back to face three pairs of eyes on her.

"What have we here?" she asked, surprised at how steady her voice sounded. "It seems to be a conspiracy. Frankly," she addressed Maggie, "you're lucky I didn't turn around and walk out."

Maggie winced, but it was Michael who answered, "Please, Ada, don't blame them. I asked them to bring you here."

Sighing, wishing she could calm the fast tattoo of her heartbeat, she tried to pretend to a nonchalance she didn't feel.

"That I can believe," Ada said. "Yet why they would acquiesce is a mystery."

"I heard him out," John spoke at last, claiming her attention. "Alder seems to be, dare I say, sincere. And as you know, for me to give him the time of day was not easy."

"Sincere?" Ada repeated. "In what regard?"

"Please," Michael said, approaching her, "I don't need Lord Cambrey to speak for me. Only look at me and let me speak to you."

"Why are you doing this? And why here? Do you wish to humiliate me?"

"No, of course not. But I must speak with you, nonetheless. I'm doing it here, because you told me I would not be admitted to your home again. And a letter at this stage seemed absurd."

If she could have put her hands on her hips and rolled her eyes without looking like a character in a farce, she would have.

Instead, Ada nodded. "If we are to do this in front of my best friends, then I am going to sit down." She took a seat next to Maggie, who patted her shoulder.

"What's more, I'm going to have a glass of wine."

John moved toward the sideboard and poured her a glass of madeira. Taking it, realizing her hand was shaking, she sipped, closed her eyes, breathed deeply, then looked at Michael again.

She noted to herself he wasn't drinking anything. *But how long would that last?*

"Shall we leave?" John asked her, looking hopeful he would be spared whatever emotional scene might follow.

"No," Michael declared, sharply, and all eyes turned to him. "I do not intend to embarrass the lady, and to speak frankly in front of her friends seems perfectly fitting since every other part of my life has been played out on the public stage of the gossip columns these past years. Moreover, she is less likely to throw something at me."

His attempt at humor fell flat, and Ada closed her eyes. She was not a creature given to violence, and even throwing his flask at him had felt abnormally vicious. She didn't want her friends to think she was the type of person who habitually lowered herself to such actions.

"Maggie once threw a—"

"John!" her friend shushed her husband.

This was getting out of hand.

"Lord Alder," Ada began, "why don't you say what you wish to say before this evening descends into a travesty."

"All right, I will. After the other night, I was puzzled to say the least. One minute, we were having an enjoyable time and the next, you vanished only to later say strange and terrible things I cannot believe you meant."

Should she tell him now she most assuredly meant them?

Before she could say anything, he crossed the distance between them and sat beside her, so she was caught between her best friend and the man with whom she'd foolishly fallen in love.

"Not that I am in any position to inform you of your feelings, of course, nor would I presume to do so," Michael added. "And perhaps in that instant of dudgeon in your library, you meant every word, but I don't understand what could have caused your wrath."

Inwardly, Ada groaned. *Was he really going to make her say it?*

Since he had fallen silent and neither John nor Maggie looked as if they were going to speak, she took in a deep breath.

"Very well," she said, looking straight ahead of her, feeling awkward at having him close beside her. "When I returned from meeting Maggie in the ladies retiring room and stopping by to see John, I went onto the terrace to find you. I saw you . . . I saw . . ."

"What?" all three of them asked.

She glanced from John to Maggie, and finally turned slightly on the cushion to face Michael.

"I saw you with your arms around another woman. You might even have been nuzzling her neck." Maggie gasped behind her.

"Nuzzling her neck?" Michael sounded so confounded, she suddenly wondered if she'd seen anything at all. But, sadly, she knew she had.

"I let you arrange this meeting, tricking Ada," John said, his voice menacingly low, his sharp gaze focused on Michael, "because you convinced me you love her. You made no mention of another woman or her neck."

Michael groaned. "I didn't know you even came outside," he said to Ada. "I never saw you."

"Because you had too much gin," she surmised. "You were stewed." Maybe being drunk was a valid excuse for his being with another woman. Perhaps he'd been confused and imagined—

"No," he shook his head, interrupting her thoughts. "I'm not proud to say it, but I'm an old hand at drinking, and I know how much I drank at Stafford House. I wasn't foxed. I didn't see you because you didn't show yourself. Is that possible?"

"True," she confessed. "I didn't make my presence known because you were—"

"Nuzzling someone's neck. Yes, so you said, but I refute it."

"Was there another woman with you?" Maggie asked.

All at once, Michael's expression cleared and his face broke out into a smile that made her stomach twinge.

"I stood out there for a long time, maybe three quarters of an hour, and for all that time, I was alone, except for about two minutes when a woman came outside, rather young, too, reminded me of—" he broke off and looked at the floor, then back at her.

"Never mind that, in any case, she mentioned going farther into the garden, and if I may say so with confidence, unlike me, she was stewed, as you said."

Resting his elbows on his knees, he looked reflective, dragging up the memory.

"She needed her mother, if you ask me, or at least a trustworthy companion. Anyway, she practically fell on me, I steadied her, told her not to go beyond the light of the terrace and walked away. Because, you see, if I stood there too long, someone was bound to come upon us, and being seen with me would have ruined her reputation entirely, although I don't even know her name."

Ada listened. It could have been exactly as he said. She hadn't watched for more than a few moments before fleeing the scene.

Michael straightened and took her hands in his, and Ada glanced over her shoulder to see Maggie watching intently. Then she looked back into his amber gaze.

"I have absolutely no interest in any other woman. I love you."

Ada swallowed the emotion welling up. *God help her if he was lying, but she believed him.* It was as simple as that. Even though she'd said terrible things to him in her library, still, here Michael was, in front of her friends, including the formidable Earl of Cambrey, declaring himself.

At last, she nodded. "I believe you. I am sorry I mistook what I saw."

Standing, he drew her to her feet.

"Sadly, it's understandable given my behavior of years past. The question is, do you think you will ever be able to trust me? I can vow my devotion to you—indeed, I have already done so—but will you be able to accept it, or will you always wonder whether I am up to no good?"

Before she could answer, he brushed a tendril from her forehead. "It may be unmanly for me to confess, but it is downright frightening."

"What is?" she asked, wishing for nothing more than for him to kiss her.

He glanced at her lips as if he knew her feelings. "It's frightening how with a change of heart, you will be able to destroy me."

Oh gracious, Ada thought as he voiced the very plan she'd come to London to enact.

"I do think we should have left them alone," John muttered.

"Do be quiet," Maggie said softly.

Ada ignored them.

"Since coming into my life, Michael, you have given me no cause to doubt you. I am sorry for jumping to conclusions, and I will *try* my best not to do so in the future."

"I believe that's the best I can hope for until time proves me true. I only hope in your anger you didn't destroy the ring or toss it into the Thames. If you tossed it into the Serpentine, then maybe we could get it back as I'm willing to roll up my trousers, but the Thames . . . ," he trailed off, a small smile appearing on his handsome face.

"Oh, Michael," she said. "The ring is safe, and I love you."

Then, even with spectators, his arms went around her, he lowered his head, and he kissed her. Not too long, of course, for that would be unseemly, but long enough for her to feel warmth down to her slippered toes.

When he lifted his head, she turned in his arms to face the silent room and the blatant stares of Lord and Lady Cambrey.

Shrugging, she said, "I'm positively famished. Is it time for dinner?"

Halfway through the third course, she remembered Clive Brunnel and nearly choked on the piece of braised beef she was chewing. While coughing, having both gentlemen stand, letting Maggie pat her on the back, and then taking a drink of wine to wash it down—Ada felt her panic rise.

She had financially ruined the man she loved. *How would he ever forgive her?*

CHAPTER TWENTY-SIX

First thing the next day, feeling in a panic, Ada directed her driver to the London Stock Exchange at Capel Court. *What could she do if the trade had already been done as she feared it had? Nothing.*

She knew how the exchange worked, and one didn't simply ask for one's shares back or un-purchase what one had bought.

Tallow! Michael's entire account emptied to purchase tallow shares. *Dear God!*

She'd barely been able to finish eating the night before, taking only a few bites of whatever else was put before her in order not to insult her best friend.

Repeatedly, she had to reassure Michael all between them was well. But her heart ached with the damage she had caused. And she was relieved they had separate carriages when the evening was over. Ada could not imagine sitting in the close confines of his brougham and not confessing her deviousness.

Instead, she'd collected Harry and Nanny Finn for the trip home, hugged Maggie, nodded to John, and let Michael walk them to their carriage.

After ruffling Harry's hair and lifting him in, Michael had assisted Nanny Finn, and then turned to Ada. He'd cocked his head, clearly about to ask her again what was the matter?

"I'm awfully glad you convinced John to ask Maggie to bring me here," she'd admitted.

"Yet something is amiss," he'd guessed.

Her heart sank. He would never look at her the same way after he learned she'd ruined him and his family. *Poor Camille!*

Unable to smile, she'd merely shook her head.

"I'll talk to you tomorrow," she had offered. For by then, she would know the extent of the damage.

With that, she let him help her into the carriage, his expression wary.

Now, traversing Fleet Street and passing by St. Paul's, so close to Queen's Head Passage and Dolly's Chop House, she recalled with growing misery their wonderful meal weeks earlier. When he trusted her. The very night he'd asked her to marry him.

Descending from her carriage, she ran to the entrance on Bartholomew Lane, up the five steps, and inside where she froze.

In the entrance, there were only a few men, but they instantly stopped and stared at her in shocked silence.

The first gentleman to approach her wore a stern expression upon his face.

"Are you lost? You mustn't come in here, you know?"

"No, sir, I'm not lost." Ada hated to utter the next words, as they would make her seem like a child, but she had no choice. "I'm looking for my father, Baron Ellis. He's a member, sir. It's rather urgent."

His countenance relaxed, finding out she was not a renegade female breaching the sanctity of the all-male trading hall. Just a helpless woman in need of her patriarch.

"I'll consult the ledger and see if he logged in. He's a broker, yes, not a jobber?"

"Yes, a broker."

And he spun on his heel and disappeared through a doorway.

She ventured in farther, past the lobby, to the double doors, open wide, through which she could see activity rivaling an ant nest or a beehive. The place fairly hummed. Drinking in the sights, sounds, and smells—all exactly as her father had described, she recited the line from Cibber's play *The Refusal:* "Every shilling, sir; all out of stocks, puts, bulls, shams, bears, and bubbles."

And every shilling could be lost, too.

"There you are," said the man who'd gone to look up her father's name in his admittance book.

Turning to him, hearing the prices of stocks shouted out, followed by names, and "buy, buy, buy," as well as "sell, sell, sell," any pleasure she might have had at being at the exchange was utterly wrecked by the knowledge of the terrible thing she had done.

"Baron Ellis is here," the man told her, "in the west quadrant. You see, miss, the room is divided up—"

"Yes, I know. Shall I go find him, or will you?"

"You? Go find him?" He laughed. "Not unless you want to create a riot! Your ears would bleed with the language on the floor, miss, and your head would spin with numbers and information the likes of which you could never understand. Go on the floor? You?" And he laughed heartily again.

What an ass! "Will you go find him then, sir? At once?"

He straightened up. "Yes, of course. Stay here," and his tone had become deadly serious again.

Tapping her foot with impatience while at the same time unable to curtail all her interest in her surroundings, Ada listened to the continental news being read out in between stock prices. *Fascinating!*

"Ada Kate," her father's voice grabbed her attention, as he hurried over. "What are you doing here? Is everything all right with Harry?"

"Yes, Papa. I'm here on a trading matter. I can't explain it all now, but would you please check on a stock purchase from Mr. Clive Brunnel to the jobber Andrew Barnes? I hope I'm not too late to stop it, but if it could be stopped, I would most appreciate it."

Her father gaped a moment like a fish on land.

"How do you know Mr. Barnes?" Then his eyes widened. "Are you trading without me?"

To her father, that would be a sin of betrayal, worse than any other.

"No, of course not. If I needed to buy or sell, I would do so directly through you, Papa. I know Andrew Barnes because you've mentioned him as being an upstanding jobber." She looked him squarely in the eyes. "Please, Papa, will you be able to determine if a purchase was made for Mr. Brunnel?"

With the massive sigh of a put-upon parent, James Ellis nodded and walked back into the fray of the trading floor.

She wondered how she could bear the suspense. Was Alder entirely destitute, his family ruined?

In a few minutes, her father returned.

"Barnes made the transaction two days ago, late, right before the markets closed."

Dear God! "I am too late, then," she muttered, feeling abject misery. "He is ruined."

Feeling as if she could weep right there and then, Ada wanted to sink to the floor with the weight of guilt upon her shoulders. Revenge was not sweet at all.

"Brunnel, ruined?" her father exclaimed. "Don't be absurd. Sharp as a needle apparently. I just saw his entire transaction history. Always comes in with the right choice. Reminds me of . . . ," he trailed off and narrowed his eyes at her. "*You* are the one who is sharp as a needle, aren't you, dear daughter?"

She felt her cheeks grow warm.

"You've been giving him advice and tips, haven't you?"

She nodded.

Shaking his head, he reminded her, "You know the exchange would frown upon it if they knew, and it would be even worse if you were using him as a proxy for yourself."

Ada shrugged. "Then they should change their rules. Remember what happened with that man they called 'The Lady Broker'?"

"Yes!" her father, said. "Exactly so. And stocks were bought and money lost because of that unconscionable woman, trading and not making good on her purchases."

He was entirely missing the point.

"It was her husband who wouldn't pay up on her bad decisions, and still the broker made *her* name public. If women were given equal access to the market, if it were all out in the open, that wouldn't have happened. Women should be allowed to buy and trade openly, then they could be held responsible. Remember President Adams' wife, Papa. You told me it was she who invested in government bonds when her husband wanted to invest in land. She made a fortune for them."

She threw up her hands in dismay. "Only think how women are robbed by the huge commissions charged us. If you weren't my beloved father, why, I could hardly afford to be in the market at all."

"*Hmm*, beloved, am I?" He smiled, having regained his good humor. "You are a rarity, but I suppose if other women had an interest in the market and read the reports as you do, they could do as well as some of the traders here."

She reached up and kissed him on the cheek. "Thank you, Papa."

"Tell me why you were worried about Mr. Brunnel's stocks."

Oh dear. The terrible, ruinous stock purchase! How could she have become distracted with her righteousness for women when she had entirely ruined the Alders?

"He has been trading for a friend of mine."

At his silence, she knew she would have to say more.

"Do you remember Lord Alder? You and Mummy met him at my house."

Her father's countenance became instantly dour.

"In fact, I do. Your mother was curious following our brief encounter with the man and asked about him afterward. She found out exactly who Alder is."

He leaned close and whispered in her ear, "He is called Lord Vile by many, and for good reason."

Then Baron Ellis straightened. "I don't think you should continue a friendship with him."

Luckily, her glove covered her engagement ring. What type of person was she, manipulating a man's trading to ruin him and hiding her intent to marry from her loving parents? She didn't even recognize herself. All in the name of revenge toward a man who'd given her a wonderful son and to whom she'd now fallen utterly in love.

Sighing, Ada knew she must placate her father if she were going to ask for his help.

"I understand your concern, Papa, and I'll be happy to speak with you and Mummy about all that later. However, right now, I must ask you to sell Mr. Brunnel's last purchase immediately. You can do it. You're more advanced than a jobber."

He shook his head. "Even if I were to take the customer away from Mr. Barnes, which would be highly irregular, I can only sell shares at Brunnel's request. You know that."

She did know that, but in her hurry, she'd pushed it aside, hoping only to stop the trade. She should have written something up and forged Brunnel's signature. After all, she'd gone this far into depravity, she might as well be a counterfeiter as well.

"Ada, why did you want to stop Brunnel's stock purchase?"

She began to pace in front of him. Even at that moment, the money was draining from Michael's account.

"It wasn't a sound investment. He will lose everything he's gained and more."

"Absurd!" her father declared.

Sighing, she wondered how her father could be so wrongheaded.

"Papa, tallow is not going up at present. Only think of the new technology and gas lamps. In fact, I read a week ago, there was a glut, and the price of stock is plummeting as we speak. We mustn't wait a second longer."

"Dear daughter, Brunnel's last purchase request was for cocoa bean stocks, and I, for one, think it a good one."

She frowned. "Cocoa beans? Are you certain it wasn't for tallow?"

Her father drew himself up. "I assure you it was cocoa beans."

She'd discussed cocoa beans with Michael before they'd quarreled.

He'd listened to her about cocoa beans? Michael had told Brunnel to buy cocoa bean shares, not tallow. The heaviness of heart she'd felt since the night before lifted. She hadn't ruined the Alder earldom. *Thank God!*

Basking in a bubble of relief, she kissed her father's cheek again.

"You had best be off before a riot ensues," he said and winked at her.

He'd said it as a jest, but they both knew it wasn't far from the truth. At that moment, however, feeling light as a feather, she didn't care.

"Wonderful! I shall see you and Mummy soon."

He nodded. "And we'll talk about this inappropriate friendship . . ."

Before he could say more, she was hurrying to the exit, giving him a wave before disappearing outside. When he found out the friendship was an engagement, she would have some explaining to do, and Michael would have to win her family over as he had the Cambreys.

As soon as she arrived home, she wrote to Mr. Brunnel of her wish to terminate their arrangement immediately.

The next morning, a note arrived requesting a meeting.

"We shall meet as usual," Mr. Brunnel wrote. "Or there will be consequences."

She read and reread his missive. *What on earth could he mean?*

Sitting opposite him in her library the next day, eleven o'clock sharp, she soon found out.

"I was surprised by your request to end our association," he began.

"Not a request," Ada insisted. "I have decided to cease our arrangement."

"I offer my sincere apologies regarding the last transaction, but Lord Alder insisted on cocoa bean stocks. If I'd not gone along with it, then he could have pointed his finger at me if he lost money. I can only buy or sell that which he has agreed to, or I would be held culpable, if you see."

"I do see, but it is neither here nor there. I am no longer interested in giving tips to Lord Alder."

Brunnel continued as if she hadn't spoken. "The good news is Lord Alder did well, and cocoa beans are a sound market." Then he looked at her sharply. "Moreover, you might wish to rethink tallow, Mrs. St. Ange, as our jobber definitely did not recommend it, and said he didn't know anyone who did. Apart from that one mistaken choice, however, your analysis of the market has been spot on. Therefore, I have no wish to terminate our arrangement."

Perhaps he didn't understand her determination. "I am not interested in what *you* wish. I shall no longer meet with you. I am discharging you from your services."

"That won't work for me," Mr. Brunnel said, his tone neutral and smooth, belying his contrary words. "After your successful first tip to Lord Alder, I began investing for myself, too. You've been making *me* a wealthy man, and I don't intend for it to stop."

"Then all my tips to you shall be like the tallow—a mistaken choice, as you put it."

He gave her a hard stare.

"That will also ruin Lord Alder," he pointed out.

She returned his gaze while considering his words. Clive Brunnel didn't know her original intention had been to do exactly that. *So, what were her options?* She could continue to make Alder—and Brunnel—wealthy men. However, she didn't like being forced to do it, not one bit.

"Or perhaps I will ruin Alder anyway," Brunnel threatened, "unless you continue with our arrangement."

She took a quick breath, then she smiled. "How do you know I don't want him ruined? Perhaps that was my plan all along."

His eyes widened, then he frowned in disbelief.

"What?" she asked. "You don't think a woman capable of hatching a plan so devious?"

"Your stock choices have all been perfect up until now," he mused.

"Exactly. Do you still think the tallow was a mistake?"

He looked thoughtful. "I see."

"If I wish to stop, Mr. Brunnel, there is really nothing you can do about it. You will never know which stock is destined to rise or fall. You will be at my mercy."

He appeared to be thinking of it from all sides. Then he said, "I might report you to the exchange. I don't believe they look kindly on someone using the market in such a manner. What's more, I know Baron Ellis is your father and a broker."

Despite how her heartbeat sped up, she shrugged nonchalantly. Mr. Brunnel couldn't really hurt her, but he could do severe damage to her father's impeccable reputation as a broker. Certainly, everyone would believe Baron Ellis was behind any stock trading doings, nefarious or otherwise, related to his daughter. No one would believe *she* was the source of good trade advice.

He could have his membership terminated and be thrown out of the exchange.

"Very well," she told him. "We'll leave everything as it is, for now."

"Yes, we will," Mr. Brunnel shot back.

Folding her hands, she added, "Except since you're making money in the market, I'll no longer pay you a penny for your unwanted services."

He stared at her a moment, then nodded and rose to his feet.

"Good day, missus."

She stayed where she was, already planning how to remove herself from this unholy arrangement.

"Good day, indeed," she murmured, as he left.

Still reeling from the near disaster of the tallow, she expected the two notes that arrived. She welcomed the one from Michael, who was still concerned about her mood at the Cambreys' dinner and asking to see her.

The other, a brief note from her father, she dreaded. Her parents would be over to speak with her the following day.

Apparently, even a pretend widow with independence and a home of her own had to answer to her parents once in a while.

Her mother's opinion was known immediately, as she grabbed Ada's hands, looked at her with loving eyes, and proclaimed, "Do not be seen with that vile man!"

"It is not as simple as that," Ada began.

Her father grimaced. "Yes, daughter, it is. Do not go riding with Alder, nor out to the theatre, and, most assuredly, do not have him here at your home."

Taking a deep breath, she held out her left hand, upon which Michael had replaced the ring when she'd seen him again the evening before. Everything had been back to normal, and she was once again happy. Not blissfully so, for there were secrets between them, but happy nonetheless.

Her parents were rendered momentarily silent, staring at the amethyst and diamond creation.

"I don't understand," her father began.

"You are engaged?" Her mother's voice was cautious and questioning. "But surely not to Lord Vile!"

"Actually, yes," Ada confirmed.

With a long, dramatic groan, her father sat down heavily on the sofa and put his head in his hands.

Her mother blanched, then rallied. "You are no fool, Ada Kate, so I know you wouldn't do anything to put yourself or Harry at risk."

"Of course not, Mummy." Although hadn't Ada, herself, suspected she'd done exactly that when she'd seen Michael on the terrace? How could she expect her parents not to be wary when she'd immediately doubted her fiancé's faithfulness at the first opportunity?

"Lord Alder might've been a tad wild, even inappropriate in the past," she said, hoping to reassure them, "but he has declared his devotion to me, and I have no reason to suspect him of dishonesty on that account."

"Ada," her father began, his voice dripping disappointment, "has it occurred to you he has attached himself to you because of your usefulness in growing his fortune?"

Goodness! Her father really did have the wrong end of the stick.

"I know positively that is not the case. For Lord Alder has no idea I am the one who has been giving stock advice to Mr. Brunnel."

"I see." Her father ran a hand over his face, and she hoped he was somewhat soothed. Then he looked at her, and she saw the worry in his expression.

"We have always stood by you, even after . . . ," he trailed off, and Ada felt tears prick her eyes. "I cannot bear for you to be hurt again," he concluded.

"Oh, Papa," she said, rushing to sit beside him. "I am not the same naïve young lady I was then. I promise you, I'm not. Nor am I letting Lord Alder pull the wool over my eyes. This time, instead of letting a situation be forced upon me, I am making my own decisions."

Glancing up at her mother, she added, "I love him, and Harry does, too. And Lord Alder cares for us both without question, even believing I am a widow and not a pure bride.

He got off on the wrong track, so to speak, when his heart was hurt years ago. I believe without your love and support, I might have had a terrible life. I was blessed where he was not." She pondered the truth of her words.

"Yes, he made mistakes, and I believe he drank too much and conducted himself with less than gentlemanlike behavior—"

Kathryn Ellis evoked a strange snorting sound of displeasure, for obviously, she had heard all about Lord Vile's behavior and passed the information along to her husband.

But Ada knew Michael was a changed man. She believed it with her whole heart.

"I think Lord Alder has transformed himself. Moreover, he makes me happy. I hope you'll welcome him as a son-in-law when the time comes."

Her father's lengthy sigh was the only answer for many moments.

Then James Ellis exchanged glances with his wife.

"Very well. Because as I said, you are no fool, we shall trust in your decisions. However, if Alder hurts you, I shall tear him limb for limb, just as I would the scoundrel who gave us Harry."

Ada decided then and there not to mention they were one and the same man.

"How about some tea and cake?" she offered. "And I'll fetch Harry."

MICHAEL WISHED SOMETHING WASN'T bothering him, but there were, in fact, two matters slicing through his happiness with knives of misgiving.

For one, he knew in his heart he'd sniffed the unknown lady at Stafford House, as he did nearly every female he met, especially in that type of setting, at a ball. He'd done it without meaning to and before he could stop himself, and Ada had seen him, thinking he was nuzzling the stranger's neck.

In truth, involuntarily and while completely in love with Ada, he still searched for his golden goddess. However, he'd vowed he would stop the imbecilic practice when he'd gone to the Earl of Cambrey and convinced him of his utter devotion to Ada.

Secondly, he knew his beloved was holding something back from him. Call it instinct, call it experience with the ability of people—even those who professed their love—to betray and to lie.

He longed to pour himself a large glass of brandy, but he was trying to be the man Ada St. Ange deserved, not a weak lout who was always reaching for the flask or decanter. He had, in fact, consigned his silver flagon to a drawer in his wardrobe the night she'd thrown it at him.

Was it important he suss out her secrets? It was. Perhaps her past and her parents held the answers. Thus, the next day when he went over, he was surprised to learn she'd told her parents already about their engagement.

"I'm still standing," he said, taking her in his arms and kissing her before she could say another word.

When at last he lifted his head, she looked dazed and utterly beddable, with her languid gaze, her pink cheeks, and her reddened lips. The engagement was, at that moment, still open-ended, something he wanted to change.

"Seeing as how your father hasn't shot me or run me through—yet—may I assume we can set a date for our nuptials?"

Her eyes widened, and then, to his delight, she smiled.

"Yes. How about in the spring?"

TWO DAYS LATER, MICHAEL took Ada's front steps at a run, always with the same feeling—he simply couldn't wait to see her. She engaged his mind, made him laugh, stirred his blood so he couldn't imagine how he could put off claiming her body until after the wedding, although he was determined to do so.

Moreover, he'd told his parents about their engagement, and they were thrilled for him. Knowing there would be no underhanded sneakiness on their part at this stage of his life was a relief. His father liked that Ada had her own money. His mother was pleased his wife-to-be had already demonstrated she was fertile.

Randall opened the door and informed him Mrs. St. Ange was in the library.

"She has a visitor, my lord. If you'll wait in the parlor, I'll tell her you're here."

Michael had not taken two steps when the library door on the other side of the marble foyer opened and Clive Brunnel emerged, a smug look on his face. It changed the instant he saw Michael. Then the man paled.

Michael's brain froze with astonishment, unable to make sense of how his investment advisor could be at his fiancée's home. *A coincidence?*

CHAPTER TWENTY-SEVEN

A da appeared behind Brunnel, following him into the front hall, her face looking peevish and displeased. However, when she saw Michael, her mouth dropped open and her expression changed to one of shock—and guilt— telling him this was no coincidence.

What could it mean? Without doubt, Ada knew Brunnel was associated with Michael. What's more, she obviously hadn't wanted Michael to know she knew the man.

With a sick feeling in the pit of his stomach, he faced them squarely.

"What is the meaning of this?"

After a brief pause, Brunnel spoke first. "I am . . . advising Mrs. St. Ange."

However, by the way Ada startled at his words, it was plainly a fabrication.

"No," she said clearly. "He is not."

Michael said a silent word of thanks. She wasn't going to lie to his face, for that would surely be the end of their relationship.

Brunnel, however, looked irritated. "Mrs. St. Ange, I warn you."

He warned her? Michael took a step forward.

"Are you threatening my fiancée?"

"I, that is, of course not." Brunnel glanced at Ada, who merely shrugged, crossing her arms, apparently unwilling to help the man out of the sticky situation.

Looking again at Michael, Brunnel added, "As you know, investing is a personal matter and not to be discussed in a foyer."

Michael's fingers twitched. He wanted to punch the man in the face, and he didn't even know why.

"That's rubbish!" he said. "I demand an explanation."

Ada lowered her arms and dropped her gaze to the floor. When she looked at him again, a streak of fear shot down his spine. Her eyes told him something very bad was happening, something akin to the betrayal by his parents that had destroyed his engagement to Jenny.

"This is all my fault," Ada confessed, her voice barely above a whisper. "Mr. Brunnel gave you advice regarding investing that I, in turn, gave him."

Brunnel winced at her disclosure, then sighed. He seemed to know his ruse was finished. Michael's gut twisted uncomfortably at learning she had been secretly conferring with another man about him.

However, she had helped him, so why was she looking so glum?

Ada straightened her shoulders and said in a firmer voice, "Now, he simply won't leave me alone, and despite having made a great deal of money from my advice, Mr. Brunnel has threatened to damage my father's reputation."

"Is that so?" Michael narrowed his eyes at the man, who suddenly seemed to resemble a common garden weasel. There was much to be explained and even more to be sorted out between him and Ada—in private—but first, he would do everything in his power to rid her of Brunnel.

"I assume your threats were made only in order to keep me in the dark. Now that I know of your association with my fiancée, there is no point anymore in your trying to harm this lady or her father, is there?"

Brunnel's mouth formed a thin line of annoyance.

"Well?" Michael prompted. "Hear me, if you say any of the trades or purchases you've done on my account were anything to do with either Mrs. St. Ange or Baron Ellis, I will gainsay you, even before a judge."

Brunnel looked as if something unpleasant was being waved under his nose.

"I see," he said at last, and tried to walk around Michael to the door.

"You will offer an apology and promise on your honor to leave her and her family alone. Perhaps you should thank her as well."

Brunnel glanced back at Ada. "I will leave you alone," he promised tightly, then to Michael, he added, "Ask her if you should thank her, too, for the instruction to buy tallow."

With that remark, he pushed past Michael and left.

He stared at Ada, whose cheeks had infused with pink at Brunnel's remark. It was true, the man last advised him to buy tallow. But so eager was Michael to follow up with cocoa beans after his discussion with Ada, he had ignored Brunnel's advice, only now to find it actually came from her, after all.

Then it dawned on him. He'd learned afterward it was a terrible stock to purchase.

If he'd put all his money into tallow shares, he would have been ruined.

Ruined!

"My father spoke the truth when he said you had an interest in stocks?"

She nodded.

"And you paid Brunnel to encounter me by happenstance and start giving me advice?"

"Yes." The small word seemed wrenched from her.

Michael let out a long breath, processing her deceit as he did.

"He was a very good actor. He should take to the stage. Perhaps you should as well."

God's truth, he wanted a drink. He wanted to numb the emotions swirling through him with some good Belgian gin.

She blinked at him, saying nothing, only worrying her bottom lip with her teeth. Normally, he would find it charming and clasp her to him to kiss her concerns away.

But she had lied to him. *Who was she anyway?* Some other man's widow, a man she wouldn't even speak about. A woman who knew the stock market and kept that knowledge hidden. A woman who'd left London hurriedly and inexplicably, cutting short her Season. *What other lies had she told him?*

"The tallow advice was recent," he pointed out, realizing the awful truth. She'd still been in contact with Brunnel even *after* saying she loved him. "If I'd followed it, the entire estate would have been in jeopardy."

Ada nodded, not even bothering to defend herself. He needed to leave at once, to get away from her achingly beautiful face, which now looked like absolute betrayal to him. He'd been along this path before—having his loved ones surprise the hell out of him with the level of treachery they could accomplish.

"I'm going now," Michael told her, and she flinched.

He intended to get uproariously drunk, if not on gin, then, at the very least, on brandy.

"Will you come back?" Her voice sounded like a child's, and his heart squeezed painfully.

"I don't know."

It was the honest truth. He might get into his carriage, go to a gin palace, and never come out.

Could he ever look at Ada again and not mistrust what was going on behind her blue eyes? He remembered how cold those same eyes had been in the beginning, which he took to be reserve, protecting herself as any woman should from an eager suitor.

Now, he understood he'd seen emotionless calculation in her gaze.

Putting his hand on the door latch, he shook his head. It had been only a few minutes—*hadn't it?*—since he'd walked in thinking the sun rose and set on her. It seemed eons ago.

Randall appeared as he always did when someone was near the door. Her butler looked from Michael's grim face to Ada's devastated one, turned on his heel, and left. *Smart man!*

Michael wanted to say something more to her, some sort of farewell, but he couldn't think of anything, so he simply walked out, closing the door carefully behind him.

Waving to his driver to follow, Michael walked toward Hyde Park.

If he got into his carriage, he would end up ran-tan drunk in some hellhole. He would awaken with a pounding head, feeling like dung, and Ada would still have betrayed him, and he would still be minus one fiancée whom he adored.

Why? His footsteps slowed as he passed Elizabeth Pepperton's residence and then reached the end of the block.

Why had she set out to destroy him?

Her words from the night of the Sutherland's ball echoed in his head: "If breaking our engagement hurts you even a little, that only makes it all the sweeter."

Made what sweeter? What was this all about?

He had known she was hiding something, but he'd never expected this. He stopped. Four years ago—*was it five already?*—he'd felt the sharp betrayal of his parents, and then he'd made a hash of his life. Unfortunately, drinking came easy to him. Wenching, too.

And now he had no better plans than to drown himself in liquor.

Had he learned nothing since meeting Ada? Hadn't he become at least a little more mature? After all, he'd made peace with his parents and was saving the earldom, stock by stock.

Was he really going to follow the very same path of degradation as before and take on the mantle of Lord Vile once again? As if loving hadn't changed him, not only his love for Ada but also the newly rewarding love for Harry.

He turned around. *No, he wasn't. What's more, he deserved a goddamn answer!*

ADA WATCHED HIM CLOSE the door without histrionics or rancor. It might have been easier on her if he'd slammed it rather than slipping out so quietly, so wounded.

Everything seemed to be in tatters, her horrible, terrible plans—*thank God*—and her horrible, terrible heart.

Slowly, she climbed the stairs. It was only midday, but she was exhausted. She knew she should go visit with Harry in the nursery, perhaps suggest a walk with Dash, but she simply couldn't rally.

Sinking onto her bed, she put her head in her hands. Desperately, she wanted to weep the way she'd done when she believed Michael was being unfaithful on the terrace at Stafford House. Yet, she couldn't.

Tears of sorrow seemed a luxury she didn't owe herself. She should have come back to London, grateful for her health, fortune, and, of course, for Harry. Instead, she'd sought revenge and ruined her own life in the process.

She loved Michael Alder with all the fascination of her former youthful self, who'd fallen for the viscount upon first sight at a dinner party, even though he was then beyond her reach. And she loved him with the full breadth and depth of the woman she had become, who now knew him deeply and adored everything she knew.

Her heart felt as if it were bleeding. *Was that possible? Was there truly a crack in the middle of it?*

As quietly as he'd left number twenty-seven, Michael returned, opening the door, peering in, and slipping inside. Standing still, he listened, most assuredly not wishing for an encounter with Mr. Randall, who might turn him away or, at the least, would warn his mistress. Michael intended to beard the lion in her den, for at that moment, he certainly viewed Ada as a dangerous opponent with the power to destroy him entirely.

Most likely, she was in the library where he knew she spent much of each day—apparently reading about the infernal stock market.

And stupidly, he thought women only read the fashion and gossip pages.

Unfortunately, with the butler's uncanny ability to guard the front of the house, Randall appeared from inside the parlor as Michael crept across the foyer.

"My lord?" Randall queried, an eyebrow arched, and Michael felt like a naughty child caught stealing cake from the pantry.

"I must speak with her at once. I shall go insane if I don't." He couldn't believe he'd spoken about such a personal matter to the butler, and in those terms, but he needed an ally.

Randall paused, taking a visible breath. Michael knew him to be torn between his duty, which had included training of utmost loyalty to his mistress, and pity toward the beseeching man before him.

Making it even harder on Randall, Michael added, "I don't want you to summon her to me. I don't want her prepared and ready. I must meet with her in an unguarded moment. It is the only way she and I will get to the truth of the matter. Will you allow me that?"

Randall's jaw was working, clenching and relaxing as he determined the best course of action.

Then he surprised Michael with a question. "Do you love Mrs. St. Ange?"

That a butler would be asking him such an intimate question! That he should feel compelled to answer. Indeed, it was once more a topsy-turvy world.

"Yes, I do."

"Very well," Randall said and nothing more.

"*Um*, where . . . ?" Michael gestured around the hall with its various doors and also toward the stairs.

The pained look upon the butler's face bespoke how difficult it was for him to betray Ada, and Michael felt genuine gratitude she had such a servant.

"Her room," was all Randall said, glancing at the staircase, before he turned away and walked down the hallway to the back of the house.

Michael didn't hesitate in case the good man changed his mind. His heart drumming in his chest, he took the stairs two at a time.

Would he find her upset? Or was she even then laughing at him?

He knocked on her bedroom door.

"Leave me, Lucy," Ada called out. "Leave me in peace."

She certainly didn't sound happy.

Without giving her any warning, he lifted the latch and entered. She sat upon her bed, which he noted was a four-poster, her face covered by her hands, her elbows resting on her knees.

Closing the door behind him, he waited.

After a moment, she lifted her head, then gasped at his presence.

"How . . . ?" she began, slowly rising to her feet. "What are you doing here?"

He wasn't sure how to answer. She was so very precious to him. And looking at her, he hurt to think she didn't think of him the same way.

"I suppose I'm here because we are not finished." He considered her a moment. "At least, *I* am not finished with *you*. I certainly cannot speak for what you are feeling."

"I am feeling wretched," she declared. "I designed my clever plan, never thinking for a moment I might not be pleased should I succeed. I was so certain of my rightness in punishing you. And I never thought I'd feel ashamed at being found out."

He ran a hand through is hair, knowing it was probably standing on end. She was speaking rationally, yet she made no sense.

Strange though—if he could turn back the hands of a clock and go back to when he'd picked up her packages from the pavement, even knowing they would end up at this particular excruciating moment, he would do it.

"Why?" Michael asked, unable to keep the tremor from his voice. Manly or not, tears were not too far away. "Why have you done all this? Why the 'clever plan'?"

She closed her eyes a moment and then sighed. "Still, you don't know? It's hard to believe."

There was only one explanation he could think of why a female would seek to exact revenge on a man.

"Because of Jenny? Some sort of retribution for the pain I caused her? For I swear to you, Ada, I wouldn't have hurt her for the world."

Her eyes snapped open, their blue depths boring into his.

"It was *me* you hurt, not her."

He was confounded.

"What do you mean?" he stepped closer. "I have tried my utmost in all the time we've known each other never to do anything which could hurt you. Remember, the scene on the terrace of Stafford House, it was a misunderstanding."

She shook her head, tears springing to her eyes, making them shine brighter.

"Not recently," she explained, her voice thick with emotion. "Before. Three years ago."

"Three years!" He considered who he was at that time and felt a little sick. But surely, he would remember her of all people, especially if he had wronged her.

"In a garden, in a gazebo, to be precise." Her words seemed to choke her. She sniffed loudly.

"In a gazebo?" He knew instantly what she meant. As if he'd had scales upon his eyes, they fell away and he realized the truth. "My golden goddess!"

She recoiled at his words, as if she'd heard them before and they had caused her pain.

No! She couldn't be. That young woman had been an experienced member of the *ton*, ready and willing for a tryst. Of that, he'd always been certain.

Snaking his hand out, he snagged hold of her wrist and pulled her close. Unresisting, she let him, completely limp in his arms as he put his face to her hair, her neck. He loved her scent. It was familiar and warm. It was his Ada.

But it wasn't the scent of his dreams, of his memories, of his goddess.

"You don't smell like her."

She drew back, a frown on her face. "I don't . . . ?" Then her expression cleared, and she gave a small, bitter laugh, devoid of joy.

"I used to wear jasmine flower perfume." Her tone was brittle.

This was all too incredible, and he couldn't begin to sort through what he was feeling. Joy at having found her, sadness at her duplicity.

"I've never smelled the scent before or since."

"My father procured it for me in a business dealing," she explained. "It's rather rare, imported from Asia."

Tugging her arm free, she went to her dressing table and pulled open a drawer. Grasping something, she returned to him. Without looking at it, she pressed a bottle into his hand.

"There is your golden goddess," she whispered. "After that night, I couldn't bear the scent as it reminded me of . . . of . . ." She stopped speaking on a half sob and then hiccupped.

Staring at the stoppered vial in his hand, he lifted it to his nose. He didn't need to open it for the fragrance to flood his senses, transporting him back to that evening. He had been rather foxed, he recalled, on both champagne and brandy, and then a luminous creature had approached him and, with very few words, she'd let him—

"Good God!" he exclaimed, staring at her. "It *was* you."

Nodding, she sat down heavily on her bed.

His pulse seemed to be pounding in his ears, and his world tilted. All along, she'd been right there.

"Why didn't you ever tell me?" his voice sounded hoarse to his own ears.

"You must be joking," she said. "I never speak of that night, not to anyone. It was my ruin, the singular most humiliating experience of my life. Why would I confess to you, my tormentor?"

He groaned and grabbed his hair with both fists, tugging in frustration.

"But I haven't been your tormentor, have I? I've loved you and cared about you for months."

She hung her head.

"Michael, I came to London to ruin you entirely. Instead, I helped you to grow your fortune . . .and I fell in love."

"I can't believe this." He sat down beside her. "I looked for you after that night at every event I went to. After a month or so, I stopped."

"You obviously wouldn't have known me, even if you'd seen me. It was dark, and you were too far in your cups to retain a memory of my face. Undoubtedly, that's why my scent made such a strong impression because your other senses were impaired. In any case, I left immediately for the country, the very next day in fact, and I never came back."

She sounded so weary, his heart hurt for her.

Keeping his feet on the floor, he tossed himself back onto the bed to stare at the canopy overhead, keeping the small vial clasped in his hand.

How many times had he wanted to be right here with Ada on her bed?

With his other hand, he grasped her upper arm and dragged her down beside him.

344

"I don't know what to say?" he admitted. "Offering an apology and saying 'sorry' seem woefully inadequate."

"Correct," she agreed. "You cannot simply apologize for something like that. It was too enormous an event. Life changing. In all honesty, though, I don't hold myself utterly blameless anymore, either."

She angled her head to look at him. "I did, at first. I believed it was entirely your fault. But I strolled out into the garden like a wool-headed ninny, and I didn't run when I saw you."

"Why?" His tone betrayed his sheer frustration and misery. "Why did you seem as if you knew me? My memory of that night has always been of a willing female. Thus, I imagined, you were also an experienced one. I remember thinking you *wanted* me to kiss you."

"I did. I suppose I can now confess to having grown a *tendre* for you before we ever truly met. I had seen you during my first Season, and I thought you were superb."

He groaned and closed his eyes.

"We spoke earlier that evening at the Fontaine's ball, when you brushed by me on the dance floor, but I was so tongue-tied with nervousness over finally speaking to Lord Alder, the handsome viscount, it turned out I couldn't speak at all."

Opening his eyes, he looked at her again. "I'm sorry I don't remember. As you know, I drank a lot then. You should, indeed, have run from me in the garden."

She nodded. "I simply didn't understand what would happen after I let you kiss me."

"No, no, no," he moaned, draping his arm over his face. To think he'd deflowered her in such a quick and callous way. Of all the sins in his life, the drinking and whoring, he'd never guessed he'd taken a virgin, especially unwillingly.

He sat up. "I should be shot."

"No," she said, wiping tears away. "Don't be ridiculous."

"I should go to your father and confess what I did."

"Then you probably would be shot," she agreed.

345

Her disinterested tone worried him.

"I have to be punished," he insisted.

"That's what I thought, too. That's what I was trying to do but failed. Luckily," she added.

"No. You didn't fail," Michael insisted. "When you told me you didn't love me and called me Lord Vile to my face, it was the worst moment of my life. Today, when I discovered you were behind the stock market advice, both good and bad, that was the second worst moment of my life."

"It could get worse," she said, and he glanced down at her.

"Are you making sport of me now?"

Shaking her head, she sat up, her expression dejected.

He groaned again. "Frankly, I'm not sure I want to know. Tell me first, what did your husband think of all this? I assume you told him."

Then the awful thought hit him. "Or did he discover it on your wedding night?"

This time, Ada was the one to groan.

Michael's imagination seemed to have sprouted wings. *Had her husband beat her for her not being a virgin? Cast her out, perhaps?*

"What? Tell me?"

Staring at him a long moment, finally, she said, "I had no husband."

CHAPTER TWENTY-EIGHT

Michael let her words sink in and even repeated them in his brain, but they made no sense. There were too many indications she'd had one.

"Your name is fictitious?" he asked when he could form a question.

"Yes, I made up the story of Mr. St. Ange, lost at sea, so I could be free in London, not under my parents' control."

"But this house? Your fortune?"

"Just as I helped to build up your account, I have created my own fortune over the past three years. With my father's help at first, of course, then I believe I was helping him."

With a slight shrug, she glanced around the room. "I bought this house with my own money."

He whistled, realizing he couldn't be prouder of her than he was. Not only was she the most beautiful woman he'd ever met, who grew lovelier the longer he knew her, she was also the smartest.

His brain sifted through the facts he had. She'd never been married, thus, not a widow, but she was evidently a mother to a boy of nearly three.

It hit him as a low hanging tree branch knocks a careless rider—*three years ago, no husband, the gazebo, Harry!* If she was the smartest, he was, indeed, the densest.

"Harry is my *son*," his voice broke on the last word. "I am truly an imbecile. No wonder he reminded me of Gabriel as a boy."

She merely nodded at him, and he found himself squeezing the perfume bottle in his fist.

By God, he had a son! A wonderful boy, whom he already loved, who gave him hugs.

Tears came unbidden and flowed unchecked down his cheeks. To Michael's amazement, Ada wrapped her slender arms around his shoulders and cried with him.

After a few minutes, he said, "I will give him my name."

He felt her nodding. They stayed silent together for a long while. At last, when he had reined in his wayward emotions and wiped his face on his sleeve, he asked, "How did you choose St. Ange? Such an unusual name."

"I named him after you."

He waited for her to explain.

"I knew Michael was the name of an archangel," she said against his shoulder.

Ah, he understood. "Saint Angel in French."

"That was even before I knew there was a Gabriel in your family."

"Beyond that," he told her, "Camille was named after another one, Archangel Camael."

Ada straightened, and they finally looked into each other's eyes.

"I suppose your parents hoped for three angelic children," she guessed.

The irony was not lost on him. He, their first born, had been re-christened 'vile.' What an ass he'd been.

After another moment of silence between them, he reached over and tucked a lock of her hair behind her ear.

"And why 'Harry'?"

She shrugged. "No significance. I just liked the name."

From weeping, he now wanted to laugh. "Perhaps we can keep St. Ange as his middle name after we marry. I prefer it to George."

Her mouth had fallen open, and he closed it with his finger on her chin. And since he was touching her, he couldn't help leaning forward and kissing her, too, stunned when she actually let him.

When he drew back and looked into her blue eyes, which were wide with surprise, he could think of only one thing that would destroy him.

"Please Ada Kathryn Ellis, don't say no. Will you still be my wife?"

SHE WAS LIGHT-HEADED FROM the turbulent emotions of the past half hour. However, one thing she knew—she loved Michael Alder with all her heart, with both his flaws and his virtues.

"I will," she said, and pure joy flooded her.

He held up the vial of jasmine perfume, offering her a quizzical look.

"You didn't destroy it. You even brought it back with you to London."

She had to be honest with him. "I hate to tell you, but I kept it in my drawer to remind me of your vile behavior and of my own childish naivete."

He winced.

"In a way, it was a source of strength," she added. "And if Harry had been a girl, I would have used it to illustrate a cautionary tale, which I would have told her one day *before* her first Season."

Leaning over, he kissed her again, tenderly, touching his tongue to hers. Then he withdrew.

"I should leave at once."

His words caught her by surprise. "Whyever for?"

He smiled and cocked an eyebrow. "We're in your bedroom, sitting on your bed."

She felt her cheeks heat. "And?"

"And if I stay, I'm going to ravish you. Properly this time."

Her heart started to pound.

"I'm a widow with a great deal of freedom. You may stay."

He laughed. "You're *not* a widow, though. Not really."

"No one need ever know that, and I might as well put my independence to good use."

Without further invitation, Michael dropped the bottle of perfume on the bed and proceeded to unfasten her gown. She ought to be irked at the skill of his fingers, for he undressed her more quickly than her own maid. But she was as eager as he was.

With his assistance, she was soon reclining on her bed, head on her pillow, completely bare to his gaze.

He stared for a long moment, swallowed hard, and then laid beside her.

When she expected him to kiss her again or even latch onto one of her breasts which were aching for his touch, instead, he pressed his mouth to her stomach in a gesture that felt far more like love than desire.

"I want to erase everything about that night," he murmured, his lips against her bare stomach.

"Except Harry," she reminded him.

"Except Harry, of course," he agreed. "I want to start over, take it slowly, enjoy your innocence and give you a new first time."

Raising his head, he looked into her eyes, and she smiled.

"I don't know about the slowly part," she told him. "I'm already undressed and, truth be told, I feel rather ready."

A strange sound came from him, half laugh, half groan. He claimed her lips fiercely, tugging on her lower one as he pulled away. Then standing, he began to strip off his clothing starting with his cravat, chucking everything hither and yon, making her giggle, until he undid the fall of his pants.

Her smile died as he dropped them to the ground and stood before her in only thin cotton drawers, which he also hastily removed. Then he climbed onto the bed again before she could catch more than a glimpse, enough to see he was as ready as she was.

"The first thing to do is always a long, lingering kiss," he said, claiming her mouth again.

When he tilted his head, fitting his mouth perfectly to hers, a tingle of desire shot through her. Parting her lips for his tongue, she sighed with happiness. For the first time, she could return his kiss with a clear conscience and a peaceful heart.

How wonderful to have no lies between them.

After their tongues seemed to dance, with her hands in his hair and her body heating up, wanting more, he lifted his head, gazing at her.

"What are you thinking?" she wondered aloud.

He picked up the perfume bottle. "I will never ask again if you say no for, in truth, I love the smell of your skin." To prove it, he nuzzled her cheek and then her shoulder, which he also licked, causing her to shiver.

"But this scent, as unusual and gorgeous as you are, suits you so perfectly. Will you wear it again? I promise, it will always remind me to be a better man than I was that night."

Would it be a constant reminder of her own ignorance and his drunken carelessness, or could she think of it as the night Michael Alder made her his woman and gave her Harry? She smiled up at him and nodded.

He unstopped the bottle that had been closed so long, pressed his finger to the opening, and upturned it, releasing a few drops. Tracing his perfume-laden finger down her neck, he let the fragrance explode between them. He swept it across her collarbones, then to the hollow between her breasts.

Pausing only to kiss each peaked nipple, he helped himself to a second dose of jasmine flower and drew it down her stomach to the warm place between her legs. He didn't stop, even though she found herself desperate for him to touch her there.

As if anointing her, he continued the trail of perfume oil down her left leg to her ankle and then up her right leg, leaving goosebumps of excitement in its wake.

"At that rate," she said, "I'll have to get more soon. It could be quite expensive."

"Luckily, my fiancée can make money practically out of thin air."

"It's not that easy," she countered, but at that moment, he began to retrace his finger's path with nibbling kisses, and she clamped her mouth shut.

This time, he did pause to tease her nipples, taking his time with each while his hands stroked her skin, which suddenly felt too tight and overly sensitive.

Running her fingers up and down his back and over his sculpted shoulders, she marveled at his form, at the breadth of him, his long body and lean waist. *This man was hers! How remarkable.*

His skilled mouth and tongue were on the move again, heading lower, pausing to kiss her belly again.

"Harry's first home," he whispered against her skin, and then as he continued, he blew a puff of air at the soft curls between her legs, before kissing down her thigh, licking behind her knee.

When he started up the other leg, she thought she might scream.

"I think this slow and *proper* ravishing is more like torture."

"Be quiet, woman. I'm worshipping you."

She bit her lower lip, but as his mouth drew close to her intimate parts gain, she lifted her hips.

"A bit advanced for an innocent's first time," he said, but rewarded her with a kiss between her folds, stealing her breath.

"*Mm*," she murmured, and he continued, until she knew she would spend as she had at his family's home in Kent.

Before she did, however, he raised his head, causing her to gasp in dismay.

"Michael," she whispered desperately.

"*Shh*, I know. Trust me."

Kneeling between her legs, he fitted his yard to her and then lowered himself to his forearms as he slid inside.

It wasn't like the previous time. Ada felt no sensation of burning or tearing, only pleasure. In an onslaught of sensation, he lowered his mouth to hers and kissed her while continuing to glide in and out with the gentle movement of his hips.

The peak of release was upon her again within a few moments of him thrusting and withdrawing slowly, then more quickly.

With eyes firmly closed, she broke free of the kiss, her head tilting back as her muscles clenched and coiled. Then, blissfully, she let go, gaining her release in what felt like a spiral of ecstasy.

As she lifted her lids and looked up at Michael, he closed his own eyes, head back, jaw clenched, as he spent deep inside her.

When he rolled to the side and took her with him, their bodies remained close together. She felt his arms go around her, his chin resting upon her head.

"That was a much better first time," she acknowledged, feeling him chuckle.

"I love you," he said against her hair.

Pressing her lips to his chest, she responded, "I love you, too."

EPILOGUE

"To this day, I'm not sure Cambrey likes me."

"Nonsense," Ada said, adjusting her hat in the mirror in their front hall. The large looking glass formerly hung in Michael's home on Brook Street, which they'd sold to the highest bidder a month after their marriage. Next to it was the framed print of the Crystal Palace, which Ada decided more people could enjoy there than in the library.

She loved having her husband's things mixed with hers and sharing their home on Belgrave Square.

"John is simply a little slower to warm up to you because he had a few years of thinking you'd done his wife's sister a disservice, and then Jenny's husband no doubt said a few unkind words about you as well."

"You say it so matter-of-factly."

Shrugging, she turned to him and touched his impeccably tied cravat, pretending to improve on his valet's work.

"You were Lord Vile, after all. But Maggie thinks the world of you for making me so happy and for loving Harry. John will, too. Eventually."

"Eventually. In the meantime, I see him looking daggers at me when he thinks I don't notice."

"You're probably imagining it."

"*Hm.* Am I imagining how he pours himself a large drink of brandy whenever we go over there? He's testing me, I tell you, making sure I don't weaken to the stuff."

She looked up into his gold-flecked eyes. "Have I told you lately how proud I am of you?"

Her husband had confessed before the wedding if he had a little liquor, he would want a lot, and thus he had given it up entirely. They had no wine in the house either, and she didn't miss it in the least. She knew for him, though, it hadn't been easy. There had been more than one occasion when he'd said he was changing his mind about abstinence.

When that happened, Ada would smile, kiss him, rub his feet, and he would purr like a big cat, forgetting all about the craving.

His arms went around her, and he lowered his head and kissed her.

"We could stay home and go to bed," he proposed, tempting her with the wicked gleam in his eyes. "It wouldn't be the first time."

They grinned at each other, and her heart raced with desire. He was a superb lover, after all. But she'd promised Maggie.

"Let's be positive and have a wonderful evening with our friends. The bed will be here when we get back. I promise." She winked at him, and he laughed.

"Where is Harry?" Ada asked more loudly.

"Here we come, my lady," Nanny Finn said, charging down the stairs after the skipping boy, nearly four years old in a month.

"Mama," he exclaimed, running at her.

At the last moment, Michael swept Harry off his feet before the boy could bang into her.

Lifting him high in his arms, her husband held their son on his hip.

"We don't want to knock Mummy over," Michael warned, "not until she gives you a brother or sister. Remember, we talked about that."

Harry nodded, looking a little solemnly at her rounded stomach.

"Won't be too long, darling," she told him, leaning in to kiss his soft cheek.

Locking gazes with Michael, she smiled. It was still hard to believe she was going to have the pleasure of seeing two children running around the house, a sibling for Harry.

"Daddy," the boy said, putting his hands on his father's cheeks to get his full attention. "Can Dash come?"

"*Hm*," Michael said. "What do you think, dear one?" he asked her.

"He is such a well-behaved dog, and Maggie's kids love him, too. In fact, Dash will keep all the children amused for hours. It'll be easier on Nanny Finn and Maggie's nanny, for that matter."

"Very well. Mummy is very wise and she says yes, so yes, he can come." Michael set Harry on his feet. "I'm surprised he's not already here underfoot."

"Dash has a bone," Harry said.

"Mary had a ham bone to spare," Nanny Finn explained, "and the dog has been in the kitchen all afternoon gnawing on it."

Ada was very glad Michael had been amenable to keeping Mary and letting his own cook along with his butler stay with the new owners of his old townhouse. The couple were beyond grateful since good help was so hard to find.

Michael had brought his valet and his driver and two maids, who had all fit perfectly into the blended household.

"Dash, come," Michael called out, and in a second, they heard the dog's toenails in the hallway as he scampered along. When he hit the marble foyer, his feet slid out from under him until he lost his footing altogether and glided the rest of the way on his belly before crashing against Harry's legs.

All of them, including Nanny Finn, laughed.

Ada's heart nearly burst with joy. She'd never expected such blessings after her disastrous adventure in the Fontaine's gazebo. Moreover, her own plans for vengeance nearly cost her a future with the man she loved, and a brother or sister for Harry.

Thankfully, it hadn't come to that. And her practical husband not only brought home the weekly business papers for her to peruse, he also paid the price of admission to the London Stock Exchange so he could take her tips to the floor, himself.

There was an alternate reason, of course. Michael vowed one day soon, when she was delivered of their child and had her trim figure back, he would help her dress up as a counterfeit man and enter the exchange as his guest.

With that prize to look forward to, how could she be anything other than the most contented woman in London? She was the ecstatically happy Viscountess Ada Kathryn Alder, wife of the fully reformed Lord Vile, whom she was certain would never be called so again.

ABOUT THE AUTHOR

*U*SA *Today* bestselling author Sydney Jane Baily writes historical romance set in Victorian England, late 19th-century America, the Middle Ages, the Georgian era, and the Regency period. She believes in happily-ever-after stories for an already-challenging world with engaging characters and attention to period detail.

Born and raised in California, she has traveled the world, spending a lot of exceedingly happy time in the U.K. where her extended family resides, eating fish and chips, drinking shandies, and snacking on Maltesers and Cadbury bars. Sydney currently lives in New England with her family—human, canine, and feline.

You can learn more about her books and contact her via her website at SydneyJaneBaily.com.

Made in the USA
Middletown, DE
09 May 2022